For the first time in a long time, everything is good in our corner of the universe.

We solved the mystery of Gaia's decline at the hands of its alien Planetary Defense System, stopped the war between the Titans, Nibirans, and Gaians before the PDS on Nibiru could trigger the same fate there, and got our asses out of there before we could all be arrested for the various forms of treason that most of us committed along the way.

But I still can't shake the belief that it's only a matter of time before something from our past catches up with us and everything goes wrong again. Maybe it's just because I've felt hunted my whole life, and never known a system that wasn't on the brink of war...but somehow, I don't think so. We've been involved in too much, and know too much, to be allowed to walk away from it all. There will be a reckoning eventually.

I submerge my head under the warm water and let those thoughts float away. They can wait. Tonight is about good news.

Praise for

KRISTYN MERBETH and
THE NOVA VITA PROTOCOL

Praise for Book One: *Fortuna*

"Kristyn Merbeth has created a desperate, gritty world in her newest book, *Fortuna*, an epic space opera about the lengths a family will go to survive not only each other, but a world out to kill them. Merbeth is a voice to watch in space opera!"
—K. B. Wagers, author of *There Before the Chaos*

"The narrative is powered by a cast of deeply developed characters. Scorpia, in particular, is impressively multidimensional.... The nonstop action and varying levels of tension make this an unarguable page-turner."
—*Kirkus*

"Merbeth's multiple narrators and plotlines converge beautifully into a suspenseful tale of family. The characters are distinct and grounded, and each interaction is filled with purpose and emotion that brings all of them, regardless of differences, into the fray together. SF fans who have been waiting for a crime family spin on space opera will find nothing but joy in this whirlwind story."
—*Publishers Weekly*

"High energy, high stakes, and lots of high notes."
—*Library Journal*

"Merbeth's world building is fascinating—five human-settled planets, each distinct and littered with alien technology—but her multifaceted characters and their troubled relationships give this action-packed family drama its heart. A good readalike for Lois McMaster Bujold's Miles Vorkosigan books, John Scalzi's *Collapsing Empire* (2017), and for those who want a grittier version of Becky Chambers' Wayfarers series."   —*Booklist*

"This is an engaging start to a series that blends crime family drama with the sort of character-focused sci-fi that made Becky Chambers' Wayfarers series an award-winning favorite."
—*B&N Reads*

"It's everything you could ask for in a space opera."
—*Arcanist*

Praise for Book Two: *Memoria*

"This satisfying sequel has more of what made *Fortuna* (2019) such an excellent read: emotional weight, thrilling action, empathetic characters, and a complex plot that raises the stakes both for the five-planet system and the Kaiser family."   —*Booklist*

By Kristyn Merbeth

THE NOVA VITA PROTOCOL

Fortuna

Memoria

Discordia

DISCORDIA

The Nova Vita Protocol:
Book Three

KRISTYN MERBETH

orbitbooks.net

Orbit
Hachette Book Group
1290 Avenue of the Americas
New York, NY 10104
orbitbooks.net

First Edition: December 2021

Orbit is an imprint of Hachette Book Group.
The Orbit name and logo are trademarks of Little, Brown Book Group Limited.

The publisher is not responsible for websites (or their content) that are not owned by the publisher.

The Hachette Speakers Bureau provides a wide range of authors for speaking events. To find out more, go to www.hachettespeakersbureau.com or call (866) 376-6591.

Library of Congress Cataloging-in-Publication Data
Names: Merbeth, K. S., author.
Title: Discordia / Kristyn Merbeth.
Description: First edition. | New York, NY : Orbit, 2021. | Series: The Nova Vita protocol ; book 3
Identifiers: LCCN 2021017169 | ISBN 9780316454056 (trade paperback) |
    ISBN 9780316454049 (ebook) | ISBN 9780316454063
Subjects: GSAFD: Science fiction.
Classification: LCC PS3613.E67 D57 2021 | DDC 813/.6—dc23
LC record available at https://lccn.loc.gov/2021017169

ISBNs: 9780316454056 (trade paperback), 9780316454049 (ebook)

Printed in the United States of America

LSC-C

Printing 1, 2021

For everyone trying to be better than they were yesterday

CHAPTER ONE

A Motley Crew

Scorpia

Music thumps through *Memoria*'s halls, and I hum along with the beat as I walk. My boots trace the now-familiar path from the captain's quarters to the mess hall. The music isn't loud enough to drown out the steady hum of the ship's engine, but the noise has become a comforting constant. And beyond them both, I hear the voices of my crew bouncing out from other rooms—the continuous, easy chatter that always fills the space between these walls.

Sometimes it's hard to believe that this ship belonged to an enemy crew not so long ago. Every night I sleep in the huge bed of the captain's quarters, with a window to the stars above my head. Mine. This whole, clunky, ugly old mess of a ship, down to the name *Memoria* scrawled crookedly in my own hand—mine. Ours. My family's and my crew's. We're building a life here, all of us outlaws with nowhere else to call a home.

We're fast approaching Gaia for another scavenging run on its stormy surface. It's been a few months since we lifted off from a freshly peaceful Nibiru. Now, we're well on our way to establishing a foothold for our new business on Deva as an importer of Gaian goods. The recent turmoil in the system means that most planets are currently off-limits even to us, with Pax's borders closed, Titan still too hotly contested for us to risk, and Nibiru likely eager to arrest us if we land. But we've survived worse.

Things aren't perfect in the system. They probably never will be. We humans are constantly finding new ways to screw ourselves up, after all. Deva and Pax are still squabbling like particularly entitled children over the resources of Titan even now that they've found out some of its people have survived, and I doubt the three peoples intermingling on Nibiru are going to have smooth sailing, with all of the messy history and cultural differences to trip them up. But because of me and my crew, they've got a chance. The rest is in their hands.

And in the little world of my ship, at least, everything is better than ever. I've never been so glad to have nowhere important to go and nothing pressing to do, and I suspect most, if not all, of the others feel the same. Boring is a relief right now, even for me, despite the fact it feels like I left a chunk of my heart back on Nibiru.

I follow the smell of something spicy and delicious into the kitchen, and pop my head in to peek at whatever Corvus is cooking up. He frowns down at the pot, but it's a thoughtful kind of frown rather than a genuinely upset one. I think. He's still impossible to read, sometimes. He looks better lately, his dark hair and beard kept neatly trimmed, his eyes less haunted than they were when he first returned from the war. But he still wears the marks of his time on Titan: the thick scar slashing across the left side of his face, the black tattoo of a war-brand on his right wrist.

"What's for dinner?" The moment I draw close, he jabs at me with a ladle. I stagger back, throwing my hands up dramatically. "Whoa! That's no way to greet your captain. Blatant insubordination!"

"I know you're just trying to steal a taste," he says, a small smile cracking through his stern expression. "Out of my kitchen."

"No respect around here," I grumble, retreating to the doorway. "Just a heads-up, I've got an announcement to make during dinner."

His frown returns immediately. "An announcement about what?"

"Gotta wait and see," I say, and leave with a bounce in my step.

I find Lyre and Apollo in the engine room next. He's balancing her on his shoulders while she fiddles with an air vent in one corner of the room. I fight back a laugh at their matching looks of intense concentration, an expression far more at home on our little engineer's face than Pol's. There's no way this is the most effective way to handle the situation, so I have a suspicion she enlisted him just to give him something to do. He's been making progress lately, recovering physically and mentally from the lingering aftereffects of an alien bio-weapon and the toll it took on his once-strong body, but I know being back on the ship has made it hard for him again. Being raised on Momma's ship, where she only doled out love according to our usefulness, made it hard to be all right with not having a part to play. Now that I'm the one in charge, I hope he understands that he has plenty of time to figure out who he wants to be.

Lyre taps him on the shoulder as she finishes changing out the air filter, and he lowers her carefully to the floor. He's sweaty with exertion despite our sister's diminutive size, and has to immediately sit down to catch his breath. He's looking more himself lately—his dark hair starting to grow out again and his body still thin but less sickly—but I'm not sure he'll ever be the wall of muscle he once was. Yet when Lyre gives him an approving nod, he breaks into a gap-toothed grin nonetheless. My heart twinges. They've never been very close, but ever since the two of them landed—well, half landed, half crashed—the ship onto Nibiru in my absence, they've been spending more time together.

I knock on the doorway to get their attention. "Make sure to take your dinners in the mess today. Got an announcement."

Pol nods without seeming to think twice about it. Lyre pushes a stray curl out of her face and folds her arms over her chest, scrutinizing me. "It's not anything bad, is it?"

"Nah," Pol says. "She looks way too pleased with herself."

"You're right." Lyre taps her chin with one finger, leaving behind a smear of dust. "What could it be…?"

"No spoilers!" I say, wagging a finger at her before leaving them to find the others.

Dull thuds of impact lead me to the training room. Izra and Andromeda are engaged in what I like to refer to as a therapy session, and what others might refer to as punching the shit out of each other in padded clothing. After enlisting in the war on Nibiru, Drom came back to us quiet and distant. She spent a full week in bed, refusing to talk to anyone. Pol delivered meals to her door, but not even her twin could get her out of her room. When Corvus tried to talk to her, she threw a bowl of stew into his face. That got *him* sulking and blaming himself, so finally Izra marched into her room, dragged Drom out of bed, and brought her to the training room. Ever since, they've been doing this every day. They don't talk, as far as I can tell, and Drom mostly seems to do her damnedest to break Izra's face, but every day she gets out of bed, comes here, and suits up to do it again.

It's odd to compare them side by side: Drom bulky and dark-haired, Izra lean and very fair. Drom is half Izra's age, but she seems much older than her scarce twenty years after she fought for Nibiru in the war. And the top of Izra's head is just above Drom's shoulders, but I know better than to underestimate the fierce ex-pirate. A scar cuts across the skin surrounding one of Drom's eyes; the empty crater left in one of Izra's eye sockets is a warning of what could've happened if it had cut a little closer.

If nothing else, they share a spectacular talent for violence. For a few seconds I just watch them dance around each other, feeling very aware of the fact that either one of them could lay me out in a second flat. One of Izra's arms is half-useless, with the black, rib cage–like Primus gun attached to it no longer operational, but it doesn't seem to slow her down.

"Hey," I say, and they pause their sparring and turn to me. Izra looks annoyed by the interruption, while Drom just looks... flat. "Uh, I've got something to tell everyone at dinner, so stick around in the mess if you want to hear it."

They both glare at me wordlessly. I hold up my hands, back out of the room, and flee to the cockpit.

Orion, at least, is always happy to see me. It may just be because long hours at the wheel are far from exciting when we're drifting aimlessly out in open space between Nibiru and Gaia, but the broad grin he flashes when I enter seems genuine. He's been through a lot lately, from his stint in Ca Sineh, to risking his life by abandoning us for the Titans, so I'm glad he's on his way back to being his usual cheery self. His buzz cut is starting to grow out into his usual brown curls, and his smile is as frequent and charming as always. But I don't think I'll ever get used to seeing him with a Titan war-brand on his wrist, and our friendship still isn't what it used to be. I've forgiven him for choosing the Titans and leaving me, and I trust him as the pilot of my ship, but that doesn't mean everything can just go back to the way it was. I hope it can, someday.

Well, minus the whole "hooking up in supply closets" part. *That* we can leave in the past.

"What's up, Cap?" he asks, giving me a mock-serious salute.

"Hey, hey." I sink into the copilot's chair, allowing myself a wistful look around the cockpit. Handing my former role as pilot to Orion was clearly the right move, but I can't deny that I miss the sense of freedom behind the wheel. I keep finding excuses to come spend time in here, even with nothing to do. "How's my ship? Looking good for the landing?"

"Sure," Orion says. "Running like a dream, as always."

I have to laugh. This ship is my pride and joy, but we both know it's far from a dream. *Memoria* has been torn apart and put back together so many times I doubt there's anything left of the original, and most of those repairs were the cheap and dirty type. She's a patchy old thing, even worse than ol' *Fortuna* was. Not that I'd ever let anyone aside from me speak that way about *either* of my ships.

"Wanted to give you a heads-up, I've got an announcement to make after dinner."

"Announcing your announcement, eh?" he asks, and then waits for me to say more, but I only grin. He slumps down in his seat and presses his hand to his forehead, feigning despair. "You're a tease."

"You should know that better than anyone." I smirk at him and rise from my seat. "Anyway. Dinner's almost ready. Be patient."

On the way back toward the mess hall, I pause outside the room of our final crew member. I know he's inside; he pretty much always is. Daniil...Daniil I still haven't figured out yet. I was happy to invite him aboard the ship at Corvus's request, knowing that my brother never would've suggested it if he had any doubt that he was trustworthy. But I still know hardly anything about him, even after months on board together. Granted, he did spend the first few weeks being horribly space-sick as he adjusted to life on a ship, but even after that he's barely interacted with the rest of the crew. All I've gathered is that he knew Corvus on Titan, fought on their home-planet's side in the recent war, and committed treason against his own people in a risky play for peace.

The last bit is all I need to know to welcome him with open arms, no matter who he was beforehand. It's not like I'm a stranger to making terrible mistakes. Some might call me an expert, in fact. And it's obvious he's trying just as hard as I have to make up for them.

I rap my knuckles on the door, and it opens so fast he must have rushed to answer. His jumpsuit—borrowed from Corvus, so it's a little baggy and short on his lanky build—is rumpled like he was lying on the bed.

"Yes, Captain?" he asks, standing with a soldier's attention. His slim body and olive complexion may not be the norm for his home-planet, but it'd still be hard to mistake him for anything other than a Titan, even at a glance.

I bite back a laugh. He's the only one who always calls me by my title rather than my name, and never making a joke out of it like the others sometimes do. I've told him he doesn't have to, but, well...if I'm being honest, I do kind of like the sound of it. Daniil is the only person on board who didn't know me during my messy years. It feels good to be looked at with genuine respect.

Still, as much as it strokes my ego, it's more important to me that he's comfortable here. "You don't have to be so formal," I say, flashing him a smile. "Scorpia's fine. And I just wanted to let you know that I'm making an announcement at dinner. Do you mind eating in the mess hall with the rest of us?"

So far, he's been taking all his meals to his room to eat alone. But he says, "Of course, Captain." His fingers twitch, and he hastily folds his hands behind his back to hide that he was about to shoot me a Titan salute.

"I'm just asking, not ordering," I say. "If you want to eat by yourself and then come back for the announcement, that's fine, too." As badly as I want to pull him into the rest of the crew, I have to be careful. I don't want to make the mistakes I made with Corvus—pushing too hard, too fast, not letting him take the alone time he needed when he came back from the war. And I know all of this must be especially strange for Daniil, who has never known a life outside of Titan. He must be lonely here, but I know it's not a simple thing to forge new bonds to replace old ones.

"I'll be there, Captain," he says, very seriously, in a way that shows he is definitely taking it as an order.

I suppress a sigh. I could push it further, but really, I *do* want him to be there. "Appreciate it," I say, and head out.

I take a long bath before dinner, both because I'll never tire of the luxury and because I need some time to calm my nerves. No matter how excited I am about my announcement, the anxiety is always there, too. And the desire for a drink. That always rears its head at moments like these. But tonight's not gonna be the night that it wins. Not with my whole crew counting on me, and not when everything is finally going right for us.

For the first time in a long time, everything is good in our corner of the universe. We solved the mystery of Gaia's decline at the hands of its alien Planetary Defense System, stopped the war between the Titans, Nibirans, and Gaians before the PDS on Nibiru could trigger the same fate there, and got our asses out of there before we could all be arrested for the various forms of treason that most of us committed along the way.

But I still can't shake the belief that it's only a matter of time before something from our past catches up with us and everything goes wrong again. Maybe it's just because I've felt hunted my whole life, and never known a system that wasn't on the brink of war...but somehow, I don't think so. We've been involved in too much, and know too much, to be allowed to walk away from it all. There will be a reckoning eventually.

I submerge my head under the warm water and let those thoughts float away. They can wait. Tonight is about good news.

I toss on a dress shirt and nice pants for the occasion, rather than the standard-issue jumpsuits most of us wear around the ship. The prosthetic fingers of my right hand fumble with the buttons, but I manage it and then drag a comb through the unruly tumble of my hair. It's growing out long and wild lately, but I'm kind of digging the look.

By the time I'm ready for dinner, everyone is waiting for me. I step into the room and pause, briefly overtaken by the sight of everyone gathered in the mess hall. I still remember the immense pressure I felt leading a crew that wasn't just my family for the first time. Hell, even taking charge of my family was a huge challenge not so very long ago. But it feels right, standing up here now, looking over my crew. A couple of ex-pirates, a Titan deserter, and of course, my siblings, raised on the smuggling ship *Fortuna*—may she rest in peace. Born all over the system, most of us in trouble with one planetary government or another, many without a single place to call a legal home aside from the one we've created on this former pirate vessel. Altogether, they're probably the motliest crew of criminals all over the system.

I'm so damn proud.

"Hey, everyone," I say, moving to the head of the table and remaining on my feet. The chatter quiets, and their eyes follow me. I don't have to work to gain their attention like I once did. "As you all know, we've all been through a lot over the last several months," I say, looking from face to face. "We've seen planets end." I think of the bio-weapon spreading over Titan; and Gaia, plagued by unnatural storms stemming from the Primus statues. "And many of us fought in a horrible war." Kitaya still burns in my memory. I suspect it always will. "And...perhaps worst of all... we've had to work for fucking politicians." That one earns me a smattering of chuckles and wry grins, along with an exasperated look from Corvus. I smile at him before continuing. "I know we've all got our scars, whether visible or not." Now I can't help but look down at my prosthetic hand, flexing my new fingers. Admittedly, now that I've gotten used to them, I barely even think about the fact it's not my real hand...but that moment of pain and loss and terror is still sharp in my memory. "But in the end, we fought for peace, and we got it. Each and every one of you helped make that possible, and I'm damn proud to have you all on my ship." I take a deep breath, letting my hand drop to my side again.

"But I've been promising for a while that I'd find a way to make it so that this isn't your only option, and I think I've finally figured out how to pull through on that. I'm working with Eri and Halon for a way to get to Pax." Most of them look surprised. Some—like Lyre—are openly disappointed. Pax is a dangerous little desert world, and nobody's first choice, but it's the only choice for most of us. It doesn't have as much government oversight as the other planets, with its lack of a formal leader, and it's also the only planet without an alien Planetary Defense System. "They say it's easier to disappear there, if that's what you want. Get a new identity. A fresh start. We can head to meet them once we finish up on Gaia." I pause, letting that sink in, before continuing.

"But before that, I'm going to ask you all to stay on board for one last mission. When this is over, should you choose to, you're free to go your own separate ways. You'll always have a home on *Memoria*, but if you've had your fair share of adventure, I'm not gonna hold it against you. Before that, though, I need you all at my side this one last time. This is important. Maybe the most important thing we've ever done." I pause and let the silence stretch out till it's ready to snap. Even Corvus is looking at me with his brow furrowed, uncertain of what I'm about to say.

"And that very important mission is…" I bite the inside of my cheek to hold back a grin, maintaining the somber facade for as long as I can manage. "…We're going on vacation in the Golden City! We'll spend a full week there before heading onward to Pax."

There's a moment of silence. Corvus shuts his eyes and sighs loud enough to be audible in the quiet room. Then Orion lets out a bright peal of laughter, and the room erupts in excited conversation.

"All of us can go?" Orion asks eagerly.

"All of us," I confirm. On our past trips, almost everyone has stayed on board while we sold our wares in the city, to lower our chances of being recognized. But we haven't run into trouble yet, and I feel confident enough to take a risk for the sake of one last hurrah together.

"*Finally*," Pol says. "I'm sick of sitting on the ship while you get to go have fun." He grimaces. "And getting knocked out whenever we go to Gaia."

"Never been to Zi Vi," Daniil is saying to Corvus. "Is it really all they say?"

"It's more than they say," Orion says, reaching over to clap him on the shoulder. "The Golden City is the jewel of the system. You'll see."

"Yes, it's great, so long as you're a fan of drugs and nudity," Izra drawls.

"Scorpia, I hope you haven't forgotten our deal," Lyre calls out, and I try not to wince as I remember my *expensive* promise to pay for an education on Deva for her.

"Right, right, right," I say, clapping my hands to regain everyone's attention. "Now, we have some business to attend to as well. Sell whatever we grab on this trip to Gaia, hopefully solidify some business connections we can use in the future. But for the most part, I just want the lot of you to have some fun. I think we all deserve it after everything." I look around the room, at the genuine excitement on everyone's faces. Even Izra has a hint of a smile, though it shifts into a scowl the moment I look at her.

It feels good to see them happy. To know that I have the power to make them happy. Once, I would've thought the best thing I could do was give them safety, and leave it at that. But right now, the future seems brighter than I've ever hoped for.

CHAPTER TWO

History of the Lost

Corvus

The ship shudders as it fights through Gaia's atmosphere, and the straps of my launch chair dig into my chest. The winds scream and claw at us. Every time I tell myself that *Memoria* will endure, and Scorpia and Orion will guide us safely through the unnatural storms again—yet it never feels certain. Gaia does not want us here; the Planetary Defense System will do all it can to rip us apart to prevent us from reaching the surface.

Yet, like every other time, we survive. The ship settles and the engine fades down to a low rumble. Outside, the winds still howl, but they failed once more to keep us at bay.

Even the bumpy landing isn't enough to dampen everyone's spirits. Scorpia's announcement that we're heading to Zi Vi isn't as exciting for me as it is for many of the others, and I'm not sure how I feel about the potential for some of our crew members to leave us for a life on Pax, but at least I can look forward to a few weeks without any trips to this desolate world. Still, as Drom, Izra, and I prepare for another venture out onto the storm-torn surface for loot, I try to keep in mind that we have one more obstacle before our little vacation.

"Focus up," I say, zipping closed my orange surface suit, a remnant from our council-funded first trip here on *Memoria*. "We have work to do."

"Oh, shut it," Drom says. "It's not like Gaia's gonna be any different than last time. Still as dead as before."

Irritation bubbles up in me, but I push it back down. Drom is always itching for a fight, lately, but I'm not going to be the one to give it to her. "If you don't want to come, I can find someone else," I tell her, as mildly as I can manage.

She bristles. "Yeah? Who? The Titan deserter? Not even you trust him."

Before I can respond to that, Izra smacks Drom's helmet. "I don't trust *you* to watch my back if you're not going to take it seriously," she says. "Gaia's still dangerous. You know how many people I watched die to storms and landslides on Titan?"

Drom rolls her eyes, but bites her tongue and finishes suiting up. I'm fairly certain Izra is the only one who could get away with talking to her like that. I shoot her a grateful look, but she either doesn't notice or ignores it.

Lyre, Scorpia, and Daniil are all out on the ramp already, bathing in the red-tinged light of Nova Vita, since the weather is calm enough for them to get some fresh air. Daniil sits apart from the others, huddled with his knees to his chest, likely recovering from the rough landing. Orion must still be in the cockpit, holding his post in case we need an emergency liftoff, and Pol is knocked out by the sleeping pills we give him whenever we land here to prevent another adverse reaction. Whenever he's conscious on Gaia, he complains about an earsplitting noise the rest of us can't hear—something related to his sickness, we've gathered.

"Remember," Scorpia says, "the more you find, the more credits we have to blow in Zi Vi. I've got some rich lady on Deva who's eager to buy—get us some pretty shit to sell." She pauses, and then adds, "Oh yeah, and be careful, and all."

"Yeah, yeah, we know the drill," Drom grumbles.

"Don't forget to check on Pol in about an hour," I tell Scorpia. I head for the ramp and pause beside Daniil—wondering, as always, if I should try to reach out to him, to say something. He always wanted to leave Titan for Pax, and soon he'll have his chance to start a new life there. I'm running out of time to try to repair our damaged relationship. But as usual, I find myself at a loss. I clear my throat, click on my helmet, and carry onward to Gaia's surface. I wait for Izra and Drom to do the same and turn on their comms, and then say, "Let's hustle. This weather won't last forever."

No matter how many times we've been here before, the extent of the devastation in Levian still strikes me anew every time I see it. Once a shining testament to humanity's resilience, one of the first cities established in Nova Vita—now, nothing but rubble. As we push deeper into the city, I spot a fallen billboard half-hidden in the mess: Talulah Leonis's face flickers up at us, half of it reduced to dead pixels. I shake my head and carry on, but Drom pauses to stomp on it, killing the image for good.

The Gaians paid heavily for the hubris of their former leader. In her push to make her proud civilization less dependent on the others in the system, she instead turned their own world against them by placing too much trust in alien technology. When faced with the consequences, she then wiped out Titan and tried to do the same to Nibiru. It still makes me sick with anger to think of all the things that Leonis did. At least she, too, paid the price in the end, thanks to my sister. My only regret is that I couldn't do it myself.

Yet, I sometimes feel guilty about ransacking a city that I once knew to be so full of life. I walk over twisted metal and ruined buildings and see the ghosts of homes, and schools, and churches. Abandoned lives and lost culture.

But it is difficult to feel too guilty when the rest of the system is too busy fighting among themselves to come here and save any of it before it is buried forever in the destruction. And my family has turned a profit off of much worse things.

Thinking of the loss of culture here gives me an idea. I turn on the lights on my fingertips and signal to the others to follow me as I head to the once-glamorous Itsennen district. I make my way to a familiar building, now half caved in, but with enough of it still standing to give me hope.

The Levian Museum of Art has the boxy architecture characteristic of Gaia, but with a playfulness the surrounding buildings lack. It has the appearance of several bricks stacked on top of one another, with a piece carved out of each to create a hole in the midsection. There, a set of lifts is meant to take visitors to the top, so the exhibits can be explored from the top down.

"A museum? Seriously?" Drom asks over the comms.

"Some of its paintings are supposed to be relics from Earth," I say. "They're priceless."

"Personally," Izra says, "I'd prefer something with a price."

I sigh. "Trust me. We can sell a lot of this. Especially if Scorpia has a wealthy Devan client."

Despite their doubt, they follow me. When I visited this place as a child on a school trip, we explored the museum the way it was designed to be explored, descending through the stories of the building, which display galleries from different time periods in reverse chronological order. Now, I don't trust the battered lifts to operate correctly, nor do I fancy the thought of being inside without an easy exit, so we break through a security door on the bottom floor. We move through a musty storeroom to what was usually reserved as the museum's final exhibit: displays of art saved from long-ago Earth.

The building—once pristine, artistic, and stylized—is a wreck. I'm surprised how much it stings to see it fallen. The shutters have been ripped off of the windows and the glass shattered, and this bottom level has flooded. The once-plush carpet is filthy, its former color indistinguishable. Many of the display cases have toppled, their relics buried under heaps of glass and metal. Shards of ceramics are scattered among the wreckage. Ancient books lie facedown on the sodden carpet. History and culture preserved since humankind's exodus from Earth, now ruined.

When I take off my helmet to get a better look, the stink of mold chokes me and glass crunches beneath my boots. Expecting the worst, I move onward—and breathe a sigh of relief as I enter the next exhibit. The holoscreens meant to display information about the paintings here have died, and the white walls are rife with water stains and mold, but much of the art seems salvageable, saved by Plexiglas display cases.

"This is all worth taking," I say, gesturing with my lights. "We'll have to extract them from the cases, then from the frames, and roll them up. Carefully." I cut my gaze to Drom. "Their value will go down considerably if they're damaged."

She gives me a mocking Titan salute. I ignore her and shed my gloves for the delicate work. Izra stays near the shattered windows, keeping watch on both our surroundings and the state of the weather overhead. This careful process would be difficult for her, regardless, with only one good hand. Her left arm was patched up decently back on Nibiru, but the Primus gun attached to it is still dead. She refuses to have it removed, so for now it's merely in the way most of the time.

A tearing sound pulls my attention to Drom.

"Shit," she says, scowling down at the painting she's crouched over. "This isn't one of the valuable ones, is it? It looks like a fuckin' finger painting."

I walk over, look down at the painting, and instantly recognize it as an old Earth classic. The kind of piece we covered in my history education on Gaia. I clear my throat, trying not to estimate how much it might be worth. "Let me handle the paintings from now on," I say, and leave it at that.

After securing the paintings I deem most valuable, we proceed to the second floor. This area holds artwork from the generation ships on their way to Nova Vita, almost all digital due to the careful allocation of resources during the long trip from Earth to here. This story is arranged as one huge room, high-ceilinged and windowless, the stairs tucked away in the corners to leave the space as open as possible. The lights are dim and yellow, and the walls painted in a metallic silver to recreate the atmosphere on the ships.

This exhibit was my favorite as a child. Most of my classmates didn't have much interest in it. The dim, enclosed space made them uncomfortable—but for me, it felt like *Fortuna*. Like home. I remember wishing I could have brought Scorpia to see it.

These art pieces are simple compared to the complex, immersive digital artwork created on Gaia, which is held on the upper levels of the museum. They don't have the same ancient feeling of the relics from Earth, either. But I admire the beauty in the simplicity, and the natural themes the space generations favored. I always found it moving to think of them floating out in the vast emptiness, a broken home behind and no guarantee of survival ahead, still taking the time to make art. And as someone who has spent much of his life on a spacecraft, I can appreciate the images they chose to replicate in order to find comfort in the darkness.

"Never understood the point of this shit," Izra says, pulling me from my nostalgia as she wanders in behind me. Drom must have stayed below. I should call her to us, but the sky is quiet for now, and I could use a break from her attitude.

"You prefer Titan art?" I went to a museum there, once, when I was on leave. Most of it was paintings depicting famous battles, and statues of old war heroes.

Izra snorts. "That propaganda? No." She walks over to one of the nearby podiums and jabs the button on top with her gun arm. A small, rotating holosphere, slowly changing colors, appears in the air above the table. I'm honestly not sure if the pixelated glitches are a result of damage, or part of the piece. It's surprising that it still works at all, but perhaps the Gaians kept the original, discrete power sources the pieces were originally made with, rather than hooking them up to their own power grid. "But at least that has a purpose. The fuck is this supposed to be?"

I walk over and touch my hand to the top of the sphere. It slowly unfurls into the shape of a flower, still changing colors. A few holographic petals drift upward and melt away into nothingness. I watch it, and then look at Izra. "Did you know that flowers grew on Titan, once?"

She looks back at me, unimpressed. "What do I care about flowers?"

I shut off the hologram and move onward to the next table. "I remember this one." I press the button, and the soft sound of rain fills the surrounding area. Above my head, holographic raindrops appear and fall upward to splash against the white ceiling. It strikes the same chord as the first time I saw it, dredging up something tender and melancholy from deep inside me. I stand, head tilted back to watch the digital rain defy gravity, for several long seconds before I realize Izra is staring at me.

"What?" I ask.

"You're into this shit," she accuses.

"I wouldn't say I'm into it." I pause, consider, and relent. "But I was raised here. You'll have to forgive some Gaian tendencies."

She walks across the room to me, and jabs me in the chest with one finger. "You're all soft, deep down, aren't you? You gonna recite poetry next?"

I stand perfectly still, watching the faint blue light of the holographic rain shimmer on her skin. That is my favorite part about the art in here—how it invites you to be a part of it—and I can't bring myself to be embarrassed about my appreciation for it right now. Perhaps there is a little bit of Gaian still in me, after all.

The sound of laser-fire downstairs shatters the moment.

Izra and I both draw our weapons and race for the stairs without hesitation. But the first floor is quiet once we reach it. Drom stands with her back to a wall, her weapon aimed at a still-smoking hunk of metal on the floor. She holsters it when she sees us.

"No worries," she says. "Only a drone. Damn thing came in through a window."

Izra walks over to the fallen drone and nudges it with a boot, but it doesn't move.

I lower my weapon. "You should've hidden and let it pass by. Shooting it down will only draw attention."

"Yeah, well, figured we didn't want it recording us and beaming it back to whoever-the-fuck," Drom says.

Assuming the drone was live-streaming its feed, the damage is already done. But judging from the flush spreading across Drom's face, I don't think shooting it was a logical move, no matter what she argues. She's been on edge ever since the war on Nibiru.

Izra picks the machine up by one broken propeller and flips it over, revealing the unmistakable barrel of a weapon beneath—and a stamp that reads *Made in Pax*.

"Since when does Pax send out armed drones?" I ask.

"Since Deva started shooting them down?" Izra retorts. She drops the broken machine to the floor with a dull clunk.

Both Pax and Deva are still picking the bones of Titan's carcass despite the fact it's technically reclaimed territory, so it doesn't surprise me that they're scavenging here on Gaia, too. But sending drones to investigate, or even to harvest materials, is one thing. Sending in automated weaponry is another entirely.

"I don't like this," I say. "Where there's one drone, there's bound to be more. Let's head back to the ship."

"Oh, come on," Drom says. "This is hardly a haul. You really afraid of a few drones?"

As if in response, a sound comes from outside. I hold up a hand, and we all listen to the growing, unmistakable buzzing noise of approaching drones.

And, from the sound of it, there's far more than a few.

"Up to the second floor," I say. "No windows. We'll funnel them through the doorway."

As we race for the stairs, the drones begin pouring in—through the shattered windows, holes in the wall, the door we left cracked for our exit. Each one is only about the size of my head, but that doesn't make them any less deadly, especially when they're swarming in the dozens like this. We make it to the second floor just as they fire off the first shots, lasers peppering the stairs at our heels.

Drom rushes to barricade the door to the third story so we won't be fighting on two fronts. Izra and I hold the doorway. The drones quickly force us back with their barrage of laser-fire, and we duck behind two of the metal podiums holding art projectors. My arm stings. I've already been grazed with a shot that would've done more damage if not for my suit taking most of the impact. Izra, too, has had her suit punctured in a couple of places, though I see no blood. They're too fast, too precise, their movements too in sync.

20

"They're automated," I shout across to the others, as we struggle to hold them back with our own fire. Good news, as it means we likely only triggered a self-defense system, rather than being discovered by someone who wants to kill us. Yet bad news, as it means we'll never outshoot them; we can't beat their targeting and reflexes with our flawed human bodies.

But we can outsmart them. Automated drones have one glaring weakness, and we are in a perfect place to exploit it. "Confuse the targeting systems, they're based on movement!" I slap the button on the podium behind me to demonstrate. The holographic art piece folds out from the top—and the sound of rustling grass is immediately drowned out by responding fire from the drones. I lean around the podium and shoot down two of them while they're focused on the hologram.

Izra grins as she catches on. She activates her own podium, sending digital flames crackling out the top, and the drones swap targets again.

Soon the room is a kaleidoscope of movement and color and sound. Drones fall to the floor one after another against a backdrop of holographic beauty. Rushing water, birdsong, and the roar of a snowstorm fill the room, all punctured with the steady ping of laser-fire from both us and the drones. By the time the shooting has died down, the metallic walls and podiums are all pocketed with dents and scorch marks. Several of the holograms crackle and pixelate. The last few flicker out after a minute, leaving us in silence.

"Fucking hell," Drom says, breathing hard, as she emerges from the back of the room. She kicks one of the smoking fallen drones to clatter into the wall. The floor is littered with at least a couple dozen of them. "Thought they'd never stop coming."

I move to the descending stairwell and listen for more drones, or additional company brought by the sounds of the fight, but there's nothing. Still, there's no telling what kind of attention we've pulled to ourselves. I'd guess there are living Paxians somewhere on the planet as well—and even if not, those back on Pax are unlikely to be happy about us destroying their property. I've no idea how much these drones are worth, but I can't imagine they're cheap. And we have enough enemies as it is.

I was hoping for a chance to explore the higher floors, but there's no time for that now.

"Pack up what you can, and quickly," I say. "Let's get back to the ship."

Our packs are only half-full by the time we notice dark clouds gathering overhead and make the final call. We're all geared up for a storm, but none of us are eager to be caught in the middle of one. The last time we were here, the weather was so bad we were forced to seek shelter in the city overnight. Drom sprained her ankle as we rushed out of the rain, and we had to drop a quarter of our haul so we could help her back to the ship.

This time, we're luckier. If we leave now, we should be able to beat it. We suit up and set off for the ship, wordlessly picking up our pace to race against the incoming storm.

Then we round a corner in Levian and come face-to-face with a group of strangers.

They're clearly just as surprised to see us as we are to see them, and in the moment of mutual stunned stillness, I take in as many details as I can. They're wearing orange suits identical to ours, though their chests are emblazoned with a dark blue emblem in the shape of a pair of wings. Their tinted visors conceal their features. There are six of them.

That's as far as my mind gets before everyone starts drawing weapons. I do so, too, though I also jut out my free hand to signal defense, not aggression. Too late, I realize it's a Titan army signal, which only Izra will recognize, but Drom seems to get the idea.

The strangers don't fire, either. Likely means they're here on official business, rather than scrappers—not that it improves the situation much for us. One of them turns toward my hand signal, and then sharply back at my helmet-concealed face. Alarm shoots through me—but they don't stand like soldiers, nor do their weapons look Titan military-issue. They're more like the compact blasters that Gaian law-enforcers would carry.

"Lay down your weapons and state your business," the one at the front says, voice muffled through their helmet.

Scorpia would know what to say here to defuse the situation, but I'll have to do my best. "Not until we know who we're speaking to."

"We are representatives of the Interplanetary Alliance, here to reclaim the land and materials that belong to our people," she says, drawing herself up tall and rigid with a righteous indignation that immediately makes me think *Gaian*. "And you are trespassing on our planet."

"The *who?*" Drom asks, before I can respond.

The Interplanetary Alliance. The name is new to me, but it can only mean that Nibiru, Gaia, and Titan are making strides to unite—and apparently take back the planets they left behind. They're moving much faster than anticipated. Bad news for us, as we're no longer on their good side. "Didn't realize the Alliance was already moving to reclaim this area. We'll leave."

"Yes," the woman says stiffly. "You will. Just as soon as you tell me which planet sent you, and hand over everything you've looted."

I hate the thought of handing over our haul. We need the credits, especially if we're going to be grounded on Deva, and then Pax, for a while. But if the Alliance forces recognize us, we could risk a lot more than this. We didn't leave Nibiru on good terms with any of the planetary governments, and Scorpia and I have always known they'd come after us when the dust settled after the war. We just didn't think it would be so soon.

I don't like our odds in a fight here, especially when we're already worn out from the encounter with those Paxian drones. So we'll have to try to talk. Lying always comes so easily to Scorpia. Not so much for me. But we already have a plan in place for something like this. I cross my arms over my chest in a Gaian greeting. "We're not looters. We're here on behalf of Shey Leonis to collect cultural artifacts of significance." I glance around, well aware that I have weapons aimed at me. "May I take my pack off and show you what I have?"

The woman seems to chew it over for a moment, and then she dips her chin in a brief nod.

Thank the stars we went to the museum today instead of getting our usual haul of the most valuable technology we can find. I'm able to lend our story some credibility by pulling out a few of the rolled-up paintings and art projectors from my bag. "I'll give you what we have, and we'll leave," I say, once I've slowly emptied out my pack. Izra and Drom surrender some of theirs, too, though I can tell they're holding on to a portion of what we grabbed, in the hopes they won't scrutinize us too closely. "But I'm sure you understand that what we're doing isn't strictly legal, so...I hope you don't feel the need to take down our information, since we're complying."

There's a moment of silence. Sweat trickles down the back of my suit.

"I understand," the woman says, finally. "It looks like a genuine case of getting our wires crossed. You're doing a good thing out here. Thank you for what you've done to help preserve Gaia." She gestures to the others. "Gather the goods and move on." They do so, though a couple of them cast confused glances back at her.

I stay where I am. Suspicion overshadows my relief.

That was too easy. Far too easy. We weren't even searched or interrogated. Could this be a trick to get us to let our guard down? Are her people setting a trap for us ahead?

The woman in charge lingers behind as the others leave, confirming my suspicions that we aren't done here. As their footsteps recede, she turns to us and says, "Okay, cut the bullshit. You're the Kaisers, aren't you?"

My hand automatically goes for my weapon, but she makes no aggressive moves herself, and she's left herself outnumbered here. So after a moment, I pull my hand away from my gun and instead remove my helmet, since the weather is calm enough to risk it.

She nods to herself. "Corvus. We've not been acquainted yet, but my name is Commander Yvette Zinne."

The name still isn't ringing any bells for me, but after a moment she takes her helmet off. The face is familiar: brown skin, straight eyebrows, and a serious expression. "You're the one who took care of Pol when he was being treated on Gaia."

Zinne nods. "And before that, to my shame, I was Talulah Leonis's head of security."

She meets my eyes, and then makes a Gaian gesture so formal and complicated it takes me a moment to parse. It's one of those I've only studied and never had the occasion to use, conveying a combination of respect and shame. "And I know more than most about what your family really did."

I tense. That could mean... a wide range of things, truly. Our family history is complicated at best. But after a moment, Zinne says, "Which is why I'm going to let you go."

She pauses. "But don't you dare use Shey Leonis's name to get yourself out of trouble again. I won't have you staining her reputation just when she's repaired it."

"Understood." Assuming that means we're done, I step back. "You won't find us here again."

"I really hope not," she says. "Now go. I'll give you thirty minutes before I call in this sighting to the IA. We're under orders to arrest you on sight."

I'm already hurrying to replace my helmet and zip up my bag, but that gives me pause. "Arrest us?" I ask, though I dread the answer. "For what?" I knew the Alliance would hold a grudge against us—but I didn't realize they would go so far.

Her brow creases. "For..." She stops, taking a harder look at me. "Stars. You don't even know?"

I shake my head wordlessly. She looks away. I can tell she's grappling with whatever she's about to say next. Finally, she grimaces, and pulls a comm out of her pack. "If anyone asks, you didn't get it from me. But you need to see this before you go."

CHAPTER THREE

Most Wanted

Scorpia

Lyre and I play cards in the cargo bay while we wait for the ground team to return. She soundly beats me each and every hand. Literally every hand.

"Are you trying to lose?" she asks, annoyed.

"Huh?" I tear my eyes away from the brewing storm on the horizon. "No. I'm just bad. No need to rub it in."

"It's just that, statistically speaking, you should win at least occasionally, if only due to dumb luck. And yet..." She gestures wordlessly.

I look at her, look at my cards—just as terrible as the last several—and let them tumble out of my hand. The wind gusting through the open ramp scatters them across the cargo bay. "Oops," I say. "Wind's kicking up."

"Scorpia!" Lyre pushes to her feet and scrambles after the fallen cards as the wind continues pushing them away. "This is our last good deck after Pol spilled curry all over the other one!"

"Wind," I repeat, and bite my thumbnail as I turn again to the horizon. A storm *is* coming.

Thankfully, the others beat it back. The sight of all three of them approaching quells the anxiety gnawing at my stomach lining, but when Corvus climbs up the ramp and pulls off his helmet, his expression brings it right back.

"What?" I ask before he can get a word out, hoping it's nothing more than a bad haul.

He runs a hand through his sweat-slicked hair and sighs. "We need to get off of the planet. Immediately."

I frown. "Okay. Launch seats, everyone." I start to head up to the cockpit but grab Corvus's arm before he can pull away. He falls into step beside me. "What's going on?"

"He let the Alliance goons steal our whole haul, is what happened," Drom says, clomping right along behind us and wrestling with her suit straps as she walks. "We could've taken 'em. Easy."

"The who?"

"The Interplanetary Alliance," Corvus says. "Seems Nibiru, Titan, and Gaia have a new name, and a new plan to start retaking their planets." He stops there, though it looks like he's holding himself back from saying more.

And this is bad news enough—not only because it'll make it impossible for us to continue scavenging on the abandoned worlds. We've been hoping they'd be too busy managing their alliance to come after us. Surely they have enough of their own problems, between trying to make peace between three peoples who were recently trying to kill one another, and the fact that Deva and Pax will undoubtedly see this new coalition as a threat.

But we always knew this would happen eventually. The Alliance leadership can't be happy about us running around the system with our knowledge about the Planetary Defense Systems, even though the Nibirans are the ones who hired us to discover the truth about them on Gaia. Plus, there's the fact that the Nibirans must hate Corvus and I for disobeying their orders to end the war, and Altair hates us for blackmailing him into peace, and I'm sure the Gaians hate us, too, just on principle. They'll find a way to punish us. If they're already moving to reclaim their lost planets, that means they're stable enough to do it sooner, rather than later.

And they know we're here, so getting off of this planet needs to be the priority. With that storm headed our way, I don't trust any of our trainee copilots in the chair today.

"All right. We'll talk more after launch. Someone make sure Pol is strapped in."

Once we're safely out of Gaia's turbulent atmosphere, I head straight to Corvus's room.

"Please don't tell me we managed to piss off some Paxians, too," I say.

His guilty look tells me everything. "I...thought it was more prudent to mention the IA incident first. But how did you know?"

I sigh, holding up my comm. "We got a message from a Silvania Azenari. I had to look her up. She was the Paxian representative at the Interplanetary Council." I vaguely remember there being some confusion about her presence, since Pax doesn't have a formal leader. "Tell me we didn't shoot some Paxian scrappers."

"Just some drones," Corvus says. He pauses, and then corrects, "A lot of drones."

I rub a hand across my face. "Shit. Well, okay. Hopefully this doesn't mean we have Pax on our ass now, too." I drum my fingers on the side of the comm before hitting the play button.

A holographic visual of Silvania expands above the device. I remember her once I see her: a middle-aged woman with brown skin, long, dark hair, and a weird metal box implanted in the back of her skull. Ugh, Paxians.

"Captain Kaiser," she says. Her smile says this message isn't a threat, but I've dealt with enough politicians not to trust that. "I just reviewed some drone footage and almost thought I saw some of your crew on Gaia. Weird, huh? Surely a reputable woman like yourself wouldn't be trespassing on Interplanetary Alliance Territory. And neither would I, of course. But, weirdest thing...the footage disappeared right after I watched it." She shrugs. "Anyway, sorry if my malfunctioning drones caused you any trouble. If you ever find yourself around Pax, I'll buy you a drink sometime to make up for it."

The image disappears. I lower the comm, frowning. "Not sure what to make of that."

"I'm guessing it's an 'I won't tell if you won't.'"

"Hmm." And the offer to buy me a drink is a clear enough message—she wants something from me. "Well, guess we might need to lie low on Deva for longer than anticipated. Whatever this is, I want no part of it."

Corvus grimaces. "About lying low on Deva...I was given some information on Gaia by a certain Commander Zinne."

It takes me a moment to place the name. "Oh, right. She arrested me once."

"I suppose we're lucky she was more sympathetic this time. She gave me..." He stops and, instead of continuing, holds out his comm. A document is already open on it, and dread halts me in my place as I see the title: *The Interplanetary Alliance's Most-Wanted List.*

"Shit," I say. "How many of us are on here?"

"I didn't read much of it without you," Corvus says, but his dour expression says much more.

"Shit," I say again, more emphatically. My fingertip hovers above the comm screen, but I pull it back and let out a long breath. "Well, let's gather the crew in the lounge. Everyone should see this."

30

The crew's curiosity is already bubbling over after our impromptu departure from Gaia, so it's not hard to get them together. Even Pol comes in, slouching on the couch and barely able to keep his eyes open with the lingering effects of the tranquilizer in his system. He's too tired to brush off Corvus fussing over him to make sure the drugged-up launch didn't do any damage. Drom sits on Corvus's other side, while Lyre and Orion take up another couch, and Izra sprawls across her favorite armchair in the corner. Daniil remains standing near the door, leaning against the wall with his arms folded over his chest.

I head to the front of the room and plug Corvus's comm into our holoscreen projector—an admittedly banged-up but still cutting-edge piece of tech we swiped for ourselves on our last trip to Gaia.

Then I turn to the others and ask, "Anyone wanna take bets on who tops the IA's most-wanted list?"

"Where did you get that?" Lyre asks, her eyes going wide.

I grin. Just for a little bit longer, I want to savor the feeling of knowing something before she does. I'm not going to feel bad about it when she spent days preening over the fact that she was the first to find out that Nibiru, Gaia, and Titan had officially announced their peace treaty and intention to live together on Nibiru.

"Oh, you know," I say with a breezy shrug, "I have my sources." Or rather, Corvus does, but she doesn't need to know that.

"Show us already," Izra snaps.

I hold up a hand for patience and wait for everyone to simmer down into grumbling before turning back to the comm. I hope nobody notices that my hands are shaking. Despite all the jokes and theatrics, I know that this list's existence means a big change for many of us—maybe all of us—and maybe forever. But we have to know. I hold my breath and open the document.

It must have been designed for advanced holoscreens like this one, because the document immediately springs into holo-mode. I scroll past the very official and important-looking text, ignoring Lyre's protests that she wants to read it. When I reach the first profile, the scrolling text is replaced by a hologram of a scowling man's face. Statistics hover in the air around him: his name, his crimes, the place he was last seen, etcetera. This man is unfamiliar to me, which is a good thing, given that there's an alarming amount of murders attributed to his name.

I scroll past the serial killers and kidnappers and the like. None of those on our ship, at least; we're a bit pickier about the types of criminals we welcome on board. "Ooh, here we go, Titan deserters," I say. "And...there! Our very own Orion Murdock, wanted for desertion from Titan forces and involvement in a terrorist plot against Nibiru!" This must be a mug shot they logged when he entered Ca Sineh, before he lost his deep tan and head of dark curls. Orion stands and bows dramatically to the room, earning some nervous chuckles and sarcastic clapping from Izra.

"Truly an honor," Orion says, straightening up and getting a closer look at his profile on the list. "My street cred has never been higher. But nothing about my daring escape from Ca Sineh?"

"Technically not a crime on Nibiru, as long as there was no violence against the guards," Lyre pipes up. "They consider it part of human nature to desire escape from confinement, so they don't see fit to criminalize it."

"But how will people know if it's not on my record?" Orion asks, clearly disappointed.

I roll my eyes and keep scrolling. "Now we're getting to the good shit," I say. "Treason! Look, there's Daniil!"

Daniil Naran: desertion and treason against Titan. I'm shocked at how hard-eyed he looks in the image they chose, wearing the Titan military uniform designating him as a colonel. The first thing he did when we hit open space was burn that uniform and launch the ashes out of the air lock.

He glances around as the room applauds again, rubbing the back of his neck with one scarred hand and giving a tentative smile, and it's difficult to believe he's the same man from the picture.

Despite all of my joking around, and the blasé attitudes of the rest of the crew, my chest constricts as I continue to scroll and find my younger siblings' faces staring out from the screen. "Apollo Kaiser. Andromeda Kaiser. Lyre Kaiser," I read out, trying to sound as casual as I did with the others, even though it scares me to know that the IA is out for them as well. I guess I should have expected it, but I'd hoped that they would escape association with our crimes and be able to lead normal lives if they chose it. Once, part of me would have been guiltily glad that the criminal record meant they were stuck on the same boat as me, even if that boat were sinking fast; now, I feel sad that they won't have a choice about what kind of lives they want to lead. "Wanted for questioning regarding the crimes of the deceased Auriga Kaiser and Talulah Leonis...Oh, hey, that's not so bad. Doesn't say you're being charged directly for anything."

"We're not?" Pol asks glumly.

"That's a good thing, dumbass," Drom says, nudging him with a shoulder. "Good criminals are the ones who don't have a rap sheet."

"I hope this list doesn't make it to authorities on Deva," Lyre says. "A criminal record won't look good when I'm applying to the Zi Vi University."

"We'll pay for a new identity for you if we have to," Corvus tells her. "You have nothing to worry about."

"I mean, if it's Deva, who knows?" I say, shrugging, and trying not to think about how expensive that would be on top of the education I already promised her. "Maybe they'll count it as a bonus. Anyway..." I clear my throat, and bang out a drumroll on the table with one hand while I scroll with the other. "Next on the list is...me!" I throw both hands up in celebration. "Scorpia Kaiser, wanted for treason against Nibiru." I lower my hands, stomach twisting. "Wow, treason. Guess I've really moved up in the world. I've come so far since my days of petty crime..." I feign wiping a tear from my eye, earning myself a few laughs, and keep a grin on my face despite the anxiety worming around in my gut. Treason. Damn. It's really going to be hard for me to stay under the radar with a warrant out for something like that. I'm not sure if anywhere in the system will be truly safe for us ever again, even outside of the IA's territory.

And funny to think that this, of all things, is considered my worst crime. I'll own up to plenty of things: smuggling, theft, drug dealing, you name it. But *treason*? For turning Leonis over to the Titans in return for a peace agreement? Fuck that.

"There have to be people in the IA who know that this is a ridiculous charge," Corvus says, with a surprising amount of venom. "Someone has to fight it."

"I'm not holding my breath," I say. "They're all bullshit. Desertion, treason...They don't really care about this. The war's over." The only reason they really want us is that we know too much. They would've found any excuse to come for us.

"Anyway, moving on, where is..." I scroll up farther and finally find Corvus's name. "There you are! Corvus Kaiser. Wow, you're listed even higher than I am?" I turn to shoot him a look. "Stars damn, Corvus, you're a better criminal than me now? You just can't let me have anything for myself, can you?"

He looks at me warily, but I can only maintain a serious face for a few seconds before bursting into laughter. He cracks a small smile. "What am I on there for?"

"Looks like...treason against Titan *and* Nibiru. Wow." I lean over and mock-punch his shoulder. "Look at you. Star of the crew. Worst of the worst. You proud of yourself?"

He shrugs, as if it doesn't matter, but he's still smiling. I had worried that hearing something like this would've sent him into one of his broody, self-loathing spirals, especially given how much respect he once had for both General Altair and the Nibiran Council. Knowing that they both considered him a traitor might have broken him in the past. But as far as I can tell, he seems genuinely unconcerned.

I scroll through the rest of the list. Some of the names on here are familiar—old business contacts, well-known criminals scattered across various planets. But nobody I consider close. Eri and Halon have still evaded attention, it seems. And as far as our crew, that leaves . . .

"Guess that official pardon did the trick," Izra says with a smirk. "Only one on the ship with a clean record. Who would've thought?"

"Won't last long if you keep associating with us," Corvus tells her.

She shrugs. "Wouldn't last long if I was on my own, either."

I'm still staring at the list, my amusement fading and irritation taking its place. The sheer nerve of putting us on a list like this, after we stopped an interplanetary war not once but twice, is pretty stars-damned astounding. Everything we did for them, and they call us criminals for not doing it their way. Plus, everything *they* did—all the death, and the lies, and the manipulation— and they'll get away with it. I wonder how the history books will rewrite this one. I wonder if they'll include me, staring down the barrel of Altair's gun or losing my hand for a planet I never belonged to, or Corvus and Daniil laying down their weapons and calling off the fight despite their orders. Choices, and sacrifices, that saved millions of lives—and they have the gall to call them betrayals.

"These fuckers, sitting all prim and pretty and calling us criminals, like they're any cleaner than us," I say. "The Nibiran Council poisoned their own food supply and lied about it, but sure, whatever, that can be swept under the rug. And Altair attacking a planet and killing innocent civilians? Nah, that's forgivable. And Khatri..." I trail off, thinking as hard as I can, but as far as I'm aware, the new Gaian president hasn't done anything awful. Yet. "Khatri may be decent, but she's still an alien fucker, so she's on thin ice in my books."

"I feel as though there was a point you were trying to make," Corvus says.

"Right. As I was saying, they'd still be tearing each other apart if not for us. And yet we're the criminals? Hah." I shake my head. Much as I want to be flippant about it, it does bother me. "This is 'cause of us, you know? We did this. But they've erased us from the story."

"Such is the way of the system. We've always known it." Corvus looks at me, one corner of his mouth lifting in a sad sort of smile. "They were never going to let us be the heroes. Not people like us."

"Well..." I wrestle with my emotions, annoyed at the fact that it stings. He's right, I should've known better. "Well, fuck 'em, then."

"Fuck 'em," he agrees, which surprises a laugh out of me. "We know the truth of it."

"Guess that has to be enough," I say. But still, it's no wonder we as a species are always falling into these endless, repeated cycles, when we sanitize the past so thoroughly it's impossible to learn from it.

"So what's our plan, then?" Lyre asks, her arms folded over her chest and shoulders braced in clear anticipation of bad news.

I think about it for a few moments, and then shrug. "I mean, as far as I see it, this is just another reason to stay out of the Interplanetary Alliance's reach for a while," I say. "Which we were already thinking about doing, yeah? Deva and Pax should still be safe enough, as long as they're not part of the Alliance." I look at Corvus for confirmation.

His expression is pensive. "There will still be a risk."

"There's a risk for us anywhere," I say. "Always was, always will be. We just gotta be a little more careful. Keep our heads down, keep the law-breaking to a minimum." I shrug. "Maybe our vacation on Deva will be more of an extended stay. That wouldn't be so bad, would it?"

While most of the crew remains to discuss the list further, I retreat to my room and flop onto my bed, staring at my comm. The most-wanted list concerned all of us, so I wanted everyone to see. But I'll admit, I haven't been completely transparent with my crew. The moment we left Gaia's atmosphere, a number of messages hit the ship's inbox, which only I have access to. The first was the one from Silvania that I showed Corvus. The others... Well, the others made a lot more sense once Corvus showed me that list. I suspect the IA was hoping to catch us off guard on one of their planets, but once their scouting party reported sighting us, they decided to try a different tactic.

Bait.

The first message is labeled *From: Councillor Ennia Heikki. To: Crew of the* Memoria.

That one I scanned already. It was, as expected, a boring and formal invitation for us to come to Nibiru to "negotiate." As if I would trust any of those Nibiran council members after the way they manipulated us and then put us on a wanted list. I considered sending back something petty in response, but I wasn't sure if that would let them track our location, so I deleted it instead.

The other two are more surprising, and more concerning. The first: from Shey Leonis, to me. A video message. I desperately want to open it and see her face... but I'm also terrified that it will break my heart. And what if the IA is trying to use her against me? But what if it's not? What if it's a personal message? What if she's in some kind of trouble and needs our help? I cling to that last thought, and try to convince myself that's the main reason I'm watching as I hit *play*.

"Hi, Scorpia."

I panic and jab the pause button, freezing the image of her face against a plain white wall. Shit, this is embarrassing. But I wasn't ready to see her again after the weeks apart and the way we left things. I've been trying so hard not to think about how everything finally seemed to be going right between us... and then went so very, very wrong. Stars, I miss her so much.

But now's not the time to get sentimental. I scrub at my eyes, clear my throat, and resume the message.

"I heard you ran into an old friend of mine," she says. She must mean Corvus's run-in with Commander Zinne, which means she recorded this very recently. "I hoped to get a message to you sooner, but they've been monitoring me closely. Planetary security personnel have been here asking about you—if you've been in contact, if I know where you are, if I believe you've told anyone else about what we learned on Gaia. They want to find you. Badly. You need to stay away from the IA worlds." She bites her lip. I try to focus on her message rather than thinking about how much I've always loved when she does that. "Please stay safe," she says, "and don't respond to this message."

And that's it. I close out of the message and press a hand to my eyes, breathing in deep. I don't know what I expected. I guess I should be glad she isn't in trouble, or being used by the IA to draw us in, but... stars damn, it hurts a lot to see her.

I shake it off, as best I can, and flip to the last unopened message. This one...this one I don't know what to do with.

Message from: Helena Ives.

I remember Ives: the hungry young general who earned herself a reputation in viciousness on Titan, and very nearly purchased the Primus bio-weapon from me. The only thing that stopped that deal was my own conscience getting in the way.

And I also remember, all too well, some of the last words Altair spoke to me: *The only peace my people will accept is one that we earn in blood.*

But the message isn't for me. It's directly addressed to Daniil Naran—which raises a whole host of other questions. The first, and the most important, is: How much can we trust the newest addition to our crew?

I gnaw my lip, considering. But honestly, at the end of the day, this just feels like more trouble we don't need. I hit *delete.*

Even when it's gone, I can't fight the sense that the system is shrinking around us, like a noose.

CHAPTER FOUR

Old Pains

Corvus

'm on my way to make dinner when the sound of a fight in the mess hall reaches me. I hurry my steps. It's been a while since the twins had one of their clashes, since Pol is always weaker than usual after trips to Gaia, and Drom has been working out her aggression in the training room with Izra, but that's still what I expect to find.

What awaits me is worse. Drom is, predictably, the aggressor. But the person on the other end is Daniil, his own arms up in a defensive position as he retreats from her assault. Izra is watching from a table, sipping coffee.

"They're fine," she says, when she notices me in the doorway. "Nobody's got a weapon."

"This is not *fine*." I storm past her and throw myself in between them. Drom pulls her punch before it hits me, growling under her breath in frustration. I hold out my arms to separate them. "Stop this. What's going on?"

"This asshole thinks he can just hang out in here drinking coffee like he's one of us," Drom says, her lip curling.

"What? He can, Drom. He's part of our crew."

"No, he's *not*. He's just here until we can drop him off on Pax, isn't he? We're not bringing some fucking Titan war criminal on board permanently." This is the most animated I've seen her since she returned from the war on Nibiru; it is unfortunate that hate is the emotion that lights her up. If it was only directed at me, I might even be glad for it, but Daniil doesn't deserve this. "He's not like us. He's just another one of those fucking machines Titan churns out." She leans over and spits on the floor in front of him. "Tell me. Were you on Kitaya, fucker? Did you burn my home? Did you give the order?"

Daniil meets her gaze with a surprising amount of calm. "No," he says. "I would never have done that."

"But you killed others," she says. "Bet you had one of those nice exosuits that let you wipe out poor Nibirans by the dozen, didn't you? Did it feel good to slaughter people who didn't have a chance? Make you proud to be a Titan?"

Daniil's eyes flicker.

"It doesn't matter what he did or didn't do," I say, before he can answer. Once it's clear Drom's not going to throw another punch, I step back and stand beside Daniil. "Show me one person on this ship who hasn't done something awful in their life." She stares at me, betrayal written on her face, but I can't let myself stop. I turned my back on Daniil for the sake of my family once before. I won't do it again. He deserves a chance at redemption as much as any of us—maybe more, because he rarely had a choice in the matter. He was born into war and never expected to see peace in his lifetime. I place a hand on his shoulder. He looks sideways at me, and I meet his gaze for a moment before turning to Drom.

"My own hands are nowhere close to clean. I spent three years on Titan, Drom. As a sergeant." I could leave it there. I've never stepped over the line before into giving the details of those years.

I've never been able to bring myself to do it. Now I see that was a mistake. I didn't do this soon enough to stop Drom from going to war herself, but maybe I can still save her from the festering hatred it's planted in her.

"I killed enemy soldiers so young they could have been my children," I say. "Barely trained Isolationist kids in uniforms stolen from their own dead. I let good people die for the sake of objectives. People under my command, who trusted me." I hate this, hate sending my brain down these dark and well-trod paths of memory, but I force myself to. I remember the chill bite of Titan's winds, the weight of a pulse rifle in my hands, a man stumbling away from me while I raised my gun to point at his back. Red spreading across the fresh snow. "I killed civilians, Drom. Unarmed civilians on our side." I force myself to hold her gaze, though the disappointment in her eyes makes me burn with shame. "I know you're angry. You have a right to be. But don't direct it at Daniil. He's no more to blame than you are. He has only ever fought because he had to, and even after being born and raised on a world like Titan, he always tried to find a way out. If anything, be angry at me. Because if I had been honest sooner, I might have spared you from this."

The room is silent after I finish. Drom is staring at me like she's never seen me before, and even Izra looks surprised. The back of my neck is hot with embarrassment after laying myself bare, but I stay where I am, my hand on Daniil's shoulder, my eyes meeting Drom's. After a moment, she makes a disgusted sound, turns on her heel, and storms out of the room.

I let out a long breath and look at Daniil. "Are you all right?" He nods, avoiding my eyes. "I can walk with you back to your room, if you'd like."

"Actually..." He rubs the back of his neck. "The reason I'm here is that Scorpia suggested you could use some help in the kitchen."

"Oh." Scorpia knows damn well I hate anyone interfering with my cooking, so she must have some other motive for sending him here. But I'm not going to send Daniil away when it must have been hard to show up in the first place, especially after what happened with Drom. No matter how uncomfortable it might be to be alone with him after everything I just said, I'll have to bear it. "By all means, then."

Daniil leans against the counter beside the stove as I pull out the ingredients, eyes following my movements, brow furrowed in a frown. His scrutiny makes me uncomfortable. I'm not sure how to read him. We spent time as brothers-in-arms, then enemies. Now we're shipmates, but I feel as though we've barely spoken, and it's difficult to know where we stand. Has he forgiven me? Or is he only here because his other option was a Titan execution for treason?

Either way, I realize now that I've failed him yet again. I thought it was best to give him space on board, considering that we nearly fought to the death back on Nibiru...but that has only allowed the gap between him and the rest of the crew to grow. I know the pain of being an outsider.

"Three years together on Titan," Daniil says, and I nearly cut off the end of my finger in surprise. I set aside the knife and look at him, bracing myself for a well-deserved verbal thrashing. "Three years of fighting side by side, sleeping under the same roof, eating and showering together...and never *once* did you tell me you knew how to cook." His eyes snap up from the food to meet mine, mischief in them now. "You asshole."

The sound of my own laugh surprises me. A smile cracks his face, and warm relief spreads through my chest. "In my defense, there wasn't much to work with on Titan. Rice and protein cubes only go so far."

43

"Don't forget the algae. Always a treat." He leans over to eye the ingredients. "What are you making?"

"It's a vegetarian take on Nibiran fish curry, but with a Devan twist of shredded sunfruit and sweet cream."

He looks at me blankly. He doesn't even know what most of the ingredients are, I realize. Titan cuisine—if one could call it that—was far from varied.

"Here, try this," I say, slicing a small piece of the freeze-dried golden sunfruit. He grabs it, gives it a sniff, and takes a hesitant bite. Shock ripples across his face as the flavor hits his tongue.

"Good?" I ask. He takes the knife from my hand and cuts himself another slice. I laugh. "You'll have to try a fresh one while we're on Deva. There's nothing in the system like it."

We fall into an easy rhythm of chopping and tossing ingredients into the various pots and pans. I pause when I need to, to guide or correct Daniil, as it quickly becomes clear he has little to no experience in the kitchen. But none of this is particularly difficult and he is a fast learner.

He is quieter than I remember him being. More serious. On Titan he was always a cheerful, social presence, touchy even for a Titan—though perhaps that was mostly with me. I remember the way he used to look at me, back then. Him and Magda both, always jostling for my attention. Craving affection I couldn't bring myself to give.

Now he barely looks at me at all, even now that we're alone together for the first time since he joined us on the ship. On the odd occasion that our shoulders or elbows brush as we're working side by side, we both tense and pull away.

Perhaps we can work together, live together, but nothing is mended between us. Not really. It is still there, lurking beneath every interaction and glance, and it will linger there until we address it. And I need to take the first step forward; I know that much, at least.

44

But how? How? No one in my family has ever been good at talking about these things, and myself least of all. It is so easy to tell myself that no good can come of stirring up old troubles. That it is better to keep my head down and say nothing. Accept the status quo.

But that has always been my problem. There is no truth behind that line of thinking—only years of having it drilled into my head by Momma.

"Daniil," I say, physically forcing his name out of my mouth so that I have no choice but to keep talking. The first is the hardest, and soon others start to spill out, though nothing close to coherent. "I...need to say something. I should have said it a while ago. I..."

He leans back against the counter and looks at me, saying nothing, just waiting for me to pull myself together enough to say what I want to say.

And what do I want to say? I'm suddenly unsure. What can I possibly say that will make amends for what I've done? I can't change the past, nor take back the damage I've done. I can't mend the broken thing between us with words, if it can be done at all. And yet...

"I'm sorry." It's not enough. I know that. But it needs to be said. "I should never have left you on Titan after I promised you I'd take you with me. I betrayed your trust."

He looks at me, pain written all over his face, and says nothing. Perhaps it was a mistake to bring this up. It may still be too raw for him to talk about, a wound only deepened by the fact that it drove us to fight on different sides of the war on Nibiru. But I push on, fighting against my instinct to bury these feelings deep and let them fester. I need to say this, and he needs to hear it, and it seems wrong to let even one more day pass with it hanging, unspoken, between us.

"I know an apology isn't enough," I say. "I don't know if it's possible to earn your forgiveness. But I'm willing to work for it, if you'll let me. And I won't leave you behind again."

He takes a deep breath, nods, and smiles. "Well. You got me out this time. That counts for something."

My shoulders relax. Small step though it may be, that smile hints there is still a chance for reconciliation. I left behind the rest of my team to die on Titan, and that is something I will have to live with. But with Daniil, I still have a chance to make different choices.

"I made mistakes, too," Daniil says. "I let my anger turn me into someone I never wanted to be, and took it out on all the wrong people." A shadow crosses his face, and I know he must be thinking of Nibiru. I want to tell him he doesn't have to feel guilty about it, but then I think of the terrified look on the Nibiran soldiers' faces as they went into battle against the Titans, and I hold my tongue. It's not my place or my right to give Daniil forgiveness, but I won't pass judgment, either.

"No one is innocent on this ship," I tell him. "But we are all doing our best to change for the better. So long as you're doing the same, you'll always have a place among us."

We walk into the mess hall for dinner together.

Everyone else is already waiting for the meal. Scorpia has taken a seat at the head of the table. Orion and Izra sit together on one bench, while my younger siblings are gathered across from them. Drom glares at us but doesn't comment as we sit down side by side.

I focus on eating, and ignore the weight of the stares. It's difficult when the whole room is stiflingly quiet. I can feel Izra looking at us, and thinking, just dying to say something. I silently beg her to keep her mouth shut.

"So," she drawls, and I suppress a wince. Here we go. "Just when our good little soldier boy reformed, we gained another one, hm?"

Daniil glances at me, and then looks up at her. Blinks. Then, against all odds, he smiles. "Oh, no. I was never so good a soldier as Corvus."

Much as I'm glad he didn't take Izra's words to heart, I'm not so pleased for the spotlight to swing in my direction. Too late to stop it, though—Scorpia is already leaning forward, latching on to his words like a fish on bait. "Don't worry," she says, grinning. "No one's ever as good as Corvus at anything."

Pol laughs. Lyre hides a smile. And after a moment, Izra gives Daniil an appraising look before returning to her food.

For now, it seems, our small world is at peace. I only wish the rest of the system was so simple.

CHAPTER FIVE

Shared Futures

Scorpia

Hours after the rest of the crew has already eaten, I pick at my breakfast in the mess hall. I'm exhausted and queasy after horrible nightmares kept me tossing and turning last night, featuring General Altair declaring my siblings guilty and executing them one by one. Now, I find myself scrolling through the IA's list again, lingering on my younger siblings' faces. Corvus and I chose this path for ourselves. Daniil, Izra, and Orion made their own choices, too. But Pol, Drom, Lyre…they're so young, and none of this is their fault.

I wish I felt more confident that heading to Deva was the best move to keep them safe. But that doesn't matter when it's our *only* move before we gain access to Pax. I'm sure the planet will bring its own problems, but we just have to hope they're the kind of problems we can deal with. Because a three-planet alliance officially declaring us wanted criminals is a *little* bit out of the realm of things I'm confident about taking on. We haven't received any more messages as we've approached Deva, but I know the IA is still lurking out there, waiting for a chance to grab us.

When Drom walks in, I shut off my comm, even though I assume she's going to head straight to the kitchen for a protein bar or whatever else exercise-obsessed weirdos eat. But instead, she slides onto the bench across from me and leans over the table, her hands folded in front of her and her expression serious.

"I wanna talk," she says.

I look up at her, halfway through chewing a bite of food. "Okay," I say, my voice garbled through the mouthful. "So talk."

She glances at the doorway, and then at the kitchen, verifying we're alone before continuing. "You and I had an arrangement on Nibiru," she says. "You were supposed to give me the houseboat for coming with you to the job on Gaia."

I take my time chewing and swallowing now, and lean back in my seat before I respond. "Right. Yeah. I remember." Stars, do I regret the promises I made on Nibiru to my younger siblings; I'm pretty sure every one of them is going to come back to bite me. "So...that's not possible now, obviously, when we're not legally allowed on Nibiru."

"Exactly." She folds her arms over her chest. "I heard you talking with Lyre about her Devan school bullshit. So. What do I get instead of the houseboat?"

"Uhh..." All of that has been far from my mind with everything that's happening lately. I'm really not so sure paying for Lyre's school is going to be possible right now, as it is; we have to be careful with our credits while we're figuring out our crew's future. But judging from the serious look on Drom's face, she's not gonna accept *We'll talk about it later* as an answer. "Well, okay, let's talk. What do you want?" I don't have a lot to give, but hopefully I can find something to hold her over until I do.

Her answer comes so quickly I'm sure she's been thinking

about it for a while. "I want the ship." Seeing the look on my face, she says, "I mean, not now. Not for a long time. But when you, y'know. Get too old or die or whatever."

"You want the..." I start to repeat her words, slowly, dumbfounded, but stop myself and shake my head. "You...really? Are you sure?" The answer is so far from what I would've expected. A Primus gun like Pol asked for, or a nice house on a planet, sure. But the ship? "That's not just a present, Drom. That'd mean handing over..." I gesture widely, not even sure how to put it into words. "Most people on this ship have nowhere else to go. When you're the captain, you're not just accepting the weight of the metal, or the business, or even the family legacy. You're accepting the responsibility of every life on board. And the responsibility of being one of the only ships left in the system that can travel planet to planet. Many people will want to use you for that. Others will want to kill you. And it's probably only going to get worse from here on out."

"You think I don't know that?" Drom asks. "I've been here the whole time, the same as you."

"Why do you even want this?" I ask, baffled. She's never shown any sort of interest in the ship before. Not piloting it, not captaining it, nothing at all. "You're twenty years old, Drom. Surely you've got better things to worry about than inheritance."

She goes a little red at that, her jaw setting, anger flaring in her eyes. "Yeah, I'm twenty," she says. "And I've fought in a war to defend my home-planet, nearly watched my brother die, and visited every planet in the system. That's more than most people can say in their entire life." She glowers at me. "And who were *you*, at twenty?"

I feel a twinge of guilt at that, because I know she's right. At twenty, I was still a good-for-nothing, drunk off my ass most of the time, thinking nothing of the future. Back then, I assumed

Corvus would be the one to get the ship, and I was happy with that. I guess I thought the same was true of the twins. "I haven't thought too much about who the ship would go to," I say carefully. I know that matters of inheritance can warp the best of relationships, and the last thing I want to do is start a feud between my baby siblings. I still vividly remember those days when Corvus and I turned against each other. It almost tore both of us—and the whole family—apart. " 'Cause I've got a lot of years ahead of me, you know. I'm not even thirty yet, for your information, so this is pretty damn early to make me worry about this. But if I had to think about it . . . I mean . . ." I shrug. "Lyre's put a lot of time into the ship, hasn't she? She's learned the ins and outs of both the engine and the pilot's seat."

"Lyre would make a shit captain and you know it," Drom says. "Anyway, she'll jump ship and live planet-side as soon as all of this blows over."

"What?" My brow furrows. "No, she won't."

"Yeah, she will. It's obvious."

I don't think there's anything obvious about that—or about Lyre at all, really, the workings of her mind are a mystery to me—but I'm not here to argue that. I lean back, raising one hand to massage the bridge of my nose. "Okay, okay. I'm not saying no to you, Drom. I'm just trying to understand. You gotta know that this seems like it's coming out of nowhere for me. You've never shown any interest in this before."

"The world was a lot different before. And so was I." She sets her jaw. "You think I can't do it?"

"That's not what I'm saying. But I . . ." I trail off, thinking. Maybe she's right. It is early for this, but maybe it's better for the conversation to happen early, to prevent a repeat of what happened between me and Corvus.

And maybe Drom isn't the worst choice. She's right that Lyre would hate the pressure of leadership, and Pol... Well, we still don't know what's going on with him, but even before the bioweapon and time in the cryosleep chamber sapped his health and left him with these strange side effects, he was always eager to follow Drom's lead.

But if I decide Drom is the one, will she end up following the same path as Corvus? Will the others resent her just like we all resented him for being the "favorite"? I understand now that nothing about that dynamic was good for any of us—Corvus crushed beneath the pressure, the rest of us turned against him rather than placing the blame on the person who really deserved it. I spent a while trying to imitate Momma, and a while trying my hardest to be her opposite, and I'm still figuring out a happy medium between the two. Still figuring out how to be me without measuring myself against her.

And after all this time, I still don't know how much of her was cruelty and how much was necessity. Did she prepare us for the world outside of our walls? Yes. Does that make it right? No. No, of course it doesn't. The harshness of the world outside is all the more reason to make sure my siblings will always have somewhere that's safe for them.

And as I look at Drom now, I realize that's what she's really looking for. I've never thought of the two of us as similar—she'd probably laugh in my face right now if I said we were—but I do remember the way she looked to me for a role model when she was scared. And as I look at her now, I see that she's scared again, as much as she's trying to hide it. Nibiru was her home, and she fought for it, and she still lost it. Now she's like me, an anomaly in the system without anywhere to call her own. That's what she wants. And who the hell am I to judge whether or not she deserves it?

Of course there are reasons to say she'll never make a good

captain. She's too temperamental, too impulsive, not responsible enough... but I could just as easily pull out a laundry list of my own flaws that make me ill-suited for the job. Hell, Momma laughed in my face when I wanted to inherit the ship and said it would never happen, and look at me now. Who's to say Drom won't come into her own just the same? Maybe all she needs is someone to believe in her, and she won't make the same mistakes that I did.

Anyway, I know that no matter what, she'll always have our siblings to back her, and me and Corvus to help train her right. In the end, I think, being captain isn't always about picking who's best suited to the job. I've met good leaders and bad leaders and all of the types in between, and I don't believe it's as simple as saying that some are born for it and others aren't. It's about picking the one who needs it most, and making sure they have the space and the right tools to become the person they need to be.

"Okay," I say. "I'm not gonna promise anything, Drom, because it's still early, and I think you don't even know what you're asking for yet. But that doesn't mean I'm saying no. If you really think this is what you want, then you can shadow me, learn the ins and outs. If you decide it's the life for you, then I'll teach you, and we can figure out an arrangement that Pol and Lyre are happy with."

She sets her jaw, but I can see a flicker of joy at my answer, buried deep beneath the hard shell she's presenting. I'm getting better at seeing it. "I guess that's the best answer I'm gonna get, then."

"For now, yes. It is." I stand up. "And... one more thing. I heard about that scuffle with Daniil the other day. I know Corvus already chewed you out for it, so I'm not gonna belabor the point, but... it's not okay. We're better than that. Part of being captain is being able to bring people together, not find more ways to split them apart like the planets do. If I ever hear about that kind of shit coming out of your mouth again, deal's off. Got it?"

"Yeah," she says quietly, looking appropriately ashamed. She clears her throat, not meeting my eyes. "I don't wanna make any excuses, but I ..." She pauses, grimacing. I wait; it's rare for Drom to open up, and I get the feeling she's trying her best right now. "On Nibiru some of the other recruits would say I looked like a Titan," she says, finally. I nod at her to go on. I can see why they'd make that comment—we've always thought that Pol and Drom's father must have been Titan, with their height and their relatively pale skin. "They were real assholes about it. I would try to bad-mouth the Titans as much as I could, to ... I don't know. Distance myself. And once I got into the fighting, and I saw the kinds of things the Titans could do ..." Her expression darkens, and she stops, seemingly unable to go on.

"I get it," I say. "And the Titans did attack your home-planet. A lot of them are probably just as bad as you'd think. But Daniil was one of the ones who helped stop the war. He's not our enemy." She nods, and I smile at her. "All right then. I'll see you bright and early tomorrow. We'll make the rounds together."

As I grab my dinner, I'm still thinking about our conversation, and about Daniil. And about that message from Ives that I deleted. I meant what I said to Drom—I don't want Daniil to feel uncomfortable on our ship. But he's also the only member of our crew who's basically a stranger to me.

Only one way to fix that. I hurry out of the mess hall and catch him on his way to his room. "Hey, Daniil."

He straightens his posture and snaps his head toward me. "Captain."

"I was thinking ... What do you say the two of us have dinner together in my quarters?" Before he can fire off one of his yes-ma'am-of-course-ma'am knee-jerk responses at me, I add, "Only if you want to. This isn't an order by any means."

He blinks at me, and shows a hint of a smile. "I'd like that."

I'm still pretty positive he would've felt obligated to say yes either way, but at least the smile looks genuine. We head down to my room. Only when we arrive do I realize I don't actually have a table to eat at, and inviting him to eat on my bed doesn't feel appropriate.

But, not to be dissuaded, I sit cross-legged on the floor and set my tray on my lap. He doesn't even hesitate to follow.

"Sorry about the lack of furniture," I say, feeling a little embarrassed now that we're both down on the floor.

He blinks at me, and then laughs. "Honestly, I assumed this was some planetary custom I was unaware of."

"Oh, damn, that would've made a great excuse. No wonder you went along with it so quickly."

We share a laugh, and some of the awkwardness melts away. Daniil has one of those smiles that changes his whole face. I can tell there's a lightness to him despite the mass-production-Titan-soldier surface. I'd like to see more of it.

"So," I say, trying to think of where to start. My curiosity is begging me to ask about his and Corvus's history on Titan, which both of them have been tight-lipped about, but it doesn't seem like something to ask off the bat. "How are you liking life on the ship right now?"

"Couldn't ask for anything more."

"Really?" I study his face. "You'd be the only one, then. Seems like everyone else on board has some kind of complaint. Drom's room is too small, Lyre's bed is uncomfortable, Orion keeps getting woken up early by noise from the training room...and they're all used to living on a ship. Surely you must be feeling cooped up. The close quarters driving you crazy yet?"

Daniil smiles again, shrugging. "If anything," he says, hesitantly, "I have too much of my own space here."

"Now that I haven't heard before."

"I'm Titan. I've never had my own room," he explains. "I grew up with six siblings. Well, not siblings as you think of them, no blood relation, but…" His brow furrows as he tries to put it into words.

"I understand." I've heard of the big, blended families on Titan. Between the lack of monogamy as a norm and the fact that many children lose their birth parents to the war, their concept of being related is a lot looser than anywhere else. "What about after you left home?"

"In basic, I slept in a bunker with many others. Once I was placed with a team, we always slept in the same room." He pauses. "Well, aside from Corvus. But I'm sure you knew that." Before I can decide whether or not I should admit I had no idea, he continues, "Teams do everything together. Eat, train, shower, sleep…or stay up." He gives me a cheeky look that makes me laugh, but then his expression turns more serious. "So someone being on the other side of a wall still feels very far away for me. My room is quiet. My bed is cold."

I think of the way that Titans act with each other, the constant touches and affection whether romantic or not, and my heart aches for Daniil as I think of him alone in his bed for the first time. He gave up everything he knew to help stop the war. I know how seriously Titans take loyalty. He will always be a traitor in their eyes.

"You and Izra are the only ones on this ship who grew up on Titan, and she chose to leave a long time ago," I say. For a moment I wonder how a woman like her came from a place like that, whether or not she had a childhood and military experience like Daniil describes. It's hard to imagine her being so warm with anyone. I've only ever seen her show affection toward Orion, but even that is guarded, and rarely physical. But I push that aside. "I can't promise that being here will ever be like that, or that the relationships you form with the crew will ever be a family like you think of one. But I hope that this ship can be a home for you someday. And if it isn't, I want you to know that we'll find a way for you to go elsewhere. It might not ever be safe for you to go back to the Titans, but like I've said, we should have a way to get you to Pax soon. But until you decide that—if you ever decide it—you'll always have a place here. And if there's anything I can do to make your stay more comfortable, let me know." I pause. "Ex...cept for the cold bed issue. 'Fraid I don't sleep with my crew."

The emotion on Daniil's face cracks into another smile. "Shame."

"Sorry to disappoint," I say, and then shove a bite of food into my mouth to stop myself from talking more. Nope, nope. I cannot, will not, flirt with a crew member, no matter how much Daniil's words reminded me about how empty my own bed feels without Shey. No matter how badly I miss her. Especially when I'm still not positive whether or not there was something between Daniil and Corvus. I had my suspicions already, but the more I hear about what life was like with a team on Titan, the more I wonder how much of a story Corvus has been keeping from us.

Luckily, Daniil's thoughts are already wandering in a different direction. "Actually, there is one thing I've been wanting to ask you," he says. "Is there anything I could do on board to help out? I'm used to a routine, and the empty hours are starting to make me lose it a bit. I've been helping Corvus out in the kitchen, as you suggested the other day, but..."

"Oh." I mostly suggested that to force him and Corvus to talk out their all too obvious issues. "I mean, if you want. You don't have to worry about earning your keep here or anything. I figured you might need some time to rest."

"With all due respect, more time alone with my thoughts is the last thing I need right now."

"Yeah, okay, I get that. Well, what are your skills?"

"Sniping. Interrogation techniques. General combat experience."

I blink. "Anything less...violent?"

He shrugs apologetically. "I'm Titan."

"Right. Uh..." I take another bite and chew as I think over the options. Lyre is constantly complaining about being overloaded with work, but she'd kill me if I sent an untrained helper into the engine room. He'd probably be good at helping Izra train the twins, but I'm not going to throw him at them without making sure they're okay with it. So..."Orion can train you up for shifts at the wheel. And, of course, I can add you to the chore list—it's boring stuff, cleaning and maintenance and the like, but it's good for filling time out here."

I thought he might balk at the mention of cleaning duty, but Daniil's expression holds nothing but relief. "Happy to help wherever you could use me," he says. "Thank you, Captain. I really appreciate this. All of it."

We stand, and I reach over to clasp his hand. "Let me know if you need anything else," I say, and smile. "I'm really glad to have you on board, Daniil. I know we're all a little rough around the edges, but I think you're going to fit in just fine here."

CHAPTER SIX

All That Glitters

Corvus

The cargo bay boils with nervous energy after we land on Deva. I'm not usually the biggest fan of Zi Vi, but even I'm not immune to a flutter of anticipation. It's been so long since we were able to travel freely. Our only trips in the last few months have involved brief stops here to off-load goods, and less than pleasant visits to Gaia. Zi Vi may be many things, but it's never dull.

And the others' enthusiasm is infectious. Scorpia has been bouncing off of the walls for days, though I suspect it's as much nerves as excitement. The twins have always loved the noise and energy of the Golden City, and Lyre is excited to check out the university that Scorpia has promised to pay for her to attend. For Orion, this is a visit to a home he thought he would never see again. It's Daniil's first peaceful trip to another world, other than dead Gaia. Even Izra seems less bristly than usual, tolerating everyone else's excited chatter without so much as a scowl.

Unfortunately, I have to put a damper on everyone's good

mood. "We can't walk into Zi Vi looking like this," I say. "They'll spot us as off-worlders a mile away, and we don't want that kind of attention. Especially with the list out."

Everyone stops to look at me, and I watch their faces fall as they realize what I say is true. Aside from Daniil, who glances around, clearly trying to figure out what is so wrong about the way that we look. Everyone else is aware that Zi Vi is known for its bold fashion and makeup trends. No half-respectable bar or restaurant is going to allow us onto the premises looking as we are—and in the disreputable ones, they'd likely attempt to mug us.

On *Fortuna*, my family had an entire wardrobe specifically for trips to Deva, but it was lost with the ship, and anything this one once had would've been seized by the Nibirans when it was in their custody.

So Lyre and Orion, the only ones with citizenship, go into the city to gather the proper clothes for us. After a couple of hours, just when I've begun to worry that something may have gone wrong, they return and drop several bags of clothing in the cargo bay. Everyone swarms around to see what they brought.

"Any trouble?" I ask.

"So far, so good," Orion says, smiling. "Nobody shot us a second glance at customs."

I allow myself to relax a fraction. Perhaps Scorpia is right, and the list hasn't made it beyond the Alliance's worlds yet.

Lyre disappears to her room, likely so she can focus on her own look without being bothered by everyone else for her expertise. The rest of us pass mirrors and supplies around the cargo bay as we dress. Orion paints his eyes and lips with a decadent golden shimmer that looks like it's dripping down his face, and gives Izra a matching sunburst design around her good eye. Drom goes for her usual dramatic black, with a dusting of crimson glitter to highlight her new scar. Pol, of course, has to counter with an even more dramatic look, slathering his eyes with black eye shadow and painting lines over his cheekbones and lips to give a skull-like impression. Scorpia forgoes anything close to standard makeup, instead choosing to draw metallic silver stars all over her face to match the shiny suit she brought from Nibiru. I give myself the same simple adornments I always do: slashes of black eyeliner and glittering highlight on my cheekbones.

Daniil looks on at it all in absolute bewilderment, and stares especially long at me. I feel a flash of self-consciousness, realizing how odd this must look to him, when he's only known me as the no-nonsense Titan sergeant. "Trust me," I say, "this is a tame look for Deva. It's a necessity if we don't want to draw attention."

"Oh, no," he says hastily. "I wasn't...you look..." He swallows. "Just, different. But I don't know anything about makeup. Could you help me?"

"Of course."

It's easy to agree. Harder to stand in front of him with one hand braced on his chin and actually do it. We've made a few small strides toward something akin to normality, but part of me feels there's just too much pain between Daniil and me for it to ever truly be possible. Unspoken words and old hurts have built a wall between us. I try to ignore his eyes on me as I give him some simple eyeliner and shadow, one hand gripping his chin to keep him steady, but the moment still feels uncomfortably close. His skin is warm enough to burn under my fingers, and his eyes bore into me while I work. I finally clear my throat, pull back, and hold up a mirror, and Daniil pulls his eyes away from me to look at his own reflection. He leans closer, and turns his head side to side to get a better look.

"Good enough?" I ask.

"I guess?" He lowers the mirror. "You promise people aren't going to stare?"

"Well, they might," Scorpia says, appearing over my shoulder to butt into the conversation, "but it won't be because you look bad. Quite the opposite." She winks at Daniil, who grins back. I glance back and forth between them, unsure what to make of the interaction or how to feel about it, and Scorpia nudges my shoulder and laughs. "Oh, relax, Corvus. We're friends now. Don't make it weird."

Once we've all finished our makeup, we move on to sifting through the pile of clothes they brought—except for Scorpia, already outfitted in her suit. Orion throws on a pair of extremely tight pants and some type of mesh top so insubstantial I wouldn't even call it a shirt. Izra scowls at him when he tosses her the dress he picked out, but slips into it nonetheless—a strappy, shiny chrome outfit that seems to change colors at different angles and shows off expanses of her pale, scar-covered skin that I've never seen before. That, plus a pair of knee-high black boots that match her gun arm well enough to make it look almost like a strange accessory. It's odd to see her like this, so...exposed, and feminine, but somehow rather than softening her it just makes her even more intimidating. It is simultaneously a little hard to look directly at her, and a little hard to look away once I do.

Luckily, there are slightly more tame options for the rest of us. Daniil gets a floral suit that complements his makeup nicely. Drom wears a jumpsuit that looks like it's made out of shimmering oil; and Pol, a lace button-up shirt tucked into a high-waisted skirt.

At first glance, I'm glad mine appears to be neither overly revealing nor in any bright colors. But, still... "Is this a cape?" I ask, looking up at Orion with my brow furrowed. "Does this outfit come with a *cape* attached?"

"It does." Orion covers a laugh with a cough. "I thought it would look dashing on you. The store clerk assured me it's all the rage right now."

I sigh, looking at the fabric in my hands again. This must be a joke at my expense, but I don't have any other options. I head into the supply closet and slip it on—the whole thing is black silk, which is bad enough, but the high neck and long attached cape really complete the absurdity of it. I grimace as I step out, preparing myself for laughter, but instead Orion and Izra are both staring at me.

"What the hell," Orion mutters.

"Don't act surprised," I tell him. "I know your goal was to make me look ridiculous."

"Yes, okay, I admit that it absolutely was, but I didn't expect..." He gestures at me, baffled. "You actually pull it off, somehow? Okay, I can see why everyone is always complaining about the fact that you're good at everything. This just isn't fair. You look like a hot supervillain."

"Please," I say, stiffly, "do not ever call me that again."

"Hot, or a supervillain?"

"Either."

Izra mutters something unintelligible and turns away. I pull at the high neck of my outfit and grimace.

But when Lyre emerges, the spotlight shifts off of me and the cargo bay goes silent. She's painted her entire face in shades of blue. White flowers trail down one side of her face; a glistening, colorful school of fish swims along the other. Her lips and eyes are lined in brilliant silver. She is a walking tribute to Nibiru. She walks through the cargo bay as if unaware of our stares, stops at the top of the ramp, and looks back at us. "Well?" she asks, tone tinged with impatience. "Let's go."

CHAPTER SEVEN

A Night Out

Scorpia

Deva is a feast of sensations. The neon lights, the smell of fried and spicy foods, the close press of the crowd, the advertisements blaring from the billboards, the swampy, sticky heat—it is both overwhelming and an absolute joy. It is *different*, and that's what I like most of all.

Our recent stops here have been brief—handoffs in the landing zone or just beyond customs, and away again. The last time we really went into the city was back during the Interplanetary Council. It's hard to think about that period of time, just after we lost Momma, when Pol was still sick and locked in cryosleep and we didn't know if he would ever wake up again. It hurts to think about who I was back then, and remember everything I did. Kidnapping Shey. Making a deal with Leonis for my brother's life. It all feels so alien to me now; it's hard for me to wrap my mind around the fact I ever was that person, drunk and desperate and afraid, trying to be like Momma because she was all I had ever known.

Thinking of it all, and freshly feeling Shey's absence, nearly sends me spiraling into a bad mood despite the current circumstances. But then I look out over my crew, and feel a burst of pride in both them and myself. None of that matters, because we're here now. And looking fuckin' great tonight, if I do say so myself.

I'm not about to get sucked into thinking about the past when the present is spread out in front of me in bold neon lights and shiny billboards. We're in the Golden City, and I'll be damned if I'm not going to enjoy it to the fullest.

Especially not when everyone else is buzzing off the city's energy. My younger siblings are all grinning and jostling one another like they're kids again—even Drom. Daniil's eyes are wide as he takes it all in for the first time. Corvus and Izra walk side by side, and Corvus cracks a few actual smiles as he watches Daniil notice new details about Deva.

And Orion is perhaps the happiest of all. "Home, I'm home," he says, spreading his hands out to the wild city around us. When we pass a glittering billboard sporting Prime Minister Jai Misha's face, he stretches up to plant a kiss on it.

"Disgusting," Lyre proclaims. But when Orion grabs her and pulls her into a whirling dance in the middle of the street, she dissolves into laughter. I feel a weird tug downward in my stomach, but even that isn't enough to wipe the smile off of my face. I'm glad everyone's happy. They deserve a night like this, even if it's a bittersweet one for me, stained by my past failures and Shey's absence.

Still, I can't help but notice that there's been a shift in the atmosphere here. First of all, there are a truly weird amount of advertisements featuring sexy factory workers and miners alongside hiring calls, which I guess is a very Devan way to attract people to a line of work in need of bodies. Life outside of the city walls is so dangerous that I can't imagine how grueling it must be to mine in the jungle—so it's no wonder Deva was after Titan's resources. And of course, Prime Minister Jai Misha is everywhere, smiling and handsome and looking more like a pop star than a government official.

But not all of the billboards and ads are as fun and lowbrow as I remember. Amid the usual glamorous celebrity faces and commercials for a million "life-changing" new beauty products, there are images and clips that give me pause. One is a life-size, deeply unflattering image of the woman I recognize from the transmission we received on Gaia—Silvania Azenari—with *x*'s drawn over her eyes and the words TOO MUCH RADIATION TO THE BRAIN scrawled above her head. Another depicts Pax as a literal ball of dirt beside the fruitful, decadent world of Deva, with the line THEY WANT WHAT WE HAVE.

Those give me a sinking feeling, like I'm watching an imminent head-on collision, as I remember the rising tensions between Deva and Pax. I knew they were clashing over wanting Titan's resources, and something about the Paxians shooting down Devan drones and the Devans seizing Paxian miners...But since the Interplanetary Alliance has laid claim to their planets again, effectively booting both Deva and Pax from Titan, I would've expected things to start cooling down. Instead, it feels like everything has heated up in the couple weeks we spent traveling from Gaia to here. What do they even have to fight about? Have those scuffles already festered into a blind hatred, or is there something deeper at play?

But none of that is our problem, and certainly not tonight. So I shrug it off and let myself be pulled along by the others' enthusiasm.

Orion, insisting he knows "all the best spots in the Golden City," takes us to a dingy little restaurant tucked away on the edge of the city. Even with a handful of whining fans struggling to keep the place cool, it's uncomfortably steamy inside, and barely large enough to accommodate our group. We all remove our shoes at the threshold before the hostess escorts us to a table in the back. We squeeze around it, seated on cushions on the floor in Devan fashion, and wash our hands with cold towels.

It's easy to forget how cramped and hot it is once the food starts coming, delivered by a shuffling old woman who kisses Orion on both cheeks when she sees him, and clasps Izra's hands without so much as a frown in return. We all share the dishes in standard Devan fashion, reaching over one another to grab bites with either chopsticks or our freshly washed hands. There are a wide range of curries and flatbreads to scoop them with, chewy, clear noodles stir-fried with an array of colorful vegetables, flavorful chilled soups, slices of fruit dusted with spices, cubes of fried tofu served with dipping sauces spicy enough to make me sweat. So many foods, rich with flavor and texture, every bite an eruption of sensation. Some of it I don't even recognize, but it's all delicious. No matter how much we protest that we're stuffed, the chef keeps bringing us new dishes to try, and we clean every plate. All of it is new to Daniil, but he tries it all even though anything remotely spicy makes him go red-faced and hiccup uncontrollably. I laugh so hard at him that I'd feel bad if he wasn't laughing, too.

Finally, we beg off, tip generously, and spill out into the streets of Zi Vi. The air outside feels cool after the stuffy restaurant, though my lips are still burning from some of those sauces. I feel so full and content that I'm half-tempted to head straight back to the ship and fall into bed, but a night in Zi Vi doesn't end with food.

"Right," Orion says, clapping his hands. "Let's get drinking, then!"

Something cold and uncomfortable swells in my gut. An awkward silence falls; Corvus is watching me, though I pretend not to notice.

"Oh," Orion says, finally catching on when nobody says anything for several seconds. "Or...not drinking. Plenty of fun nondrinking things to do here, too. Like..." He trails off, his brow furrowing in thought, and a few seconds of silence pass while he struggles to come up with something.

"A sober night in Zi Vi? I don't think so," I say, fighting back a surge of embarrassment. Stars, I'm supposed to be the captain, not the one everyone has to look out for. Before Corvus can butt in to contradict me, I add, "I mean, I'll be your designated sober person tonight. No worries. You all drink to your hearts' content, and I'll make sure nobody ends up arrested or handing their life's savings to a sex worker."

"Are you sure that's a good idea?" Lyre asks, her eyebrows knitting together.

"I mean, it's about time for her to pay her dues," Drom says. "Think we've all babysat drunk Scorpia at one point or another, right? So why not?"

They all laugh, and I smile and shrug even though it does hurt a little to hear. "Exactly. So go on, you lot, have fun. That's what we're here for, isn't it?" I clap Daniil on the back, grinning. "Someone buy this man his first glass of fireberry wine."

I wanted something different, and now I guess I've got it, since this is an experience I've never had before: being the only one stone-cold sober while everyone else is working hard at getting as drunk as possible. Orion and Pol make a bet over who can handle more shots, Drom and Corvus work their way through multiple pitchers of beer, and even Lyre breaks her usual two-drinks-only rule, indulging in an expensive bottle of fireberry wine. Daniil flirts with the bartender while tasting a wide array of colorful cocktails, and Izra makes her slow but steady way through a few of her usual gross-as-hell vodka on the rocks.

It is fun, for a while, as these nights always are. Pol and Orion are soon surrounded by a small crowd egging them on, and Daniil launches into a bawdy Titan drinking song that earns him several dirty looks from across the bar but a rare smile from Izra, and Drom and Corvus finally get drunk enough to bow their heads together and appear to have a heartfelt conversation. A pink-cheeked Lyre sits beside me and tells me, with occasional interrupting hiccups, how proud she is of me—which is touching, hilarious, and embarrassing for both of us all at once.

And yet, much as I want to relax into the night, I can't seem to shake the feeling that people are staring at us. Staring at *me*, especially. The woman who turns to do a double take at me as she walks in, the bartender who looks at me a little too long as he pours someone else a drink, the table of patrons in the corner who all get quiet when we sit down nearby...Maybe I'm just being paranoid, but it feels like I'm being watched. But most of the time, when I get that itchy feeling on the back of my neck, I turn and there's no one looking. So I tell myself I'm just being paranoid. After all—there's no way that IA list has made it here already, right? And even if it has, the Devans aren't too keen on the IA from my understanding, so they'd have no reason to want to turn me over to them. Maybe I'm just more sensitive to being noted as an off-worlder after our time on Nibiru, when we actually started to fit in, for a change.

So I do my best to shake off my paranoia and enjoy the night. Everyone else seems to be having a good time. Corvus occasionally glances around and frowns, and he always sits with his back to the wall and his face toward the door, but that's just how he is, not a sign that something's wrong.

It's hard to pinpoint exactly when and why things take a turn for the worse, but all of a sudden Lyre is crying on my shoulder, and Drom is yelling at Corvus, and Pol and Orion are both in the bathroom getting sick. Corvus storms out of the building, leaving me to deal with the others in the midst of an increasingly hostile-looking bar crowd. At least Izra and Daniil have kept their heads enough to help me out. We work together to get our drunker companions out into the street. I drag Drom by the arm and Lyre follows, still sniffling and hiccuping intermittently. Behind us, Izra half carries a staggering Orion while Daniil helps Pol along. Corvus is sulking with his back against the building outside. I corral everyone into a side street, look around at the disastrous state of my crew, and start to laugh.

"Oh, stars, this is a mess," I say. "I guess we've had enough of Zi Vi for tonight, then."

So begins the long trek back to the ship. The streets are less crowded now, but time holds little sway here, so the city never really sleeps. I usher the drunks ahead of me and fall in step with Corvus at the tail of our caravan.

"Is this what it's always like for you?" I ask.

He glances sideways at me. "Nobody tried to run off on their own and kidnap a president's daughter or anything, so really, this is one of the good nights."

"Yeah, okay, I deserve that." I rub the back of my neck. "But you could loosen up a bit, you know. Have some fun, for once."

"Not my type of fun," he says, but there's something wistful in his eyes. I follow his gaze ahead to see Daniil and Izra walking side by side, talking quietly.

I fall into silence. Maybe Corvus can't loosen up, not really, not when he's always expected to be the responsible one. Even with me being sober, I'm sure he still feels like he has to take care of us all. He never lets his guard down. All his life, he's lived with expectations on his shoulders. I can't imagine the weight of it all.

"You know, I can handle this tonight," I say. "I'll get everyone into bed. Why don't you go have another drink? Daniil should see more of Zi Vi than one shitty bar. Maybe take Izra." I nudge him with my shoulder. "You could use a night to relax. I'll handle the kiddos. Go on."

Corvus looks like he's going to say no again, but then we both look over and catch Daniil casting a longing glance over his shoulder at the lights through the trees. Corvus sighs. "I guess a couple more drinks can't hurt," he says. "But I'll help you get everyone back to the ship first."

I watch for a little while, smiling and feeling all nice and selfless and shit, and then Pol yanks me back to reality by vomiting on my boots.

CHAPTER EIGHT

Three War-Brands

Corvus

Back in the ship, I make sure our drunk mess of a crew is safely settled in. I half carry Pol to his room and leave him snoring on his side, while Scorpia nudges a belligerent Drom into bed. On my way back out to meet Izra and Daniil on the ramp, I glance through Lyre's open door and see her sitting side by side with Orion in her bunk—him talking animatedly while she nods along, her eyes mostly shut. His arm is looped casually around her shoulders.

"I can introduce you to some friends in the city and help you get settled," he's saying. "And of course I'll visit you at university whenever the ship stops on Deva—"

Before I go and do my best to relax, there's one thing I've been meaning to handle, and the alcohol has given me the courage to do it.

"Orion." He stops midsentence, his head jerking toward me. "Come talk to me."

He follows me out into the empty hallway. When we stop, he

has considerable trouble standing still without leaning on the wall to help his balance. He also keeps glancing over his shoulder and wiping his palms on his pants. I frown down at him, unsure what to make of the behavior, and he shrinks further inward under my gaze. "What?" I ask. "Why do you look like you're heading to the chopping block?"

"Well, I don't know." He finally meets my eyes. "Am I?"

My brow furrows. "Of course not. You haven't done anything wrong." I eye him. "Have you?"

"No!" He throws his hands up, sways on his feet, and hastily grabs the wall for support again. Now I'm wondering what exactly he's done that has him looking so guilty.

But this is going off track. I rub the bridge of my nose, trying to get my thoughts in order. Perhaps it was a bad idea to have this conversation while neither of us is sober. I forgot that Orion can be about twice as insufferable and half as clever as Scorpia sometimes, even when he isn't nine shots deep.

"It's about your father—" I start.

"I haven't done anything with her, I swear," he blurts out at the same time.

We both stop and stare at each other. I recover first. "What are you talking about?"

"What?" He shoves his hands under his armpits and rocks back on his heels, clearly trying very hard to look casual. It's not working. "Never mind, I...What about my father?"

At this point, I just want this conversation to be over before it gets any worse. "The last time I saw your father face-to-face," I say, "he told me that I'm his biological son. He could have been lying but..." I think back to the conversation, to the timeline I already knew of when my late mother left her position on Murdock's crew, and shake my head. "I believe he was telling the truth."

Orion stares at me for several long seconds, his eyebrows drawing together, and then says, "Is that all?" I blink at him, and he bursts out in a sudden laugh, brushing sweaty hair out of his face. "Oh, stars above," he says. "Is that why you've been staring at me like you want to toss me out the air lock this whole time? That's what you want to talk about? *That?*" He laughs again. "Fucking hell. I thought you were about to tell me that you were going to dump me here in Zi Vi and leave me."

"I won't say I hadn't considered it," I say, getting annoyed at his laughter.

"Okay, okay, okay. Sorry. I just...I had built this up into some huge awful thing in my mind. I thought you hated me."

I decide not to comment on that. He wipes a hand over his face, smearing what's left of his makeup, and pulls on a more serious expression. "I mean, I'm glad you told me, I guess, but I don't think it has to change anything. Do you? It's not like we share any blood, or any heartwarming childhood memories, or anything else that would make us anything close to siblings. Forgive me, but I don't see why it's a big deal?"

All this while, it's felt like some burning secret within me. I resented him for the reminder of where I came from, but in reality... "You're right," I say, finally admitting it to myself. "It was never anything to do with you. Or us. It was my own shame over it." Momma had always drilled it into me that blood came first. So what did it mean that I came from her and Murdock? Two selfish people who would've gladly contributed to the end of the system if it meant satisfying their own greed.

"You're nothing like him, if that's what you're so concerned about," Orion says. "Take it from one of the people who knew him best. Never would've guessed you were his son in a million years. I would've assumed your father was some Titan warrior. All broody and tragic and heroic-like."

That drags a laugh out of me. "I spent most of my childhood dreaming it was the same," I confess.

Orion grins. "Of course you did." After a moment's hesitation, he claps me on the back with one hand, and almost seems to be going for a hug, but he recoils when I look sideways at him. "Right. Not a hugger. Anyway, uh, good chat. I'm gonna go... vomit several times, I think."

And off he stumbles. I watch him go, huffing a laugh under my breath, and head to meet up with Daniil and Izra.

As we walk into the Golden City, us three former Titan soldiers, I'm struck by a moment of self-consciousness that we will stick out among the crowds. But of course, this is the one place in the system where we don't have to worry as much about that, especially when we're all dressed in our Devan fashions. Izra looks so strange in hers that I keep not recognizing her out of the corner of my eye—not a bad strange, but... certainly different. Daniil, on the other hand, has taken to his like a second skin. It suits him better than a uniform ever did.

And it is easy for us to get lost in the riot of color and noise that is Zi Vi. The city is even more headache-inducing after spending so much time on quiet Nibiru. This has never been my favorite place in the system, and the decadence feels even more abhorrent than usual after watching starving Titans and terrified Nibirans and stranded Gaians kill one another to survive. Here, in the heart of the city where the wealthy and beautiful reign, the people have never known hardship or hunger. I doubt they ever pause to think about the less fortunate who live beyond the walls, scraping out meager existences in the jungle villages, let alone the suffering of other planets.

They also have no idea how easily this life—this world—could be taken from them. This planet may be rich and luxurious, but it has a Planetary Defense System, too. It could fall as quickly and easily as Gaia did, and become another husk of a world stripped of life and plagued by storms. No amount of wealth would be able to save its people then. A sobering thought.

But this is Deva, and no one here remains sober for long, in any sense of the word. It's hard for me to remain so when I see Daniil's reaction to it all. I think he was struck dumb by shock when we first arrived, but now—with some time to acclimate, and several drinks in him—he stares openly at the lights and crowds, his head turning toward every new sound and sight. As we pass by a brothel pulsing with music, glass windows offering tantalizing glimpses at dancers with blacklight tattoos, he wanders too far into the street. I grab his arm and pull him back just in time to prevent him from getting flattened by a speeding hovercraft.

"Watch your step," I say. A more dire warning is on the tip of my tongue; I want to warn him that there is danger here, too, beneath the dazzling neon lights and casual decadence—but I can't bring myself to wipe that look off of his face.

"Sorry," he says, flushing as he pulls out of my grip. "I'm just... I never knew anything like this existed. Even when I dreamed about traveling the system, I never imagined it could be like..." At a loss for words, he lifts his hands and gestures to the wild neon city stretching up toward the sky. I try to imagine what all of this looks like through his eyes, after so many years with nothing but the bleak, rolling tundra of Titan and a future of endless war, and it makes me appreciate it a little more.

"Can we stop ogling and get ourselves a drink?" Izra asks, looking bored by it all, though her eye keeps wandering back to that windowed brothel. When she catches me watching her, she looks away. "I'm sobering up alarmingly fast, and this city is a fucking nightmare without alcohol."

"Oh, yes," Daniil says. "I want more of that...what was it? Corn whiskey?"

The first bar we enter has a NO OFF-WORLDERS sign on display, and I suspect Izra chose it out of spite. But I don't think they had a group of three Titan veterans in mind when they created the rule, because not a soul challenges us when we walk in. Izra may be looking for a fight, but most of the bar patrons are too focused on the television screen above the bar to pay much attention to us. The TV plays old footage from when the Interplanetary Council met on this planet, focusing on clips of Prime Minister Jai Misha talking with Silvania Azenari of Pax. There wasn't much interaction between the two of them, judging from the frequency they're replaying the same clips, but the newscast keeps bringing up a moment where Silvania questioned if Deva was responsible for the attack on Titan. Beneath the clip, the news line reads: *Silvania Azenari—queen of the hive mind, or just another drone?*

The bartender catches me watching, and must mistake the cause of my incredulous look. "It's that thing she's got in the back of her head," he says, tapping his own skull. "Some kind of mind-control device, I heard."

"I see," I say, as neutrally as I can manage, and then order a round of drinks before Izra gets a chance to jump into the conversation.

We don't get the bar fight Izra is itching for, but it's impossible to relax with the undercurrent of tension in this bar, so after one drink we head to the next.

We have a few drinks beneath a lazily spinning disco ball before wandering onward, where headless holograms dance in suspended cages. Zi Vi has a seemingly endless supply of bars, and Izra appears to know her way around. We take our time sampling drinks and atmospheres. Outside, it begins to rain, a soft drizzle that soothes the night's heat.

I can't remember the last time I had a night like this, with nothing and no one to worry about. It feels strange; I keep thinking there must be something I've forgotten, some responsibility I'm shirking, some reason I can't let my guard down—but there isn't. There's nothing. And if I occasionally get the sense I am being watched, surely that is only my paranoia, too. After a few drinks, that feeling goes away and is replaced by a pleasant aimlessness. What a luxury it is.

So I have another drink, despite the fact that reality is starting to blur around the edges in a way that would normally be my cue to stop.

"I feel like I can still taste the fireberry wine I had at the beginning of the night," Daniil says, as we stumble out of another bar. "Yes. Definitely still there. Definitely still burning. Ugh."

"I'm sorry," I tell him. "Nobody but the Devans can stand it, but it's something you have to try once."

"I want to try it all," Daniil declares, but despite the confidence, he's already tilting sideways, leaning against my shoulder. I let him. I'm surprised how natural it feels to stand so close, to touch. I thought that was something the two of us had lost forever, but maybe not.

Izra eyes us critically. "We're never going to make it through the night like this," she says with a sigh. "Unless..." She smiles. Even after the time we've shared, that knife's-edge smile of hers can still be frightening. "I have an idea."

Izra goes off to speak to someone while Daniil and I huddle under an awning to avoid the rain. He seems to only get drunker as we sit, soon slumped back with his head against my shoulder, and I rub his back with one hand and wonder if it's time to call it a night. But then Izra returns with a grin and a fat wad of dried Sanita.

"It's been a while," I say, but when Izra rolls and lights a cigarette stuffed with it, I don't hesitate to take a puff myself. The drug sparks through my veins, sharpening my vision and clearing the fog from my brain. "Is it a good idea to mix this with alcohol?" I ask, handing the cigarette to Daniil. He sits up, takes a hit, and exhales upward, watching the smoke dissipate over our heads.

"This is Deva," Izra says, snatching it from him to take another drag. "We'll worry about good ideas tomorrow."

Another bar. Everything is brighter after the Sanita. Energy fizzes beneath my skin, and I barely feel the drunkenness that was creeping up on me before. That's probably not good, I think distantly, but when Izra presses a shot into my hand, I take it. Daniil has bounced back as well, drumming his fingers on the table, his eyes flickering around with that same sense of wonder.

His eyes find Izra's wrist, the black box inked there, and he reaches over to take her hand without a hint of hesitation. She tenses beneath him, but lets him pull her hand closer and tilt it so he can get a better look at the tattoo. Still, she's bristling—dangerous, as she always is. I, too, am tense, and suddenly wondering why this seemed like a good idea. I should have seen the inevitability of these two clashing, especially while drunk.

"Couldn't you have had that removed?" Daniil asks.

"Yes. I could have." Izra yanks her wrist back. "But trying to erase the past is a fool's errand. The goal wasn't to forget what I lived through. It was to reclaim it, and my body." She looks up at Daniil and smiles in that sharp-edged way. "Plus, I like the way people flinch when they realize what it means."

But Daniil doesn't flinch. He smiles back, no sharpness in his. "I think," he says, "if I come face-to-face with Kel Altair again, I would like to do it with my own war-brand covered. If it wouldn't offend you to be copied...?"

Something flickers across her face. "You don't need permission to reclaim your own skin, soldier boy."

"Well, I would prefer to have your blessing."

She clears her throat and sips her drink, and though I still can't read her expression, I do consider the fact that Izra is the only person I've ever seen with her brand covered. "Fine, then," she says. "You have it. The more traitors, the merrier, in my opinion."

She bumps her glass against his, and while Daniil hurries to slurp the rising foam off of the top of his beer before it overflows, Izra leans back in her chair and looks at me. "And what about you? Keeping the brand?"

The question catches me off guard. I look down at the numbers and lines marking my wrist. This brand carries many memories, most of them terrible. The way Momma sacrificed me for the sake of her own ambition, the people I killed in Altair's name, the soldiers I lost, the fall of Titan... As Izra said, the idea is not to erase any of that, if such a thing were even possible. It would be a declaration of change rather than an erasure. A choice rather than something forced upon me. But...

"No," I say eventually. "For now, it is a reminder that the fight isn't over yet."

CHAPTER NINE

Answers

Scorpia

After everything my crew has been through over the past year, it feels so luxurious to pass a few days doing little of consequence. Our first wild night was fun, but now it feels like a real vacation. Corvus stocks up the pantry with new spices and cooks some incredible meals with fresh ingredients we rarely have access to, with Daniil's help. Lyre goes on a tour of Zi Vi University, and returns with a stack of brochures and stars in her eyes. Orion and Izra check in with old friends and business associates from their days aboard the *Red Baron*; he seems especially thrilled to be on Deva, and though she grumbles about being dragged off to socialize, she always returns looking begrudgingly happy. Pol is exhausted for a few days after overdoing it on the first night, but Drom cheers him up by bringing home plenty of street food.

I'm surprised by my own reluctance to spend much time in the city. But that uneasy sense of being watched the first night still lingers, making me feel safer on the ship and monitoring the news both local and system-wide. And despite the placid few days, I can't ignore the sense that something is brewing here on Deva beneath the surface. Not in my crew—it seems like we've conquered the worst of our problems for now, and thank the stars for that—but in the city itself. I remember Zi Vi as a place primarily obsessed with celebrities and other pop culture, but lately it seems like every screen is playing the news instead of the latest popular game show. Prime Minister Jai Misha seems to be making an awful lot of speeches about the IA, and the work conditions in the mines that have been reopened now that access to Titan is cut off, and most of all, about Pax. But despite all of the blustering and "breaking news" and "emergency updates," nothing seems to actually happen, so I tell myself it's nothing but the usual Devan sensationalism.

Anyway, vacation or not, we still have a few important matters to check off of our to-do list before we head onward to Pax. I get in contact with the wealthy client who expressed interest in our wares last time we were here. And once Pol recovers and emerges from his room, I pull him aside for a conversation. "So," I say. "You know one of the reasons we've been trying to get to Deva for a while is that we wanted to meet with a doctor."

He grimaces, looking down at the floor. "Today?"

"We don't know how much longer we're staying, so yeah. I found someone in a list of Murdock's old contacts in the ship's database." I scrutinize him, unable to read much in his expression. "I've heard of them. Got a good reputation. They're not gonna do anything that'll hurt you."

"I'm not *scared*," he protests, but he still doesn't meet my eyes. "What if they find something..." He trails off, shrugging like it's no big deal, but his face is creased with unmistakable worry.

"Something like what?" I ask, frowning. For the first time, I wonder if he knows more than he's been letting on this whole time. He's always claimed that he doesn't remember any of what the Gaians did to him, but...what if he does? "You know you can tell me anything, Pol, right?"

"Yeah, yeah." He lets out a gusty sigh and shakes his head. "Whatever. Let's just get it over with." His expression shuts off, telling me I'm not going to get anything more from him.

"Okay. Someone should go with you, but it doesn't have to be me."

"I guess you can come. I mean, if you want." The quick way he says it is entirely at odds with the forcibly casual tone.

"All right. Anyone else? I bet Drom's free."

"Not Drom," he says—again, too quickly, though this time I'm not sure why. "Maybe...Corvus. I guess. If he's not busy." He rubs the back of his neck, looking self-conscious. "He can translate the medical bullshit for us."

"Sure. I'll ask him for you." He nods a silent thanks. I scrutinize him for a moment longer before deciding it's not worth trying to drag anything else out. Instead, I give him a playful push. "Now go shower. You stink."

He rolls his eyes and obediently heads off, and I watch him go, trying my best not to worry.

Murdock's contact is tucked away in a back alley on the outskirts of the city. The trees have crept close enough to this area to cast shade over the street, a reprieve from the constant sun overhead. The building is so squat and nondescript that I never would've paused to look at it without the information I have—and even so, its windows are boarded up and its plant inspection signs are out of date. Clumps of black weeds sprout from cracks in the building's exterior. But Murdock's database claimed that this doctor was still operating, at least up until the former captain was imprisoned on Nibiru, and I know that appearances can be deceiving, on a planet like Deva most of all.

True to Murdock's notes, a small window on the door creaks open the moment I knock, revealing only a pair of dark eyes.

"Uh, Dr. Mora?" I ask. "I'm here on behalf of Aldrin Murdock."

"Password?"

"Mayflower."

The window slams shut. A moment later, the door swings open, and a gloved hand ushers the three of us inside.

The interior of the building is far cleaner and better kept than the outside, all pale tile and fluorescent lights, not a hint of the unruly plant growth or other signs of abandonment from the front. A good sign, again; anything that can survive in Zi Vi without advertising itself with flashy signs and bright lights has got to be one hell of a business.

The person locking the door behind us is short and solidly built, with a shock of dyed-red hair and dark clothes covering every inch of skin from the neck down. They stick their gloved hands in their pockets and look each of us over, in a way that seems more like they're casually cataloging us rather than actually interested.

"You're not Murdock's crew."

I blink, taken by surprise. "Oh, uh...yeah."

"You're the Kaisers."

Corvus tenses next to me. I eye the doctor, but they don't seem hostile. "Yeah."

Dr. Mora folds their arms over their chest and nods. "I was sorry to hear about your ship, and your mother."

My skin prickles in alarm, and I resist the urge to run for the door. But judging from Murdock's notes, Mora is no more reputable than us, so I doubt they're going to sic law enforcement on us. "Thanks. Didn't think many people knew about all that."

The doctor laughs. "When one of the last interplanetary ships in the system disappears, of course people notice. Questions get asked, answers get spread, along with plenty of rumors." They lock eyes with me, head tilting. "And when the *Red Baron* shows up with a new name painted on its side, registered to a Captain Kaiser, well. People notice that, too. Half thought it was Auriga back from the dead."

"Nothing quite so exciting," Corvus says dryly.

The corner of Mora's mouth curls. "Not sure if your mother would be appalled or pleased to have her spawn wandering the system in her old rival's ship."

"Considering I'm the captain? Definitely appalled," I say.

Mora gives me an appraising look and shrugs. "Well, anyway, I'm guessing you're not here to gossip. What can I do for you? Looking for something better than that piece of scrap?" They motion to my prosthetic hand.

I curl my fingers around the plastic limb, defensive for a second before I realize that's not a half-bad idea. "I mean, how much would that—" Corvus clears his throat, and I shake off the thought. "Never mind, that's not what we're here for. Actually…" I look over my shoulder at Pol, who is doing his best to disappear into a corner of the room. Not very successfully, considering he's the tallest person in here. When our eyes land on him, he takes a deep breath and steps forward.

"Him?" Mora asks, one brow lifting. "I mean, he could certainly stand to put some meat on his bones, but he looks like the most put-together of the lot of you. What's wrong with him?" They step forward, and one hand darts out to grab Pol's chin, turning his face from side to side as if expecting to read the answer somewhere in his features. His face reddens, but he doesn't resist the scrutiny.

"That's the question we're here to answer," I say. "A few months ago, he was affected by a…um…" I hesitate, my eyes darting to Corvus, who is watching the doctor carefully.

"Speak plainly. If you weren't willing to trust me, you shouldn't have come," Mora says, without looking away from Pol.

"The Primus weapon that wiped out Titan," Corvus says. "He was infected."

The doctor goes still, and draws their gloved hand back from Pol as if suddenly worried he's contagious. They look at Corvus, and then at me, and then back to Pol. "How did he survive?"

"First the cryosleep chamber, then a treatment by the Gaians. We have no idea what the latter consisted of," Corvus says. Grateful that he's taking charge, I move to Pol's side, touching his back with one hand just to remind him I'm here. "But he's still..." Corvus hesitates, shooting Pol an apologetic look. "Not himself. And he has moments of...strangeness. Most notably intense fits whenever we land on Gaia."

"Only because it's so loud there," Pol says, defensively. When we all look at him, he drops his head and scuffs a shoe across the floor. "Hurts my head," he mutters.

I'm afraid that Mora will kick us out on the street and berate us for bringing our trouble here. Most Devans would quail at the mere mention of anything Primus related, let alone someone touched by a deadly weapon that wiped out a planet. But instead Mora grins like they've been handed a present. "Interesting," they say. "Follow me."

Pol is obviously uncomfortable in the sterile metal exam room, and when the doctor asks him to lie back on the table, his face shows pure panic.

"It's all right," I say, squeezing his arm. "I'm gonna be right here with you the whole time."

"And the doctor's not going to do anything without warning us first," Corvus says, fixing Mora with a threatening glower, but I'm not sure the doctor even notices. They're busy grabbing a variety of vials and tools I've never seen before from the cabinet. When Pol sees a syringe come out, he squeezes his eyes shut, his entire body stiff with tension.

I don't know how to do this. I've never been the comforting kind of person. Growing up, that was usually Corvus, but that was a long time ago—and anyway, right now he's in tough-guy mode keeping an eye on the doctor. "You've got nothing to worry about," I say, trying to sound reassuring even as I eye one of the sharp-looking tools the doctor picks up.

"Stars, you sure you're real criminals? Seem awfully soft," Mora mutters, rolling their eyes. "This is my job, yeah? Let me do it."

That sends Corvus and me into simmering silences. We both watch quietly as they examine Pol. First, they run through a basic physical checkup. Then they draw a couple vials of blood from him, which he tolerates with only a tremble of his lower lip, and feed those samples into a machine on the counter. While it analyzes them, the doctor runs a handheld scanner over his body. They don't say anything, but I see the way their eyebrows shoot up at one point, the machine hovering over Pol's head for an uncomfortably long amount of time. I want to ask what they see, or what they're even looking for, and about a thousand other questions, but I hold my tongue for Pol's sake.

When the doctor goes into another room, murmuring something about checking their samples, Pol sits up on the table and takes a deep, shuddering breath. "I knew it was gonna be bad news," Pol says, putting his face in his hands. "I shouldn't have come..."

"Whoa, hey, whoa. No bad news yet." I wrap an arm around him, shooting Corvus a please-help-me look. He moves over, placing a hand on Pol's arm.

"It's always better to know," he says. "Once we know, we can figure out how to deal with it."

I would've gone with something a little more uplifting, but I guess I can't expect much of that from Corvus. We stay as we are, clustered around our baby brother, until the doctor comes back. Their face is unreadable, and they're flipping through files on a comm.

"Well?" I prompt, when they don't say anything.

Mora looks up and sighs, a little, in a way that makes my heart drop. "You should probably sit down."

I don't understand half of the numbers and terms the doctor throws at us, but I see the progressively dourer look on Corvus's face, and that tells me everything I need to know.

A numb haze settles over me. It feels like I'm not really here in my body—like I can't be here, hearing this. Not after everything we've been through. Not this, too.

"Okay, now can you tell us what the fuck all of that means, and how you're going to fix it?" I ask, cutting the doctor off. There's more anger in my tone than the doc deserves, I know, but right now it's the only thing keeping me together.

"It means I'm dying," Pol says, his voice muffled by his hands over his face. "Right?"

I glare at the doctor with all of the strength I can muster up, willing them not to say that even if it's the truth, not while Pol is sitting here like this with his shoulders shaking.

"Frankly, it means you should already be dead," the doctor says. "But clearly you're not. You're walking and talking and, all things considered, far more okay than you reasonably should be." They tap their fingers against their comm, looking thoughtful—and a little bit excited, which angers me all over again. My brother's life isn't some fun puzzle for them to figure out.

"So how do we make him better?" I ask, my voice again coming out sharp. I realize I'm gripping Pol's arm hard enough that it probably hurts, and force myself to relax. "What can we do?"

"Well, to answer that, first we need to understand what's causing it. And that's especially complicated in your brother's case. There's little research on the effects of cryosleep, and none on this Primus weapon, nor the treatment the Gaians used. It's difficult for me to parse out which is an effect of which, and how they're affecting one another." The doctor looks up at Pol now, their expression intent in a way that makes my hackles rise. "But that's not even the most interesting part."

"I'm afraid I don't find any of this *interesting*," Corvus says darkly, at the same time I say, "That's our brother's life you're talking about."

"Can I go wait outside?" Pol asks, before the doctor can respond. His arms are wrapped tightly around himself.

"You can go in the lobby," I say. "But—"

He gets up and leaves before I can say more. I sink down in my seat and turn my attention back to the doctor. "So what's going on?" I ask. "It's not like the virus can kill him now, right? The Gaians cured him."

"Well, no, not exactly," the doctor says.

My heart stops. "What?"

"He's not cured, per se. The virus is still inside him, still alive."

"I...wh..." I don't even know what question I want to ask in response. I thought I had braced myself for the worst when I came here, but this just threw me for a loop. What does that mean, he's not cured? Does that mean he's still dying? It will still kill him eventually? I think of that black oozing out of his mouth on Titan, and have to fight back tears. I knew something was wrong, but I never considered that possibility. I couldn't, not when it's my baby brother, and not when he's already been through so much. "Is that why he's not getting better?" I ask, my voice coming out a croak. "He's still sick? Is it still going to...?" I trail off, unable to even say it. Everything we did for him...did we only prolong his suffering? Buy ourselves a few more months, or a year? For fuck's sake, the poor kid hasn't even had his twenty-first birthday yet. Now all I can think about is how fragile he looks. How different he's been. I knew all along that there was something really wrong, but I just didn't want to see it.

"Let me think of the best way to explain this," the doctor muses, setting down their comm and pressing their fingers together in their lap. I wait in agony, dimly aware of Corvus taking my hand and squeezing. "He is still, technically, infected. The virus is still there, and the damage has not been reversed. But nor is it progressing. It's alive, but it's no longer targeting his cells."

"How is that possible?" Corvus asks, reassuring me that I'm not a complete idiot for thinking that sounds ridiculous.

"Well…" The doctor clicks their tongue, tilting their head thoughtfully. "It made a little more sense as soon as I remembered I was looking at the effects of the same weapon that decimated Titan. I remember the reports. It didn't damage structures, nor soil…not even animals and plant life. It specifically targeted humans. It recognized something in our DNA and knew to attack it."

"And…that explains it how?" I ask. "What are you saying, exactly?"

"You wanted to know what the Gaians did," the doctor says. "Well, there's a small piece of your answer, though it raises many more questions in itself." They tap their fingers, looking from Corvus's face to mine. "They made your brother a little less human."

CHAPTER TEN

Beneath the Skin

Corvus

U h, excuse me, but what the *fuck*?" Scorpia asks.
Not exactly the way I would have framed the question, but it does do a concise job of conveying what I'm feeling right now. That and a boiling anger, a need to defend my younger brother. He may be different, he may be stranger than he was before... but of course he is *human*.

"Only a little less," the doctor says, their voice slow and patient. "The slightest tweak to his DNA. Just enough to make the virus accept him as something benign."

"Okay, maybe you could've led with *that*," Scorpia says, letting out a strangled, half-hysterical laugh that means she's right on the verge of panicking.

I squeeze her hand before focusing again on the doctor. "So what can we do?"

"Frankly, I'm not sure there's much to do," the doctor says. "The virus won't kill him. I'm not sure whatever the Gaians did is reversible, and even if it was, that would mean succumbing to the virus. As for the damage from entering cryosleep, there are some things I could try, but…" They wave a hand. "Honestly, most of the treatments they tout are bullshit. I'm pretty sure we're all aware of the dangers of cryosleep. You made a calculated risk, and it paid off in the end, but that doesn't mean you can magically make the side effects go away."

"So he won't get worse," Scorpia says, half question and half statement.

"You should likely get him checked out frequently—this is all new ground, of course—but as far as I can tell, no. The virus is dormant."

"But he won't get better, either," I say, because someone has to.

"Likely not."

Scorpia puts her face in her hands. "How are we supposed to tell him that?" she asks, without looking up at me. "He's twenty. He's *twenty*."

"Plenty of people lead fulfilling lives with far worse conditions," the doctor says. "Honestly, he should be grateful he survived at all. And so should the two of you." They shrug. "And if you're looking for another plus side, I know plenty of scientists who would pay a pretty penny to get their hands on a case like him."

"No," Scorpia and I say at once, her voice muffled by her hands and mine sharp enough that it's practically a threat.

The doctor only shrugs again, unruffled, their expression saying *Well, it's your loss.*

I do have one more question. Though I hate to ask it, I have to. "If the virus is still alive inside him, is he dangerous?"

The doctor hesitates. "Well," they say slowly. "I can't know for sure. I'd have to run some more tests. But even if he's not contagious…" They hesitate again, tilting their head back and forth like they're fighting with something. "There's a live sample of a planet-killing weapon in his blood. That's dangerous no matter how you slice it."

I catch their meaning immediately. There is a reason that we destroyed all of the vials of the bio-weapon, vowing not to let them fall into anyone's hands. If anyone knew what Pol is, what he carries in his blood...there are many people who would find a way to use it.

Part of me always wondered at the fact that Leonis came through on her end of the deal, and safely returned our brother to us, even after we sabotaged her plan to wipe out the Nibirans. I was so relieved to have my brother back that I was willing to ignore the question marks. But now, knowing this...I wonder if this is part of why Leonis let him live. Maybe, if she hadn't been imprisoned and eventually killed, she would have found a way to use the weapon lying dormant in his blood. Or maybe she just knew how cruel it would feel when we eventually found out that our brother is a walking blueprint for a weapon that could end the system.

The walk back to the ship is tense. Though Deva is as loud and busy as always around us, the three of us are silent. Pol trails behind, his hands in his pockets and his shoulders slumped. He didn't even ask what the doctor said, he only told us that he wanted to go home. Both from the asking, and from how readily we agreed, he must assume the news isn't good.

I want to tell him that it also could be worse, which isn't untrue, but...I'm still at a loss about how to explain any of what we just learned to him. Scorpia keeps stealing glances at him when she thinks he's not paying attention, and I have to resist the urge to do the same. The doctor's words keep ringing in my ears: *a little less human.* There in that office, we didn't think to ask, *and a little more what?*

Because, really, we don't have to. Between the strange new behaviors and the fact that he was "cured" on Gaia, of all places...

I think we both have an inkling of what exactly the Gaians put into his genes. And knowing how Scorpia views the Primus, I can only hope that it doesn't change her feelings toward him. That her looks at him are only worry, and not the disgust and fear she always shows when faced with alien relics.

When we reach the shipyard, I stop and turn to Pol. "Okay," I say. "We should discuss this now, without the others around, so that you can decide how much you want to tell them."

Pol stops in his tracks, looking cornered. "Right now? I have a headache."

"I'm sorry, but yes. Now. You need to hear it." I know that he's afraid, and I know that he's desperately trying to hide it, but he needs to understand it, and all of its implications. I look over at Scorpia and nod my head toward the ship. "You've got a client to meet, right? We should get everything wrapped up here."

She opens her mouth, but shuts it again, and nods at me before she heads up the ramp. I know she understands what I mean. Now that someone on Deva has this information, it likely isn't safe for us to be here any longer. I don't trust that doctor any more than necessary, even though we paid them handsomely for their silence.

Which, of course, raises another issue: We have nowhere else to go. Our access to Pax isn't fully verified yet. But for the moment, I think we need to focus on getting Pol out of here and discussing our next move.

I sit on the ramp and pat the space beside me. Pol sighs and reluctantly drops onto the metal, his shoulders angled away like he's half thinking of making a break for it.

We sit in silence for several long seconds while I search for a way to begin this conversation, but he beats me to it.

"I'm not going to get better, am I?"

I close my eyes, let out a breath, and open them again. I wish I had a better answer for him, but he deserves honesty. "The doctor said it's unlikely. But they said you won't get worse, either. The virus is still inside you, but dormant."

He nods, looking down. I expected rage, or sorrow, or some combination of the two, but the subdued resignation on his face is even worse. I want to comfort him—want to tell him everything the doctor said about him still being able to lead a long, full life— but the doctor doesn't know Pol like I do. It's true he can, and I believe he will, still be happy. But he has to deal with the grief over the life he had, first, and I'm not going to try and take that away from him.

"And the weird shit?" he asks, after a short while. "The noise on Gaia and all?"

I suppress a grimace. I was hoping he wouldn't ask about that yet, when I've barely processed what the doctor told me. "Um..." I rub the back of my neck, and he turns to me, brow furrowing as he homes in on my discomfort. I clear my throat. "This is going to sound very strange. But the doctor believes that the way the Gaians stopped the virus from killing you was to...change your DNA."

"Change it how?" His brow is still furrowed, his eyes watching me carefully. I know Pol is more observant than we often give him credit for, and I am a terrible liar. He'll know if I dodge the question. Maybe Scorpia should have stayed for this conversation.

Again, all I have to offer is the cold truth. "They didn't say. But given the sudden proclivity for Primus technology..."

Pol blinks. Blinks again, his face crinkling and then going slack as he processes the information. Then he breaks into a grin. "*Hell* yeah," he says.

Now it's my turn to stare. "Yeah?"

"I'm some kind of mutant alien hybrid with a dormant super-weapon inside me?" he asks. "So fucking cool." He scrambles to his feet. I continue to watch him warily, half expecting him to burst into tears or shout at any second as the truth sinks in, but he only looks giddy.

"Can I tell Drom?"

"Uh..." I hold out my hands, at a loss. "Yeah. You can tell whoever you want—" He bounds off into the ship before I finish, so I shout after him, "But only family!"

Inside the bowels of the ship, I already hear him yelling his twin's name. I sit on the ramp for a few seconds longer, shaking my head, before I follow.

CHAPTER ELEVEN

Into the Parlor

Scorpia

A s I head back into Zi Vi, my mind is still reeling from the information about Pol. But I have to trust that Corvus can handle the fallout while I handle this sale. With the future uncertain, it's more important than ever to have our accounts as full as possible. And when this woman contacted me last time we were here, she gave me the impression that she was very interested in off-world goods *and* very rich.

Once I seal this deal, we're free to head onward to Pax or wait everything out in open space for a while. As I navigate the crowded streets of the city, I let myself dream about it. The rest of the system might be after us, and Deva may not be as safe as I originally thought, but I still have hope for Pax. Even if Silvania Azenari—whoever she is—wants something from us, surely there must be some truth to the stories about Pax being a wild frontier world where no one is truly in charge. No Planetary Defense System to worry about, either. I'll feel a whole lot safer with a place like that to touch down. And even if Lyre wants to stay and attend university here, we'll be only about a week's trip away. It'll be hard not to have her on board, but of course it won't be forever.

Some of my dreams are selfish, too. I'll have a new world to explore, untouched even by Momma's memory, since it's the one place she never had access to. I can build something for myself without the past hounding me, for once. Escape all of the politicking and interplanetary conflict. It'd be nice to be able to disappear for a while.

When I arrive at the address my client gave me, I pull myself out of my daydream and triple-check the directions I got to determine this is the right place. I knew that a house this close to the heart of the city would be expensive as all hell, but still, this place is...wow. I wasn't sure houses like this existed outside of Devan billboards and ludicrously over-the-top holoshows. It's built out of real wood and glass rather than metal or concrete, which makes it look flimsy in comparison to most of the buildings here—but that flimsiness is a boast in itself, stating that its owner can afford to repair any damage from invasive plants or Deva's near-constant rain or other problems. And the yard around the building is huge, and empty—a luxurious waste of space in a city where most people live crammed on top of one another in tiny apartments.

I kind of feel like I might get arrested just from looking at it too long. But of course, there isn't much law enforcement on Deva. Which is probably why this house has private security instead. No one's standing outside the gate, but multiple cameras swivel to follow me as I walk up to the main entrance. They're so large and obvious that they must be a threat as much as a practicality.

I almost turn around, but the thought of Lyre's college tuition, and Pol's doctor fees, and paying for fake papers on Pax keeps me going. Someone who can afford to live in a place like this can also afford to pay a hefty price for these goods. And probably isn't savvy enough to second-guess me when I name a ridiculous price for them, either. Rich, novelty-seeking clients are the best kind.

When I wave to the cameras, I expect a security escort or something, but instead I hear the click of the gates opening. I glance around, shift the weight of the pack over my shoulder, and walk in. Past the gate, the yard is filled with smooth, pale stones, with a darker path of steps winding through. On other planets, the wealthy might show off a nice array of carefully cultivated plants; on Deva, the lack of any signs of plant growth is the display of power and privilege. I'm so busy taking it all in that the click of the gates closing behind me makes me jump. I turn to look, and the realization that there's no clear way out without help from the homeowner makes my mouth go dry.

But I've come this far. No point in turning back now. I wipe my palms on my pants and follow the winding stone steps toward the house on the horizon.

The door opens automatically, just like the gate: two glass panels sliding outward and releasing a breath of air so thoroughly conditioned that it almost tastes like my ship. The cool dryness is startling after Deva's humidity, and when I step inside, it feels like every bead of sweat on my body chills at once. The doors slide shut again noiselessly, and I am left alone in a huge entranceway, with vaulted ceilings and unnatural lighting so bright and white it hurts my eyes.

There's something off-putting about the place. It's too clean, too understated—the kind of wealth that doesn't need to declare itself, but lives in all of the little details, like the automatic doors and the huge yard without a single weed. I feel like I'm out of my league.

And there's still no one here. I eye the staircase on one side of the room, and the closed door on the other, and opt to stay where I am, just past the entranceway. I clear my throat. "Hello?"

I check the client's name on my comm again. "I'm here for Ms....
Marigold? Alessiah Marigold?"

For a good thirty seconds, there's nothing. I glance back at the
door, considering walking away, but a moment later I hear the
click of high heels approaching.

I stare as my client walks over. I stare a lot. She politely pre-
tends not to notice as she finishes descending the staircase.

It's hard to gauge her age, given she has a pale face that belongs
on one of Zi Vi's flashing billboards: both drop-dead gorgeous
and clearly more plastic than flesh. And her face isn't the only
place she's had work done, judging from... certain bodily propor-
tions. Not that I'm looking. But they *are* pretty prominently on
display in her skin-hugging dress, if one was to look.

Which I'm not, because I'm here on a job.

Obviously.

Her hair is long and silver, which makes her age all the more
difficult to place, because it's impossible to tell if it's due to age or
just some new Devan fashion trend. Her nails, too, are a bright
silver of the shiny and metallic variety.

"Darling," she says. She takes my hands—making me stiffen
in surprise—and kisses me on both cheeks. I'm not sure if it's
the press of her lips or the rush of perfume that dizzies me, but
I recover just in time to return the gesture and avoid being rude.
"I'm glad you made it. Come." She releases my hands and walks
toward the door I noted previously. I follow, a little dazed and
willing my eyes to remain on respectful areas.

Through the door is one of those rooms that only rich people
have, occupied with just a few couches and bookshelves. Huge
windows cover one wall, but the glass is colored to negate the characteristic red tint of Nova Vita's natural light, leaving the room
as weirdly white as the entrance room was. A small glass table sits
between the couches; on it rests a tray with two drinks in crystal

cups. A huge television screen across from the couch is playing some kind of "emergency press conference" from Prime Minister Jai Misha, but the sound is muted and I can't tell what it's about at a glance.

"Sit," Alessiah says, and gestures to one of the couches. I tear my eyes away from the screen and sit. It can't be that important, if my client seems so unconcerned about it; there's some new "emergency" every day on Deva, anyway. My client takes a seat right beside me, ignoring all of the other furniture in the room to remain distractingly close. She crosses one slender leg over the other before raising her eyes to meet my continued gawking.

She grabs both cups, pours one into the other, and then pours it back before handing me one—another Devan mannerism, showing me it's safe. I grab it without thinking and gulp a rather unbecoming amount as I try to quash my nerves. It isn't until the taste hits my tongue that I realize I'm not sure what I'm drinking. But there's no bitter bite of alcohol. It's all sweetness and fizz, something fruity and cold that bubbles all of the way down my throat and stomach, not at all unpleasantly. I'm very aware of the sticky film of sweat that formed on my body on the walk over, and resist the urge to discreetly sniff myself to check how I smell.

"So, uh…" In an effort to make some kind of conversation, I glance at the news again. "What's going on there?"

She doesn't look at the screen, but her perfect smile curdles into an expression of distaste. "An important update regarding Pax, apparently, but our dear prime minister is taking his time getting to the point of it."

I eye her, and then the crowd on the screen. I've always gotten the impression that Misha is quite popular here; she's the first Devan I've heard express such open dislike. "Not a fan, huh?"

"Certainly not. Misha is a fool." Her eyes laser in on me. I feel stripped bare under her gaze. "Are *you* a fan?"

101

"Uh..." I look away from her to get my brain to work again. "I don't have much of an opinion, I guess. I'm not from around here, as you know." So much for small talk. Discussing inflammatory politics with a client seems like a bad move, so I scramble to shift the subject to business. "But you didn't want me here to talk politics, right?" I set down my drink and remove my pack. I place a few items on the glass table, handling them much more carefully than necessary to inflate her idea of their worth.

While I stall with my overly cautious handling, I glance sideways at my client again, trying to get a read on her. All of the glitz and glamor could be blinding, which is probably its intent. But I focus on what it means. She's rich, so she's probably not the type looking to buy this off of me and resell it for a profit; a few gadgets and trinkets from Gaia wouldn't be worth the effort for a woman who already lives like this.

I'm guessing chances are slim that she's some preserver of Gaian culture or a scientist with an interest in Primus tech, too. I remember the look that Shey would get when presented with something new and exciting—that desire to pick things apart and figure them out, the hunger to *know*—and when this woman sweeps her eyes over me and my collection of goods, she doesn't look like that. It's a hunger, all right, but it's not that kind. She strikes me as more of a collector of curiosities. When I glance around at the bookshelves, the assortment of old-looking book spines and small statues and the like support my guess.

I know this kind of client: someone who wants *stuff*, no matter the kind, to show off. And as an upper-class person in the most expensive city on the wealthiest planet in the system, I'm not surprised she's had to turn her attention toward the illegal variety of goods. Everything loses its shine when you can get it too easily, and for a lady like this, there aren't too many things that would be hard to get her hands on.

So I've got my in. Good. At least my brain hasn't *entirely* lost its function in the face of the most gorgeous woman I've seen in a while. I definitely don't want a repeat of my first encounter with Shey. Not that it turned out too badly, all things considered, but...I think I've had enough pining for a woman way out of my league for at *least* a couple years.

"Did you gather all of this yourself?" the woman asks. Her eyes are very large and luminously blue. I wonder—with the small part of my brain still able to properly function with those eyes turned on me—if they're natural. Probably not. "From the surface of Gaia?" she prompts, when I take a second too long to answer.

"Oh. Well, yes. Mostly." I flash her a smile, trying to regain the confidence I had a few seconds before she looked at me like that. "I'm not the sort of captain who lets her crew go on dangerous missions without her. I'm always the first one in and the last one out when it comes to jobs like this." And thank the stars no one is here to contradict me.

"That must have been very frightening," she says. She slides closer and places a hand on my knee.

I blink. The intent is obvious, but so baffling that I just keep talking as if it isn't happening. "You get used to it, in my line of work."

"I imagine you must. Especially as a space-born."

Even with her fingernails trailing along the sensitive skin above my knee, that yanks me out of my daze. "Wait. Wait. How do you know that?" I pull back—even though it hurts me a little—and stare at her. "I didn't mention that."

She arches one perfect brow, her equally perfect lips forming a small smile. "Did you think I wouldn't know who you are, Scorpia Kaiser?" She tilts her head. "Surely this mustn't come as too much of a shock. Did you think I would invite you into my home without knowing who I'm dealing with?"

103

I suppose that makes sense—but still. There shouldn't be any information about me floating around Deva. I've hardly done any deals on Deva before, and I've used a fake name on our last couple trips here. So if there's information, it's coming from outside of this planet, which means she could know...too much. Way too much. Including things linking me to Leonis, and the Nibiran Council, and all sorts of messy business that I was really hoping not to drag here with me. "And where did you get this information, exactly?"

She looks surprised at that—actually surprised, not at all like the little reactions she's been faking—and then laughs, covering her mouth with one hand. "Oh, dear. You really don't know, do you?"

"Know what?" I ask, hastily scooping up all of the things I brought and dumping them into my bag. I don't care how attractive she is or how much she'd pay, this isn't worth it. My family was supposed to get a new start, and I'm not going to screw it up for them. Not this time.

"Everyone here knows about you, Scorpia," she says, watching me with no attempt to stop me. She stays where she is, lounging on her couch with her long legs stretched out, looking like a self-satisfied cat. "Everyone who matters, at least." She tilts her head and studies me. "Oh, come, now. Don't be paranoid. We're on the same side."

I stand up, slinging my pack over my shoulder. "I don't have a side."

She stands, too. "That's where you're wrong." She takes a step toward me. I nearly trip over my own feet as I back away. "Don't pretend you're indifferent. You're a woman who's worked with planetary governments, no? Worked toward a united future. I want the same thing." She gestures toward the television screen, where Jai Misha is gesticulating animatedly, his words inaudible.

"And so long as Deva has a prime minister like him, that vision can never be a reality."

"I've got no idea what you're talking about." And, as much as she seems convinced it's safe to talk here, I know how dangerous a conversation like this can be, on a planet like Deva. I need to get out of here.

"Misha will never work with the Interplanetary Alliance," she presses on, determined, as I retreat toward the door. "Especially not after they reneged on their deal for Leonis. He's about to find an excuse to start a war with Pax to drum up support for building a fleet and distract from the problems on his own planet."

"What fleet?" I ask. "I haven't even heard about a fleet. Seriously, lady—"

"Oh, don't be dense. Why do you think Deva and Pax were so desperate for Titan's resources in the first place?"

That...makes a lot of sense, now that I'm thinking about it. But no, no—none of this is relevant to me. I'm not going to get sucked into another planet's problems. "Listen, you've got the wrong idea," I say. "I don't know what you're looking for, but you're not going to find it in me. I don't want any part in whatever political games you're playing." I saw how that ended up when we were forced to leave Nibiru. Lies, upon lies, upon lies...I'm not dumb enough to get involved in all of that stuff again. Especially not on Deva, one of my crew's last refuges in the system.

But as I inch for the door, Alessiah follows me relentlessly, her eyes boring into me. "We can help each other," she says.

"I don't want your help." I turn and walk more quickly toward the door now, my heart pounding in tune with the click of Alessiah's heels behind me. Stars above, the woman will not give up. "I don't want anything from you. I'm not getting involved in this shit." I finally get to the door, and reach for the handle—and, of course, it's locked. I whirl around to face her, and find her very close, uncomfortably close.

"I'm offering you an opportunity," she says. "You're going to need allies, with what's coming for you. Staying neutral won't be an option for long."

"Not interested," I say, trying to calm my thumping heart and put together some coherent thoughts. I *could* probably knock this lady out, break through a window, and climb the gate to freedom, but it's not my preferred style. I shift my bag to one shoulder and slowly raise my hands. "Please," I say, more softly, hoping I can get through to her without this getting ugly. "I'm leaving all of that behind. I just want a quiet life. Please just let me go."

She purses her lips and looks me up and down, this time far more critically than before, but she takes a step back. "Then you came to the wrong city, darling," she says. "This isn't the sort of place that does *quiet*. Especially not for someone like you." But she pulls out a comm and flicks a finger across it in a lazy sort of way. The door clicks behind me, and some of the tension unravels in my chest. "I'm afraid you won't find others as forthcoming about their interest, nor will they be looking for something as simple as I am. But no matter. You'll figure it out eventually."

"I'll be sure to remember that," I tell her, with every intent to stay as far from her and this place as I possibly can. "Thanks for the, uh…interesting conversation." I step through the door before she can respond, but I can feel her eyes on me as I hurry down the path.

I'm halfway back to the ship when I realize I'm being followed.

It's a sort of sixth sense that I honed real early, as a person with a tendency to make less-than-legal choices both on personal and business bases. I cast one quick glance over my shoulder to confirm it—catching a glimpse of one, two, three faces who seem to aim toward me with their body language in the otherwise-indifferent crowd, all of them wearing black.

No distinguishing characteristics that I can see, no recognizable uniforms or markings, but this is Deva, after all. They're far more likely to be someone's private security than any kind of official law enforcement. It could be someone sent by the woman I just parted with—but why would she have let me leave when she could have easily kept me trapped there? Again her words rattle in my head: *Everyone here knows about you.*

So someone else? But I've barely even done anything illegal here—recently, that is—so why now? Did Alessiah let me go just to toy with me? Or, a worse option—does this have something to do with the doctor and Pol's situation?

Either way, I'm not leading these people back to my ship and my crew. I can worry about getting myself away later. The first and most important step is making sure I don't endanger the others.

I linger outside of a street food stall, pretending to peruse the sticky-sweet rice balls. While I do so, I surreptitiously tighten the strap on my bag and glance around at various escape routes.

I don't have much faith in my ability to outrun them, especially not when I'm still unaccustomed to the heat and humidity of Deva and not too familiar with these streets. My best bet will be to lose myself in the crowd. I knock over a bottle of sauce with my elbow, apologize profusely to the vendor while I bend over to grab it, and then dart into the busy street, narrowly avoiding being hit by a hovercraft. I wind my way through traffic and people as quickly as I can, hurried but not so hurried that I'll cause a big ripple in the crowd, making my way toward a narrow side street I spotted from the food stall. I'm nearly there when I hear a shout behind me, and I glance back to see at least one of my pursuers has given up on subterfuge and begun shoving their way through the street.

In true Devan fashion, the crowd is giving them a rough time, throwing elbows and occasionally food at them as they try to force their way past. But despite the general anti–law enforcement attitude, I doubt anyone is really going to help if they catch me. Nor can I make it to the alley before they get close enough to see me. I pivot and dart into a nearby bar instead. It's a sweaty, smoky little building, packed with patrons who don't seem the type to give any outsiders the time of day—meaning both me and the people after me, or so I hope. A good place to disappear, and if I have any luck at all, one with a rear exit and a shady back alley I can escape down.

I squeeze my way through the crowd, dodging drunks and virtual pool tables. My comm buzzing in my pocket nearly gives me a heart attack, but I quickly shut it off; Corvus can get a call back when I'm done running for my life. I make my way to the back of the room—but my heart sinks as I find nothing but a wall and some corner booths. No back exit. Just my luck. I groan, running a sweaty hand through my hair and glancing over my shoulder. My pursuers are already shoving their way through the crowd at the door. The only reason they haven't reached me yet is that the bar's patrons are even more annoyed at being shoved aside a second time and are putting up a fight over it.

But it's only a matter of time. I've got nowhere to go.

The realization is almost a relief at this point. My feet come to a stop. No more running, no chance of fighting, no more clever ruses left up my sleeve. Guess this is it.

"You the cause of all this commotion, sweetie?"

I turn to find an older woman in bright makeup, a thick cigar in one hand and a drink in the other. She and a gaggle of friends are all crammed into a corner booth and staring at me, more curious than hostile. They're all wearing the long, puffy, colorful dresses that must be in style right now.

"Awfully sorry to disturb your night, ladies," I say, distantly aware that I'm hitting that hysterical point of anxiety. But, hell, it's not like I've got anything better to do with my last living hours than flirt with some good-looking older women.

"Never apologize for injecting a little excitement into the world," she says, waving a hand that trails smoke. But when her eyes move toward the door and presumably find the people following me, her expression changes, lips tightening and posture going stiff. "My, my, you did piss off the wrong people," she says. And then, before I can muster up a response, she says, "Get under the table."

"What?"

When I don't move fast enough, two of her friends get up and push me down, and soon I'm on the floor under the table surrounded by an array of colorful skirts and shoes. I nearly choke on the smell of perfume, which layers over the bar's general aroma of sweat and stale beer rather than covering it. But I press a hand over my nose and make myself as small as possible as the heavy boots of my pursuers arrive at the spot I occupied just a few moments ago.

The ladies carry on their conversation above me. The boots swivel slowly.

"Can I help you?" the woman who initially spoke to me asks—loudly enough to make me cringe. If she's trying to be subtle, why antagonize them now?

But a moment later, a different voice from the bar yells, "Get the fuck out!"

The words are followed by a thrown drink, which splashes across two pairs of boots and splatters me as well. I grimace at the spicy smell: fireberry wine. Of course.

"I would suggest you take their advice," the woman above me says, her voice deceptively mild. "I'm afraid this isn't the kind of place that takes kindly to your profession."

And a few moments later, the boots walk away, back toward the door.

Once I'm sure they're gone, I crawl out from under the table and climb to my feet, dazed and wondering if it's possible to get high from inhaling too much perfume.

The Devan women have already returned to their drinks and conversations, as if they didn't just conceal a wanted fugitive and send off someone's powerful security with a casual fuck you.

"Um, wow. I...thanks," I say, not even sure what to say other than that. Why would they risk themselves for an off-worlder they don't even know? There's only one reason I can think of. "You... recognize me, I guess?"

The woman closest to me puffs on her cigar and arches an eyebrow. "Should I?" she asks, and then shakes her head. "Never mind. I don't want to know. All I know is that I never could say no to a dashing rogue." She smiles broadly and raises her cigar in a salute. "And when I see an opportunity to wave a middle finger to the prime minister's secret police, who am I to reject it?"

CHAPTER TWELVE

Dashed Dreams

Corvus

'm stocking the pantry with fresh supplies when the news hits. One glance at my buzzing comm, and the whole world shifts. I don't need to read more than the headline before I start sending messages to the crew: *Return to* Memoria. *Now.* I call Scorpia, but she doesn't answer. She must be meeting with our client, still.

The others trickle in one by one. Daniil and Orion return from clothes shopping, and the latter hands over his findings before running to the cockpit to prep the ship for an emergency launch. Lyre returns from another trip to the university campus, shadowed by Izra, who went along to make sure she was safe. The twins stumble in smelling of alcohol and smoke, with armfuls of snacks and street food they must have stopped to grab.

I can't bring myself to scold them. "Pack everything up," I tell them. "Fast." They head off into the ship, just as the others did. Only Izra remains behind in the cargo bay with me. Waiting.

Everyone must have questions, but they keep them to themselves.

Nobody is panicking yet. They seem to take for granted that our captain will have some kind of plan.

But Scorpia isn't here. She hasn't responded to my messages. She hasn't even *read* my messages.

I pace in the cargo bay, glancing down the open ramp and into the empty landing zone every few seconds, but there's no sign of her. If this is all due to some distraction or one of her usual poor choices, I will never forgive her. But if it's not... if it's something worse, then...

"I should go into the city," I say, continuing to pace. "Look for her."

"No." Izra leans against the wall beside the open ramp, her arms folded over her chest and her eye on the ceiling. "Then we'll just have to hunt down two of you." She lowers her gaze to me. "Your sister can handle herself."

"But she probably hasn't even seen the news," I say. "If she's with the client..." I trail off as I hear footsteps, and look down the ramp to see Scorpia finally approaching at an exhausted half run, half stumble. I draw my weapon and position myself at the top of the ramp, ready for trouble, but I don't see anyone following her.

She clambers up the ramp, slaps the pressure pad to close it, and half collapses against the wall, breathing hard. "We have a problem," she says, between pants for air.

I holster my weapon and step back. "I know."

"You do?" She looks up at me, her forehead creasing. "Did the prime minister send his secret police after you, too?"

I stare at her. "Well," I say, "we have two problems."

"Shit. Fuck. Okay. At least let me catch my breath first."

I give her a few moments to recover, and collect my own thoughts. The prime minister being after her—after *us*, most likely—is most certainly a problem... but her assumption also means she truly has no idea what I'm about to tell her. I make eye contact with Izra in a silent plea for support, but she shakes her head and walks away, leaving me to deal with this on my own.

"Okay," Scorpia says, once she's done heaving for air. "Hit me. What is it now?"

"Deva just declared war on Pax." I take out my comm and show her.

Breaking News, the feed reads. Behind the text, Jai Misha is egging on a cheering crowd. "If they want a fight, we'll bring them one," he says, to roars of approval.

"What?" Scorpia asks, despair in her voice. She grabs the comm from my hand to get a closer look and lets out several colorful curse words. "Why? Why now?"

"I'm sure they have their supposed reasons, but I suspect the real cause is that they're afraid of the IA's expansion." I pocket the comm once she hands it back to me. "Deva likely sees Pax as an easy target. Small, unorganized. And a war will give them a good excuse to build up a military force to rival the Alliance." I don't need to tell her the problem with that plan: The Devans don't realize that their defense system makes them vulnerable. One lucky attack from Pax could turn their planet hostile.

Scorpia runs her hands through her hair and lets out a long, slow breath. "Starting a war to drum up support for a fleet. She was right."

"Who?"

"Nobody. Never mind." She shakes her head. "Misha must want to drag us into this. So we need to get off of Deva."

"That's the problem. We have nowhere else to go." The Interplanetary Alliance's worlds consider us criminals; Deva and Pax are at war, and the latter is still off-limits to us, anyway. It will be difficult to secure access to Pax now that they're at war, and there's no guarantee Eri and Halon will be able to meet with us, given their risky situation in a Devan-Paxian marriage.

With the direction the system has been heading, I wouldn't be surprised if all borders were soon closed to wanderers like us. We were already some of the last; this may mean the extinction of those who would travel the stars.

"We can't get stuck somewhere with a PDS again. We'll have to head to Pax," Scorpia says. "We might still end up caught in the middle of the war, but at least it's safer. And maybe we can find a way to hide out until things blow over with the IA. We can reach out to our contacts and..." She pauses, looking down at her comm, and blanches. "And we just got a message from Prime Minister Jai Misha. Shit, he really wants us, doesn't he?" She lets out a shaky laugh. Her finger hovers over the screen, but then she pockets the device. "We'll watch once we're safely out of here." She turns and walks farther into the ship, calling over her shoulder, "We're launching. Get ready."

Despite my misgivings, I can't deny my relief as the ship pulls free from Deva. I unclip myself from the launch chair in my room—and stumble as the ship's acceleration abruptly slows. The sudden change sends me crashing to the floor, but I barely feel the pain of my knees hitting the metal, because my mind is already racing ahead to wonder what's happened. Did we just flee one problem straight into the grip of another? Could it be a Devan fleet, keeping us trapped? Paxians here to attack Deva?

The wisest move would be to stay strapped in, as I expect the rest of the crew is doing, but I have to know. As the ship slows to a standstill, I grip my chair to pull myself up, and lean against the wall to keep my balance as I struggle out the door and down the hallway.

As I enter the cockpit, I don't even have to ask. Through the viewing panel, and on the various cameras showing on the screens, I see the problem: We're surrounded by a cohort of gleaming metal warships with their weapons trained on us and a now-familiar emblem of blue wings displayed on their sides.

The Interplanetary Alliance has us surrounded.

"Shit," Orion says, his fingers hovering over the controls. "Do we retreat to Deva?"

"No," Scorpia says from the copilot's chair. "But stay here. They can't get much closer to us without risking an interplanetary incident."

"They already are," I say grimly. Bringing armed, Titan-made warships so close to Deva is an unmistakably risky move. Then again, escaping from the Devan prime minister's secret police right into the hands of the IA feels like a coordinated trap. We may be in even more trouble than we thought.

Scorpia gives me a sharp, surprised look. "Stars, Corvus, you shouldn't be in here. We might have to land suddenly."

"The cockpit has emergency launch chairs for a reason." And I don't want her to deal with whatever this is alone. I stand behind her chair and squeeze her shoulder, which is knotted with tension. "They're not firing or chasing us yet."

"Maybe we're too close to Deva."

"Then why wait here?" I scan the screens, taking in the warships forming a loose net around us. "I believe they want something from us."

A transmission request pops up on the console moments later, confirming my suspicions.

Scorpia takes a deep breath and lets it out slowly. "All right. Orion, keep an eye on them in case this is a diversion. Any sign of trouble, and we flee to Deva."

"Got it, Captain."

She glances up at me in a wordless plea, and I nod and stand just behind her chair where I'll be visible, folding my arms over my chest. She accepts the comms request.

A live broadcast comes through on the main screen, displaying a larger-than-life version of a familiar face.

"Councillor Heikki," Scorpia says. "Always a pleasure."

"Let's not make this any more complicated than it needs to be," the silver-haired woman says, her hands folded neatly in front of her. Then she pauses, faltering for a moment as she stares at us; I realize we're both still in Devan makeup and clothing, which must look absurd to a woman from understated Nibiru, and fight the urge to turn away. She clears her throat. "We have you surrounded. Come peacefully into our custody, and none of you will be harmed. If you attempt to move past us, we'll be forced to take aggressive action."

"Try it," Scorpia says. "I've got a recording ready to broadcast with one press of a button. All kinds of dirty laundry about the IA's leadership and the alien you-know-whats."

Her eyes narrow. "You expect me to believe you'd throw the system into chaos in order to save yourselves?"

Scorpia leans very close to the mic. "Just give me an excuse, Heikki."

Heikki's face remains neutral. "Contact me when you're ready to surrender." She ends the broadcast.

I relax my posture while Scorpia leans back in her chair and lets out a shaky breath. "Not sure pissing her off is the right move."

"Gotta keep her in the mindset that I'm complete scum. If she thinks I'll hesitate to send that broadcast, it'll be the end for us."

Even with that threat, it's hard to see any possibility of a way out of this. The situation was bleak even before these recent developments. Gaia and Titan are dead worlds. Nibiru has almost our entire crew on a most-wanted list. Now Deva and Pax are at war. Going to Pax was a long shot as it was, and now, not even the emptiness of space is our refuge.

Though I fear for our immediate safety, the worst part of this is the loss of all the potential futures. An education for Lyre, recovery for Pol, a peaceful life for Daniil...each of us has a dream dashed to pieces now. There will be no return to normality for us. No better lives for our younger siblings, despite everything Scorpia and I have done to build a future for them. Scorpia had finally made a home for herself on *Memoria*, but not even that is safe anymore. And just when I was beginning to figure out who I want to be without someone making the decision for me, my freedom is being snatched away.

"So what are we going to do?" It's almost painful to hope— and yet, my sister always seems to have some wild scheme ready even in the worst of scenarios.

"Well..." She looks up at me with an expression that is somewhere between a grin and a grimace. "I've got an idea, but you're not going to like it."

CHAPTER THIRTEEN

Last Resort

Scorpia

We hover just outside of Deva's atmosphere. The IA ships have cloaked again—whether to hide themselves from us, or Deva, or both, I'm not sure—but I'm certain they're still surrounding us, ready to pounce the moment they get the go-ahead from their leadership. It's possible they already have some kind of tech to scramble our comms and are just waiting for us to leave Deva's vicinity. Even if they don't, I know we can't keep them at bay with threats forever... and they know we can't stay here, burning through our fuel and supplies. We need to land eventually. But where can we go, when nowhere in the system is safe for us? When our only options are to turn ourselves in as criminals or to end up in the middle of another war?

Which reminds me...

"Wait," I say, allowing myself a tiny flicker of hope. Maybe we don't have to go with my last-resort plan. "First, let's see what Misha has to say." I link my comm to the ship's system and load up the video message on my screen.

An image of Jai Misha himself appears on my screen. He has the same airbrushed, not-quite-real look he always does on billboards—handsome, but a little bit plastic.

"Whoa," Orion says, leaning over to take a look. "No *way*."

I playfully shove him out of the way. "Not the time to fanboy," I say, and then glance at Corvus—deadly serious, as always—and school my features into more appropriate solemnity. Not the time to crack jokes, either, no matter how badly I want to force levity and break the tension. I take a deep breath and hit *play* on the message.

"Captain Kaiser." Despite my time dealing with the Nibiran Council and other government figures, it still gives me an odd shiver to hear my name in the mouth of someone I've seen plastered all over billboards. Jai Misha, even compared to other planetary leaders, has always felt like a larger-than-life figure—half politician and half beloved celebrity. "I hope my request for a meeting didn't frighten you off!" I laugh under my breath. Some request, sending his secret police to tail me. "All I fancy is a chat. I have a feeling we'd have a lot to talk about. I'd love to hear what kind of stories you have about the early days of the IA. You worked for them for a period of time, didn't you? And now they seem very eager to get you back...hm. Strange." He taps a finger against his lips, filling the message with a pointed pause. "Well. Just wanted to let you know you have a potential friend on Deva. And if you decide to leave...good luck out there!"

As the message concludes, I stare at the frozen ending image of his face and chew on my thumbnail. "I think he was trying to warn us," I say slowly. "And offer us sanctuary from the IA? Are they *not* working together?"

"Like I said before, I think both Deva and Pax are wary of the IA," Corvus says. "But that wasn't an offer to help us for free. He wants information. Leverage."

I pause, mulling that over. It wasn't an option I realized was on the table. We could trade him the info on the Planetary Defense Systems…But it'd mean throwing ourselves into another war. Same if we go to that Silvania Azenari on Pax—she must want the same thing. I shake my head. "We can't. It might be different if they both had Planetary Defense Systems—it could be a way to scare them both off of war. But in this case, it'll just make things messier. And we'll lose our only leverage against the IA." Which is especially important now that they've proven they're willing to come after us in open space. Even if we allied with Misha, he wouldn't be able to protect us out there, so we'd be trapped on a planet at war, with a Planetary Defense System that could trigger at any moment. I won't do that to my crew again. "We'll have to stick with my original idea."

"Which is?" Corvus asks.

I hate knowing that the hope on his face is about to wither into despair. But I have to make him see the logic of this, no matter how much he wishes there was another way. I stand up, leaving Orion at the wheel to keep an eye on the IA ships, and step into the hallway. Corvus follows me, and once the door seals behind us, it's just the two of us alone.

"I'm going to turn myself in to the IA," I say.

"No." Of course, he doesn't even think about it. "That's not a possibility. Be reasonable."

"You be reasonable. We've got nowhere to go, Corvus. Literally nowhere. Our only option is to face this."

He shakes his head. "We're all on that list. The crew needs you. If anyone has to do it—"

"Not a chance in hell." I knew he would try this, and luckily I have an answer ready. "If you go, they'll kill you."

"So I'm supposed to let you go to the same fate?"

"Maybe not." I take a breath, trying to both organize my

thoughts and sound more confident about this plan than I feel. "Listen: You'd be dead for sure because you're a Titan who committed treason. That's a clean-cut execution case, yeah? And we know Altair won't hesitate to lay claim to you, and the right to punish you, and go through with it. But here's the thing…" I lean forward, holding my hands up. "What are they going to nail me for? And under whose authority?"

"The Nibirans will…" he starts, and then trails off, frowning.

"Now you're starting to see," I say, encouraged by his lack of an immediate argument. "If they try to punish me for disobeying their orders and handing Leonis over to the Titans, they'll be forced to publicly admit the peace deal was never their idea. The IA would self-implode."

"Then Altair—" He stops again.

"Uh-huh," I say. "He could tell everyone I helped Momma sell the bio-weapon that destroyed Titan, but then he'd be forced to admit that he's the one who bought it. I'm guessing he doesn't want me testifying publicly about that." I force a smile even though my stomach is still twisting itself in anxious knots. "And yeah, I reneged on a deal with the Gaians, too, but there's no way Khatri is going to try to hold me accountable for refusing to release a bio-weapon on Nibiru. That's the beauty of it. Everything I've done has involved one of them. Gonna be real hard to make a case for it without collapsing their entire alliance, and I don't think any of them want that, no matter how much they hate me."

"They could still pin you with some minor charges if they wanted to," he says. "Smuggling. Drug dealing. Illegal planetary entry."

"Okay, sure. They could find an excuse to put me away for a few years if they really wanted to. But even if they did manage to get me for something, punishing me will be another nightmare. Which planet's laws do I fall under? Who gets to decide what to do with me? How are they going to explain this to the public when the Nibirans still view our family as heroes? I'm gonna cause problems for them every step of the way, and I think when they realize that, they're gonna want to find a way to end this nice and quiet. I doubt they'll even want to put me anywhere near a court of law when they think about it a little bit longer. I'll bet we can work out a deal. Then we can wait out the war on Nibiru."

"They could still imprison or kill you," he says. "It doesn't matter if they can find a way to do it legally. They're some of the most powerful people in the system. No one is going to stop them if they want to find a way to punish you."

"But you'll still be free, with the information about the PDS and a whole list of other things they don't want the system to know," I say. "That's why I need you to stay with the ship and the crew. Let me go make a deal."

His face is a war of emotions. Uncertainty, and guilt, and concern. I know without a doubt that he'd choose to be the one throwing himself into danger any day, but I can't let that happen. I may not be nearly as confident about this plan as I'm pretending to be, but it's not a lie that this is the best shot we have.

"I know what you're thinking, but this isn't some grand self-sacrifice. You should know that's not my style." I force a grin. "Give me some credit, Corvus. I'm not ready to die just when things have started getting good for me. I'm gonna find a way out of this."

In the days after I give Heikki the terms of my surrender, I act far more confident than I feel. Swaggering around the ship like I don't have a care in the world, laughing too loud, brushing off anyone's attempts to say goodbye. Trying my best to ignore the fact we are being escorted by a full cohort of Titan warships.

I explained to the crew that this was our only option, and they accepted it, but nobody is happy about it. Even aside from the worries about my plan, Nibiru holds bad memories for many of us. Drom, who was starting to relax in our days on Deva, is back to obsessively training and ignoring us as we approach the planet where she fought a war not long ago. Daniil barely leaves his room, undoubtedly dreading the thought of facing the Titans again after his betrayal; as soon as I explained our plan, he pulled me aside and suggested offering himself up to the IA instead of me, but of course I refused. I catch Lyre sitting on the engine room floor, staring down at a pamphlet from Zi Vi University. Corvus haunts the halls late at night, shadows growing beneath his eyes.

It hurts to think back on how happy everyone was on Deva. Was it a mistake to leave? Would I have been better off dealing with Misha, rather than the Alliance? But no, I can't let myself think of it. Nothing is worse than the threat of ending up in the middle of a war again. This plan is risky, but it's our only shot at real freedom.

Still, the guilt eats at me. When it's too hard to keep up the cheerful facade, I retreat to the cockpit. I'm not the pilot anymore, but I'll never get tired of looking out at the stars.

Yet on the final day of our approach, there's not much to see other than the blue orb of Nibiru growing closer and closer. I run my fingers over my prosthetic hand and stare at it, thinking of all the problems, new and old, waiting for me there. Thinking, too, of Shey. All of the unanswered messages I sent her last time I was here. I wonder if she'll come visit me when the Alliance throws me in a cell.

Footsteps approach the cockpit, and I brace myself for another conversation with Corvus trying to talk me out of this, but instead Orion joins me. He sinks into the pilot's chair and sighs, staring out at Nibiru.

"I was hoping I'd seen the last of this place," he says.

Shit. I've been so wrapped up in my own issues that I almost forgot how afraid of this place he must be, too. "You don't have to worry," I tell him. "The deal I made specifies that you and all the others will stay free. I've got leverage."

He waves a hand dismissively. "Oh, don't worry about me. I've already had Izra dragging me off for self-defense drills every day, which I'm pretty sure is how she expresses concern. But I'll be fine."

It's obvious he's trying to change the subject, but it's not so easy to forget that the last time we approached Nibiru, he was so desperate to avoid the underwater prison of Ca Sineh that he abandoned ship in an escape pod. "I just want you to know that I'd never agree to this if I thought you'd end up back there." Along with the others. It makes me sick to imagine my younger siblings trapped in that horrible place, or Corvus, Daniil, and Izra left to the brutal judgment of General Altair and the Titans. Making this deal is the best shot I have at keeping them safe. No matter what it means for me.

"Scorpia." Orion bumps an elbow against mine and smiles. "Don't you worry about me. Or any of us. Last time I made the mistake of underestimating you. Now I know that if anyone can pull this off, it's you."

Try as I might, I can't force myself to grin back at him. "Just promise me that if things go wrong, you'll get the others out of there," I say. "Don't let them stay behind for me."

His smile fades as he searches my face. After a moment, he nods.

Together, we stare out at Nibiru drawing ever closer.

As I take my first step onto the ramp leading down to Nibiru, my heart feels like it's trying to break out through my ribs and run free. The familiar scent of the salt-touched air, once comforting, now makes me dizzy with panic.

I know that this might be the last time I see my family and the rest of my crew. But I also know that the second I show any doubt or hesitation, they're going to break down, so I refuse to glance back over my shoulder even as the peacekeepers swarm the dock and surround me. I have to trust that Corvus will take care of them now.

I slowly raise my hands in the air and fold them behind my head. "Aw, a welcome party," I say, loudly enough that I hope the others can hear me. "Isn't that nice?"

The moment I hear the ship's ramp thunk closed behind me, and only then, I let myself release a shaky breath. So far, the IA is holding true to the deal I cut with Heikki: I come along nicely, and they leave the rest of my family alone. I'll buy their freedom by handing myself over. And despite everything I've told the crew over the last few days, I suspect that I'll get a life sentence at best.

It feels bad to lie to Corvus. I've been doing pretty good lately as far as keeping things honest between us. But this time, I know he wouldn't be able to handle the truth. I'll have to hope he can eventually forgive me for this final letdown.

I hold out my wrists and don't resist as the peacekeepers slap handcuffs on me and lead me down the dock. They seem to be in a hurry—likely trying to avoid too much public attention—but nonetheless, my ship's arrival has already brought a curious crowd of onlookers. Some of them cheer as the peacekeepers rush me past. Whether they're cheering for me or for my arrest, I'm really not sure.

Then one face detaches from the crowd and rushes toward me, and all of a sudden it's hard to care about anything else.

Shey Leonis. Bane of my existence and probably the love of my life. Is it a little dramatic to declare that at age twenty-seven about

125

a woman I've been in a steady relationship with for, uh, maybe a week or two altogether? Absolutely. Do I doubt it's true? Not a bit.

She is poison for my heart, and way too good for me, and I'm probably never going to stop trying to make this work, even though the universe seems to be trying its hardest to dangle her just out of my reach for all of eternity. I wish, just once, we could meet as two normal people without the fate of the system at stake and a prickly, painful history hanging over our heads. But the best I can do is shove it all to the back of my mind, hold my head high, and look at her like she didn't break my heart into a million pieces a couple months ago. She shoves her way through the peacekeepers to my side.

"Scorpia, what have you done?" she asks.

Stars damn it, I've thought about this moment so many times, prepared so many words and all those little gifts from Gaia for her. I even practiced what I might say to her in the mirror a couple times, though that goes to the grave with me. But I never imagined it quite like this, and now all of a sudden I'm not ready. I swallow hard.

"Nice to see you, too," I say.

She shuts her eyes and takes a deep breath. When one of the peacekeepers tries to push her away, she grabs onto my arm and shoots him a fierce glare. Judging by the uncertainty of the law-enforcers, I'm guessing she's only increased her political pull since we last met.

"I'll be accompanying her to wherever you're taking her," she tells the peacekeepers, with a look in her eyes that dares them to argue. "I consider it my personal responsibility to ensure that all off-worlders receive fair and equal treatment under the Interplanetary Alliance."

After a few seconds of trying to figure out what to do with that, the peacekeepers give up and resume moving forward. Shey stays attached to my side, one of her arms looped around my elbow, clinging tight enough that it almost hurts.

"You shouldn't be here," she murmurs to me.

"I shouldn't do a lot of things, and yet—"

"And if you were planning on pulling this stupid stunt, you at least could have warned me," she continues as if I hadn't spoken. "You're lucky Lyre had the good sense to send me a message. But I can't protect you from this, Scorpia."

I've got nothing to say to that. But—useless, lovesick idiot that I am—the whole way to our destination, I'm not thinking about the peacekeepers around us or the planetary leaders who want me dead or the possibility of a lifetime locked up beneath the ocean in Ca Sineh. Instead, I'm just thinking about how good it feels to have her at my side again, no matter how short-lived it may be.

I expect to be taken directly to jail, or possibly into a back alleyway somewhere to be shot, but instead they march me into the heart of Vil Hava. I look around as we walk, drinking in as much of the island as I can. Nibiru hasn't recovered completely from the war, of course. Instead of food stalls, there are ration stations, with lines that stretch around corners. And there still seems to be a healthy push for military recruitment. But there are also scenes that didn't exist in wartime. Children playing ball in the streets. Open windows with music drifting out.

And also an awful lot of people goggling at me as we walk by.

"Must have gotten pretty boring around here, if everyone is coming out to witness my walk of shame," I say lightly, trying to distract myself from the crawling self-consciousness of having so many eyes on me.

"I may have spread the word that the hero of Nibiru was returning," Shey says, still holding tight to my arm. I look at her in surprise, and she says, "And it is most definitely not a walk of shame." She glances sideways at the peacekeepers. "Not for you, at least."

Now that she points it out, I can see that the hard-eyed looks I assumed were meant for me are instead aimed at the peace-keepers. Of course, now that I think about it, the council can't have made my crimes public knowledge without inviting a lot of uncomfortable questions. As far as the average person knows, I left a hero and came back only to be thrown in handcuffs. And all of the attention will make it quite a bit harder for the council to make this go away quietly.

"Smart," I say, flashing Shey a grin.

"One of us has to be." She huffs. "You should have thought about it yourself. You're not just some criminal, anymore. Not to a lot of people. You and your brother have more allies here than you think." She meets my eyes. "So stop trying to do everything alone, and let them help you."

I stare at her, taken aback. It's a little embarrassing, when she puts it like that. Never once did I consider reaching out to her or anyone else for help. But there's no time for coming up with a response, because we're approaching the steps of the Council Hall.

The peacekeepers escort us into the building and down the familiar, winding hallway. I suppress a groan. I've been here a handful of times at this point, but now, more than the others, I feel certain that the people waiting at the end will be distinctly unhappy to see me. Still, I steel myself with the warmth of Shey at my side, and the memory of the crowds watching me, and the thought of everyone waiting back on the ship. It feels dangerous to hope that this will end in anything other than self-sacrifice, but maybe, just maybe, it's not the only way.

But the moment I step into the council's meeting space and

look up at the half circle of chairs on the raised dais, that tentative little hope is crushed beneath the heel of reality.

While I understood, on a surface level, that most of the people here would be familiar faces, it's still jolting to look around and realize that I recognize everyone. These are some of the most powerful people in the system. Many of them even more powerful than they were last time we met, now that they've formed the Interplanetary Alliance.

And most of them hate me.

There's Ennia Heikki and the rest of the Nibiran Council—minus Oshiro, who hasn't been replaced, it seems—seated on one side of the table, all of them glaring daggers at me. They no doubt remember last time we met, when I accepted a job from them, and then took their high-priority package to an entirely different destination and got her killed.

On the other side is General Kel Altair, leader of the remnants of Titan, whose master plan I ruined when I stormed onto his ship. I knew I would face him here, but nothing could have prepared me for it. The sight of him makes me break out in a cold sweat and sends phantom pains shooting through my missing hand. His lip curls as he looks down at me, like he senses my fear and finds it utterly repulsive.

And then there's President Khatri of Gaia, who—oddly enough, given my history with her planet—is the only one who I don't believe has a personal reason to despise me, aside from maybe the fact that I got her predecessor killed. But she's Gaian, which means she probably still loathes me on principle, whether for my blatant disregard of law and order or the simple fact that my birth out in space makes me a walking legal conundrum.

And even aside from all of that, every person sitting at this table is no doubt aware of the fact that I blackmailed them all into a peace agreement by threatening to tell the whole system about the Planetary Defense Systems. So, all things considered, I'm not really feeling the love as I step into the room. I'm pretty sure the temperature drops a few degrees from the sheer chill of the gazes directed at me.

"Scorpia Kaiser," Heikki says, giving me a look of cool assessment. I focus on her face. Councillor Heikki doesn't scare me. I don't even think she's a particularly bad person, as far as politicians go, though she's made it clear she's far from fond of me. "We were thinking we'd have to chase you to the ends of the system to hold you accountable. And yet here you are, on our doorstep."

"Let me guess," Altair says. "You're here to cut a deal for yourself. Hold the information about the Planetary Defense Systems over us again."

"She came to us willingly," Khatri says, surprising me. "Let's give her a chance to speak."

I swallow hard. Here it is: the moment of truth. I nod at Shey, and she slowly loosens her grip on my arm and steps back. I take one last, long look at her, hoping she can sense the apology in my expression, and turn away just as suspicion starts to dawn on her features.

She's probably going to hate me for this, if she doesn't already. Corvus and the rest of my crew will, too. But I can't think about that, or the slim chance that Shey is right and we can pull something off to free me. I can't risk it.

"You're right," I say. "I'm here to make a deal." I glance over the half circle of people, taking in the glares and suspicion. "But not for my safety. The deal is that you get me, and everyone else goes free."

Affronted murmuring spreads across the room, but Altair hushes it with one raised hand. "Don't be absurd," he says, his eyes boring into me. "We already have you. And we could board your ship and take the rest in minutes."

I do my best to meet his eyes, ignoring the imaginary hot

needles stabbing at my nonexistent hand. Damn, that hurts. "And the moment you step on board, we'd broadcast all kinds of secrets you'd rather not have the whole system know. Cut the shit. You get me, and only me."

"You think all of this is about you? Your arrogance is astounding. Every person on your ship deserves to be held accountable for the things they've done. Desertion, treason—"

"No." I lean forward. "Look, I know how this works. This isn't about justice or holding people accountable. This is about you being scared that we'll tell the system the truth about the Planetary Defense Systems and the way I had to blackmail you all into a peace agreement. And I bet it'd be real nice for you to have someone to blame for Leonis's impromptu execution, and how exactly the bio-weapon that destroyed Titan was released, and all the rest of the mess, right?" I hold my hands out and throw on a smile. "So here I am. Let the others go, and I'll say whatever you want on the stand. Take the fall for everything. Or..." I lean back again, folding my arms across my chest. "Or you can be difficult, and I'll tell the truth, and drag all of you—and your fragile little alliance—down with me." I pause, pursing my lips as I pretend to think. "I wonder who will come for you first—Deva and Pax when they learn how vulnerable the Planetary Defense System makes you? Or your own people dragging you out into the streets and stringing you up for all of your lies?"

The room is quiet after I finish speaking. None of them like this, I can tell, but nobody has a good retort, either.

"So we're meant to let the rest of your crew travel around the system with the knowledge they have? And trust that they won't immediately announce it to all the worlds of Nova Vita as revenge for imprisoning you?" Altair asks.

"As long as you have me as a bargaining chip, they'll keep their mouths shut." Dying sounds a fair bit better than rotting away in

Ca Sineh for the rest of my life. But I'm willing to commit to the horror of that place if it keeps my crew free.

Altair scoffs, leaning back in his chair. "This is ridiculous," he says, addressing the other leaders instead of me. "I'll call my fleet and have them seize the ship. They'll never make it past us."

I take a step forward, looking directly at him and refusing to let my fear show. "If you try it," I say, "you'll probably succeed. But we will make it hell for you. We will sow as much chaos as we can, and trust me, we're good at it. We will tear your fragile alliance apart before it's really even begun." I glance over the other leaders and shrug. "Or, like I said, you could take my deal and I'll happily be your puppet in front of the whole system. You can get a nice, neat victory for your alliance, without lifting a single finger."

They meet my words with silence. They don't look happy about being told what to do like this. Never imagined that we'd manage to turn the tables on them and make any demands at all, I think. But I can tell, too, that they like the sound of what I'm saying. They're hungry for a chance to wrap up this messy chapter of history and move on. And this way, none of them have to accept any blame for it.

It's not fair. I know it's not, and deep down, there is a part of me that is spitting with rage: at myself for letting it happen, at them for being cowardly enough to consider accepting it. But this is the way the world works. I've always known that.

"I think it's safe to say that we will have to discuss further," President Khatri says, when none of the others speak up. She crosses one leg over the other and looks toward the Nibiran councillors. "Surely there's somewhere we can hold her until we make our final decision?"

"Certainly," Heikki says.

"Discussing" it, my ass—I can tell from one glance that they're going to take this deal. Though I will myself to feel relief, instead

132

my stomach is tying itself in knots. Time to kiss my freedom goodbye. I might never make it out of whatever hole they decide to stuff me in for "holding."

Still. This is how it has to be. Again, I don't try to resist as the peacekeepers step forward.

But Shey flings herself in the way before they can reach me, and wraps her arms around me. She stands on her tiptoes to bring her face closer to mine. For a moment I think she's going to kiss me, but instead she whispers, "Tell me you don't actually intend to go through with this." She pulls back a little, searching my face. Behind her, I'm aware of the peacekeepers slowly closing in, but just like before, none of them are eager to touch her. "Tell me you have some brilliant plan to get on that stand and tell everyone the truth."

I wish I had something to tell her that would wipe that look off of her face, but I don't. "Telling the truth has never really been my strong suit."

"No," she says fiercely. "No. I won't accept this. You have people who love you, Scorpia." My breath hitches at that, but a moment later, she says, "People who believe in you. All over Nibiru and—and stars know where else. Let them be on your side."

"It doesn't matter if that's true or not," I tell her. "They'd turn their backs on me in a second. Once the council and the others start talking about the things I've done, they'll know I've been a sham this whole time." I shake my head. "I don't even have to lie that much to make myself the villain of the story, Shey."

"Enough of the melodrama," Altair snaps. "Take her, peacekeepers. Or do I need to call in my soldiers to do your jobs?"

As they finally close in, I remember being pulled away from Shey like this by the law once before—on Gaia, when I was sure I was going to my death. I remember the way my heart broke when she sat back and watched them take me. This time, she clings to my arm, her eyes full of unshed tears, until they pry her fingers off.

CHAPTER FOURTEEN

A Visit from the Past

Corvus

Normally Scorpia is the one who can never stick to a plan, but I can't bring myself to waste time on the ship while she's risking her life for us.

Walking out onto Nibiru alone would be far too big of a risk. There's no possibility of getting through customs without my name and face being recognized. But luckily, we still have some allies left on Nibiru.

I head down to the cargo bay after breakfast, leaving Izra with instructions to keep an eye on the ship while I'm away. She's not happy about being left behind, but she understands the need to have someone I trust keeping guard. And Daniil has withdrawn to his room since he learned we were returning to Nibiru; he is not yet ready to face the planet he invaded, or the general he betrayed for the sake of peace.

I'm hoping to make it out before anyone else notices—but I find company already waiting for me. Pol, Drom, and Lyre are all lounging by the cargo bay door, and turn to me simultaneously as I enter.

"Told you so," Lyre says smugly, glancing at the other two.

"Not planning on going anywhere without us, are you, Corvus?" Drom asks with a scowl.

"We can help," Pol says.

I sigh, stopping at the bottom of the stairs. "Don't be ridiculous. We can't all go walking around on Nibiru. We're wanted criminals."

"Then why are *you* going?" Drom asks, bristling.

I glance over them, taking in the looks of indignation, and recognize this for what it really is. They're scared. "I'm not leaving you," I say, more gently than before. I meet Lyre's eyes in particular, knowing without a doubt that she's the one who orchestrated this. "I promise you. I'm just going to meet with Shey, to try to secure a plan to free Scorpia, if it comes to that. But I need you here. I need you safe." I look at all three of them now. "Watch the ship, all right? I'll be back soon."

There's a moment where I'm afraid they'll refuse to budge, regardless. But then Drom grumbles something, pushes away from the wall, and heads for the stairs. Pol is close behind. That leaves only Lyre, standing between me and the ramp with as much scowling disapproval as she can manage while being as small as she is. She steps forward and looks up at me. "You better not be lying to me," she says, frostily, and walks away before I can respond.

Shey waits at the end of the docks. She greets me with her open palms in the way of a Gaian meeting with a member of her in-group, and I return the gesture without a second thought. But before anything else, she turns and starts to walk. "Hurry," she calls over her shoulder. "We'll catch up later."

"Wouldn't it be safer for them to meet us here?" I ask, as we head toward the customs building, but Shey shakes her head.

"It's not good for any of us to be seen in public together. Especially if you're here to ask what I expect you're going to ask." She glances sideways at me, and her expression softens. "I'd do almost anything for Scorpia. You know that. But I can't risk bringing the legitimacy of my entire movement here down with me."

Given that *Memoria* is the only foreign spacecraft docked here among the Alliance warships, it's impossible that the customs agents don't realize who I am. But whether it's due to the Alliance holding true to Scorpia's deal—at least for now—or Shey's generous bribe, they let us through without any trouble.

Shey leads me along the outskirts of the island toward the Gaian refugee camps. The sea and sky are restless today, and there aren't many people this close to the water. We only pass one group—young people with drinks clustered close to the edge of the sea, playing some type of game that involves daring each other closer to the drop-off.

It isn't until we draw close that something about their postures and mannerisms makes me take a second look. Despite their casual, colorful Nibiran clothing, I realize, with a jolt, what I'm looking at. Pale skin, tall height, fair hair—even before I catch a glimpse of a war-brand on one young woman's wrist, I know that this is a group of Titans. Seeing them like this, acting more like kids than I've ever seen any Titans act before, it's hard to imagine them dressed in uniforms and holding pulse rifles. But my chest aches as I realize that's where they must've been not so long ago.

I tug my sleeve over the brand on my own wrist and keep my face turned away as we walk by. Still, as we pass near them, the group goes quiet, and I feel their eyes on me.

Shey takes us to the edge of the Gaian refugee camps. The area looks like it's become more livable since last we were here, but it's still full of too many bodies. Yet the Gaians have found little ways to make it their own—there's artwork on the walls, and a woman playing traditional Gaian music on a street corner, and the atmosphere is far less bleak than I remember it being.

The building Shey leads me to looks much like any of the others. But inside, all of the windows are covered, and the door she shuts behind us has several mismatched and hastily installed padlocks. The place is clean but cluttered. I catch a few glimpses of information pamphlets and maps of Nibiru before my gaze catches on the table across the room, and—seated in one of its several chairs—none other than former councillor Iri Oshiro.

They stand as they see us, and bow to me at the waist—deeper than they ever would've when they were still a councillor, but now we're social equals, or at least closer to it. I bow back, just as formally.

"Oshiro," I say. Once I would've called them by their first name; once, things were a lot different between us. But though their presence here, and Shey's intel, suggests I can still call them an ally, we're no longer anything close to friends. "Thank you for meeting us."

"Of course." Their face betrays no emotions. "I still owe you a few favors."

Before I can say anything more, Shey abruptly whirls around, plants her hands on my chest, and shoves me. I stumble back a step, more out of surprise than any actual force on her part.

"I can't believe you let her do this," she says. Her expression is caught somewhere between fury and the verge of tears. She takes another step toward me, and I hold up my hands in surrender.

"We didn't have any other options." The argument sounds weak even to me. But ever since Scorpia told me what she wanted to do, I've been searching my mind for another way, and I still haven't found one.

"There had to be something better than this." Shey folds her

137

arms over her chest, glaring at me. "At least tell me you have something planned rather than leaving her to the Alliance."

"You think I would've let her go otherwise?"

Shey relaxes a fraction. She lets out a sigh, brushing hair out of her face. "I suppose not."

"But plans are all well and good until they go wrong," I say. And—though I keep this part to myself—I'm not so sure I trust Scorpia with her part of it. She'd sacrifice herself for the rest of us, I have no doubt about that. I'd have done it myself, if I thought it would work. "That's why I'm here. I need your help securing a Plan B."

"Which is?" Oshiro asks.

"Breaking her out if things go wrong," I say. "And getting her off of the planet."

The two exchange a glance. I know what I'm asking of them. They'd be risking far more than I would be; I can leave the planet if things go wrong, but they'd be stuck with the consequences, and both of them have reputations and careers they'd be putting at stake. It's a large favor I'm requesting, but I don't think I need to explain to either of them that I wouldn't ask it unless I didn't see another way.

"For Scorpia?" Shey asks. "Anything."

"As I said, I owe you," Oshiro says.

Oshiro departs to put things in place, and Shey remains to escort me back to the ship, just in case of trouble. I find myself walking slowly despite the danger, unable to resist the urge to drink in the sight of Nibiru while I can. This place may have turned against us, in the end, but it is still full of good memories, and good people, and I am glad to see it recovering from the war. I suspect the scars of it will always be here, but that doesn't mean it can't heal.

"How are things here?" I ask Shey.

"Difficult," she says. "Integrating the Gaians and Nibirans was a challenge. The Titans are perhaps even worse. Their laws are so very different than ours. The mandatory years of service are controversial enough to the other planets, but the fact that citizens can't even *vote* until they serve, and the way the military is inextricably linked to the government..." She massages her temples, letting out a small, frustrated sigh.

"Their society is built for war," I say. "But they can change."

"First we have to convince Altair to let them change. The man is absurdly stubborn." She shakes her head. "Though I understand his concerns. The Titans are so few, and so young... He fears the erasure of their culture, the same as I do."

"And how goes your fight?" I welcome the change in subject; perhaps someday I will be able to discuss the Titans without a strange twist deep down in my gut, but that day hasn't arrived yet.

She smiles at me, a little sadly. "We haven't lost it, yet, and sometimes that seems to be the best we can hope for."

The dejection on her face makes me want to tell her about Scorpia's collection from Gaia, but I hold my tongue. It's not mine to tell, and even if Scorpia is away from us for the foreseeable future, I haven't given up my hope for her yet.

"Sometimes," I tell her, "that's all you need."

The group of young Titans we passed on our way in are still hanging around the dock. They seem quite a lot drunker than earlier, and judging from the damp and rumpled state of their clothes, most of them managed to overcome their fear of the water.

I cover my brand again as we walk by, averting my gaze and hoping my limp will keep them from recognizing me as an ex-soldier as easily as I recognized them. Most of them glance at us and quickly away again, disinterested, but one young man with his bare feet dangling over the water follows me with his eyes. I avoid meeting them. The others don't seem to notice his scrutiny, chatting among themselves and carrying on as before, but I am fully attuned to his attention, every nerve alight with warning.

We've almost made it past when he says, "Corvus Kaiser?"

Feet stop; heads turn. I stand where I am and suck in a deep breath before turning to face him. He's Titan-pale and blue-eyed, his head shaved down to stubble, a raised scar across one cheekbone.

Shey steps between us. "Excuse me," she says, "I'm afraid we're in a rush—"

I put a hand on her shoulder, and she stops, shooting me an uncertain look. But I can't run away from this. I do my best to avoid confrontation, but when it comes, I am not a coward. I look the Titan in the eyes. "I am."

The conversation among his friends goes quiet at my admission, and he climbs to his feet, stretching out to a good few inches taller than I am even without shoes. He takes a step closer, and frowns down at me. "You're shorter than I thought you'd be."

I blink, unsure what to make of that. It could've been an insult, but instead he sounded genuinely puzzled.

"Stars, Adel," one of his friends hisses, before I can muster up a response.

The Titan standing in front of me flushes bright red, and all of a sudden he no longer looks like an ex-soldier or any kind of threat, but an embarrassed young man fumbling for words. "I didn't mean it like—I just, the stories make it sound like you're *huge*—"

"Stories?" I repeat.

"Because he was in an exosuit, you moron," one of his friends murmurs helpfully, and the boy turns an even more vibrant shade of red.

"Shut up, you're ruining this for me," he whisper-shouts at them, and then turns back to me, rubbing the back of his neck. "Sorry. I just wanted to say...thanks. For what you did." He clears his throat, and when I say nothing, he continues on, the words coming out quicker and more nervous. "The ending of the war, I mean. I was there, at Aluris." My mind conjures up an image of this boyish Titan amid the gore and terror of that final battle in the Nibiran-Titan war, and I wrench my mind away, sickened. "The official story goes that General Altair and the Nibiran Council made the peace agreement, but there are those of us who remember that you and Colonel Naran were the first to call for a cease-fire." A flash of memory: Daniil and I grappling in the mud; later, his hand reaching out to clasp mine. "I'm really grateful," the young man blurts out, grounding me in the current moment again. "A lot of us are. Um. Just wanted to say that." He pauses, hesitates, and taps his fingers to his chest in a Titan salute. *For heart.*

It's been a long time since I saw that salute. Longer still since it was directed at me. Words stick in my throat—about how I'm not Titan enough, not honorable enough, not *enough* for a gesture like that anymore—but then my eyes shift behind him and see all of his gathered friends doing the same, waiting for my response, and the words die down. Who am I to tell the next generation of Titans who, and what, to believe in? Who would I be if I turned away from their respect without returning it?

It's been a long time, but my hand still knows the way to my heart. *For homeland.*

CHAPTER FIFTEEN

The Dotted Line

Scorpia

've been locked up more than a couple times in my life. Certain things always stick with me: the sense of creeping panic that comes with being trapped, the obsessive and usually useless scouring of the cell for a way out, the universal cruelty of security guards who work at these kinds of places. Yet somehow I always manage to forget the sheer *boredom* of it. The hours and hours spent sitting on a lumpy cot or cold floor, staring up at the ceiling, waiting for someone to decide my fate. I can't even bring myself to sleep, because every whisper of a noise makes me jolt upright, convinced someone's decided it's easier to come slit my throat and be done with it.

But morning comes, and I'm still alive. And very, very bored. I guess I had better get used to it—this is what the rest of my life is going to look like.

Days pass in a blur. They feed me three decent meals per day, and even give me private, daily showers and changes of clean clothes. All things considered, it's far from the worst jail I've ever been in. Whether it's because I'm on Nibiru or because of my newfound status as a high-profile criminal, I'm not sure. Still, despite the bearable treatment, I'm hit by waves of anxiety whenever my mind wanders to what's going on outside of these walls. Will the IA take my deal? Or could they be going after my crew right now, while I'm trapped, helpless and oblivious, in here?

Finally, my answer comes. My first hint that today is different is that they give me the clothes I arrived in, rather than a new change of a prison uniform, after I shower. Then, instead of taking me back to my cell like usual, the guards escort me out a back door of the prison and into a waiting hovercraft. A peacekeeper is at the wheel, and when they open the rear doors, Heikki is waiting beside an open seat. When one of the guards moves to put handcuffs around my wrists, Heikki waves them away.

The driver takes small side streets rather than any main routes. For a few minutes I'm content to stare out the window and take in the stimulation I've been starved of for the last few days. Sunlight that doesn't filter through bars, people who aren't wearing guard uniforms, all of the colors and sights I've missed. I try to find a button to roll down the window, but of course, this is a peacekeeper vehicle, not built for the enjoyment of its passengers.

"You're not going to ask what we've decided?" Heikki asks, when I remain silent.

I shrug, still staring out the window. "You don't have a choice. You're taking the deal." I glance over at her. "Honestly, the most surprising part is that you managed to decide this quickly. I'm guessing Altair and Khatri gave the council a good kick in the ass to speed things up?"

"We're all eager to bring this chapter to a close," she says.

I drum my fingers on my lap, trying to focus on the sights outside my window rather than the inevitable future. Questions flit through my brain—Will I be going to Ca Sineh? Will my family be able to visit me? Will Shey? *Would* Shey?—but I dismiss them as quickly as they come up. I can't think about any of that now and risk losing my resolve.

"You're doing the right thing." Heikki surprises me by speaking up. I look at her again, but she's gazing steadily ahead and doesn't meet my eyes. "Your sacrifice is not only for your family and crew. It will help stabilize the Alliance and make it easier for us to build ties with the other planets as well." She finally looks at me now, and dips her chin in a nod that's almost a bow. "It... noble." Her expression crinkles in displeasure, like it's physically painful to force the compliment out, but she says it anyway. "I'll ensure that you're treated fairly."

Weirdly enough, I get the sense she's telling the truth. Heikki's not my favorite person, but she's never struck me as a liar, either. Still, it's not very reassuring. Regardless of what she intends, I've always known how this will go. Someone will see me as a loose end. And sooner or later, they're going to find a way to handle me.

Things happen fast when the hovercraft comes to a stop. A full escort of peacekeepers hurries Heikki and me into a building I don't recognize. I can hear the roar of a crowd somewhere, and I think I hear my name, but they're not close enough for me to tell if they're calling for my death or my freedom. Whatever route my handlers have picked lets us avoid them entirely. Inside, I'm hustled down a hallway into a room full of bright lights and cameras and people watching me.

"What is this?" I ask, turning to look at Heikki. Despite our mutual dislike, she's the only face in the room I recognize, and I find myself grateful for her presence. "A trial?"

"No. Not yet." Someone presses a comm into my hands, but I'm still looking at Heikki and waiting for a response. She sighs. "There have been some complications. We have been trying to deal with this quietly, but a few news stations have been spreading footage of you arriving on the planet. There's some understandable confusion about the charges against you, since some people still consider you the 'hero of Nibiru.'"

All of that seems very far away now. It was so easy to forget that not everyone I left behind here harbored hatred for me.

"I don't understand why that matters," I say. "The public's got nothing to do with our deal, right?"

"It means that a public trial would be troublesome. For all of us." She looks at me steadily. "I'm sure you'll agree that you don't want that kind of controversy. Such a high-profile case would have an impact even beyond the Alliance worlds. You don't want everyone in Nova Vita to think of these accusations every time they hear your name, do you?"

My chest tightens. I don't want every person in Nova Vita to know my name, *period*. I'd never be able to live a quiet life again. Nobody on my crew would, since I'm sure their names would be dragged through the mud as well. It'd make us all targets, even more than we are now. We already have planetary leaders after us, but this would mean *everyone* would recognize us, *everywhere*.

"So how would we avoid a trial?" I ask.

Heikki—who waited patiently while I thought this all over—gestures at the comm I almost forgot I was holding. "If you sign this agreement, we can deal with this quietly."

I look down at the screen. A growing buzz of panic makes the words swim before I blink and refocus. My eyes snag on key words and phrases as I scan it, making the meaning obvious at once. It's a confession. An admission of the various crimes the Alliance leadership wants to pin on me. Plus a nondisclosure agreement about the Planetary Defense Systems and other details the Alliance leadership would rather keep private—such as Altair's involvement in the deal for the bio-weapon that destroyed Titan, and the fact that I blackmailed both Nibiru and Titan into the peace agreement that ended the war.

"And if I agree to this?" I ask. "What happens to me?"

Heikki gestures to the comm again. "It's all on there."

I scroll through the document, struggling with my anxiety and the legal jargon. Fuck, I wish Lyre was here. Or Shey. Someone smarter than me. But once I reach the end, the terms I'm agreeing to are laid out in brutal clarity.

"Twenty years in Ca Sineh," I read aloud, under my breath. Trying to wrap my head around the mere idea of that.

"It's a generous offer, given the gravity of your crimes," Heikki says. "It will mean that the rest of your family stays out of this. You'll take sole responsibility."

"And the rest of my crew, too," I say. "Orion Murdock, Izra Jenviir, Daniil Naran, Shey Leonis. I'm not even considering any of this unless you agree not to go after any of them."

She nods. "It can be arranged. They'll all be free. And in twenty years you will be, too. By that time, the rest of the system likely will have forgotten you were ever involved. There will still be plenty of time for you to live a good life, with the people you love, without all of this hanging over your head."

Damn it. She makes it all sound so simple, so tempting. I look back at the comm and flip over to the statement they want me to read again. I feel cornered, and I know that's exactly what they want. But it's not as though a written document, or a lawyer, or a trial is going to be able to protect me from the Alliance leadership. They're going to do whatever they want with me, no matter what I choose. And it's not like I wasn't planning on going along with this, anyway. Pleading guilty will only make the process move faster, and maybe that's good for everyone involved. Maybe it will help my family move on with their lives quicker, rather than waiting out a lengthy trial. They'll understand that there's no coming back for me and, hopefully, that I'm doing all of this for their safety.

And eventually, I'll be able to fade into obscurity and lead a quiet, uncomplicated life. Isn't that what I've dreamed of, lately?

Still...twenty years in Ca Sineh. Imprisoned beneath the waves, without feeling the sunlight or wind on my face. Twenty years without seeing the stars. It's one of my greatest fears...but if the others are alive, and free, it's far from the worst outcome I can imagine.

I look up at Heikki. "Okay. I'll do it."

She smiles. "Excellent. We'll need your signature on a physical copy, and a video recording of you signing of your own free will."

There's a flurry of action that I can barely follow. I feel numb, distant, like I'm watching all of this happen from behind a screen. Somebody fixes my hair and powders my face, and then I'm in a chair, sweating under too-bright lights that it hurts to look at. They make me read through the statement once, twice, three times, asking multiple times that I'm sure I understand. I tell them I do, although it's all a blur of noise at this point. I numb myself to the atrocities I'm admitting to and the consequences I know this confession will have. I keep telling myself this is what I wanted. Let them villainize me. The easier I make it to hate me, the easier this will be. I'll keep their eyes on me and away from the others.

Then it's time. They set out a stack of papers in front of me and hand me a pen. One woman keeps a camera focused on my face. I try to swallow past the lump in my throat, and think of my family as I set the pen to paper.

Then the wall explodes.

The world rings, and my ears are upside down—no, wait, other way around. I shut my eyes and groan, in too much pain to process it all. My hearing comes back first, though distant, like it's all rippling through water to reach me—screams and shouting and a stampede of rushing feet. I slowly open my eyes again, and focus on the facts: I'm on the floor. On my back. Everything hurts. I wiggle my fingers and toes experimentally before slowly rising into a seated position. It makes everything hurt even more, but the fact I can manage it is comforting.

The sight of the room is less so. Smoke and blood and panic and rubble. One wall of the building is gone—just *gone*—and sunlight leaks through. I can't seem to process what's happened. I raise my hand to make sure everything is intact, but touching the side of my head makes me hiss in pain, and when I draw it back my fingers are bloody. The sight makes the ringing rise again, and my vision whites out at the edges.

Then a peacekeeper is at my side, helping me up and ushering me toward the back of the building. "This way, ma'am. We'll get you somewhere safe."

"What's going on?" I ask, my voice coming out distant and slurred, but he only pulls me along. I stumble behind him, still stunned. More sounds start to filter through the haze inside my head: screams. Sirens. I think of breaking away from this one measly peacekeeper and making a run for it, but...why? Where would I go? I'm not even sure what's happening, or if that blast was meant to kill me or free me, or...

My thoughts grind to a halt as the man pulls me into the alley behind the building, turns, and all of a sudden he has a blaster in his hands. A *blaster*. Peacekeepers don't carry deadly weapons, only stun-sticks.

"Shit," I say, raising my hands. "Please don't, I'm cooperating, this isn't—"

The man jolts, and I flinch, expecting the burn of laser-fire to hit me any moment. Instead, the man slumps to his knees and then falls facedown in the alley, and I see the person standing behind him with a crackling stun-stick in hand.

"Izra?" I'm shaking—whether from shock or fear or adrenaline, I'm not sure. "What the fuck is happening?"

"Someone is trying to kill you," she says matter-of-factly. She holsters her stun-stick, steps forward, and grabs my chin, forcing me to tilt my head one way and then the other. "They failed. You're fine. Come on."

When I don't react fast enough for her liking, she grabs my arm and pulls me, stumbling, along. "Oh," I say. I think back to the explosion, the wall caving in, the bodies trapped under rubble, and hysteria bubbles up inside of me. "Oh, that was for me? Wow. What a surprise. What an honor—"

Izra turns and slaps me across the face. "Get it together."

"Mmf." I blink, shake my head, and focus on her. Damn, that didn't do any favors for the sharply throbbing pain in my head, but at least the ringing has subsided a bit. "Right. Emergency. Got it."

We resume walking. I expect peacekeepers—either real ones or fake ones with blasters—to come at us any moment, but instead all I see are people running away from the direction of the explosion. All civilians, as far as I can tell. "Listen, I mean, I'm grateful for the help and all, but why are you here?" I ask. "We had a plan."

"We also had a Plan B," she says. "Or, rather, your brother did." She glances back at me. "But neither of those plans took into account that someone would try to blow you up, so now I think it's time to start working on a Plan C."

I thought the panic would be centered on the building I was in—it seems much too fast for the news to have spread far—but the whole island seems to be in chaos, from what I can see. There's a siren wailing somewhere, and people are rushing through the streets. Away from what, I'm not sure, and Izra doesn't slow down enough to let me try to figure it out. I suppose for the moment I should just be grateful that this is granting me an easy escape route. But there's a seed of dread in my stomach that grows and grows as we walk, throbbing just as intensely as the pain in my head.

When we emerge from a side street and get a clearer look at the horizon, it confirms it. I stop in my tracks. There's a cloud of smoke rising in the sky, dark and thick and deadly, just like the one behind us. I wasn't the only target. Something else is going on.

"I think that's the Council Hall," I say. "Holy shit, Izra. What's happening? Who's doing this?" I can think of plenty of reasons someone might want to kill me, both personal and strategic, but the fact that they targeted the Council Hall as well speaks to a larger plan. And whether that blast was big enough to trigger the defense system or not, something is very, very wrong here. I can feel it in my gut.

Regardless of who is responsible—whether another planet or someone within the newly formed Alliance—I suspect that the fragile peace won't be able to withstand such a devastating blow. Everyone on this planet is in danger.

"Not our problem right now," Izra says, and jerks her chin. "Let's keep moving."

"Wait." I grab her arm. I'm pretty sure the shock at my audacity stops her more than my grip, but at least she stops. "I'm not going anywhere without Shey." I'm not going to leave her behind again.

"She's probably at the docks already," she says, yanking me forward again. "She's been helping us organize an escape route for you."

The combined shock and relief of that is enough to let her drag me onward without hesitation. As we rush to the space-docks, I'm dimly aware of the chaos all around us, and half-grateful for the fact that it helps us disappear into the crowd. We're just a couple others in a wave of people rushing away from the explosions and toward the ocean. The air tastes like smoke and fear. As we draw closer to the edge of the island, I realize that there's signs of yet another attack nearby. And I have a horrible feeling that one's centered in the Gaian refugee camps.

As we're approaching the water, there's the distinct, terrifying roar of another explosion. Another cloud of smoke rises into the sky—directly above the space-docks.

My stomach drops. "No," I say. "No, no, no." I turn to Izra. "Tell me that wasn't . . . It couldn't have been . . ."

But her expression is stricken, and she offers no comfort. She looks at the customs building—swarming with people rushing either toward or away from the docks, intermixed with peacekeepers who are desperately trying to maintain a line of security—and rushes for the shoreline instead. She dives into the water without looking back at me. I swear under my breath before following.

The cold shock of the water grounds me in my body. It pushes away my panic, thoughts of the chaos I'm leaving behind and the potential horrors waiting for me, as I focus on kicking toward the surface and then moving in smooth strokes toward the docks. Normally these waters would be patrolled by peacekeepers on hoverboats, but they must have better things to do right now than keep a lookout for a couple stray swimmers. I'm grateful for my childhood years on Nibiru as my limbs fall into the easy rhythm of swimming, and I soon overtake Izra—struggling with the weight of her gun arm—and reach the docks first. I pull myself up to the edge and turn to look at the remnants of the explosion at the end of the docks.

The smoking wreckage of a spacecraft floats in the water—along with a massive spill of fuel turned into floating fire and face-down bodies.

And beside it floats *Memoria*. My ship. Intact. She's okay; my crew is okay; we're going to be okay.

I let out the sob I've been holding down for the last several minutes, and take a few deep breaths to keep myself from spiraling into a full breakdown. On the docks beside me, Izra finally hoists herself up and half collapses, spitting seawater. She pushes herself up, follows my eyes to *Memoria*, and lets out a shaky breath.

"Oh, thank fuck," she says.

We race toward the ship. The docks are crowded, but most people are too focused on the wreckage to pay much attention to us. Emergency personnel are working to contain the fuel spill and search for survivors, though from the looks of it, I doubt they'll be successful. The explosion tore a chunk from the docks as well, and the shrapnel has torn into a handful of other Titan vessels nearby. I have to cling to the hope that *Memoria* won't be too damaged to fly. But she's a sturdy thing, a survivor, and it isn't too hard to believe we'll be all right.

As soon as I know my ship is intact and my crew alive, my thoughts return again to Shey. Izra said she'd be waiting here, but we didn't yet know the extent of the destruction. Would she have left when the Gaian refugee camps were attacked? Or went to help when the ship exploded? Or could she be back at customs, trapped in the panicked crowd? I know we have to rush off of this planet as soon as we can, and yet, I don't know if I can bear the thought of leaving her again...

And then we approach the end of the docks, and she's here. Rushing toward me. I can hardly believe my eyes, but when I run forward to meet her, and wrap my arms around her, she is real and solid and warm in my arms.

"Scorpia," she says, breathlessly, clinging to me. "Thank the stars you're okay." She holds on to my hand, but her face shifts from relief to concern as she looks up at me. "You're bleeding."

"Shey," I say, and stop, unsure of where to go from there. I swallow hard. No time to soften her up with any dumb jokes or sincere compliments or anything else. I just squeeze her hand, and say, "Come with me."

"I—" She hesitates, and turns to look over her shoulder at the floating remains of the ship that exploded, and the panicked island beyond. I can imagine she must be thinking about the Gaians she'd be leaving behind, and the rest of the planet, and all sorts of other things I can't comprehend. Shey has always been one to take the weight of the world on her shoulders. I'm already bracing myself for a rejection when she looks back at me and says, "I will."

I blink. "Really?"

"But I need a favor."

"Yes." I blink again, trying to shake myself out of my surprised stupor. "I mean—probably? What is it?"

She pulls on my hand, and I follow along helplessly as she heads down the dock. "The Alliance was sending a diplomatic mission to Deva today," she says. "An attempt to make peace after the, um—" She pauses only briefly. "Failed deal for my mother. But the ship that was supposed to take them was…" She looks at the wrecked ship again, and I follow her gaze and understand. I don't yet understand the goal of the attack today, but they clearly picked their targets with a purpose. "The diplomats weren't on board yet, thank the stars, but they need a new method of transportation."

"Okay." My feet keep moving automatically, letting her pull me along, but I'm getting a bad feeling that I'm not going to like where this is going. "But the Titans have a whole fleet, right?"

"Yes, but…" She glances back at me, letting me see the worry in her expression. "We have no idea who's responsible for what's happening today. It could be a betrayal by Altair. Or it could be someone on the Nibiran Council, or…" She shakes her head. "It could be anybody. And if the defense system triggers here, it's more important than ever that we solidify a deal with Deva. So…" She stops walking and looks at me, holding my gaze. "You're the only person I know for sure that I can trust right now, Scorpia."

"Shit," I say automatically. "I mean...I'm glad you trust me, really, but..." I squeeze my eyes shut, trying to think without her pleading face turned in my direction and reducing all my thoughts to sludge. The last thing I want to do right now is get dragged into more of a political mess. The IA leadership is already out to get me, and agreeing to this will mean putting ourselves into the middle of the Devan-Paxian conflict, too.

It's a big risk. It'll put a target on our backs—or, rather, slap another one right on top of the one we already have—for whoever planned this sabotage on Nibiru. But I can't deny that it's also an opportunity. A favor will put the IA in our debt. Being on Deva for official Alliance business might make us safer there, too. Might even grant us access to Pax, if we play our cards right. Overall, it's another bargaining chip, and we need as many as we can get right now.

"Okay." I open my eyes again and look at Shey. "We'll do it. But...wait, are the diplomats going to agree to this?"

Her expression shifts. "Um...I hope so."

"You *hope* so?"

"If not, some light force may be necessary."

I pause to absorb that. "So the plan possibly involves kidnapping IA officials. Could've led with that, Shey." I blow out a breath and shake my head. "Whatever. Fuck it. I already said I'm in." I turn to look at Izra, who has been trailing along behind us with an increasingly annoyed expression. "Go get our muscle," I say. "We've got some diplomats to kidnap."

As she rushes off, Shey squeezes my hand and draws my attention back to her. Her expression is apologetic. "There's one more thing you should know," she says. "I believe you might be acquainted with one of these diplomats...a Titan woman by the name of Helena Ives?"

CHAPTER SIXTEEN

Isolation

Corvus

I rush down the docks with Drom and Izra at my side. Nibiru is in chaos around us; one of the ships docked next to *Memoria* exploded not long ago, and smoke is rising from numerous other attacks out on the island. We still have no word about what is going on, and I want to get off this planet as soon as possible. But I trust that Scorpia has a good reason for delaying our escape.

Shey and Scorpia are talking with two figures who must be the diplomats we're meant to transport. The first is a reedy older man whose silk gloves mark him as a Gaian.

The second is former Titan general Helena Ives.

The last time I saw her was at the disastrous attempt at peace talks between Titan and Nibiru. She didn't say much then, but the same raw anger as always smolders in her eyes as she turns to face us. I remember how they loved to plaster her on posters all over Titan, flaunting her as a perfect soldier. She does have the classic Titan look: tall and muscular and icy pale, with blue eyes and long brown hair. Even the thick slash of the scar across her throat looks more like a badge of honor.

The Gaian blanches and takes a step back, half hiding behind Ives, as he sees us approaching. His gaze flickers nervously between us, pausing on Izra's gun arm and the weapons Drom and I wear at our hips.

"There's no reason to be concerned," Shey says, holding up her hands and making some placating Gaian gestures. "This is for your own safety. We need to get you off of the planet as soon as possible, and the Kaisers can get you to Deva. I'll explain more when we're away from Nibiru."

"With all due respect, Ms. Leonis," the man says stiffly, emphasizing her last name in a way that highlights her association with her mother, "I will take my chances here."

He looks at Ives beseechingly, but she is still standing stock-still, her eyes on me. After a moment, he clears his throat, seems to summon up his courage, and steps forward, making a move to slip between me and Drom and head down the dock.

I step into his way, holding my hands up, palms out, to show we mean no harm—but Drom steps forward as well, and before anyone can stop her, she grabs the man around the torso and hauls him over her shoulder. He lets out a choked sound of outrage.

"Drom!" Shey says, shocked. "This is not what we intended, I'm so sorry Diplomat Tommasson!"

"We're wasting time," Drom says, and heads back to the ship with the diplomat on her shoulder.

Ives braces herself for a fight—but when none of us immediately move toward her, she raises her wrist to her face and speaks into the comm strapped to it. "This is Diplomat Helena Ives. Diplomat Tommasson and I are being kidnapped by the crew of the spacecraft *Memoria*—"

Izra lunges for her. Ives cuts off and seizes her by the wrist, twisting out of her attempted grab. The two women grapple with each other, both full of snarling fury. I hover on the edge of the fight for a moment, hand on my blaster's hilt in case Ives tries to draw a weapon. When she doesn't, I lunge forward and grab one of her arms, twisting it behind her and pulling her away from Izra. She leans into me and uses my grip on her to raise her legs and deliver a solid kick to Izra's stomach. Her unexpected weight sends me stumbling, and she twists half-free and rakes her nails across my cheek.

Ives is a whirlwind of finely honed violence, but between the two of us, Izra and I finally manage to wrestle her into submission and drag her to the ship. Scorpia and Shey follow us, the latter fretting the whole time, though I can only imagine she's the reason we're involved in any of this. Even after the hatch shuts behind us and the ship's engine thrums to life to prepare for launch, Ives doesn't give up. As I shove her into a launch chair in an unoccupied room, she head-butts me in the face, and it takes all of my willpower to subdue the urge to knock her out and be done with it.

"Fine," I say instead, stepping away from her. "Strap in or die in the launch. Your choice."

I stride out of the room—grabbing Izra's arm on the way out, since she looks like she's contemplating throwing another punch at Ives—and into the hallway. Lyre is already waiting there, typing a code into the lockpad to keep the door secured from the outside.

"I take it we're remaining on the IA's list, then?" she asks, glancing up at me.

"Guess so. Not sure what happened, but Scorpia's back with us."

"And Shey, I saw." She sighs. "Somehow I feel as though we've ended up even deeper in trouble. But I suppose these things never quite go to plan, do they?"

After the panic on Nibiru, the quiet of the ship is deafening. After what we've seen, it is easy to sink into the belief that we are all alone out here. And maybe we are. It seems we have left disaster after disaster in our wake.

I didn't see much of what happened, but I saw enough. The diplomatic vessel across from *Memoria*—an old, unarmed disk of a ship that must have been of Nibiran origin—blown apart with the crew on board. News coverage of the explosion at the Council Hall and the one that nearly killed my sister. And I have no idea if the devastation ended there when we launched. Who would do such a thing? Is this the work of Deva or Pax, launching an assault on the Alliance? Or is it a betrayal from within, one of the three united planets turning against the others?

But worse than those initial attacks is the threat of the Planetary Defense System. Were those explosions enough to activate it and doom the rest of Nibiru?

The moment it's safe to leave my launch chair, I head for the cockpit. Images of tragedy on Nibiru play in my head, superimposed over the ruins of Gaia. We saw how quickly Gaia was devastated, with all of its tech and gleaming civilization—how can anyone on Nibiru hope to survive, with only their houseboats and human-made islands to stand against the endless ocean, if their Planetary Defense System activates?

Even a normal storm on Nibiru can be a threat. And now... Now I picture waves tearing at the shore and sucking houseboats beneath the surface, the ocean rising to reclaim the planet.

They have the Titan fleet to evacuate with, if it comes to that. That alone gives me a shred of hope. But I can't begin to imagine that they will save everyone. Not only the populace of Nibiru, but the already once-transposed Gaians, and the young Titan survivors. And even if they do escape the planet before the defense system kills them all, where will they go?

I wrench myself away from the thoughts as I reach the cockpit. Orion and Scorpia are in their respective chairs.

"Scorpia—" I begin, and pause, realizing I've barely welcomed her back. And that there's a wound on the side of her head, still sticky with blood. "I need to have a look at that."

"In a minute." She barely glances at me, her hands moving diligently over the console in front of her, though most of the screens are blank.

"Where are the Nibiran newsfeeds?" I ask, surprised that they're not already playing across our screens.

"That's what I'm trying to figure out. We're not getting any."

"What do you mean?"

"Just that. We're not getting any signals from Nibiru. I tried pinging them, too, on all of the channels we have, but…" She shakes her head, wincing slightly as it jostles her wound. "Nothing."

"How is that possible?" I stare at the static on the screen, trying to make sense of it. "The damage it would take to knock out all of their communication channels… there's no way it already…" I can't even bring myself to complete the thought, though my mind effortlessly conjures an image of the ocean swallowing all of Nibiru's islands at once, instantly undoing humankind's efforts to render it habitable.

Orion lets out a small, strangled sound and takes his hands off of the controls to bury his face in them. "Fuck."

I'm surprised at how affected he seems, until Scorpia reaches over to touch his arm and says, "They'll evacuate Ca Sineh. They have to."

Of course. His father and the rest of his former crew are still there in the underwater prison. I've no love for the old pirate myself—no matter our biological ties—but still the thought makes bile rise in the back of my throat. If the water rushes in, Ca Sineh will be one of the first places lost.

"We saw what happens if the prison floods," I say. "There are protocols in place."

"And I'm sure the planet's worst criminals will be high on the priority list, right?" Orion asks.

Neither Scorpia nor I can find anything to say to that. We know he's not wrong. After a moment he stands and pushes past me to the door, leaving us. I sigh, looking at Scorpia.

"Maybe it's something else affecting the comms," Scorpia says, though she sounds doubtful. "Maybe the defense system is blocking transmissions somehow. I mean, Primus tech can do that, right? Maybe something similar happened on Gaia?"

"We can ask Shey."

She nods. "Yeah. Go get her, would you? And Lyre, too, I want her to have a look at our systems."

"Then promise me you'll come to the med bay."

"Yeah, yeah."

I find that the others have started trickling out of their rooms. This should be a joyous occasion, Scorpia returning to us, but everyone stands around looking lost. I send Shey and Lyre off to the cockpit. Pol's still in his room, but Drom hovers outside of her door, looking at me like she expects me to say something.

Before I can, there's a loud *bang* on the other side of one of the doors.

"Let me the fuck out of here!" Ives screams.

I move over to the door, but hesitate. After a moment, Izra joins me.

"I say we just leave the bitch in there," she says.

I can't deny the thought is tempting. My cheek still stings from where she raked her nails across it.

"It's going to be a long trip to Deva with her screaming like that," I say. "Maybe she'll calm down when we explain the situation. If not, we'll throw her back in to cool off for a while."

"Just say the word," Izra says, already slipping into a fight-ready stance.

160

I brace myself as well, and release the lock on the door.

Ives rushes out, spitting curses, and slams into me before I can react. I nearly punch her in the face before realizing she's just grabbing on to me, not attacking. Still, she grips my shoulders hard enough to hurt. "What the *fuck* is going on?" she snarls, her face inches from mine. "Where are you taking me?"

I still can't believe that Ives, of all people, is one of the Alliance's diplomats. After Daniil defected to our side, I suppose Altair didn't have many other options, since the vast majority of his army was made up of fresh-from-training grunts. But still... Ives is a military woman, through and through; and though I suppose that's as close as Titans get to politicians, she has always struck me as particularly hungry for violence. She was popular among the younger members of the Titan ranks because of it. Recruits would fall over themselves for a chance to serve under her and get their shot at glory.

But perhaps that's exactly why Altair sent her—to get her away from Nibiru. I'm not sure what happened between them, but I do know that sometime between the attack on Titan and their arrival on Nibiru, she lost her position as a general and gained that scar across her throat. I can't imagine the abrupt ending of the war improved matters between her and Altair.

"Calm down." I grab her by the wrists and wrench her hands away, grimacing with the effort.

"Calm down? Are you fucking kidding me? You and your stars-damned traitor family, for all I know *you're* the ones who planned all of this—"

Izra's standing back—for now—but looks ready to throw a punch at any second. Drom's approaching from her end of the hallway, too. I'm contemplating whether or not it's better to just shove her back into the room before this gets violent when Daniil emerges from his room and rushes over. He pushes his way between us, his back to me, and places both hands on Ives's shoulders.

"Helena, shh," he says.

She stiffens in his grip, her expression going blank with shock. "You," she says, through gritted teeth, but she doesn't try to pull away from him.

The familiarity surprises me—but it shouldn't. They were Altair's two highest-ranked officials, after the fall of Titan. They must have been very close.

Before I can fully digest that, Ives finally pulls away from Daniil. "Get your traitor hands off of me," she hisses, though it's a little late for it to have its full effect. She stands back, her eyes darting accusingly from him to Izra to me. "Someone tell me what the fuck is going on."

After I half drag Scorpia to the med bay to clean her wound and assess the damage—a mild concussion—she brushes off my urge to rest and instead gathers everyone in the lounge to explain the situation. The only one who doesn't join us is Pol, who is in his room complaining of a horrible headache, according to Drom. By the time she's done, Ives has calmed down. The stiff-looking Gaian diplomat seems vaguely panicky and has barely said a word, so I suspect he still thinks we're kidnapping him, but at least he isn't causing trouble over it.

"As soon as we get our comms system back up, I'll let you contact your people back on Nibiru," Scorpia finishes, looking at each of the diplomats. "And if we can't, for whatever reason, then we'll just focus on getting you safely to Deva. I know my ship isn't the kind of transportation you're accustomed to, but, well . . ." She trails off and shrugs. "You'll get used to it. Just let me know if you need anything." She pauses. "Anything reasonable, I mean. Don't be a pain in the ass."

I huff a laugh despite myself. She leaves it at that, and Shey goes over to speak to the diplomats privately, likely attempting to smooth things over.

"I'll get started on dinner." I glance at Daniil, but he takes a few seconds to notice because he's busy looking at Ives.

"Oh, uh. I think I should…" He nods his head at her.

"Right." I hesitate, about to say more, but I swallow it and leave to head toward the kitchen.

Izra follows behind me. As I start preparing the meal, she perches on the counter and watches me.

"Better be careful with those two," she says.

"Hm?"

"Daniil and Ives."

I frown down at the vegetables I'm chopping. I can't deny that it bothered me to think of Ives and Daniil being close, for some reason. And I am surprised at how much I miss him working with me in the kitchen, even for one night. Strange how quickly I grew accustomed to having him at my side. Our easy conversations. The way our shoulders would occasionally brush as we worked. But still… "It's not my business."

"Not a good sign that they're civil. She could try to drag him back into Titan patriotism."

"Daniil's free to do what he pleases," I say. If he decides to go back to the Titans, it will be shattering, but it will be his choice. I'm surprised Izra, of all people, would argue otherwise.

"That's the problem. He's never been free before. He doesn't know how." She shakes her head. "Probably hasn't so much as picked what he wants for breakfast, or what to wear, for years. People like you, who didn't grow up on Titan in their military complex bullshit, don't get it. You think getting out feels like a relief. I'm sure it felt that way for you. But for the ones who have never known anything else, it doesn't, not at first. It's fucking terrifying. It's as much about losing your purpose as it is about gaining your freedom."

I'm taken aback by the heat in her voice. I never got the sense Izra cared much about Daniil. But maybe there's more to it than I thought. Or maybe she just wants to see another Titan get out like she did. Until him, she was the only one I ever met who managed to make her way free. I have to admit, even beyond my personal feelings for Daniil, I feel a desire to see him succeed for bigger reasons as well; he could be living proof that there is hope for the Titans. That they are more than the soldiers they've been trained to be for all of their lives, stronger than the conditioning that started when they were born.

Or, if what Izra is saying is true, he could be the opposite.

"If I try to push him, it will be the same," I say. "He'll be craving an authority figure." I may not have been born Titan, but that I understand all too well. "I don't want to be that for him. I can't." Especially since I already was, once.

"Better you than..." She gestures vaguely, and I know she's not just talking about Ives. She means Altair. Momma. Govender. Murdock, for her. All the people who would notice a hole in someone's heart waiting for a purpose to fill it, and see it as an opportunity.

"He's vulnerable. If I take advantage, I am no better." And I still remember that the way Scorpia became an authority for me almost broke our relationship beyond repair. I sigh. "He has to make the choice on his own."

CHAPTER SEVENTEEN

Relics of a Lost World

Scorpia

I curse, jabbing at the interface in the cockpit, but my attempts to send a message informing Deva of our approach are met with the same error message as the one when we tried to contact Nibiru. I was so focused on trying to figure out what was happening on the planet we left behind that I didn't realize we can't contact anyone else, either. Whatever problem we're having, it seems to be on our end. And that makes it a *big* fucking problem.

Hearing nothing from Nibiru was worrisome. Being unable to reach Deva is downright dangerous. We're an unknown ship approaching without announcing our intentions. They're not as strict as the Gaians were about those things, so just a few months ago I wouldn't have been overly concerned about it, but now? Now they're at war, and I've seen for myself how fast situations can change with that kind of threat hanging over a planet.

But this also adds another concern to the list. Something's wrong with *Memoria*, and I don't understand what or why, which is a terrible feeling both as a captain and as a human being on a vessel that's the only barrier between me and the bitter cold of outer space. Especially because living on a ship for most of my life has taught me that where there's one mysterious problem, there's usually more, or will be soon.

Even with all the years on a spacecraft under my belt, I can't understand this, and neither can anyone else. I've talked to Lyre and Shey, and Orion and Izra since they know this ship the best, but everyone is stumped. The hardware seems to be working fine. Lyre says it's all systems red. There's no computer issue, no wiring problem, not so much as a sticky button on the console. But when I try to send or receive anything on comms, all I get is static.

"So what the hell's your problem?" I ask, staring down at the screens from the pilot's chair. I tap my plastic fingers against the dashboard. I've been in here for hours, trying everything I can think of to locate the problem, but there's nothing. At this point I'd be relieved to find anything, even something terrible, because nothing is as terrifying as an unknown threat. I don't like the idea of landing without figuring out what it is—but I don't like sitting around in open space in a potentially damaged ship, either.

Leaving the cockpit feels like giving up, but I'm too exhausted to think up any useful ideas right now. And anyway, the ship's halls are filling with the smell of the dinner Corvus is preparing, and I'm eager to have something other than jail food for the first time in several days.

I was hoping for a chance to catch up with Shey at dinner, but she chooses to take her meal with the diplomats, who retreat back to the spare room we've given them. Daniil, too, goes with them. Maybe I should join them and try to make them feel more welcome, but I'm too exhausted to deal with prissy interplanetary officials right now, when I'm still reeling from all of the events of the day—and mildly concussed, according to Corvus.

I share a quiet meal with Corvus, Izra, Orion, Drom, and Lyre.

Pol is still in his room. Nobody's in a mood to talk much, but it feels good just to do something half-normal, and have my crew around me. The system may be going down in flames around us, but at least I've got them.

After the meal, I go to my room to shower off the smell of sweat and smoke. I'm about to climb into bed when I realize I've still barely had a chance to talk to Shey. Maybe it would be better to leave it for the morning, give us both some time to recover from the events of the day, but... I've never been a very patient person. So instead, I show up at her door with a box of Gaian tea I've been saving for her.

She opens the door wearing a pair of pajamas she must have borrowed from Lyre, and blinks at me, clearly surprised. I hold out the tea like a peace offering. She stares down at it for a moment, and then cracks a smile, takes it, and gestures for me to join her in the room. We sit on the edge of the bed, and I try not to fidget as she turns the tea over in her hands. She raises it to her face, inhales deeply, and sighs.

"It's actually been a long while since I had this," she says, smiling sadly as she lowers it. "Nobody thought to bring the little things with us when we fled Gaia." She looks at me. "Thank you for thinking of me."

I think about you constantly. The thought rests on the tip of my tongue, but I swallow it down before it can jump out and embarrass me. It's way too soon to delve into all of that. Right? But now she's staring at me like she expects me to say something, so I blurt out, "Well, nobody else likes the stuff, anyway."

She lets out a small laugh. "I suppose not."

Shit. Damn. This is more awkward than I thought. I had a lot of things I planned on saying, but they're all jumbled in my head now, and this moment is so fragile I'm afraid the wrong move will shatter something irreparably. I curl my hands together on my lap, resisting the urge to reach for her, and similarly stifle the desire to crack a joke to break the tension. It feels like it's always my instinct to ruin things—moments, relationships, myself. But I don't want to do that right now, and the sense of teetering on the brink of something dangerous terrifies me. "Actually, I have something else for you, too."

I rush out of the room before she can respond, and head to the armory where I've been storing various things set aside from our trips to Gaia. Lugging the huge crate to Shey's room nearly throws out my back, but the thought of asking anyone to help is worse than the physical pain, so I bear it. I throw the box down on the floor beside her bed, and stand back with my hands on my hips, panting.

Now that I'm doing this, it feels ridiculous, especially with everything else going on with our lives right now. But surely nothing can be more embarrassing than sitting here and trying to talk about feelings and shit, so, here we go.

"Uh, so, yeah," I say, gesturing toward the overflowing crate. "Just a couple things we've found on our trips. Thought you might want to take a look at them."

She's staring at the crate, a dumbfounded look on her face. She stands up and takes a hesitant step toward it, and then another. "All of this is...from Gaia?" She crouches down, gently touches an instrument I don't know the name of, and then gasps as she spots a rolled-up painting. "Is that..."

"The paintings are from the museum in Levian," I say, following her gaze to the various objects we collected, since looking at her face right now makes me feel like I'm witnessing something private. "I don't know shit about art, so, uh, that's all Corvus. Then there's some pottery, some physical books that looked kind of old and important, and...oh, wait, that's not supposed to be in here." I hastily reach down to grab a book from the top of a stack and hide it behind my back, hoping Shey didn't get a glimpse of the cover, which features a rather sultry image of a Primus alien with a half-naked human wrapped in its tentacles. I clear my throat. "Anyway. Yeah. Just a few things we picked up on Gaia."

Shey takes a moment to recompose herself, straightening up and looking at me with eyes that are just a little bit dewy in a way that makes me want to melt. "These items are irreplaceable cultural relics, Scorpia. Thank you for saving them." She pauses for a moment, and then asks, "How much would you like for them?"

"Oh, what, this junk?" I ask, looking from her to the crate and back again. "I mean, I don't think anyone would want it except for you Gaians. I would've just tossed if it you didn't want it. So…" I shrug. "A million credits should do it."

She blinks.

I crack a smile. "Kidding. I'm kidding. It's free, of course." My voice softens. "I got it for you." She looks at me, and I amend, "I mean, for you and your people." I thought she'd eat that up, but when she only continues to stare, I amend again, "Well, mostly for you."

Shey is quiet for a long moment. Then she says, "I hope this isn't a way to apologize."

"What, me? Trying to buy your affection back with worldly goods? I would never—"

"Because an apology isn't necessary," she continues, completely ignoring my anxious babbling. She takes a deep breath, and when she lets it out, her posture relaxes, like she's finally giving up on the effort of holding herself perfectly upright. "On your end, that is. I am sorry for the way I handled the situation." She looks me in the eye, her hands twisting nervously against one another. "I know it's no excuse, but I was overwhelmed. The future of my people was at stake, my mother was dead, peace was here but no one knew if it would hold, and I..."

"You don't have to explain if you don't want to," I say, when she seems too overcome to continue.

"I do want to. And you deserve to hear it." She steadies herself again. "I knew my choice was to leave behind my people and the movement I helped build, possibly forever, to be with you. It would have been a difficult choice either way, but given the fact that my mother was also dead, and my father was mourning, I..." She shakes her head. "It wasn't so much that I made a choice. More that I refused to make one until it was too late. If I could go back, I would change that."

Stars, for all the reasons I adore this woman, sometimes I wonder if she deliberately speaks in riddles just to mess with me. Is this a polite rejection meant to spare my feelings, or a polite invitation for me to ask her again, or something else entirely? For the hundredth time, I wonder why, oh why, I had to fall for a stars-damned Gaian.

But oh well. She might not be saying what she means in any way I can decipher, but that's not going to stop me from doing so. "Well, like I've told you before," I say, "there's always a place for you on my ship if you want it."

She smiles. "I'm here, aren't I?"

Now *that* definitely feels like an invitation...but something holds me back from reaching for her. Instead the silence stretches out like the space between us, awkward and cold. Maybe I'm too tired from the day. Maybe it's too soon. Maybe I've just been burned too many times. But...whatever was broken between us, I don't think this conversation has fixed it, and I'm at a loss about where to go from here.

"Well, um." I clear my throat, and rub one hand against the back of my neck. "Glad to have you back, Shey. Uh...good night."

Surprise flickers across her face, but then disappears into a mask of politeness. "Good night, Scorpia," she says, and doesn't move as I head for the door.

Before bed, I go to check on Pol. I haven't seen my baby brother since I got back on the ship, and I'm feeling in desperate need of one of his hugs.

Instead of his usual enthusiastic welcome, though, I find him holed up in bed with the covers pulled tight around his chin. There's a sheen of sweat on his forehead, and he barely opens his eyes when I walk in. "The light," he mumbles, and I hurriedly shut the door behind me. His room is so dim it's hard to see more than silhouettes once it's shut.

"Hey, kiddo. Sorry you're not feeling well." I lower myself to a seat on the side of his bed. He reaches out with one hand, and I take it, rubbing my fingers over his sweaty palm.

"That's okay. Just a really bad headache," he mumbles. "It's so loud. That lady..."

"Right. Yeah. Sorry about all of the yelling." I half smile. "Had to kidnap a couple of diplomats. You know how these things go."

He nods, and says, "I'm glad you're here, though."

"Yeah, me too."

He opens his eyes a little wider to look up at me. "I didn't think you were coming back."

I'm not sure what to say to that, so instead I squeeze his hand, fighting back a pang of guilt. After a few moments, his eyes slide shut again, and he lets out a long sigh. I lean forward to press my lips to his clammy forehead before I leave.

CHAPTER EIGHTEEN

Questions of Loyalty

Corvus

I t seems that every time I turn a corner, I find Daniil and Ives
locked in conversations that go silent as soon as they notice
they're no longer alone. I can't fight the sense that they're planning something, though I tell myself I'm only being paranoid,
and letting Izra's words get under my skin. It's always hard for me
to have new faces on the ship.

It isn't the only thing bothering me—that Gaian diplomat is
a grating presence at every meal, Pol is still locked in his room
complaining of constant headaches, and our communications
system is down for unknown reasons. But I can't help but worry,
especially, for Daniil. I feel as though he's my responsibility, and
I'm failing him in some way I can't seem to understand. Finally,
after a few nights of cooking alone, I ask him to help me in the
kitchen.

This used to be routine, but now it feels so uncomfortable to
have the two of us alone in here. I take my time pulling out cutting boards and knives and pans, mostly to stall as I try to think

of what to say to him. He helps patiently, and quietly, though I catch him casting sideways glances at me.

"You and Ives are spending a lot of time together." I force the words out, fully aware that they sound strange and petty.

He stops what he's doing and glances at me. "Is that a problem?"

"You tell me." He doesn't say anything. "I would've thought she'd hate you, after you disobeyed Altair's orders and deserted."

"Me too. But it's very complicated, Corvus. We were two of the only ranking officers to survive Titan and make it to Nibiru, so…" He trails off. I know enough about Titan culture to fill in the blanks. They would have worked closely together. *Lived* closely together. Known each other intimately. "And being here, on neutral ground, away from Altair and the rest…it gives us a chance to speak in a way we couldn't, otherwise."

I wait for him to go on, but he doesn't. "She wants something from you."

He's quiet for a few moments. "Yes." He pauses, and then continues, "She told me there might be a way back into the Titan ranks for me, if I was willing to work for it."

"And what did you say?"

"I told her I would think about it."

Silence stretches out, again, as I grapple with my feelings about that. I have the sense he's waiting for me to speak. Finally, I say, "I was under the impression that you always wanted to get away from all of that."

"I wanted to get away from the war, yes. I never wanted to be a part of it. But I never imagined Titan might have a future that looked so different, either. Nor that the opportunities outside of Titan would be so bleak."

"They're not bleak. There's a whole system out there."

"Sure," he says bitterly. "I spent many years dreaming about it. Imagining finding a way to get to Pax, and meeting the father

I never knew." He glances at me, and I'm forced to remember, again, how I once promised I'd take him there, and then abandoned him on Titan. "I dreamed of other worlds, peaceful worlds, peaceful people... but even if any of that was real, I would've realized eventually that they would never be *my* people. Wouldn't know what it is for others to be the only comfort in the cold. Things were hard on Titan, but I was never alone. Never. Now I always am." He stops and shakes his head. "But even if I go back now, it will never be the same. I know that. I can't regret what I did. I bought peace for my people by sacrificing my chance to ever be with them again. But I do miss it. I miss home. I miss Drev Dravaask, and our drinking songs, and the feeling of standing on a mountaintop and looking out over the empty tundra. I miss the fresh snow..." He trails off, his expression growing wistful. "Shameful as it is, I even miss the war, at times. Because it gave me a reason to wake up every morning. And it gave me people I loved. Uwe, and Sverre, and Magda."

Even after all of this time, it still hurts to hear their names. "You still have me," I say, quietly. "I know I'm not enough to replace them, I know I may not be as Titan as you'd like, but—"

"You don't understand," he says. "I don't think you ever will. It's not the same for you. It's not about you not being Titan enough, it's that you're..." He holds out a hand like he's grasping for something, and shakes his head, frustrated. "I haven't even heard you say their names since I got here. I don't understand how you could leave it all behind. And you...not even you are the person I remember."

I feel like I've heard that a hundred times from a hundred different people. Everyone seems to want some different version of me that I'm not sure truly existed—and even if he did, he's long gone now. "I'm sorry I can't be who you want me to be. I can only offer myself."

"You can't even offer that. You never do. I've realized this, now—you only give people pieces of yourself. You give them the parts you think they want, and keep the rest hidden. I'm sure you think it's noble, but it's not. It's *selfish*. It makes it impossible for anyone to really know you."

His words cut deeply, mostly because they have the uncomfortable ring of truth. I swallow hard, unsure what to say to him. If what he wants is vulnerability...I'm not sure I could give him that, even though part of me wants to. "I'm trying, Daniil. I'm trying. It's all I can do." He shuts his eyes, as though he's trying to tune me out, but I'm not going to give up so easily. Not this time. I take a step closer and press my fingertips to his arm, and say, quietly, "Be patient with me."

He lets out a long breath, and his eyes flutter open. When he looks at me, his mouth twitches at the edges. "I've already waited an awfully long time, you do realize." I study his face, unsure what to make of that, and he lets out a half laugh, half groan, dragging his fingers through his hair and leaving it wildly disheveled. "All of you non-Titans," he says, "make things so complicated!"

I don't know what to say to that—so after a moment, at a loss, I move to the pantry and begin to pull out the ingredients we need for dinner. But I stop, and look over at Daniil as a thought occurs to me, a niggling concern about what Izra said. I clear my throat and ask, awkwardly, "What do you want for dinner?"

His eyebrows lift. "Weren't you planning on stir-fry tonight?"

"We don't have to. Your choice."

"Stir-fry is fine. Why wouldn't it be?" He's staring at me as though I'm being strange, making me feel self-conscious, and I know trying to press him further will only make him more certain that something is up.

"Never mind," I say. "Stir-fry it is."

He hesitates for a moment before helping me unload the

ingredients—some of the last of our fresh produce from Deva. He's already familiar enough with the recipe to know what to look for. It bothers me now, to see how readily he fell into the role of helping me, without even considering giving his own input. Is it already too late? Have I become that person for him that I never wanted to be? Become the kind of person who will continue the same cycle that has happened to me, taking others' freedom because I could not seize my own?

He pauses with his hand on the container of dried pepper and frowns. "But maybe," he says, thoughtfully, "not as spicy as last time?"

I look sideways at him, and smile in a way that I'm sure makes me look like a fool, but I can't stop it nonetheless. "Of course. That's fine."

Or maybe he will be okay. Maybe we both will.

CHAPTER NINETEEN

A Matter of Diplomacy

Scorpia

Just when our ship had finally settled into a comfortable routine, the newcomers have thrown everything off-kilter again. A bubble of unease follows them around the ship. It doesn't help that the Gaian diplomat is constantly harassing me about when we'll arrive on Deva, and I don't know what to tell him. We'll be within range of the planet early tomorrow, but I still haven't figured out how we're supposed to land while our comms are down. We can't approach a planet at war without warning. But I can't blame the diplomats for wanting to get there, and contact the IA, as soon as possible. We still don't know what's going on back on Nibiru. And whether Nibiru's defense system has been triggered or not, it's essential for the Alliance to secure Deva as an ally and trading partner.

Right now, I'm still holding out hope that we'll figure out the issue with our comms system soon enough that I won't have to make that choice. At least Ives isn't hounding me as much. But she's the kind of person who takes up a lot of space in a room regardless—even without all of the messy past issues involved.

I was worried about Drom picking fights with her, but instead she spends most of her time in Pol's room. Corvus and Izra avoid Ives, and she and Daniil seem to revolve around one another without ever quite touching. If they do—*when* they do, if I'm being honest, these kinds of things always come to a head eventually— I'm honestly not sure if they're going to end up fighting or falling into bed together or both. I still remember that message Ives sent him, which I deleted from the ship's inbox without reading, and now wonder if that was a mistake. Corvus certainly eyes the two of them like he thinks something suspicious is going on...but then again, he might just be jealous. Hard to say.

And, speaking of that shit...then there's Shey. She'd be impossible to ignore even if she was trying to keep away, but I swear it feels like she's intentionally showing up around every corner I round. I find her sipping tea with Lyre in the mess hall in the morning, discussing Devan food with Corvus in the kitchen, even in the cockpit interviewing Orion about his home-planet's etiquette. With each of them, she laughs and talks like she used to, but the moment I step into the room she goes quiet and excuses herself. I'm the only one she's cold to, and every time it's a needle in my heart.

I'm used to pining after Shey. But this time is different, because I'm not even sure what I want anymore, let alone how to get there. Thinking about it too much is like poking a fresh bruise.

Maybe it's better for us to keep our distance right now. Shey and I have been a lot of things to one another, but I can't say we've ever made each other's lives easier. So maybe that's what she needs right now. Doesn't mean it hurts any less, though.

After a particularly embarrassing incident where Shey and I try to pass each other in the hall and move the same way *three* times, I half run to the mess hall for a distraction. Luckily, I find one.

"Hey, Helena."

Ives looks up from her glass and stares at me like I just walked up and told her the most disgusting joke she's ever heard.

"No? Not there yet? Okay, my bad." I slide onto the bench across the table from her, trying to ignore the fact she's still glaring at me. That, and the bottle of vodka, and the glass of what seems to be the same stuff over ice. These Titans…sometimes I swear they enjoy being miserable. "Y'know, there's plenty of other options in there that don't taste like watered-down rubbing alcohol. You can help yourself."

She sips her disgusting drink. It burns my nostrils even from here. "What do you want, Captain?"

I clear my throat. "Thought it might be good to clear the air a bit. I haven't seen you since…well…"

She thumps her glass down on the table. "Since your mother wiped out my planet?"

I hold up my hands. "Since…I *didn't* sell you the weapon that would've gotten you killed?"

She glares at me as she takes another sip of her drink. "I suppose there is that," she says. "You did save my life, though entirely by accident. I would have tested it myself. Not sent some off-worlder and a handful of rookies to do it for me while I sat in the safety of Fort Sketa."

It takes me a moment to realize who she means by *some off-worlder*, and I shiver at the image of Momma heading off with that vial in hand. "Yeah," I say, trying to shake it off. "So there's that." She says nothing, so I eye her across the table. "Now here we are, going from a deal for a horrible alien weapon to working together for peace. Who would've thought?"

"Peace," she repeats, and smiles bitterly. "Read a history book sometime. Humankind has never been at peace, and it never will be. It is not in our nature. We always need more, and more, and so we invent excuses to take it from each other."

I frown, unsettled. In my darker moments I've thought the same way, but... "If you believe that, seems like you'll be a pretty shit diplomat."

"I'm not here to negotiate peace with the Devans, little space-born," she says. "I'm here in case things go wrong."

"Meaning?"

"Meaning our mission is classified. And leagues beyond your comprehension, I'm sure."

"Trust me, I'd rather not know. I prefer to stay as far away from politics as possible." I stand up. "Just don't cause any trouble on my ship, Ives, and we'll be fine."

She gives me a tight-lipped, dangerous smile. "Then get us to Deva and let me do my job, Captain."

Later that night, in bed, I toss and turn despite my exhaustion. I think of Shey, and Ives, but mostly, I'm unable to stop my mind from walking in circles around the problem of the communications system. We're nearly at Deva now and still haven't figured out what the issue could be—which means we don't know if we'll be able to safely land or not when we arrive. I wouldn't be happy about trying to land with a mysterious problem in my systems in any situation, but with the IA, and the diplomats, and a Devan-Paxian war involved, I'm even more wary. It feels like something is closing in on us... but I'm not sure what it is, or which direction it's coming from. The stress follows me into sleep. I dream of howling winds, and dead planets, and alien statues towering over the crushed remnants of a city.

I wake up covered in sweat, and know what the answer is.

CHAPTER TWENTY

A Sabotage Within

Corvus

Scorpia shakes me awake. I have no idea what time it is, only that it's so early it's hard to force my eyes open. I mumble an incoherent question at her.

"I think someone brought an alien artifact on the ship," she says.

That wakes me. I sit up, rubbing a hand across my face, and try to focus. "Explain."

"Alien shit blocks comms."

"There are plenty of other reasons the comms system could be down."

"Sure. But we've run through about a million mechanical options and can't find anything." She holds up another finger. "Plus. Pol's headaches. I haven't seen him get this bad since his freak-out on Gaia, which is full of alien fuckery."

I sigh. "He gets a lot of headaches. He's sick. Not exactly compelling evidence, Scorpia."

"He said it was noisy. Same thing he said on Gaia." Her expression shifts to pleading as she sees my doubt. "Listen, I know it's a stretch, but something's wrong here. I can feel it in my gut. What if these supposed diplomats weren't really on a peace mission? What if we just got tricked into delivering some kind of weapon again?"

I consider it. If Scorpia is right, then whatever Primus artifact is on board has to be large enough to disrupt the communications of our entire ship. This is no small trinket or alien weapon—it must be substantial. It'd be hard to get their hands on something under the nose of the IA, so it makes sense that they could be in on it. And it does feel like another of Govender's tricks, sending slaughter to the Devans under the guise of a diplomatic mission. But how would they sneak it onto our ship? The scene on the space-docks was chaotic, but still . . .

Even if this idea of Scorpia's is far-fetched, we're only a few hours out from Deva at this point. If something is happening on our ship, we need to figure it out soon.

"Okay," I tell Scorpia. "It can't hurt to make sure there's nothing amiss."

I wake Izra first. Her, I know I can trust. "I need you to search the ship," I say, without any preamble. "And I need you to do it quietly. Get Drom to help. No one else."

She stands immediately, eyes me, and asks, "What am I looking for?"

"You'll know if you find it."

Next I gather the two diplomats in the leisure room, which is empty but for a few aluminum cans and a game of cards someone left scattered all over the couch. Neither of them question my order to come, nor show any sign of worry as I have them sit. I look them over. The Gaian sits on the very edge of the couch and wrinkles his nose. Ives leans back with her boots up on the footrest. I don't trust either of them, or the Alliance, but I can't assume they're guilty, either. I watch them until Scorpia joins us.

"What's the meaning of this, Captain?" the Gaian asks, drawing himself up. "Has there been word from the IA? Otherwise, I'm afraid I'm quite busy—"

"Shut up," Scorpia says. "Come with me. Ives, stay here."

The Gaian huffs and blusters and rolls his eyes, but still follows Scorpia. I shut the door behind them and lean back against it.

Once he's gone, Ives stands and stretches. I watch her carefully as she wanders the room, flicking a card off of the footrest to flutter to the floor, picking up an empty beer can to fiddle with. I'm aware of time passing like blood leaking from a wound.

Finally, a knock comes at the door. I expect Scorpia, but instead Izra and Drom are waiting outside, their faces grim.

"You found it?" I ask, keeping my voice low.

They exchange a glance. "Pol did," Drom says. "He insisted on helping despite the headache, and that's when I realized...he kept complaining about a *noise*, so I asked where it was coming from, and..."

"He led us right to it," Izra says.

"Show me. Drom, stay here and guard Ives."

My heart sinks as Izra leads us to Daniil's room. I don't want to believe it, but as she jerks open the closet door, the truth is irrefutable. Inside, spreading over the walls is a quivering, fleshy black mass. I recoil in disgust. Izra, though she holds her ground, is tense from her head to her toes as though she expects it to leap at her at any second.

I don't blame her. I've seen this substance once before, in the Titan base I infiltrated on Nibiru. But without the containment of the cold that the Titans were using, the thing looks even more alive. It's spread over the walls and ceiling and floor of the closet like an oozing, growing mass, and pulses slowly, like a heartbeat.

It makes me feel sick to look at it for too long—especially because of where we found it.

"I don't understand," I say quietly. The evidence is difficult to ignore: not only this location, but the fact that I know this came from the Titans. Still, I think of Daniil burning his uniform; Daniil staring up at the lights of the Golden City with awe on his face; Daniil laughing as he helps me in the kitchen. After all of this time, all of this pain, the way we found our way back to one another despite it, why would he do something like this?

Izra slowly lets the closet door shut and turns to me. "Like I've said. Titan brainwashing is hard to shake." She studies my face, and then says, "I'll get him."

"No. I'll do it myself."

She follows me anyway, and I am grateful for her presence at my back.

We find Daniil in the mess hall, brewing coffee. "I hope I did this right," he says as we enter. "I didn't know where everyone else was, so…" He stops as he sees the looks on our faces. "Is something wrong?"

"I need you to come with me."

He searches my face, and then nods. Questions bounce around my mind—why would he not run, or fight, if he did what we think he did?—but I suppress them for now. "Hands up," I tell him. "Let me search you, first."

He slowly places his hands behind his head. "I have a knife in the sheath on my left leg," he says, his voice remarkably steady given the situation. "That's all."

I take it, and find nothing else in my search. Something about this doesn't feel right. I know Daniil is a talented soldier, but he's not a spy trained in deception, and nothing about the way he's acting right now screams guilt. Yet I can't ignore what we found.

Nor can I stop my mind from returning to Izra's warning to me, again and again. I should have listened. Should have found a way to get between Daniil and Ives. If anyone talked him into doing this, I know it was her. I know, too, how insidious the idea of Titan loyalty is. And how easy it can be to do terrible things when you tell yourself it is for a good purpose.

I stand back, folding my arms over my chest, and he remains silent where he is, hands still raised. "Do you want to explain what we found in your room?" I ask.

He frowns at me. "I don't understand."

"Hard to believe you missed the huge alien artifact in your closet," Izra says dryly.

Daniil's eyes widen, flicking to her and back to me. "Alien—I don't—" He shakes his head. "I've barely been in my room for the last two days."

"Then where have you been?" I ask.

His mouth twists before he says, "Helena's room."

"We've all seen the two of you sneaking around the ship at odd hours," Izra says, stepping forward so we're shoulder to shoulder. "Are you working together?"

"Not... precisely the word I would use," Daniil says, never looking away from me even when she speaks. "Look, yes, it's a bad habit, but..." He shakes his head. "I don't know anything about an artifact."

I exchange a look with Izra. She seems as perplexed as I am. I'm not sure what to make of Daniil's reaction. No excuses, no insistence of his innocence, no display of emotion I would expect from either a falsely accused man *or* a guilty one. "How are you so calm about all of this?" I ask him.

Daniil looks at me levelly. "Because I trust you to get to the truth of the matter."

I want to trust that he's telling the truth. That he is being calm and blunt because he has nothing to hide. But paranoia is in my nature, and it has saved my life many times before.

After laying eyes on the thing in his closet, Daniil finally looks rattled. He stands several feet back from the door, and refuses to move forward even at Izra's prompting. I hold up a hand to stop her from pushing him farther.

"You know what this is?"

He doesn't take his eyes off of it. "No."

"Don't lie to me. I know this came from the Titans. I saw it on Nibiru." I give him a hard look. "Tell me what it is."

"I don't know!" His expression seems genuinely fearful as he continues gazing at the alien thing. "I knew Altair had Primus weapons, but I never worked with them. Never. I refused." He tears his eyes away from it and looks at me. "You can't truly believe I had anything to do with this? I would never..." He trails off, looking from me to Izra and back. Something in his expression changes. He lowers his hands and moves them behind his back, then sinks to his knees on the floor and bows his head. My throat constricts. It's a Titan gesture—one of surrender. Shame. A pose usually taken before an execution. "I had nothing to do with this," he says. Not begging, simply stating it as a fact. "But I submit myself to your will, Corvus."

There is a tearing, clawing, desperate part of me unwilling to fully trust anybody outside of my blood, a thing hand-fed and carefully shaped by Momma to keep the world out, which makes it difficult to believe that he's telling the truth.

But I'm not going to listen to it today.

"Get up." I hold out my hand to him. "I believe you."

He raises his head, looks at me, and—after a moment—takes my hand and rises to his feet. Izra frowns at us.

"That easy?" she asks.

"We shouldn't have entertained it for a second. The diplomats must be trying to frame him." I shift my grip from his hand to his arm and squeeze. "I'm sorry, Daniil."

He squeezes back. "All forgiven."

"Well." For a moment I'm worried Izra will lash out in anger, or insist on not trusting Daniil's word so easily; but instead, there is unmistakable relief on her face. She steps forward, lightly touches Daniil's shoulder, and nods. "Then let's find the fuckers who tried to frame you, and stop whatever they have planned with this alien mess."

As I look at the Primus relic spreading across the ship's wall, I can only hope we're not too late to prevent whatever it's put into motion.

CHAPTER TWENTY-ONE

An Enemy Within

Scorpia

It doesn't take me long to figure out that I don't make a very good interrogator. Neither of them takes me seriously. The Gaian is full of blustering condescension and thin-lipped disapproval that I would dare accuse him of such a thing, and Ives just laughs at me when I try to question her. I should've put Corvus in here and let him scowl at them, but it's too late for that.

After questioning both diplomats, I'm no closer to an answer. I was hoping one might try to throw the other under the bus, give me a weak point to exploit. But even when I try lying and saying the other diplomat gave them up, I get nothing from either one.

I throw them back into the leisure room to simmer for a while, figuring I'll see if their stories change after they have a chance to talk. But if they're working together, they must've planned for this kind of situation.

Unless...they're not working together. That thought gives me pause. Instead of the Interplanetary Alliance sending a fake diplomatic mission, this could be one of the planets working alone and turning traitor against the IA. Altair was reluctant to enter a peace agreement in the first place—maybe this was his doing. Ives seems like she'd be more than willing to do that kind of job. But if I'm right that it's a Primus weapon, that seems like a Gaian tactic. And the Gaians have always been so proud of themselves that they think of everyone else as less than human. Maybe this is a ploy by Khatri to give her people more power while the Nibirans and Titans are weak from the war. It's not hard to imagine that some Gaians would be eager to finish what Leonis started . . .

While I'm mulling over that, Corvus shows up again, with Izra and Daniil on his heels.

"You're right," Corvus says. "We found a Primus artifact on board. Now we need to figure out a way to get rid of it. Where are the diplomats?"

Fighting back a surge of terror at the thought of an alien menace somewhere on my ship, I jerk a thumb at the door behind me. "In there. Making 'em sweat a bit. I already questioned them separately." I chew my lip. "But now I'm starting to think it might not be both of them. It might be that one is sabotaging the Alliance."

"Might not be wise to lock them up together, then."

"Yeah, yeah, it's only been like five minutes. And I checked them for weapons beforehand."

But he does have a point. We can't keep them locked up forever. I turn, open the door, take one step, and stop so abruptly that Corvus bumps into me. Someone is asking me a question, but I can barely hear them over a low buzz in my ears as I stare into the room. It takes me several moments to process what I'm seeing.

My eyes slowly move over the toppled furniture, the wild splashes of blood on the ceiling and walls. They climb from the body's feet to its bloodied throat to its face: the Gaian diplomat, his eyes still wide open and his features twisted in shock. There's blood around him. So much blood, way too much for him to be anything but dead. It was a messy job, from the looks of it. A trail of blood leads from his fallen form to a torn-apart beer can that must've been the murder weapon, to the wall, and up it, to...the air vent.

"Shit," I say, dazed. "Well. I guess that answers the question about them working together." Corvus tries to move past me, but I grab his arm and shake my head, both as an order and to clear it.

I need to get my shit together real fast if we're going to stop whatever Ives has planned. "Nothing to do in there. We need to make sure everyone is safe." My mind races, trying to follow what Ives could be planning. I scramble to the nearest screen and activate the emergency alarm before turning to the others. "Shey. She might go for Shey. Corvus, go to her first." If her goal is to sabotage the negotiation plans, she'll want to be thorough. "And— and Orion! Izra, go." Killing a pilot is a perfectly effective way to cut a diplomatic mission short, too.

"I'm going to make sure Pol's okay," Drom says before I can say anything, but she waits for my nod before taking off. That leaves Daniil, hovering and waiting for my order.

"You go keep an eye on that alien whatever-it-is, in case Ives is planning something with it," I tell him.

"Yes, Captain," he says, and rushes off.

The thought of anyone on the ship in danger makes me want to panic, but the others are already on the move, and I have to trust that they can keep them safe. Not that any of us are safe right now, really. Ives brought an alien freak show on board, which makes it hard to believe she intended for any of us to survive this. Maybe herself included. It would be an awfully Titan way to go out, dying for whatever fucked-up cause she believes in.

My mind is whirring as I rush down the hall, trying to guess what her plan is and how to stop it, but I know it's going to take a bigger brain than mine to figure it out. "Lyre!" I find her in the engine room, and thankfully unharmed. Shit, now that I think about it, I should have sent some of our muscle down here to guard her and the engine, or at least asked for a blaster. I always think of spacecraft as so durable, but now that there's a threat I realize how many weak points there are to poke at, especially with a crew as small as ours. We're spread too thin already.

Lyre looks up at me, her expression wrinkled in annoyance about her work being interrupted until she sees my face.

"What's wrong?" she asks, stripping off her gloves and setting them aside.

"If someone was in the air vents, where could they exit?" I ask in a rush. No time to explain, and thankfully she doesn't ask; her brow is already furrowing as she thinks it through.

"Practically anywhere. Where did they enter?"

"Leisure room."

"It would be hard to get up to the top deck from there through the ducts. Not impossible, but hard, and time-consuming. Easiest exits would be in the training room and the armory."

The fucking armory. I'm an idiot. Of course that would be Ives's first move, and that puts her . . . right down the hall from us.

"*Damn* it." I press myself to the doorway and peer out into the hall, suddenly very aware of how unarmed and vulnerable I am. There's no sign of Ives now, but if she came this way, Lyre and I would be no match for her. Even if she is unarmed. Even if we *were* armed.

"And who is this hypothetical person in the air vents?" Lyre asks, dropping her voice to a whisper and creeping behind me.

"A certain murderous Titan diplomat who may have also brought a creepy alien monstrosity on board," I whisper back.

"Of course," she says in a small, resigned voice. "Always the worst-case scenario with these things, isn't it?"

Before I can respond, I hear the dull clang of footsteps in the hallway outside. We both go silent, our eyes on the doorway, waiting for the worst-case scenario.

CHAPTER TWENTY-TWO

The Enemy Revealed

Corvus

I rap my knuckles quietly against Shey's door, looking up and down the hallway for any signs of Ives. There's a pause that raises my heart rate and makes me wonder if I should force my way in. But then Shey opens the door, frowning. She lets out a small squeak of protest as I push past her, but swallows her complaints when she sees the knife in my hand.

"Oh, stars. What's happened now?"

"Ives smuggled an alien relic on board and killed the Gaian ambassador."

Her eyes widen. "So you think she might come for me next."

"Possibly." It's frustratingly difficult to guess at her targets without knowing her end goal. She could be aiming to sabotage the Gaians to avenge the Titans, perhaps in an effort to force them out of the Interplanetary Alliance. Or the Titans could be turning against the Alliance itself, in which case she wants to prevent the entire diplomatic mission. In that case, taking out the whole ship with her still on it wouldn't be out of the question; perhaps she planned on a more subtle approach, or thought the alien weapon would do her work for her, but now that we're onto her she's being forced into a more heavy-handed play.

"An alien relic," Shey says under her breath. "So that's what's been interfering with our communications system. Is it a weapon?"

"Don't know."

"Perhaps I can help with it?"

I almost refuse immediately, tell her that it's safer to stay in this room—but in reality, I don't know if it is. We can't know if Ives will come for us, or go elsewhere, and staying holed up in here will be pointless if she takes down the entire ship.

"Do you have any weapons in here?"

I expect a firm *no* and perhaps a shocked look, but instead Shey walks over to her bunk, reaches under the mattress, and reveals a sleek laser pistol small enough to fit into her palm. She offers it to me without hesitation, and I hand her my knife in return. The weapon looks tiny in my hand, but it's still good to have a gun. I look at it, and then her, lifting my eyebrows.

"I've spent enough time around your family to expect trouble," she says with a shrug.

"Smart."

We move through the hallways, pausing often to listen for footsteps or voices, but the ship is eerily still. Part of me yearns to go check on the others—the cockpit, the engine room, Pol's room—but I can't defend them all at once. Better to focus on what I can do.

Daniil is waiting outside his room, guarding the doorway.

"I'm going to have Shey take a look at the alien artifact," I tell him. "Would you go check on the cockpit?" Part of me wants to tell him to go defend my siblings, instead—but right now, our priority has to be avoiding landing on Deva with this on board. He nods and goes to obey.

I leave Shey in the hallway while I step into Daniil's room. The sight of the alien relic nearly sends me stumbling backward. The thing is growing, and fast; it's spilling out of the closet door now, tendrils of it stretching out nearly to the bunk on one side and the door on the other.

Once I'm certain it's not moving rapidly enough to be a threat—yet—I check the rest of the potential hiding spots in the room, but there's no sign of Ives. I bring Shey in, and she gasps as she spots the alien relic—though I'm now starting to think of it in terms of a *creature*—and presses a hand to her lips.

"Is it alive?" she asks.

"Don't know. But it's spreading. Fast. It was inside the closet when I first saw it, less than an hour ago."

As we both pause to weigh the implications of that, a tendril of the creature oozes out, probes the wall, and begins to climb.

"If it moves this fast, how could Ives have hidden it?" Shey asks, taking a tentative step closer to eye the thing. I resist the urge to pull her back.

"Maybe it was tiny when the trip began," I say. Though even if it began the size of a pebble, with this rate of growth, it would have quickly become difficult to conceal. But it's growing too slowly for it to overtake the ship by the time we reach Deva, if that was the intent. That nags at me. I find it hard to believe that Ives would bring something like this on board solely for the purpose of deactivating our communications. If she had access to something like this, surely there must have been an easier option at her disposal than some...living, growing, unpredictable thing. So what is its purpose?

"Do you recognize it?" I ask, hoping Shey will have some insight.

"No, it's not anything I've studied before." It's impossible to miss Shey's curiosity, and I'm sure she'd be dying to study the thing under less dire circumstances, but she shakes it off after a moment. "But the goal isn't to understand it. It's just to contain it. Ives and whoever she was working for must have had a way to do so safely, if she was able to transfer it onto the ship."

"Not just onto the ship, but into Daniil's room. He swears he wasn't working with her, and I believe him. But he's only been out of his room for the last couple days, so she must have moved it here." Likely when he was sleeping in her bed, I think, but push the unimportant detail away.

"Perhaps it adjusts to whatever confines it's given," Shey says. "We could attempt to trap it in something."

I was about to suggest shooting it—if it's alive, logic follows that it can be killed—but her idea does seem less risky. We comb through the room together and eventually come up with a plastic storage container from under Daniil's bunk. We dump its contents out on the bed—just a stack of old photographs that I resist an urge to take a look at, a small bag of Sanita and some rolling papers, and a bottle cap from a Devan beer—and I move toward the closet.

"How are we supposed to get it in?" I ask, unwilling to touch the thing with my bare skin.

Shey hesitates, looking at her gloved hands before quickly thinking better of it. "Try this," she suggests, handing my Primus knife back to me.

I tentatively probe at one edge of the oozing substance, and it recoils. Encouraged, I begin to pry it off of the walls, letting it drop into the storage container. I chip away, careful not to make contact with it. By the end, I'm sweating, and there is barely any room left in the box—but all of it fits inside. I set it down, grab the top of the container, and lock it.

Shey and I exchange a look. "Could it really be so easy?" she asks, sounding doubtful.

"We should move it somewhere more secure. The med bay has a quarantine area."

"I don't think we have time to get there," Shey says, watching the box with clear apprehension.

I step forward anyway, ready to grab the box and run, but it quickly becomes obvious that she's right. The substance has swelled to fill the box already. There's a pause. I hold my breath. And then, slowly but surely, the plastic walls begin to bloat outward, the box's shape mutating.

Shey and I both take a step back.

For a few moments, I maintain hope that the box will hold, and this will be the end of it. But it's not. I realize what's about to happen just before it does. I turn to grab Shey by the shoulders and push her out the door ahead of me, narrowly saving us both from contact with the thing as the box erupts outward and the substance within splatters all over the room. Blobs of it coat the walls, the bed, the floor, one piece even reaching the ceiling—and a moment later, each one begins to grow and spread at a pace even more rapid than before. Shey and I step into the doorway, but move no farther.

"Fuck," I growl under my breath. If we can't contain the thing, then we have to kill it. And quickly, judging from the way that it's progressing. I raise Shey's gun, aiming at the closest glob clinging to the floor. Not much of a weapon, this tiny thing, but it will have to do.

Shey grabs my arm and yanks it down before I can fire, giving me a stern look. "Not the solution to everything. It may just make it worse."

"So did trying to contain it," I say, yanking out of her grip. "We can't just let it keep growing."

"I know. I know." She shuts her eyes and takes a breath, likely trying to calm herself and organize her thoughts. "It's becoming more reactive. Its growth and movement are accelerating. But why? How did Ives know it wouldn't happen until now, allowing her to control it in its early stage?"

More questions, and no answers to speak of. The thing is getting more unnerving by the second. The room is stifling, seeming to shrink with each passing moment—and grow hotter. It isn't until I notice the sheen of sweat on Shey's forehead that I realize it may not be just panic making me overheat.

"The room is getting warmer," I say.

Shey frowns, and holds a hand out over the alien substance. "It doesn't seem to be emitting any heat…" Something in her expression shifts. She pushes past me to the door, and checks both ways before stepping out. "It's not just the room. It's the temperature on the whole ship. There's no way the alien substance is having that much of an impact already, so…" She turns to me. "It's the other way around. Something or someone is changing the temperature, and the substance is reacting to that."

"Ives," I say. "Temperature controls are on the lower level, in the engine room."

Lyre. Ives never would have gained access to the engine room without going through her.

Torn between worry for my family and my duty to protect the people who could change the system, I stay rooted where I am. Before I can make the decision, footsteps approach from the direction of the cockpit. I push Shey behind me and take aim with her pistol, listening and waiting. Just one pair of footsteps. Too heavy to be Lyre or Scorpia…

Daniil comes around the corner. He's alone, knife in hand, but he flips it so it's hilt-out when he sees me.

I lower my gun. "Izra and Orion?"

"Safe. The cockpit is secure, and we're staying just outside Deva's atmosphere. No sign of Ives." He reaches me and squeezes

197

my arm with his free hand, a brief and surprisingly comforting contact. "Have you seen her?"

"No," I murmur. It's a relief to hear that the others are safe—but concerning, as well, for what it could mean. My entire family isn't yet accounted for. I swallow down the urge to panic, trying to think clearly. Ives didn't go after Shey or the pilot, as we thought she would. So where is she? What is she doing? Who will she target? "Take Shey to the others. I need to find my siblings."

CHAPTER TWENTY-THREE

Feeling the Heat

Scorpia

A bead of moisture slides down the bridge of my nose, dangles on the tip, and splashes to the floor.

"If you wanted to make me sweat, Ives, there are easier ways to do it," I say, twisting my hands in their bindings. I'm tied up on the floor in a corner of the breaker room. My wrists are growing increasingly slippery as the temperature rises, and I'm fairly confident I could wriggle my way out of this rushed knot. Unfortunately, me being free wouldn't solve the problem of Ives holding a gun to Lyre's head. In fact, according to the former general, making any move she dislikes will end with my sister's brain splattered all over the breaker room.

And I believe her. This is not the cool, collected woman from earlier on our voyage. Ives is disheveled and sweaty, strands of hair ripped free from the untidy knot at the back of her head, shirt drenched in the rusty shade of dried blood. She looks unhinged. Still, she was able to overpower both Lyre and me within the span of ten seconds, tie me up, and march both of us here to continue with whatever nefarious plan she has underway, so I know better than to underestimate her no matter how ruffled she seems. I'm not sure what turning up our temperature is going to accomplish, other than making everyone on board severely uncomfortable, but I can't imagine it's anything good.

"Quiet," Ives says. "I'll get to you in a minute."

She's watching the temperature gauge tick up. One hand taps against the glass, while the other holds her gun—her *stolen* gun, as I'm pretty certain that's one of ours rather than something she brought on board—aimed at Lyre's head. She's not even looking at her, but when Lyre shifts her weight, Ives's gun follows like a magnet.

I was hoping I could get her to turn the gun on me, instead, by being sufficiently annoying, but maybe it's time to try another tactic. "She's the person who keeps this whole ship running, by the way. If you kill her and something goes wrong, we'll all be dead."

Her only response is to press the barrel flush against Lyre's temple. Lyre lets out a quiet whimper, and I shut my mouth.

"There," Ives says, finally, in a tone I don't like at all. She grabs Lyre by the arm and yanks her over to me, never lowering her gun even a smidgen. She is every inch a professional at this; she's not going to give us any sort of opening. Even if the others show up, what can they do with us at her mercy? It's funny, in a way—we gravely outnumber her, but that's not enough. It's both the strength and the weakness of my crew: Even the smallest loss would be an unbearable one.

"What do you want?" I ask, desperate to get her talking. Even if it only delays the inevitable, even if I can only buy time for the others rather than my life, that's good enough for me. "Let's talk."

"At the moment..." She presses the gun against Lyre's temple again, and I suck in a breath through my teeth, my whole body tensing. "What I want is the code for the emergency escape pods. I know you locked them down."

I glance at Lyre, who shakes her head just a little despite the fear in her eyes, and then back at Ives. "Sure, sure," I say. "Just one problem. I don't remember it. It's like twelve digits long."

Ives's already-cold expression goes frosty. She shifts her gun from Lyre's head to her arm. "Liar."

"I'm not!" I strain against my binds. "I swear. You'll have to go to the cockpit to get it. I'll show you where."

"Twelve fucking digits," she says, "for an escape pod? A password so long you can't remember, and you expect me to believe you'd take the time to input it in an emergency?"

I pause. "I guess we didn't think of that."

"Not even you're that stupid."

"Wait, maybe I can remember if I—"

The sound of her gun is deafening. So is Lyre's scream. I scream as well, and launch myself at Ives's legs, sending all three of us toppling to the floor in a sweaty, bloody mess of limbs. Lyre manages to scramble to her feet and run for the door, but Ives pins me down with a knee in my back and aims her gun at the back of my head.

"Don't fucking move," she barks at Lyre, who freezes in the doorway, blood streaming down her arm and tears in her eyes. "I can kill her and shoot you in the legs before you get anywhere. Trust me."

Lyre stays where she is. I can't move with Ives's weight on top of me, though I got one hand free from the ropes in the tussle.

"Escape pod codes," Ives says. "Now." I try to speak, but she shoves my face into the floor. "Not you. *You*," she barks at Lyre.

Shit. Not good. Lyre can be a devious little thing, but she's never been a very good liar, and there's no way she'll be able to talk us out of this. She could've claimed she doesn't know the codes, but the silence has gone on too long already. She must be panicking. Maybe holding out for as long as she can in the hope that someone will come chasing the gunshot and the scream to this room.

Or maybe she's just going to hold her tongue and keep her pride. Let me die to keep Ives here. I squeeze my eyes shut, bracing myself for that possibility. I wouldn't blame her for it. If Ives is so desperate to jump ship, it probably means she's confident that anyone who stays is dead.

When Lyre still says nothing, Ives removes her gun from the back of my head. I barely have time to consider whether it's worth struggling when she presses the cold barrel into the back of my hand instead. My flesh hand. I'm already sweating, but now my heart is really pounding.

"What is it with you Titans—" I start, my voice muffled by the floor, and she yanks my head up with her free hand and slams it back down. I gasp in pain, my head spinning.

"Last chance," she says. "Escape pod codes. Now."

Lyre lets out a small, strained sound, almost a whimper—but she says nothing.

"Fine," Ives says. "If that's your choice…"

"Let her go, Ives."

Oh, thank fuck, Corvus is here. The relief is instantaneous, though it probably shouldn't be, since I'm still pinned on the floor with a crazy, armed general on top of me.

"Daniil," Ives says, her voice softening. I shift until I can see him, standing behind Corvus in the doorway. "Enough of the ruse. You're better than running with this scum. There's still time to build a better future for our people, and make the dead proud of what they sacrificed for." There's a quiet intensity to her voice, almost an intimacy, as if the rest of us aren't here at all. And we might as well not be; all of us are frozen with her gun still trained on me. "Our soldiers didn't die so we could live alongside our enemies and have our culture stripped away. We deserve our own world. One without the alien threat hanging over our heads. There's still time to do all of the things we once talked about, Daniil. Burn it all down, and start anew."

Daniil hesitates. He stares at her for a long moment. One of his feet shifts forward, as if he's going to take a step, but then his eyes flick to Corvus, and he stops.

Ives's tone drops, low and icy. "That's an order, Naran. Show me you're not the coward they all say you are."

Daniil flinches like he's been struck, but still doesn't move. "Give it up, Helena," he says, gently. "It's over. Let the dead rest."

Ives lets out a harsh laugh. The bitterness isn't quite enough to hide the hurt beneath it. "You too, then?" she asks. "Fine."

"Just because Altair wants this—" Daniil begins.

"Altair," Ives spits, interrupting him. "Altair has become a coward. He is too old and tired for war. What kind of person makes peace with the enemy who slaughtered his people, when the war still could have been won? Agrees to live among them? Certainly no Titan." Her lip curls back in disgust. "I knew he was too soft from the moment he delayed our counterattack. We could have had the Gaians before they reached Nibiru. We could have had them after, too. Instead he told us to wait, and begin to starve, and warn them even when we were finally on our way there. He stripped me of my rank for daring to speak the truth. Nearly killed me because he was afraid that the others would follow me instead of him."

An eerie calm settles over me. Maybe I've escaped near-certain death enough times that I'm finally resigned to it. My mind goes back to facing Altair on the Titan mothership, and his words to me: *The only peace my people will accept is one that we earn in blood.* I thought I fixed everything with the deal I made, but it looks like my risk and my sacrifice may have only prolonged the inevitable. It was naive of me to think that anyone could be forced into lasting peace.

"Doing this will just get more of your people killed," I tell her, straining to form the words with half my face squished against the metal floor. "And, I'm just saying, you don't have a whole lot of lives left to spare. Don't you want Titan to live?"

"Better a brave death than a cowardly life," she says. "Any real Titan knows that. We deserve a glorious future, or an honorable end."

"Okay, sure." My mind is working overtime now, trying to figure out a way through this. Despite all of her blabbing about honor and bravery, she's hounding us for the escape pod codes right now. She wants to live. She also sounds like she's not working alone—but judging by her earlier words, it's not with Altair, either. "So you're willing to die here and leave that 'glorious future' in the hands of a bunch of Titan kids?" I ask. "Altair's a coward, and Daniil's with us now. Who's gonna lead them, when you're gone? 'Cause surely this plan of yours doesn't end with us. You've got bigger and better things to move on to, yeah?" I shift to allow some more air into my lungs. She doesn't argue, which encourages me. "So let's make a deal. We all just wanna get through this alive."

"I don't need to deal with scum like you," she says.

"Well you're gonna *die* with scum like us if you don't," I say. "So how about this. We'll trade. You tell us how to deal with that alien bullshit you set loose on my ship, and we'll give you the code for the escape pods. We all walk away from this."

There's a long pause. It's tempting to fill the silence and try to persuade her further, but I hold my tongue. Her inner battle right now, I suspect, is mostly about her pride. Better for me to stay quiet and avoid reminding her how much she hates me. The rest of my crew remains silent, too, though I can feel them all watching us.

"Fine," Ives says, finally. "You first."

"No." Corvus speaks before I can. "You tell us what you know. Then we'll let you take Scorpia to the escape pods for you to verify our information is true. You know we won't do anything to endanger her."

Ives pauses again to consider. Her weight shifts on my back, and she sighs. "All right," she says. "It's harmless on its own, but explosive if it's exposed to a spark. I'm sure you've already figured out that it expands in heat and shrinks in the cold."

"So how do we destroy it?"

"No idea," Ives says, sounding all too satisfied with herself. "Even if it explodes, it just spreads more pieces. We haven't found a way to fully destroy it."

"For fuck's sake," I mutter.

"That's all I know," Ives says. "Your best bet is to shrink and contain it. Now, your turn."

"Wait," Lyre says. "One more question. How did you get it on board?"

Ives pauses. I can tell she was hoping we wouldn't ask this. "I ate it."

"You...what?" I sputter, and then gag as I think more about it. "*Ew.*"

"Bullshit," Corvus says. "Not even you're that insane. The deal was that we get the truth—"

"She's not lying," Daniil says. I can't see his face, but he sounds shaken. "I've heard of this. There was a plan Altair considered early on. He said there was a substance we could ingest that would turn our bodies into living bombs. He decided it was too risky."

"You crazy bitch, Ives," I say. "You really swallowed some alien weapon and puked it up on my ship? All of this just for us?"

205

"It wasn't supposed to be you fuckers," she snarls, increasing the pressure on my back. *"You* were supposed to die in the explosion on Vil Hava, not force me onto your stars-damned ship. I wanted someone more important. Someone who wouldn't have realized what was happening before—" She cuts off with a growl, realizing I goaded her into revealing more. But I can see the blueprints of her plan, now. She must've expected some oblivious Nibiran higher-up would take her to Deva, desperate to make a deal for their people, agonized that they couldn't even reach home with the hidden alien relic blocking their comms. They would have no idea what they were transporting with them. I suppress a shudder, thinking of how easily that alien weapon would have spread in Deva's muggy climate.

I'd love to insult her some more—both to glean more information and because she deserves it—but the weight of her on top of me is making it hard to breathe at this point. "Code," she snaps. Her knee grinds into my spine, and I groan. "Now."

There's a pause, in which I imagine we're all weighing our options. But in the end, I suspect everyone reaches the same conclusion I have. A firefight in such close quarters is risky for us all, and we need time to deal with that alien shit before it spreads over my poor ship. Stars only know what kind of effect it's going to have if it gets into the wiring.

Letting Ives go feels like giving up, but in the end, I'd rather keep us alive than ensure her death.

I tell her the code so no one else has to make the choice: 2-02188-1036. *Fortuna's* Gaian registration number.

CHAPTER TWENTY-FOUR

Primus Problems

Corvus

A s the ship gradually cools, I clean and wrap Lyre's arm in the medical bay. Beside us, the cryosleep chamber rests open, waiting for the others to arrive.

Izra and Drom soon shuffle into the room, carrying the alien mass between their gloved hands. I'm relieved that I was excused from that particular duty. The weapon is visibly shrinking as the temperature drops around it, but it's still around the same size as me, and shifts and stretches as they carry it, like it's trying to escape.

Once they heave it into the cryosleep chamber, Pol wanders in behind them, holding his hands over his ears. He lowers them as the women shut the chamber, and lets out a satisfied sigh. "Better," he says.

Daniil comes in behind him, looking like he's trying not to be sick. The others must be in the cockpit waiting for our comms to come back online.

Ives, true to her word, didn't shoot anyone on her way out.

I suspect Scorpia is right—whatever plan she concocted is more important to her than making sure we die. Her main goal here must have been to interfere with the IA's plans for diplomacy, and get this weapon to Deva. Even though we've foiled the second part, she succeeded with the first, and took one of our escape pods. I'm sure there's more to come.

But for now, we have to focus on staying alive.

As I finish treating Lyre's wound, I join the others crowded around the cryosleep chamber, watching with horrified fascination as the alien sludge gradually shrivels into a perfect sphere about the size of my fist. Despite the intense cold, it's still not completely frozen, somehow. Instead it still vibrates. Like it's waiting for a chance to break free.

"Are we really going to land on Deva with this thing on board?" Lyre asks, voicing what I suspect we're all thinking. "If it gets into the wrong hands, or even just gets loose on accident..."

Ives picked her weapon well. In Deva's hot, humid climate, this growth would spread like wildfire. Her plan must have been to block our comms, in case the IA caught on to her betrayal and warned us, and force us to land on Deva with it on board.

If she had ended up on a different ship, instead of being dragged onto ours, it likely would have worked. She couldn't have anticipated our knowledge of the Primus, or Pol's unique affinity that helped Scorpia realize what was happening. I think of the alien mass oozing through the dark jungles, overtaking the helpless villages spread across the planet, crawling over the neon lights of the Golden City, and my stomach lurches.

"We should take it back to Titan, where it was found," I say. "Bury it in the cold."

"You really wanna fuck off all the way to Titan with everything going on right now?" Drom asks.

"It's a good long-term plan, but it'll take weeks. And we need to get Shey to Deva to try to salvage the IA's diplomatic mission," Lyre says.

"But we don't know what kind of reception we'll get there," I say. "Misha was already after us last time. He could apprehend us, search the ship. I don't want this weapon falling into Devan hands, especially given the war with Pax."

"We can't toss it out the air lock, either," Lyre says. "Even if we weren't just outside of Deva's atmosphere, we don't know if it would destroy it or not."

I nod. I don't like the idea of this unknown factor floating around in space, either. "So what do you suggest?"

There's a moment of silence. I can tell from Lyre's expression that she has an idea, but she doesn't want to say it. After a few seconds, I realize what it must be.

"We're not going to *eat* the damn thing," I say.

"She did seem to think it was a safe way to transport it," Lyre says, though her nose wrinkles in distaste.

"We don't know what kind of effect that would have on us."

"Altair believed it was safe enough," Daniil butts in, sounding regretful even as he says it. "I think the idea was that your stomach acid contains it, despite the heat of your body..."

"I am already regretting asking this," Lyre says, "but how would one get it *out*, then?"

"Your system won't process it naturally. So you have to, um." Daniil grimaces. "Force yourself to throw it up."

"Fucking Titans," Drom mutters. Then she glances sideways at Daniil and adds, "Uh, no offense."

"In this case, none taken."

There's a long, tense silence as we all stare into the cryosleep chamber.

"Well," Lyre says, her expression queasy. "How should we decide who the unlucky carrier will be, then? Draw straws?"

"I'll do it," Pol volunteers immediately.

"What? No. You already got cool alien shit, my turn," Drom says, pushing him aside and reaching for the hatch of the cryosleep chamber.

I grab her wrist. "It's too dangerous. If anyone is going to do this, it's me."

"But of course," Lyre mutters, "I forgot I'm on a ship full of heroic idiots. Consider me out of the running, then."

Daniil steps back, holding his hands up. "I'm all for noble self-sacrifice, but this one's going to be a no from me."

I'm still grappling with Drom over the cryosleep chamber.

"Just once, let me have this," she says. "It's not fair that you and Scorpia get to do everything."

"It's too risky, Drom. And you're not exactly averse to the line of fire."

"You get shot way more often than me!"

I'm so busy keeping her away from the chamber that I don't notice Pol stepping behind me. But when Drom shoves me, all of a sudden his leg is in my way, and I trip and crash down to the floor with a grunt.

"Go, Drom!" Pol cheers, ending up on the floor right beside me.

"*Apollo*, this isn't a joke!"

Drom races over to the chamber. The moment it opens, I hear a quieter version of that strange, warbling song I remember it emitting on Nibiru. I didn't notice it before now, so I imagine it must only make the noise when it's being contained. But Drom reaches inside, pulls out the alien mass, and stuffs it into her mouth. The noise disappears as she swallows.

"There," she says. "Done."

I stare at her from the floor, winded and horrified. "Drom..." I glare over at Izra, Lyre, and Daniil, none of whom moved to interfere.

"What?" Izra is the only one who meets my gaze. "*I* wasn't about to eat the fucking thing."

Before I can respond, Scorpia walks into the room. "Okay, there's good news and bad news," she says, and then stops. She looks at me and Pol still on the floor, Daniil and Izra and Lyre standing off to the side, Drom beside the open cryosleep chamber. She does a double take at the latter. "Oh, did we already find a way to deal with the alien shit?"

"I ate it," Drom says, matter-of-factly.

"You..." Scorpia blinks. "Y—Ate..." She gags and slaps a hand over her mouth.

While she's pulling herself together, I take the opportunity to get to my feet, and grudgingly offer Pol a hand up. He looks way too pleased with himself.

"You said there was news?" Lyre prompts.

"Yes. Right." Scorpia gulps one last time, takes a deep breath, and straightens up, still green in the face but seemingly past the point of actually retching. "The good news: Our comms are back online, and it looks like Nibiru is okay. The bad news: The IA definitely thinks we kidnapped their diplomats and have sent us several threatening messages about it. So...that's not great. We should probably toss that Gaian's body out the air lock before we get to Deva."

"Perhaps better to incinerate it," Lyre says. "Then we know there won't be any evidence."

Scorpia snaps her fingers and points at her. "Right. Incinerator. Definitely a better call. So we'll do that, and then go down to Deva, where hopefully we can find some way to talk it out with the IA and..." She frowns, face wrinkling with thought. "But I guess Ives must be going to Deva, too. Probably going to make sure we get an unfriendly welcome, so maybe..."

As she trails off into thought, I realize the same thing that must be crossing her mind: Something doesn't feel right about that. "What was her plan when she reached Deva?" I ask. "It's a hostile planet. She wouldn't have a guaranteed way off once she reached it. And if her original plan was for us to land with that alien thing on board and take it out, then..."

"A good ol' Titan self-sacrifice?" Scorpia suggests, though she sounds doubtful.

"Then why the escape pod?" Lyre pipes up. "She could've easily damaged our engine enough to crash us, rather than go through all of that trouble."

There's only one answer that makes sense. "She made it clear she wasn't working alone." I pause, remembering a detail that I forgot amid all of the turmoil: the mention of claiming a planet *without* the alien defense systems. "She's not going to Deva. She just wanted to get the weapon there. She must have some way to get to Pax."

"*Shit*," Scorpia says. "There must be a ship out here—maybe more than one—the fucking Titans can cloak! We need to land on Deva, *now*."

She races for the cockpit—but she doesn't even make it out of the room before an impact shakes the ship.

CHAPTER TWENTY-FIVE

A Captain's Choice

Scorpia

I claw my way into my copilot's chair as the floor tilts beneath my feet. The three Titan warships linger just long enough for me to see them on our screens before they cloak again. Like they're gloating. And of course they are. We've fallen right into Ives's plan. Her escape pod made it back to the ships that must have been waiting to take her to safety, and now they'll be able to head off to carry out the rest of her plan. The only thing left to do was handle us.

"Autopilot is shot," Orion says. "So is the engine. They hit us right as we were entering Deva's atmosphere." He doesn't need to tell me what that means, but he says it aloud anyway, sounding like he can hardly believe it's true. "We're going down."

Memoria is crashing. And I've crashed before—both gracefully and not—but this is different. We're going down fast and hard. And the surface we'll be hitting isn't the forgiving ocean of Nibiru, or the wide-open spaces of any of the other planets. Here on Deva, we'll be crashing into the jungle. The trees will rip the ship to pieces, and stars know what other kinds of plants will be waiting for us if we venture outside. Even if we don't die during the crash, the chances of making it to civilization alive are slim.

But I can't think about that right now. First things first.

I hit the video recorder. The screaming alarm and flashing lights will make the message a nightmare, but I need them to know it's really me. "This is Captain Kaiser of *Memoria* pinging Eridanus and Halon," I say, struggling to keep my voice as steady and clear as I can. I don't have time for a second run through this recording. "We're going down on Deva. I don't think the ship will survive. We'll be trapped and possibly in need of an evac. Please, guys—" My voice cracks, and I pause and swallow. "We need your help. You're the only ones I trust out there." I smack the button to send it off, one last hope drifting out in the stars. It might not reach them until it's far too late, or they might not be willing or able to get to us, but at least I tried.

Step two: Survive the landing.

"How many can fit in the escape pod?" I ask. We still have one left.

"Three," Orion says. He looks shaken, but doesn't tear his hands or his eyes off of the controls, holding his post.

"I know there are only three seats, but if we cram—"

"No," he says, with a quick shake of his head. "We're too close to the planet. It won't slow enough before it hits the surface. Anyone not strapped in will die on impact."

"And if they are strapped in? Will they be safe?"

Orion shrugs. "They'll have a better chance than anyone left on the ship, that's for sure. They're built for emergencies like this. And if they aim for Zi Vi, they'll land closer than us."

"Okay." I bite my lip. Three in the escape pod. Which means I have to make the decision who goes, and quickly. There's no time to consult Corvus or the others. "Can't be us. We both need to be here controlling the ship as much as possible."

214

Orion nods. Judging from his expression, he had already reached and accepted the same conclusion before I said it. "But they need a Devan with them for when they get to Zi Vi."

"Right. So Lyre goes." I let out a breath. "And...Shey. Shey should go. To manage the diplomatic situation."

"Then at least we won't die for nothing," Orion agrees.

It's the right choice. I know it is. But it also means I can't send both of my other little siblings. I can't bear the thought of sending one of the twins over the other, either. I've made a lot of choices, but I won't make that one.

And I need to think logically. Make a choice as a captain rather than a sister. This isn't about who I want to try to save the most, it's about who needs to go. And Lyre and Shey will need someone smart and brave and capable enough to handle the jungle. Someone who will bring them to Zi Vi no matter what happens. There's only one person I trust with a job like that.

"Corvus." My voice is barely a whisper. "Corvus will get them there."

Even if that means he won't be here with me, for better or for worse, to deal with whatever happens. And it means I have to ask him to leave not only his family behind, but Izra and Daniil as well. He'll hate me for this. But it has to be done. And I think he'll understand that, too, even though it will tear him apart. I know my brother. He'll agree, if I ask him to do this. Not to save himself, but because it's the best chance for all of us.

"Izra—" Orion says, like the start of an argument, but then he trails off and shakes his head. "No...her arm. You're right."

"Fuck. Okay." I unstrap myself with shaking hands, trying to shove my emotions as far down as I can. This choice can break me later—if I live long enough to see the consequences—but not before I get it done. "Hold her steady as long as you can, Orion."

"Got it, Captain," he says, taking his eyes off of the screen just long enough to flash one of one of his usual grins. It helps steel me to know that he, too, will do what needs to be done.

I make my way back into the bulk of the ship, clinging to furniture and walls to hold my footing as the craft shakes around us. Everyone else is strapped in and waiting. Trusting us. I feel a pang of horrible, twisting guilt at the thought of what I'm about to do—but the choice has to be made. It's not possible to get everyone to safety, as much as I wish it were. All I can do is give as many people as possible the best chance they can get.

I gather Corvus, Shey, and Lyre from their rooms, trying not to think about the others waiting behind their closed doors, all of their lives in my hands. They come along without too much questioning, sensing the urgency, but all stop as I bring them to the single escape pod.

"Where is everyone else?" Shey asks, her eyebrows drawing together. She doesn't understand, but I can tell that Corvus and Lyre both do. Lyre goes very pale, but she takes a deep breath and steps into the pod, strapping herself into the pilot's chair without a word of argument.

"I'll get us as close to the city as I can." Her voice wavers but doesn't break, and I feel a fierce surge of pride in her.

"I know you will." I turn to Shey. "There's only room for three. We're prioritizing the diplomatic mission. You need to get to Zi Vi, talk to the IA, and foil whatever plan Ives is launching, no matter what." I force a smile. "Make it worth it, all right?" My voice trembles, but I fight past it. "No time for sappiness. We're crashing. Get in there." I give her a little push to get her started. She takes a step, and looks back at me. Just a look—that's all we have time for—but I nod at her. "I'll see you again." I know I can't promise that, but I have to believe it.

She gets in, leaving just Corvus, staring at the final seat with a stricken expression.

"Corvus, there's no time," I say quietly. "I'm sorry. But you're the person I trust to get them there and finish this." He still doesn't look at me. "It's the best chance we have. You'll need to send help back once you reach the city."

He nods. "I'm doing this for all of us," he says. "Make sure Daniil and Izra know that, if they—if you—"

"I know. I know. I will. But you gotta go. Now."

He finally looks up to me, and reaches over to give my arm a brief squeeze, and before I can think of anything more to say the door is sliding shut behind all of them. I swallow my grief and my guilt and run back to the cockpit.

Instead, I hit a locked door. I slam my palm on the pressure pad three times, my panic growing, trying to figure out what the hell is happening, before the intercom to the side crackles to life. Orion's face appears on the screen.

"Orion," I say. "The fucking door is jammed—"

"Yeah, I know."

It takes me a second to process that, and the look on his face. "Did you lock me out? What the hell do you think you're doing?"

"'Fraid a copilot's not going to help with this one," he says. "I've got this. You go strap in."

"Don't be ridiculous. It's my ship—"

"And I'm the pilot," he says, his voice full of forced cheer. "So let me do my job. The rest of the crew will need you. The back of the ship is safer."

My stomach drops. I understand the logic in what he's saying. He's probably right that I'll be safer elsewhere, and that having a copilot won't help much in a crash, especially with most of our systems down. It only takes one person to handle the wheel and aim for a good crash zone, and that's about all we can do right now. But still. Still. There's no way I'm letting him do this alone. Especially when I know he's right: The back of the ship is safest.

And the most dangerous spot to be in a crash? Right in that seat. "You don't get to make that decision. It's my ship. Let me in."

"Sorry, Captain. No can do." He shows me that damn smile that won me over the first time we came face-to-face, his eyes crinkling in the corners. "I'll see you on the other side."

He cuts the connection before I can say anything back. I stand there for a moment, my hand resting on the screen, thinking about pinging him again and trying to talk him out of this, or finding a way to break the door down, or, or...

Then the ship jerks under my feet, and the alarms start to scream, and it's too late. The decision's already been made. All I can do is run for my quarters, skidding across the shaking floor, and hope I'll make it to a launch chair in time.

CHAPTER TWENTY-SIX

Lost

Corvus

Lyre puts in the coordinates for Zi Vi, but the second we detach from the ship, the escape pod is falling. It's not built to fly this close to a planet, its engines not strong enough to combat the insistent tug of gravity, barely strong enough to slow our descent. So we drop toward the surface. Pressure slams into me and my thoughts hiss away into nothingness. I barely think to grab my mouth-guard, my fingers slow and clumsy as the world spins.

It feels like we drop for only seconds before we hit something. Not the surface—a tree, probably, since soon we drop again, with a great tearing sound, and then hit again, and jerk to a stop. I jolt in my seat, the straps digging into me hard enough to bruise, and let out a grunt of pain around the goo of the mouth-guard between my teeth.

Finally, we come to a stop. I'm breathing hard, my head still spinning and my stomach rolling wildly. For a second there's nothing but ringing in my ears, but gradually, the noise kicks in again—a screaming emergency alarm from the pod's system, and nothing else. I spit out my mouth-guard, fumble to release my safety straps, and fall forward onto the back of Lyre's seat. I was so disoriented I didn't even realize the pod must be tilted forward, nose-down. I grab the handholds on the side to keep myself from tumbling farther.

"Everyone okay?" I ask. "Lyre? Shey?"

"Yes," Shey says, half sobbing the word out.

"Lyre, say something." I want to get to her, but the craft shudders when I move. I stop, realizing I don't know if we're on stable ground or not.

After a heart-stopping moment, Lyre lets out a small groan. "I'm okay," she murmurs. "Hit my head a bit, but…"

"All right. Just stay still for now. What can you see out the front panel?"

"Um…" The grogginess in her voice concerns me, but her answer is the more pressing concern for the moment. "We're caught on something. Some kind of tree. But I can see the surface, too—I think we're hanging just a few feet above it."

"Okay." Could be worse. Could be a lot worse, since the pod is still intact. "Both of you stay strapped in." Maybe I should, as well. If we're close enough to Zi Vi, the Devans should send someone to check out what happened, and the escape pod will undoubtedly be safer than the jungle outside. But, no—we can't risk it. Especially since the safety of the others may depend on us reaching help. "I'm going to go check it out."

I maneuver myself carefully around the side of Lyre's seat, glancing at her as I do. Her head is bleeding, and the bandage over the wound on her arm is soaked through with blood, but neither looks too serious. I brace myself on the wall with my back against her seat and crank the manual lever to open the exit door. It releases with a hiss, and the humid air of Deva rushes in, warm and earthy.

Lyre was right, the drop isn't far, so I jump down to the surface, careful not to touch any of the plants we're tangled in until I get a better look at what they are. Once I'm down, I feel even more disoriented than in the pod. This is Deva, but not like I've ever experienced it before. Gone are the bright lights and crowds of Zi Vi; gone, too, is the constant presence of Nova Vita overhead, blotted out by the tangle of dark foliage above us. All around us, the world is dim and hushed except for the whisper of leaves. It must be just a breeze—but still, I think of the stories of strange Devan plants I've heard about, and imagine the entire jungle gradually closing in around us. We are completely alone here.

I'm not well versed in Devan plants, but nothing around us seems threatening, so I help Lyre and Shey down next. I have Lyre sit once she's out, and do what I can to assess the wound on her head. The bleeding is slowing on its own, at least, and the gash isn't deep. She's dizzy, and a slight concussion is likely, but she's not showing any symptoms that set off immediate alarms. I retrieve the escape pod's first-aid kit, and wash and dress both of her wounds again.

Shey tries to contact Scorpia on her comm, and then ours, but none of them are receiving any signal.

"How far from the others do you think we landed?" she asks, once I straighten up again and turn away from Lyre.

"I don't know."

"Maybe we could get to them. Meet up and make our way to the city together."

"Even if we knew where they were, the last direction we want to head is away from Zi Vi," I say, as patiently as I can.

"But the others—Scorpia—"

"Stop." I cut her off as my sister's name floods me with a panic I've been trying desperately to keep at bay. "We deal with the situation at hand first. And you heard her as well as I did. Our best shot, and what she wants us to do, is to get to the city as soon as we can." That's why she chose me. Because she knew I would do it, even if it meant walking away from her and the others without knowing if they're okay. She knew I was probably the only one of our crew that could. "Our first order of business is figuring out which direction Zi Vi is in. Lyre, do you have any ideas?"

When I turn back to her, she's huddled with her knees to her chest and her forehead resting on them. She takes a deep breath, slowly lets it out, and raises her head. Her eyes are dry, but I know from the look on her face that she's feeling the same pressure and guilt that I am. It is a heavy weight, to be the responsible ones of the family, but she bears it with her shoulders squared, just like I always have.

"The pod's navigation system," she says, climbing to her feet. "It will at least point us in the right direction. Lift me up, Corvus."

I do so, and hover just outside the door as she clambers inside, in case it becomes unsteady. While she tinkers with the half-broken pod, I glance over at Shey. She seems to be composing herself now, hands clasped in front of her and her eyes closed, but she opens them when she feels my gaze on her.

"You all right?" I ask.

"I have to be."

I nod. The only way to make it through this is to keep our eyes forward. Once we're in Zi Vi and the danger is behind us, then we can face all of the rest.

Once Lyre reappears, she tosses down the emergency supplies from the escape pod and accepts my hand down to the ground, carefully avoiding touching any of the entangling vines around the pod. I swear that they're tightening around the vessel, like they're making a concerted effort to trap it there.

"Okay," Lyre says, putting one of the emergency kits onto her back. "Zi Vi is northeast of us, but if we head east—" She points out the direction. "We'll hit a river we can follow straight north. It looks like it passes close enough to the city for us to see it."

"Good. There are likely villages situated near the river as well. They might be able to help us along."

"There are people living out here in the jungle?" Shey asks, lifting her own pack. "So we don't need to get all the way to the city to reach safety?"

Lyre and I exchange a glance. "There are, but the villages probably aren't what you're expecting," I say, and leave it at that. Gaia had plenty of its own troubles, but I doubt someone from a life as pampered as hers can imagine the extreme poverty and constant struggle with the world itself that takes place in Deva's smaller settlements. "And I doubt they have vehicles, if that's what you're hoping for. But we should be able to pay them for more supplies and directions, at least." I sling the last pack over my shoulder and look up at the darkness of the jungle ahead, a dense tangle of trees with no visible path whatsoever. "Stay behind me and try not to touch anything."

We don't talk. It's hard enough just to keep going. Hours pass, with little progress to show for it. Getting through the jungle is less of a walk and more of a battle. I have to use my knife to hack through vines and bushes, and despite my warning not to touch any of the unknown plants, it quickly proves impossible. Soon my sleeves are torn from the thorns and whipping branches. My skin itches beneath. Whether it's a product of one of the plants, or the sweat soaking me, or the buzzing insects, or just a product of my own paranoia, I'm not sure.

Lyre points out the plants she recognizes as we go—most of them horrifying—and we give them a wide berth, even if that means taking a longer route. But as well educated as my sister is, I know there are many things out here she won't recognize. Even someone born and raised here wouldn't know all of the things that lurk in the jungle. And we are deep in the thick of it, far from even the dubious safety of the smaller villages. We're trespassing in the home of plants that don't have names. Now I'm thinking of all the stories I've heard, ones that used to frighten me sleepless when I was a child. Brain-rot fungus and Medusan Man-Eaters. Carnivorous plants. Sentient ones. The stories are endless, and I don't think anyone knows for sure whether or not they're true. I don't want to find out.

It would be foolish to imagine we get through this completely unscathed. All we can do is hope that the dangers we encounter are the kind we can survive.

At one point, there is a loud *pop* in the distance, and all of us stop short. Shey turns toward the noise with wide and hopeful eyes, while I instinctively tense and crouch, and Lyre darts behind a tree for cover. No sound follows but the continued whispering of the jungle and the buzz of insects.

"Probably just a blood-boiler pod," I say, wiping my forehead with the back of one hand. Only afterward do I realize that's a mistake—if I've touched anything that will cause a reaction, I've just spread it—but it's pointless to worry about. "It's hot enough for them to explode."

Judging from the look on Shey's face, she's heard the stories. "Aren't those dangerous?" she asks.

"They're the least of our concerns out here," I tell her gravely, and continue forward. She follows a little more closely than before.

Soon enough, we hear the rushing sound of the river, and after hacking through a tangle of bushes with thorns that tear open my hands, we emerge onto the bank of it.

"Thank the stars," Lyre says, rushing to the edge and crouching down. She pauses, eyeing it and likely wondering if it's safe. But the plants around it are lush and healthy, and the stream is heading toward the city rather than away, which makes contamination from people unlikely, so she quickly decides it's safe enough to splash on her face.

I test it with a strip from my kit, just to be certain, and when it comes up clear, we all refill our water bottles from the stream. The air is cooler near the river, and we can see the sun; it's easier to breathe without the trees creeping in from every direction. Still, there is no sign of the city or any villages on the horizon, just endless jungle stretching out on both sides of the river.

"Let's keep walking," I say. "I don't want to sleep out here, if we can help it."

But further hours of travel soon render us exhausted and stumbling. A light rain begins to fall, making the rocks along the river slippery and dangerous, and thickening the mud that makes every step a chore. My bad leg aches and threatens to give out, and though I can tell the two women are suffering under the weight of their kits, I can't offer to take them without making myself lag behind. I fight it for as long as I can, and Shey and Lyre keep plodding along determinedly even as their steps slow further and further, but eventually I come to a stop.

"We'll have to make camp for the night," I say. The two of them look back at me, dismay evident on their faces. "I know it's not what we hoped for. But if we keep going like this, we're just going to hurt ourselves or make a mistake. And we can't afford that."

At least we're not completely exposed to the elements. Our emergency kits contain inflatable tents. It's tempting to cram into one for safety, but I know the Devan heat would make that unbearable, so we each set up our own clustered closely together on the most level ground we can find.

"I'll take first watch," I say. "We won't stay here the full night. Just long enough to get our energy."

225

They're too tired to make any complaints. We eat a cold meal of dried rations, and they crawl into their tents. I listen to the quiet for any signs of danger, but there are only the same hushed sounds we've been hearing all day, so I walk down to the stream and cup water in my hands to wash the sweat off of my face and neck. I settle again in a spot with a good view of the river. If someone wants to sneak up on us, they'll come from there; the foliage is too thick for anyone to make their way to us silently through the trees.

Only then, alone with the jungle and my thoughts, do I allow my mind to wander to the others. My siblings. Izra. Daniil. Orion. My family, my crew. We left them behind. We had to—for everyone's sake—but that doesn't stop guilt from tearing at me. Did any of them survive the crash? And even if they did, will they be able to survive the jungle long enough for help to reach them?

I will keep pushing forward for as long as I have to. But when it's done, when it's over, and I'm left with my choices and their consequences...I can only pray that I won't be the only survivor once again.

CHAPTER TWENTY-SEVEN

The Damaged
and the Dead

Scorpia

Pain. The wail of the alarm. The smell of smoke.

I come to with a groan, every part of my body throbbing, my throat raw. Flashes of memory reach me: the ship shaking like it was going to come apart, being thrown around in my launch chair like a rag doll, an intense pressure in my head as we rocketed toward the surface. And then...

I force my eyes open. The room is hazy through the smoke. I cough, my hands slow and numb as they fumble to release the straps. Once I'm free, I stumble forward and fall to my knees. The ship is tilted, and my mind reels as it tries to reorient itself. I barely suppress the urge to vomit. I feel like I'm about to pass out, my head spinning and my body battered, but I force myself up to my feet. The more I fight off the dizziness and pain, the more panic takes its place. My ship. My crew. My siblings.

Orion.

I stumble down the hallway toward the cockpit, heedless of the smoke clogging the air and my own injuries. Orion. I have to get to Orion. I have to make sure he's okay. But just as I reach the doorway, Drom steps out from the cockpit and into my path, blocking me off. There's a gash on her forehead, crusted with dried blood, but it doesn't look bad. I let out a sob of relief at seeing her alive, clutching at her arm, before trying to move past her. She plants herself in front of me.

"No," she says.

"Get out of my way," I say, trying to shove my way through, but she stands immovable. "I need to get in there, I need to—"

"No," she says, again, and I realize that despite her stubborn stance, the look on her face is one of despair. "You don't need to see that."

I know what that means. I know, deep down, but I have to see for myself before I'll believe it. "I'm the fucking captain. Get out of my way." I try again to push past her—and get just an inch of space, enough to see a sliver of the cockpit, the shattered viewing panel, and glass, and blood—and then she scoops me off of my feet and carries me back down the hallway while I struggle. "Drom, you asshole, put me down! Just let me—"

"He's dead," she says bluntly. "There's nothing you can do. You don't need to see it."

I fight her still, clawing and struggling in an attempt to break free, not even sure why—other than the need to fight *something* to release the swelling, wild wave of grief growing inside of me. "No." It comes out more of a whimper than a word. "No, no, no."

She carries me out, through the emergency escape hatch. A couple of the others have started to gather outside in the flattened space where *Memoria* tore through the trees. Pol is there, looking rattled but relatively unharmed, and Daniil, bruised but intact. I hold myself together just long enough to verify they're okay before sinking down to my knees on the muddy ground, sucking in a deep, shaky breath. "Izra?" I ask, turning to look back at Drom, terrified of the answer but needing to know.

"I haven't found her yet," Drom says. "That area of the ship is…" She shakes her head. "I haven't found her yet," she says, again, smaller this time.

"Shey, Lyre, and Corvus took the escape pod." I want to shut my eyes and turn away as I say it, but I force myself to keep looking at them, watch it sink in that I chose for them to be safe. I want to say more, to explain myself, but I know it would only come out hollow. Either they'll understand, or they won't.

"And Orion?" Daniil asks, his voice hoarse from the smoke.

Drom just shakes her head. I suck in another deep breath in an attempt to keep from crying, and press my palms to my eyes.

"I'm going back to look for Izra again," Drom says.

"I'll help," Daniil says.

Their footsteps recede, and I stay where I am, covering my eyes, just trying to breathe as my chest feels tighter and tighter. Pol drops to his knees and wraps his arms around me. No empty apologies or comforts or lies, just that. I bury my face in his shoulder and let myself cry, great racking sobs that make it sound like I'm choking for air, and he rubs circles on my back in silence.

A few minutes later, a sound tears through the wreckage to us—a scream of grief and rage. Izra. She wouldn't have let Drom keep her from the cockpit like I did. I feel a sickening rush of emotion—relief that Izra is alive, fresh pain over the loss, fear that she will blame me for it, a deep sadness that I deserve it if she never forgives me. Pol clutches me tighter to him.

Drom joins us a short while later and sinks heavily to the ground, letting out a long breath. "They're burying the body."

I pull myself out of my brother's grasp and struggle to my feet. "I should help."

"No." Drom doesn't move, but the firmness of the word stops me in my tracks. "Let Izra do it."

I want to argue, but again I think of that layer of rage in Izra's scream, and the surge of fear that it was directed at me. I'm so tired that my legs go shaky and make the decision for me, sending me crumpling back to the ground. We sit in silence, what's left of my family. Beside us, *Memoria* burns.

By the time I work up the energy to think about putting out the fire, the clouds send down rain and smother it for us. We huddle near the ship for cover despite the smell of smoke and a more acrid, chemical stink leaking from it. I don't even want to think about the state of the ship. If Lyre was here, I'm sure she'd be cataloging the damage and tallying up the cost of repairs—but thinking that is just a reminder that she's not here, she's out there somewhere, maybe safer than the rest of us but maybe not, and either way I'm going to have to live with my choice to send her away.

Izra and Daniil return, soaked through and filthy. Izra's defunct gun arm looks worse than before, its deadweight making her gait uneven, her pale skin red and inflamed and crusted with blood; the jostling of the crash must have done further damage. I can tell that it's hurting her, but she keeps her jaw set and doesn't make a sound. Doesn't look at me, either, when she joins us. Daniil stands on the edge of the circle, looking lost; he must be thinking of Corvus, and his place here without him. I should say something to him. I should do a lot of things, right now, but I am just so stars-damned tired.

"We should stay with the ship." My voice comes out small and weary, but the silence is complete enough that I know they can all hear me anyway. "Corvus and the others will send help when they reach Zi Vi. We have food and water here, so..." I almost say *We'll be okay*, but it feels like a horrible false promise at the moment, so instead I trail off into nothingness.

"And if they don't reach the city?" Izra asks, still looking down at the ground instead of at me. "Those pods aren't the sturdiest. And the jungle isn't friendly."

I almost shut my eyes at the thought—I can't take any more loss, definitely can't take the thought that I might have sent them to their deaths in trying to save them—but I force myself not to. I made the decisions that got us here. The least I can do is look the consequences in the eye. "If no help comes within a few days, we'll pack what we can and head for the city ourselves."

Izra's mouth twists, and I know she's thinking about what a long shot *that* would be, but at least she refrains from saying it aloud. The others are still silent, shell-shocked, probably. There's no reason we can't move inside the ship for better shelter, but no one seems eager to set a foot inside yet, despite the rain. Instead we settle in the dirt. Daniil and Drom make a brief trip in for our emergency packs. Nobody has an appetite, but we pass around some bottled water. None of our comms are working; we must be too far out from civilization.

It's hard to tell how much time passes. Eventually the exhaustion catches up with us. Pol is the first to doze off beside me, and then Drom on my other side. Daniil falls asleep with his back against a tree. I catch only a few fitful hours of rest. I don't think Izra sleeps at all; every time I wake, she's staring out into the dark trees with a bloodshot eye.

"Scorpia."

When her voice jolts me awake again, the rain has stopped. I sit up, rubbing my eyes, and catch movement and lights in the trees. For one delirious moment I think it's Corvus and the others returning to us.

But as I watch, the lights spread out to surround us, and I think of Izra's earlier words: *The jungle isn't friendly.*

CHAPTER TWENTY-EIGHT

The Tangled Depths

Corvus

The jungle is endless. The heat saps my strength and the constant assault of bugs tests my sanity. The plant growth is less dense along the river, but that only means that moving is possible, not easy. Even so, branches tear at my clothes and sting my skin. Something I brush up against leaves an ugly, red rash all along my left arm, and it itches maddeningly. At some points, we have to wade into the river to avoid particularly nasty-looking patches—such as a clump of dolor-trees, whose touch is painful enough that a handful of Devans commit suicide every year to escape its long-lasting rashes, and a cluster of unidentifiable flowers that release thick tufts of black spores, which we avoid out of caution. But the river leaves us all wet and filthy from the knees down, and hours later we are all still damp and uncomfortable, the humidity making it impossible to dry out.

Soon I've determined I would rather be stranded anywhere but Deva. The middle of Nibiru's ocean, Titan's tundra, Gaia's storm-ravaged surface, or even the deserts of Pax...I'd take any of it above here.

But I keep my misery quiet. Lyre and Shey plod through the jungle thickets with a grim determination that would make any Titan sergeant proud, and I'm not going to be the first one to complain. But midday, when I suggest we make camp for a brief rest, we've barely finished setting up the tents before both of them collapse. I sit outside and keep watch first again. Despite my own exhaustion, the constant rustling of the jungle makes it easy to stay awake. It is impossible to fight the creeping dread that something is out there, watching us.

I try to focus on our situation instead. We have food and water, so we aren't on a dire timeline yet, but still I'm all too aware of the ticking of the clock. The others could need help. We can't reach them—can't even know if they're safe, or alive—until we reach the city.

And then there's the wider system to think of. What kind of welcome will be waiting for us in Zi Vi, and what news of Nibiru, and Pax, and all of the rest have we missed? We're the only ones who know of Ives and her treachery, and stars only know what she's been up to in the time we've already been gone.

Our only hope of survival is to reach the city, so we must press on. But who knows what kind of world will be waiting for us once we get there?

There is an undeniable beauty to the jungle, despite its many dangers. Beautiful arrays of blooming flowers, tree trunks twisting and growing together like works of art, even the weeds like strangle-vines rustling their way through the undergrowth. Deva feels more alive than the other planets, more occupied; the flora here is so diverse and plentiful compared to the sparse worlds like Titan and Gaia, and on Nibiru most of the life exists hidden in the depths beneath the waves. In all of those places, many of the plants are crops transplanted from old Earth. I suspect much of the planets' original life must have been wiped out along with the Primus when the defense systems first triggered, many years ago.

Yet Deva's hearty native plants survived that apocalypse—and thrived, in the absence of any intelligent species to cut them back. No wonder they are so reluctant to give humans a foothold here.

I know thinking in that way ascribes a superstitious level of sentience to the plants... and yet, is it superstition? Even after many trips to Deva, I'm not entirely certain. But I have heard the locals whisper, and I have seen the city folk shudder when they look out at the jungle, and I have witnessed the way certain plants will invade any crack in humanity's defenses like it is a planned attack. In the end, I'm not sure anyone truly knows how intelligent or not the plants may be, and it strikes me as a far more grave mistake to underestimate them than to assume they may be different, and may be more, than the Earth-originated plants we understand.

Lost in my thoughts, I don't watch when I step—and as I put my weight on my bad leg, it crumples out from under me, and the ground under goes, too. A moment later—so fast my mind barely keeps up—I am sliding and stumbling downhill, branches whipping at me, mud slipping beneath my shoes and providing no traction. I desperately grab for something to hold on to, but my hands find only slim branches and vines that snap from under my weight, and something thorny that tears into my skin before I reflexively let go.

I finally come to a stop with a jerk—and a surprising lack of pain. There are stings and bruises catching up with me now that I'm still, but no hard impact, no crunch of bone.

It takes me a few moments for my mind to finally catch up with my body, and I realize I've been caught by—or on?—something. A plant, I think. I can't see much this deep in the jungle and far from the reprieve of the river, with the overgrowth so thick over-head that sunlight barely filters through the leaves. Something vinelike and sinuous stopped my fall, trapping me like a web.

Shey and Lyre are coming down the hill behind me with far less speed and far more grace than I managed, shouting my name. "I'm here," I yell back. My tumble has ruined any chance at hiding ourselves from anyone or anything that might be listening already. "I'm fine. I think. Just...stuck." I admit the last part with no small amount of embarrassment. I try to yank my arm free, but it's fully wrapped up in whatever plant I've collided with; try to move my legs, but they, too, are entangled. Frustration urges me to thrash to free myself, but instead I take a deep breath and try to relax enough to loosen their grip on me. Once the others get here with a light—I can't reach my own pack—it will be much easier to get free.

And then I feel the vines tighten around my legs. The soft rustle of movement is only audible in the near silence.

One tendril winds around my chest. Another climbs my arm. Now that I'm aware of it, I can feel them moving across me, the movement faster than even the notoriously eerie strangle-vines that crawl along the ground. Panic wells in my chest, but I hold it back—just barely. I slowly reach for the knife on my hip, moving as little as possible, but one of the vines is wrapped tightly around my shoulder, preventing me from bending enough. I'm too afraid to try to pull free without better understanding my situation.

"Don't come any closer," I warn the others as they approach, nothing more than silhouettes in the dimness. "I'm...caught on something." No need to make them panic yet. I focus on taking deep breaths to steady my own body's response, though the feeling of one slender vine probing at the side of my neck makes me twitch violently. The other vines tighten their grips in response, and I let out a small, inadvertent grunt.

"Are you hurt?" Shey asks. "I can barely see..."

"Not. Badly." Small words. Shallow breaths. Don't panic. Panic will only make it worse. "Something... holding me. Vines. Tighten when I move." I swallow hard as another vine slithers across my chest, securing the hold of the first. "Lyre?" I ask through gritted teeth, afraid to say much more. She's the smartest of us, and the best acquainted with Deva—if anyone can get me out of this, it will be her.

There's a pause, and then she says, in a small voice, "I might know what it is. I've heard of something like this. Stay as still as you can. Shey, can you shine a light?"

There's the sound of rummaging, while I try to focus on keeping my breathing slow and steady. Then the light clicks on. I stop breathing for a moment as the beam of Shey's flashlight sweeps over me and reveals a horror.

The vines are all over me. Wrapped around my arms, my legs, my torso. I'm lucky to be able to move my hands and my head, but I suspect those, too, will be lost to me soon if we don't do something to prevent it.

Once the initial shock of it fades, I realize the hideous thing I'm wrapped up in isn't the only plant moving here. Down this deep, the entire jungle seems to move, branches and vines snaking away as if trying to hide from the too-bright beam of Shey's light. Whether they're multiple plants, or all part of one huge monstrosity, it's hard to say.

The light skitters back and forth over me, and a moment later, Shey clamps her free hand onto her other wrist to steady it. She sucks in a shaky breath and says, with only the slightest tremble in her voice, "Okay. What now?"

Lyre's face has gone very pale, one hand raised to cover her mouth, though it does little to hide the stark fear in her expression. "I'm thinking," she whispers, lowering the hand.

Something tickles behind my ear, and a moment later a slender tendril of the plant begins to crawl across my neck. Every instinct screams to try to rip myself free, but I know it will only make things worse, so I force myself to stay as still as I can. "Think fast," I say in a low, quiet voice. I wish I could say more, but every word, every breath feels like a risk. I can't even take a deep breath without feeling an uncomfortable pressure in my chest. Soon, very soon, this situation is going to go from bad to dire.

"Okay," Lyre says. "First of all, keep doing what you're doing. Stay still. Not just because of the tightening, but if you snap or cut any of the vines, they'll—" She pauses and swallows. "Well. You don't want to find out."

"How can we free him, then?" Shey asks. "Should we merely wait? Will they release him eventually?"

"There's…a chance." At first I mistake Lyre's hesitation for uncertainty—but as I glance at her face, I suspect it's merely that she's withholding further information. Whatever could happen if I stay trapped here, it's bad enough that she doesn't want me to know the details. "But as you can see, there, if it keeps pulling him backward…"

Shey shifts the light, and they both stare at something I can't see behind me. I try to move only my eyes, but can't see anything. Stars, I hate this. The helplessness is making my skin itch to do something, anything, no matter how foolish. And the urge is getting harder to ignore with each passing second that Lyre doesn't suggest a way to get me out of this. Better to die fighting than to succumb slowly.

Lyre bends down and searches through her bag with increasing desperation. She doesn't have to say anything; her face makes it plain enough that she's not finding anything useful.

"If only we had something of a Primus nature," Shey murmurs. "The plants tend to be repulsed by them. I used to study their interactions…"

"Mmf," I say, too afraid to move enough to produce an actual word, and cut my eyes toward my leg.

Shey's eyes widen. "Right. Your knife." She moves toward me, stepping over a few suspiciously rustling plants on the ground, and very carefully extends her free hand toward the knife. She uses two fingers to remove it from its sheath, her eyes on the dangerously close vines all the while. My heartbeat pounds in my ears; if two of us end up trapped here, it is hard to see a future in which we manage to find our way out.

But Shey evades the vines and slips the knife free. Then, just as carefully, she holds it up to my neck. The vine there twitches—tightening against my skin for one terrifying moment—and then begins to slither away from the blade. I suck in a deep breath, and then another, and nod my head very slightly at Shey. She nods back, grimly, and moves on to the next one, working her way down my arm.

But just when I almost have a limb free to help with the process, the rest of the plant shudders suddenly, and I'm pulled backward. In instinct, I lash out with my nearly free arm to grab on to something, and the vines covering the rest of my body all tighten in response. Lyre reaches forward and grabs my almost-free arm, straining to hold me.

We remain locked in a tug-of-war for a few seconds—and then, finally, as Shey waves the Primus knife near the vines again, the pressure releases. I stumble forward and fall to my knees.

"Well," Lyre says. "Congratulations, Corvus. You escaped a Medusan Man-Eater."

We trek uphill toward the light, struggling not to lose our footing with loose soil and rocks all around. Soon we are all soaked in sweat and coated with grime. My entire body aches, and I feel bruises starting to form on my arms and chest where the vines gripped me most tightly. But there is nothing to do but keep fighting toward the sun. Once we climb back to solid ground, we all stop to breathe and rest.

The plants we encountered down there left me with a crawling, paranoid feeling—and I am still not entirely convinced that either my tumble or that horrible plant didn't leave me with any dangerous residue on my skin. Knowing what's out there, and seeing how little open ground there is near us, another night in the jungle sounds unbearable. We lost our way when I fell, so we will first have to find our way back to the river, and then...

And then I look up, and my breath hitches.

"Lyre," I say, quietly. "Shey."

"Please no more bad news," Shey groans, but she opens her eyes and looks, and so does Lyre once she manages to catch her breath. We all stare upward with the same awe, because it's not just the red light of Nova Vita we were following up that hill.

There—shining through the black leaves of the jungle like a beacon—is the neon glow of the Golden City.

CHAPTER TWENTY-NINE

The Price

Scorpia

My grief, my fear, my worry for the others—none of it matters right now. I push it down, deep down. I know it will just come back worse later, but I need it to be later. Because right now, my crew needs me to be their captain. I climb to my feet—moving slowly, just in case any of our as-of-yet unseen company in the jungle has weapons trained on me—and step forward, putting myself between my crew and the strangers.

"Okay," I say quietly, looking around at them. "Weapons on the ground, hands in the air, everybody. Stay calm. It's probably just some villagers, but we don't want to give them any signs that we're hostile."

Pol and Daniil surrender their weapons to the ground without a fuss, though Daniil still stands like he's ready for a fight, his eyes never leaving the jungle. Drom grimaces, hesitating for a few moments before she does the same, though she looks none too happy about it. Izra stares me down, her grip on her blaster tightening. I can practically feel the rage simmering off of her skin.

She looks like the pirate she once was, nothing like the woman I've come to know since we liberated her from Ca Sineh. But I know that's not who she is anymore—and it was never all that she was, that seething anger and violence. Beneath this rage is a grief even deeper than my own.

"Izra," I say softly. "The Devans aren't the ones who did this. Killing them isn't gonna make things any better."

"You don't know that," she snaps at me.

"They're just some villagers." I take a step to the side, placing myself directly in front of the barrel of her gun. "Look, if you wanna take this out on someone, take it out on me. But not right now. Not when everyone else is gonna pay the price, too. All right?" She doesn't answer, her arm trembling like she's barely restraining the urge to pull the trigger. But I reach out, grab the barrel of the gun, and lower it toward the ground. After a moment, she lets out a growl under her breath and drops the weapon.

"This isn't over," she says, her voice low enough that only I can hear.

Once, the way she's looking at me now would have terrified me. This whole ordeal would have. But I'm surprised to find that even when I was standing in front of her gun with her finger on the trigger, I never once felt truly afraid. Just deeply, terribly sad. "I know," I say. I want to tell her more, but now's not the time. Instead I turn back to face the trees and take a few careful steps forward with my hands above my head. "We're unarmed and friendly," I call out. "Just some off-worlders looking for help getting to Zi Vi."

There's a rustling quiet, and then a few figures emerge from the darkness. I can tell at a glance that they're indeed villagers, their faces roughened by sun and hard lives, their outfits plain and simple clothes rather than the outrageous fashions of the Golden City. Of course, they're also toting some pretty big guns. Aside from one, who seems to be wielding a flamethrower instead. That utterly baffles me until I realize it must be a tool used to fight back the jungle... but it still seems like it would do a pretty good job of roasting us, too, so I raise my hands a little higher.

"Hi," I say, my voice squeaking with nerves. Usually Devans offer touchy, friendly greetings even to strangers, but I'm not going to try to hug anyone pointing a weapon in my direction. "Just some merchants, here to pick up a food shipment for Nibiru. Er, that was the plan, at least, before..." I nod my head toward *Memoria*.

The Devans keep approaching, making no move to lower their weapons. I swallow hard but hold my ground. One man walks up to me and places the barrel of the gun right under my chin, forcing my head up. I hear the others shift behind me, and someone mutters a curse, but the fact I have a gun aimed at my brains must stop them from making any moves.

"Scorpia Kaiser?" the man asks.

Oh no.

"I don't suppose you're a fan?" I ask, forcing a wobbly smile.

The man smiles back. His teeth are black and rotted. "Big fan," he says, "of the price on your head."

At least they want us alive.

I cling to that scrap of good news as the villagers close in on the rest of the crew. I can tell the others want to fight, but even if we weren't grossly outnumbered and there wasn't a man with a blaster pressed to my temple, we're in no state for a brawl right now. We're all exhausted and hurt and grieving, and with Izra's gun arm out of commission and Corvus gone, we're down two of our best fighters. Maybe Drom and Daniil could take out a handful of villagers each, but even if we did manage to fight them off and hole up in the ship, the Devans would probably just come back with a bigger force and seize us. We're far too tempting of a prize to ignore.

So, the others grudgingly follow my lead and surrender to the Devans. They collect our fallen weapons, tie our wrists, and walk us into the jungle.

My chest tightens with every step away from the ship. We're abandoning not only our home and our only way off of this planet—assuming it can be repaired, which I'm forcing myself to believe right now for the sake of my sanity—but our best way of getting back into contact with the others. Now, even if Corvus and the rest successfully make it to Zi Vi and round up help, they'll come back only to find an empty husk. Should I have forced a fight? Hid right away after the crash? I don't know. It would be easy to give in to self-hatred over all of the mistakes I've made, but there's too much danger ahead for me to dwell on the past.

The villagers lead us along a narrow path where the plants have been cleared away. Mostly away, at least, because I still stumble over roots and end up whipped by stray branches that cling to me like fingers. I swear every plant on this damn planet is out to kill humans, or maybe just out to get me in particular, and soon I'm bleeding from a dozen cuts, and itchy from stars-know-what, and sore from tripping at least a half-dozen times.

But it'll take a lot more than a deadly situation and some annoying plants to get me to keep my mouth shut. Especially when my mouth is keeping them distracted from the fact that I'm slowly rotating my wrists and loosening the binds around them. They really did a half-assed job with these.

I talk as we walk, alternating between trying to cut a deal, and begging, and threatening, trying every angle from offering to get them off of the planet to mentioning that I know some very important people in the Interplanetary Alliance. They barely respond to any of it.

As we go farther, I need to save my breath. My body is already battered from the crash, and the sticky heat makes every step harder than it should be. I feel like I'm bathed head to toe in sweat, and my legs are wobbly, threatening to give up. If I fall one more time, I'm not sure I can get up again.

But I'm not the one who falls. When our line comes to a halt, at first I'm weak with relief at the thought of a break, but then I hear the scuffle behind me. I turn to see Pol on his knees in the dirt, his head hanging. A member of our escort jabs him with the barrel of her gun. When he doesn't respond to that, she hits him, hard, across the back with it.

"*Hey.*" I try to move toward them, but the man at my side jerks me to a stop, holding tightly to my arm. Pol's still not getting up. "He's sick. Give him a sec."

The woman hits him again. He falls to the side and stays there.

Drom is straining against two men holding her back. Izra watches the scene unfold, her entire body tense. Daniil looks relaxed enough that the escort at his side is barely looking at him—but he's watching me carefully, just waiting for a signal.

I test the binds on my wrists; they're slack enough for me to slip out of. I can't be the only one who managed to wriggle my way out of some ropes. But I was hoping to make it to the village before we made our move. If we do it now, we'll be stranded in the middle of the Devan jungle, at least an hour from the ship and stars know how far from the village ahead, with no promise we can follow this path either way. Since the villagers know the area and have motivation to keep us alive, we're safer with them than without.

"Let's just rest for a minute," I say. "Please. You want us alive, right? I'm about to collapse myself." I try to sit down, to make a point, but the man at my side jerks me back upright.

"We might have to carry him," the woman says, prodding Pol

with her boot. I can't tell if he's even conscious; he's completely limp in the dirt.

"Someone that size? For another hour and a half?" a man at the head of our caravan asks. "Which one is that?"

Another man pulls out a piece of paper and squints at it. "Apollo Kaiser," he says. "Just a Nibiran kid. He's not worth much."

"Then leave him. He can crawl along behind us if he wants to live."

"Listen, asshole," I say, turning to face the man who's speaking. "We've been awfully cooperative this far, but it's not gonna stay that way if you try to leave any of us behind." I meet his eyes, hoping he can see how very serious I am. "You keep us together, we'll follow along nicely. You don't..." I shrug. "Well, you'll get a front-row seat to a live demonstration of what a couple of Titan soldiers can do to some untrained Devan villagers."

The man eyes me for long enough that I'm just starting to think he believes me, even with all of us unarmed and tied up and apparently at their mercy. Then he scoffs, and says, "I know a bluff when I hear one. Let's move. Leave the kid."

The front of the caravan starts to move. The man at my side drags me forward as my boots scramble for a way to dig into the sludgy mud beneath us. I turn to look over my shoulder—at Izra and Daniil and Drom being unwillingly pulled along, at Pol still lying in the dirt, at the woman striding from his side to catch up with the rest of us—and give the tiniest nod before twisting my hands and slipping free of my bindings.

Daniil slams his forehead into the woman guarding him, with a resounding crack and a howl of pain. Izra turns and throws the weight of her bound arms—dead Primus gun and all—between the legs of the man holding her. I run for Pol. Along the way I kick one of the men gripping Drom in the shins, giving her just enough wiggle room to tackle the other.

Shouting and gunfire erupts all around me, but I stay low and ignore it all, heading straight to my fallen brother.

I drop to my knees beside him and shake his shoulder. "Pol," I say. "C'mon, bud. Get up." It takes a frightening amount of shaking, but finally his eyes flutter open and he rises up with a groan. While I help him to his feet and pull him into the trees for some cover, I look back at how the fight is going, and my heart sinks. The others are giving these villagers hell, taking down many more than I would've thought possible for people who began the fight bound and unarmed—but we're just too outnumbered and outgunned. The villagers already have Drom on her knees with a gun to her head, and Daniil is in a standoff with his one stolen blaster versus three aimed at him. Izra is struggling with the man with the flamethrower, but there's no way that will be enough to turn the tide in our favor. We took them by surprise, but that advantage has run its course, and it wasn't enough. Pol and I joining the fray won't do much, either.

As soon as he regains his bearings and sees what's going on, Pol lurches forward to help, but I grab his arm and pull him back. "Wait," I murmur. My heart is thudding in my ears as I grapple with what to do. If I turn myself in to them, will I spare the others, or will they hurt Pol or someone else they deem worth less as punishment?

Before I can make my decision, one of the men notices me and swings his blaster in my direction. Not at my head, but at my legs, no doubt thinking of the credits I'm worth. I scramble back—not nearly fast enough to outrun laser-fire—but before he can take the shot, a blurred shape barrels his way. Izra takes him down to the dirt, slams her gun arm into his head, and looks up at me.

"Run, you idiot," she snarls.

There's no way to know what these Devans will do if I turn myself over. But I do know one thing: Out of everyone here, I was the one ranked the highest on that list.

"Hey, assholes," I yell, and am rewarded with at least a couple of heads turning in my direction, even though most of them are still engaged in the fight. "If you want your paycheck, you better think fast!"

I bolt into the jungle, dodging roots and branches as I go. Shouts and gunfire come from behind me, and other bodies crash through the jungle. Whether it's my crew or the Devans, I'm not sure. Either way, all I can do is run.

CHAPTER THIRTY

Reaching for Light

Corvus

With our destination in sight, the remaining trek feels easier and yet agonizingly long at once. Most of it is uphill from here, especially due to my tumble, and my whole body aches. But Lyre and Shey charge ahead with renewed vigor, and I grit my teeth and follow, spurred on by our closeness.

The triumph of seeing Zi Vi fades as we grow closer. All of my concerns from before surge back—about what news will be waiting for us, of the rest of our crew, and this planet, and the system beyond—but even before we face all of that, there is a more immediate problem.

"They could turn us away at the gates," I say, when it is no longer possible to stay quiet. Shey and Lyre slow now, looking back at me. Lyre's grim expression says she already knows what I mean. "It may be best if you go on without us, Shey. Lyre and I are wanted criminals. If you have trouble about not being Devan, Lyre can join you."

"He's right," Lyre says. "It will be faster if you go on alone. Then you can send help to the others. We'll find another way in."

"Absolutely not." Shey looks shocked at the mere possibility. "We came this far together. I'm not leaving you here."

"We can handle ourselves," I tell her. "You need to think of everyone else. The Alliance, and the people here—"

"No," Shey says. "It's not up for debate. I never would have made it this far without you, and I'm not leaving you here."

Despite our protests, she refuses to keep moving until we do, and cuts off further attempts to argue. So we all arrive at the gate together. There is a long, winding line of people waiting for the lengthy process of entering the city. People and their belongings are identified, searched, and decontaminated before they're allowed past the city walls. The whole area stinks of chemicals, and a crew with hazmat suits is making another sweep of the perimeter right now, spraying a fresh coat of whatever they use to push back the plants.

I was worried that in our bedraggled, jungle-torn, days-of-travel state we would stick out among the crowd, but a quick glance tells me that isn't the case. We are far from the only ones covered in sweat and mud, with leaves tangled in our filthy hair.

Many people look even worse off than us. There is a couple wearing little more than rags, and a man carrying a small child covered head to toe in horrible, open sores. I overhear another, larger group saying that their village and the local mine were overtaken by an infestation of brain-rot fungus and had to be abandoned; they're carrying only a few packs of supplies between them, since the rest had to be abandoned for fear of bringing the fungus with them.

The sight of the line ahead fills me with dismay. We're so close now that every further wasted minute feels unbearable.

"You're a political figure, right, Shey?" Lyre asks, as we step to the back of the crowd. "I'm sure you could cut to the front."

Yet judging from her expression, she knows, just like I do, exactly what Shey will say to that.

"These people don't need help any less than we do," Shey says. And—catching the look that passes between us—she adds, "Our principles matter more, not less, in situations like this."

"Right," Lyre says, her voice holding a tired and resigned sort of annoyance. "Our principles. That's what's really important, here." She looks as though she wants to say more, but she stops herself, pressing her lips firmly together, and looks away.

I sigh. I have a feeling that if I pressed—guilting Shey with the reminder that the rest of our crew sacrificed a better chance at survival for her to be here—I could convince her, but I don't want to do that. And I'm too tired to argue. I take a seat at the back of the line, stretching out my aching leg. Lyre plops down next to me.

Shey, her jaw set stubbornly, refuses even to join us in that. Instead she rummages through her pack, finds what remains of her emergency food and water, and walks over to the group from the abandoned village to offer it to them. They eye her suspiciously and verify multiple times that she doesn't expect anything in return before accepting it from her, and even then, they keep frowning at her like they suspect she must be up to something. Unperturbed, she returns to us, and I fish into my own bag and hand over the last of my bottled water and nonperishable meals. She takes them without a word and heads on to the next group who seems to be in need, crouching down so she can hand a bottle of water to a teenager huddled up with her legs to her chest. After a moment, she reaches out to accept it, and offers a tentative smile to Shey.

Lyre and I exchange a glance, and I let out a low chuckle.

"She really is something," I say. Scorpia has made many poor choices throughout her life, and at the start of it all, I thought

Shey was one of them. But at this point, I'm starting to think that choosing Shey was one of the wisest things Scorpia's ever done, even with all of the heartbreak it's brought her. I hope they work it out. I'd like Shey to stay in our lives.

"I suppose it's nice that we keep her around," Lyre says. "The rest of us aren't so . . . well . . ."

"Good?" I suggest.

She smiles. "That's one word for it."

"Well. We all do our best." Despite the ache in my bones, I push myself up to my feet, biting back a groan of pain as I put weight on my poor, overworked leg. "You stay here. Hold our spot."

"Happy to be of service," she says dryly.

I grab my first-aid kit from my bag and make my way over to the parents with the suffering child to see if there's anything I can do to help.

"Identification, please."

We've been waiting in line for hours, alternating between resting on the ground and shuffling forward like zombies alongside the others. Shey and Lyre both dozed off a few times, but I can't sleep, even though we trekked halfway through the night and well into the day. I am too tightly wound, my mind running again and again over what comes next. We must get into the city, find transportation, go to the others. And then—then my mind goes blank. My plan only gets me that far. It is too hard to think about all of the possibilities that may come next.

"Sir?"

I jolt back into the present, realizing the bored-looking officer seated by the gate is speaking to me. We're at the front of the line, and I didn't even realize it. I nudge Lyre with my shoe, and she startles, awakening and unfolding from the ground.

"We don't have any identification," Lyre says. "We—"

"No identification, no entry," the man says. "Next."

"Officer." Shey climbs to her feet "My name is Shey Leonis, and I'm a representative of the Interplanetary Alliance—"

"No identification?" the man asks. When there's no answer, he says, flatly, "No entry."

I weigh our options. We're likely hard to recognize in our current state, but showing them our identification might prompt him to realize who we are, and I'm not sure if we can risk that.

Before I can decide, a woman from the group who passed through the gate before us—the villagers who dealt with the brain-rot fungus—comes back, and holds out her comm toward the guard.

"They're with us," she says.

He scowls, and looks like he wants to argue. But then he looks down at her comm, raises his eyebrows, and takes out his own device. He accepts whatever credits she gave him and waves us through.

"Thank you," Shey says, and the woman nods and moves ahead.

Inside, they bring us into the disinfectant showers. There is only one big metal room taking two dozen at a time, and between that and the guards on watch, there is no room for modesty. I strip down and line up with all the rest, and barely have time to shut my eyes and mouth before the showers blast us all with the bitingly cold and acrid disinfectant. Every cut and scrape on my body shrieks in sharp pain, and the rash on my arm burns like it's been plunged in acid. It lasts so long my lungs begin to burn from holding my breath, but I don't dare to move out of the way and incur the anger of the guards and likely another run through the showers. Finally it stops, and I have time to suck in one burning breath, so thick with the chemical stink that I nearly choke on it, before we're blasted again, this time with water.

After that, we're allowed to dry and dress—in a clean jumpsuit provided by the facility, paid for with part of the entry fee, since our old clothes will be burned. You can pay extra to have them disinfected instead, but I didn't bother. I do pay the extra fee for a set of pills to ward off common fungal infections, though, and advise Lyre and Shey to do the same. Stars only know what we were exposed to in that jungle.

When we emerge, my eyes are still stinging from the chemical bath, and it feels as though the smell coats the inside of my nose. I can't even enjoy the sensation of being clean for the first time in days when every inch of my skin feels like it's been scrubbed raw and stretched too tight. Every scrape and cut on my body is still fizzing with pain. I could use a rest, and a warm meal, but there are more pressing matters than comfort. As soon as we step out into the city—truly, the neon lights and busy walkways have never been such a welcome sight to my eyes, even though it instantly induces a dull ache in the back of my head—I turn to the others.

"Let's find our ship," I say.

CHAPTER THIRTY-ONE

Into Darkness

Scorpia

I stumble through the jungle with Pol on my heels, crashing through thick foliage, our pursuers close behind. My lungs are burning, and Pol must be ready to collapse, but he soon overtakes me and forges ahead with a single-minded determination, almost like he knows where he's going.

Then we stumble into a clearing, and a Primus statue looms above us. The trees grow around and above it, thickly enough that hardly any light reaches us, but around the statue's base is a ring of empty ground where nothing appears to grow.

Pol walks forward, as if in a trance, and presses his palms against its surface. I stop in my tracks, stunned with a mixture of relief and the memory of one of those statues, warm beneath my hand on Gaia, while the winds tore the planet apart. Was Pol drawn here because the same thing is happening on Deva? Did something trip the Devan defense system and ruin another one of our system's dwindling worlds? Maybe a Paxian attack we don't know about, or...

A terrifying thought strikes me for the first time: What about our ship, careening down onto the planet's surface? Is it possible the alien defense system would mistake that for an enemy assaulting the planet? Did we doom Deva by coming here?

I swallow thickly and force myself to move forward, creeping closer to the statue and my still-silent brother. "Pol," I say in a low whisper. "Is it...?" But I can't bring myself to finish the question, and he doesn't answer. I step forward, slowly reaching out and swallowing my fear. I place one hand on the statue's surface.

Cold.

I breathe a sigh of relief, and yank my hand back. Thank the stars it's not activated, but that doesn't mean I'm any more eager to touch the thing. The way I see it, these Devan plants are the smart ones, giving this alien relic a wide berth.

But the statue gives me an idea. One of the bad ones, an idea I know from the start is something I'm probably going to end up regretting—and if even I can recognize that, it's really bad news. But we don't have a whole lot of options right now, with the shouts of the villagers still coming toward us.

I search around at the base of the statue, quickly ending up covered in leaves and mud and stars know what else. Pol, finally seeming to jerk himself out of whatever trance he was in, blinks and looks down at me.

"What are you doing?"

"Tunnels," I say, without pausing. "Shey said the Primus built the tunnels on Gaia. Underneath the surface. If this place has statues, too, then maybe there's a way down."

Pol looks skeptical, but out in the jungle, the voices are getting closer. He crouches down and helps me search.

After another couple minutes, it sounds like the villagers are practically on top of us, and my search has proved futile. "You see anything?" I ask Pol, wiping a grimy hand across my forehead.

"Just a lot of mud and rocks."

"Yeah. Same. It's...wait." I pause, looking around with fresh eyes as I think back to the tunnels on Gaia again. I remember walking into that huge cavern that looked like nothing more than another cave, and realizing it was an alien database with the system's biggest secret instead. And Shey accessed it with... "Rocks. The rocks." I see one near the base and drop to my knees next to it, fumbling around to see if I can feel anything. Pol stares at me like I've lost it, but after a few seconds, my fingers find purchase on the sides, and with a small click, the top comes off.

My triumph is quickly squashed by the thought of what comes next. But there's no turning back now. I gulp back my disgust, shut my eyes, and shove a hand inside. It sinks into something soft and pliable and gooey, all the way up to my elbow. I gag, nearly wrenching back in instinctive disgust.

Open, I think, not sure what else to do. *Open, open, open*—

There is a flash. A sensation like something is slithering across my brain.

I come to with a gasp. Pol is gripping my shoulders and staring at me in absolute horror. "Scorpia, what the *hell*?" he asks, not releasing his hold on me. "They're almost here, and your face just went all scary, and—"

"No time," I say, standing up. "I *think* I opened an entrance. It should be somewhere right about..." I take a step, and the earth crumbles beneath my feet. Pol lurches forward to grab me as I slide, and instead we both go tumbling down, down, into darkness, too fast for either of us to even scream.

We land in a pile of limbs, dirt and leaves and rocks tumbling down on us. At least the mud provides a reasonably soft landing. I spit out a mouthful of dirt and scramble to my feet, slipping on the wet ground, and turn to look back at the sloped tunnel. Distantly,

I can still see a glimmer of sunlight, and hear faint voices echoing down.

Judging from the state of the tunnel, we're not going to be climbing back up it anytime soon. The one on Gaia was excavated by humans so we could travel it easily, but this is all earth and rock, and has the stale stink of a place that hasn't been aired out in quite a while. Getting out is going to be a problem...but one for later. With the amount of issues life is throwing at us right now, the best I can hope for is dealing with one at a time.

And knowing the Devans' distrust of Primus technology, I'm hoping we don't have to worry about them following us down here without knowing what's waiting. I turn around, scoping out the rest of the area we've landed in, but there's not much to see. It's just a simple, muddy cave, with a tunnel continuing on a downward slope.

"I guess we know where we're going, then," I say, and turn to Pol, only to realize he's still on the ground. "Hey, you okay?" He's trembling, wide-eyed. I crouch down next to him. "Are you hurt?" I look him over, but it's hard to tell when just about every inch of both of us is covered in mud. "C'mon, bud," I whisper. "Please don't freak out on me right now."

He takes a shuddering breath and finally meets my eyes. "This place...feels..." He swallows hard. "I don't like it here."

Shit. He's freaking out. And I'm not sure how to deal with it, especially not when it's just the two of us and we're trapped underground. "Okay," I say, taking one of his hands between both of mine. "I know this is hard, and scary as hell, and you have all kinds of shit going on right now that I can't begin to understand...but can you please do your best to hold it together, just for a little while?" I look into his eyes. "I need you with me right now."

He stares at me, and slowly his shakes subside. He swallows

hard, again, and nods. I let go of him and stand, and he takes my hand to get up as well. "Farther down?" he asks, looking into the tunnel, and his voice cracks.

I follow his gaze into the darkness, and bite back my own fear. I've got to be the strong one right now, even though this place is creeping me out even worse than the ones on Gaia. At least they had the touch of a human hand. This feels…different. Ancient. "Trust me, I'm not too happy about it, either," I say. Especially since we have no flashlights or fancy Gaian suits to keep us safe. "But it's the only way to go."

It feels like we've been walking downward forever. I don't even want to guess how deep beneath the surface we are. And I don't want to think about how much farther we have to go, especially when thirst is starting to set in. Did we really go through all of this and escape those villagers only to wander to our deaths down here?

At least we don't have to worry about the darkness. Just like the tunnels back on Gaia, these ones light up with patterns of blue and green moss growing along the walls. I stay close to the middle of the tunnel to avoid getting near them—this one is quite a bit narrower than I remember the Gaian tunnels being. But despite my warnings, Pol seems enamored by the glowing swirls, trailing his fingers along the side of the tunnel as we walk. I might make more of a fuss about it, but right now I'm just happy it seems like he's shaken off the panic that gripped him before.

Unfortunately, that panic is setting in for me, now. This place is making my skin crawl. I try to distract myself by talking. "These are just like the ones back on Gaia," I say. "Guess the Gaians weren't as special as they thought, with their Primus relics. They were just easier to find there."

And, sure enough, the tunnel soon opens into a familiar-looking cave. When I look closely at the walls, I realize it's the same membranous material from the database room in the tunnels on Gaia—*not* rock, which I first thought it was back there. Not gonna get tricked again.

"This must be another alien database," I say, looking around. "Like the one where we discovered the Planetary Defense Systems." If Shey or Lyre were here right now, they'd be having a field day. But finding anything useful last time took days of our crew's most brilliant minds at work, so I really doubt Pol and I are gonna be able to even figure out how to access it. "We should probably not touch anything in here," I say, turning in a full circle to look around at the room. "Just in case. I mean, it's probably been like a thousand years since anyone touched this stuff, and we've got no idea what we're messing with. The Gaians probably had to do some kind of science bullshit even to use it, right? It's not like anyone could just walk in and..." I pause as I complete my circle just in time to see Pol plunging his hand into one of the fake rocks. A violent shudder goes through his entire body, and then his face goes slack.

And all around us, the cavern rumbles like it's about to come crashing down.

I fall on my ass and scramble back, nearly brushing against the creepy, fleshy walls that are pulsing with alien runes now. But the tunnel doesn't collapse.

I remember watching Shey and Lyre struggle with the alien database back on Gaia, spending grueling hours just to navigate the menu. But Pol manages the technology with disturbing ease. Alien runes flicker across the walls of the cavern at a dizzying speed, but Pol doesn't even seem to be reading them; instead, his eyes appear focused on something in the distance, twitching rapidly back and forth. They look almost black in the dim light. His forehead is creased—not with concern, but with thoughtfulness.

I extend one hand toward him, struck with the instinct to pull him away; alien tech has rarely meant good things for us in the past. But I stop myself. As creepy as this is, if he can really use this thing effectively, maybe he can help us find a way out of here.

"Pol." My voice comes out as a whisper, and he doesn't react. I swallow hard and try again. "Pol. Can you find a way to escape on there?"

He doesn't respond for a few seconds. Just when I'm bracing myself to give in and yank him free from the alien device, consequences be damned, he mutters, "Escape..."

The pattern on the walls shifts in a wave, their dim blue coloring turning to violet instead.

And after a few moments, a hologram unfolds in the center of the room: a huge orb, slowly rotating.

When I look at Pol again, he's smiling, his eyes fixed on the hologram now. "Wow."

It's not the escape route I was hoping for, but I can't fight my curiosity. I take a closer look at the hologram, and realize it's a planet. But not one of the ones I recognize. It looks most similar to Gaia, but it's not. I mean, I'm no geography expert, but the land masses are definitely off. And when Pol does something that makes it zoom in, I see that it's covered with foliage more lush than anything Gaia has ever been able to boast. And all of it is *green*, not black. "What is this place?"

"It doesn't have a name," Pol says, his voice distant.

It takes me a second to process that. "It's not in our system," I say, questioningly, and then take it a step further. "It's...somewhere new? Somewhere the Primus discovered?" And it's surrounded by the same red glow we saw around the planets other than Pax, back in the tunnels on Gaia. All of the planets they settled. The ones they found... "Habitable," I murmur, looking up at the mystery planet. As it sinks in, I slowly lower myself to the ground, staring up at it. But more than an answer, all that raises is more questions, each of them more alarming than the last. *Escape*, I told Pol to look for. I meant escape from here, but what if he found something that they intended to be an escape from the whole system when it turned hostile? I tear my eyes away to look at Pol. "Did they... did they make it there?"

"I don't know," he says, seemingly unable to take his eyes off of the image. "But they wanted to."

If they knew this was out there, and enough of their civilization survived the initial triggering of the Planetary Defense Systems, it's possible they did. I imagine a bunch of the aliens down here, huddled around this very image, while the apocalypse of their own making howled aboveground and tore apart everything they had built. It would've been a ray of hope amid complete devastation. I'd find the mental image a little heartwarming, if not for the fact it involves the slimy Primus bastards. My favorite thing about them has always been that they're long-dead enough that I never have to worry about meeting one.

Except... this could be evidence that they're maybe not so dead, after all. This planet's discovery would've happened thousands of years ago, or whenever the fuck they were still sliming around in Nova Vita; I don't know, I've never been in a history class. If even a few of them managed to make it to this new planet, then they could have a whole other civilization over in this new system. They could come back one day, to find out what happened to the worlds they left behind.

The thought makes me want to panic-vomit a little bit, but I squish it down. Anyway, maybe I should worry about my own species first. "How many people know about this, d'you think?" I ask, again looking at Pol, though I'm mostly just thinking aloud. The Gaians knew about the Planetary Defense System for a long time before we discovered it, and so did Altair and some of the others on Titan. I'm not gonna be so arrogant as to assume we're the first people to stumble upon such vital information this time.

But would Altair have really risked launching his people into another war if he knew there was a potentially habitable planet out there for them? Would Leonis have taken this secret to the grave knowing it would doom her people to live as refugees on Nibiru? Both hard to believe. Especially the latter, actually...The Gaians have always been all about the tentacle bullshit; there's no way they wouldn't have tried to make contact if they knew there was a possibility that the Primus were still out there. But someone had to have considered the possibility, right?

Ugh, this is all making my head hurt. I wish Shey was here to work it out. Or Lyre, or Corvus, or...pretty much anyone aside from Pol and me, who are possibly the worst choices when it comes to putting together planet-sized puzzle pieces to work out huge mysteries like this.

"And here I thought handling the knowledge about the Planetary Defense Systems was a big deal," I murmur. That mysterious new world hangs above us, and I still can't seem to tear my eyes away from it, though I feel it like a weight on my shoulders slowly crushing me down. "Now I guess we gotta think about the fate of the whole human race."

CHAPTER THIRTY-TWO

Wounds and Wreckage

Corvus

S hey brings us to a local government building, where she's able to get in contact with someone who verifies her identity. She has to stay to contact the Interplanetary Alliance about Ives's betrayal, but she's able to arrange a ride in a hovercraft to search for *Memoria* as well.

She can complete her mission. Lyre is safe. Now that my duty to them is over, I can think of nothing but the others I've been trying so hard not to worry about. The only way I can convince myself to attend to anything else—including hydrating and eating, though I know my body desperately needs them—is by telling myself that I won't be able to go on if I don't. But I push away the medic who tries to tend to my wounds and rashes from the plant life. My injuries are all minor. The others are more important.

I insist, too, on riding along in the hovercraft despite my bone-deep exhaustion. Lyre comes along as well, though I try to convince her to stay behind.

"I don't know if you should see whatever we find there," I say, plainly, because I am too tired to come up with a lie.

She places a hand on my arm and squeezes. "I'm not going to let you see it alone."

I can tell it tears at Shey to stay behind, but in reality, we all know she can do more good here. And she needs to, to make this worth it. We were able to find out that Nibiru is still fine, its defense system not triggered yet, but we still need to figure out what Ives is planning.

So Lyre and I ride in the hovercraft together, seated side by side in silence. We're accompanied by a small crew fully geared for the jungle. The craft itself is an advanced thing, its engines powerful enough to skim above the tree line and search the tangled darkness for signs of the crash.

It isn't difficult to find. *Memoria* left a tear through the jungle that is impossible to miss. The moment I see it, and think of our ship skidding across the surface and slamming into trees, bile rises in the back of my throat. Lyre squeezes my arm hard enough to hurt, but I don't try to pry her off.

When the craft lands, and the ramp opens, the silence outside is total. No one comes running to us for rescue.

I hesitate on the threshold. Now I will have to face what I've been avoiding thinking about all of this time. Lyre steps up beside me, and we take the step off of the hovercraft at the same time, ready to face the truth together.

The damage to *Memoria*'s hull and systems is clearly due to the crash, but there are signs of the insides being rifled through as well, and none too gently. The kitchen is left in disarray, every cabinet torn open and plundered. Some of the bedroom doors have been cut through when the locking system resisted entry. In Shey's room, a torn painting and broken Gaian instrument sit

264

beside an overturned and empty crate; in Lyre's room, pamphlets for Zi Vi University lay scattered and trampled on the floor. Scorpia and the rest of the crew never would have done this, even if they had to scrounge for supplies in a hurry. Someone else has been through since they left, picking through the bones of our fallen home.

But that is not the worst of it. A ship, even one that means so much, can always be repaired or replaced. But when I see bloodstains on the launch chair in Drom's room, a low buzz starts to build in my ears. I wander through, room to room, noting against my will whose quarters took the most damage in the crash, which areas are blackened the most by fire. There are no bodies here, but that does not mean anything. Whoever came here since the crash could have cleaned them out just like they did everything else. Or, the survivors of the crash, if there were survivors—there *had* to be survivors—could have buried them.

I go to the cockpit last. One step inside, glass crunching under my boot, and my body comes to a halt of its own accord. I slowly turn, taking in the state of the room. The viewing window has shattered. The control system is torn apart.

There is blood everywhere.

The buzzing in my ears rises to a high-pitched whine that drowns out all else. The blood is dried and brown and flaking, but I know it for what it is, and I know that no one could lose that amount of it and still be alive. Someone died here, in this cockpit, in this chair. I step forward and lay a hand on the back of the pilot's chair, taking deep breaths. Part of me is desperate to look for hints, or a body. The rest of me recoils from the thought with every ounce of my being.

"Scorpia..." The word is just a breath. I don't want to think it, don't want to imagine that she could have put me in that escape pod, and came here, and died. Yet it is impossible to imagine that she would have been anywhere but here. She would've known it was the most dangerous place to be. Maybe Orion was sitting in this pilot's chair, where most of the blood is, but she never would have let him be here alone...and from the extent of the damage here, it is impossible to believe anyone could have survived the crash in this room.

I'm not sure how long I stand there, staring at the broken cockpit, before Lyre comes and places a hand on my shoulder. She doesn't say anything; doesn't have to. Her presence here is enough for me to pull myself together, for her sake. But when I collect myself and turn to her, more bad news is written all over her face.

"Tell me," I say.

"They found signs of disturbed earth nearby." Her voice is clipped and almost clinical, the emotions hammered down in a way I recognize because I do it, too, when things are too terrible to bear. "A mound where...something...has been buried, recently."

"A grave," I clarify. She nods, her mouth pressed into a thin line.

"Just big enough for one body, they think."

Just one. When I was a soldier, that news often came as a relief. *Just one.* One was always far less terrible than it could have been. But now, even the thought of losing one member of our family is too much to bear. I shut my eyes for a moment, tearing myself forcibly away from imagining the rest of the crew taking the time to bury someone. All of them gathered around without me there. And who in the grave? Whose face covered with Devan soil and left behind?

But I cannot let myself get bogged down by this. "So the others left. Where would they have gone?"

"They wouldn't have left the ship unless they had to," Lyre says. "It's in bad shape, but still the best shelter the jungle has to offer, and a beacon for help to find them. We didn't take long to get to Zi Vi, so they shouldn't have assumed we had failed in getting there yet. So..."

"No signs of attack," I say, finally turning my back on the awful, bloody cockpit and retracing my steps through the ship with fresh eyes roaming for a hint of the truth. "Someone could have been hurt, prompting them to seek immediate care."

"But taking them on a trek through the jungle would have been foolhardy. Scorpia would never have done that." Lyre pauses, and I know we're both thinking again of that unmarked grave and the unknown body within. "None of them would have done it," she corrects, though she sounds guilty for it.

"Unless they knew for certain that there was a village they could reach," I say. I head out onto the ramp and stare at the dark jungle around us. "Would Orion have known the area?"

Lyre anxiously twines her fingers together at the mention of his name. She shakes her head. "He never lived outside of Zi Vi."

"Well, there's nothing else here that would indicate a village nearby. So..."

"Someone came here," Lyre says, following my train of thought. She stops beside me, hands still twisted together in front of her. "It's the most likely scenario. I agree. It explains why the ship is so thoroughly cleared out, too. The crew never could have carried all of it, not by themselves."

I nod. "I'll ask the Devans to take us to the closest village."

As it turns out, we don't need to. When we get back to the hovercraft, we discover that the Devans have already received word of a nearby village trying to sell a group of off-worlders to collect an IA bounty. In a rare stroke of luck for us, they contacted the same agency that Shey is now working with.

We return to Zi Vi to meet them. The moment the hovercraft ramp opens, I break into a run. Lyre follows me, leaving Shey to apologize to the officials outside as we rush past. In the lobby of the government building, wrapped in blankets and still damp from the disinfectant showers, I find them. Some of them, at least. Daniil lets out a shout when he sees me. He crashes into me with a hug so unabashedly eager he almost takes me off of my feet. I embrace him without restraint, one hand gripping the back of his neck, my forehead pressed to his, but the moment of elation doesn't last long. I've already seen Izra and Drom seated beside him—and the fact that it is *only* them. No sign of Scorpia. Pol. Orion. I think again of the blood in the cockpit and on one of the launch chairs, the grave outside of the ship.

Daniil releases me as the others rise. Drom clasps my arm, but I yank her into a hug anyway, and she crumples against me like it stole the last of her strength. Her breath shudders out of her, and then she says, "I'm sorry."

"Don't. Don't apologize." I don't even need to hear what happened to know that there's no way I'm letting her shoulder the burden of it.

"You don't understand." She pulls back, though she still grips my arms like she needs them to stay upright. "Scorpia and Pol—" Her breath hitches again, and my heart seizes for a moment, fearing the next words out of her mouth. "They...escaped. We helped them run off. The villagers—We thought they would be safer out there, but now..."

She's not making much sense, but all I can process is the fact that they're alive. At least, they were the last time she saw them, and that means I can hold on to hope. Especially since they were together. They can take care of one another, like all of us do.

That also means I know who was in that grave. Whose blood was splattered all over that cockpit. Scorpia never could have survived the wreckage of that room. If she survived the crash, she wasn't there—which means Orion must have done it alone. And

Scorpia never would have let that happen easily. He must have made the choice, and he would've known exactly what it meant.

I pull away from Drom—conveying my understanding and my gratitude with a nod—and turn to Izra. She looks at me, her expression closed off and her shoulders tense. I don't know what to do or to say; I never have, with most people, but Izra especially confounds me. And she has just lost family. The last remaining piece of her old crew, gone. The relationship between the two of them was always bewildering from an outsider's perspective, but I still remember the way she hugged him when he came back to us. I cannot imagine the scope of her grief, let alone think of any way to ease it.

Not with her, or with Lyre. When Izra finally looks away, I turn to my sister. She's still standing near the doorway, yet to embrace anyone. I wonder if she suspected the truth the moment she saw them. Now, she has a hand pressed to her mouth and her eyes shut.

"Lyre..." Before I can get out more than her name, she opens her eyes, takes a deep breath, and looks at Izra.

"I'm guessing you're the one who buried him?" Izra meets her eyes and nods. "Good. Thank you. That's proper, for Devans. We'll have to go back to the crash site at some point and plant something over...over his grave." She swallows hard. "And someone should send word to his father, I suppose. And—" She stops again as her voice trembles, and she shakes her head. "Oh, but I'm being ridiculous. Of course the priority right now is finding Scorpia and Pol. We should alert city officials, go back to the ship in the morning in case they go there, and..."

"Lyre." I cut her off gently, before she can wind herself up any further. She looks through me rather than at me, valiantly fighting tears. I reach out to touch her shoulder, and she shuts her eyes; a few tears squeeze out at the corners. "Get some rest," I tell her. "I'll handle this."

For half a moment I think she's going to lurch into my arms, like she might've as a child—but instead she pulls herself together, nods briskly.

"I'll walk with you to the hotel," Shey says, and slips an arm into hers as they leave the room together.

"Guess I'll go, too." Drom's eyes are watery, as well, and she refuses to look anyone in the face as she rushes out. Daniil also heads for the door, pausing only to brush his knuckles against my arm and tilt his head subtly in Izra's direction.

Leaving only me, and her, and the inescapable specter of her grief.

"I'm...sorry." What worthless words. Embarrassingly lacking. "I know what he was to you. And that nothing can replace that. But...you have us. You have me." There is so much I want to say—have been wanting to say even before this—but my tongue is clumsy at the best of times, and it has never felt as worthless as now. "Tell me what I can do, Izra."

"You want to help?" Her voice is low and raw. I can hear the ache in it, but the look she gives me is all sharpness and rage. "Then give me revenge."

Sometimes I think I am rid of my violence. That the anger in me has finally died. At moments like this, I am glad to be proven wrong.

"I will," I promise. "I will."

CHAPTER THIRTY-THREE

Onward and Downward

Scorpia

'm not so keen on sleeping belowground in the creepy Primus tunnels. Very much the opposite of keen. Just the mere thought of it makes me want to throw up a little bit, in fact. But when I ask Pol, "Your creepy sixth sense showing you a way out of this tunnel?" he only blinks at me, and I'm too tired to think of any other ideas. We wander for a short while longer, while I search in vain for a hint of the natural red light of Nova Vita or a place where the path seems to go up rather than down, but we only seem to be walking farther down into this dark, creepy, alien hole.

Eventually exhaustion wins out. We return to the room where we found the planet, since at least that's the kind of creepy I've been through a couple times already, and curl up on the floor in one corner. All things considered, it's not the worst place to sleep. We're out of Deva's constant rain, and the fact that we're underground eases the unrelenting heat of the planet. No plants or angry villagers to worry about, either. And when I close my eyes, the pale blue and violet of the Primus lights almost looks like the soothing nighttime hues we use on the ship. Despite my uneasiness and the mind-boggling weight of what we found today, I nod off quickly. But I dream of running down a dark tunnel, deeper and deeper beneath the earth, with the sound of something horrible slithering behind me.

I wake with a dry throat and a gnawing hunger in my belly. Pol is still asleep, lying flat on his back. His eyes twitch back and forth behind closed lids, like he's reading something, and he lets out a noise that almost sounds like a half-formed word. I grab his shoulder and shake him awake before he can say or do anything unnerving, and he jolts up, gasping before his eyes focus on me.

"All right, kid," I say. "Today we gotta find a way out of here." There's no way I'm going to die down here in the dark, surrounded by alien bullshit, though I keep that part to myself.

I regret messing around with the alien technology yesterday rather than exploring farther, because I'm feeling terrible today. My body aches, both from sleeping on the stony floor and running through the jungle yesterday. Pol seems even worse off. One side of his face has an ugly bruise, and he keeps scratching at a growing red rash on his arm. But no matter how shit we both feel, there's nothing to do but walk. And walk, and walk. Always downward. I think of all the dirt packed above our heads and the wild jungle above that and how very far we are from any help, and it makes me want to scream. Only Pol's presence helps me keep it down. But when we hit a fork in the path, the indecision renders us completely impotent, and we both sit down to take a break.

But after sitting for a few minutes feeling sorry for myself and even worse for Pol, a thought finally occurs to me. "Wait," I say, looking at my brother where he's huddled in the corner. "You found that statue in the jungle. Did you...like...sense it?"

"No, I heard it," he says, a little sullenly, as if the distinction is important.

"Okay," I say. "Right. You heard it. Can you still hear it?"

He shuts his eyes, considers, and nods.

And if the tunnels are beneath the statues... it's possible they *connect* the statues, beneath the ground. Which means if he could lead us to another one, it might mean a way out. "Do you hear any other statues, besides the one we were at before?"

He opens his eyes to look at me. "I don't know. I usually don't try to do it, it just happens."

"Well, try. Please." I resist the urge to say more, afraid of stressing him out if I heap too much on him. He nods, and shuts his eyes.

He's silent for a long time, sometimes tilting his head in one direction or another. I shove my hands under my armpits and bite the inside of my cheek to subdue all of my nervous tics. The tunnels branching out around us are completely silent except for a quiet, far-off sound of something dripping. Slowly, Pol's head turns toward the tunnel on our left, and he opens his eyes and stares down it uneasily, like he's expecting something to jump out at us.

"That way?" I ask. "You hear a statue that way?"

"I hear... something," he says haltingly.

I don't like his tone, but this is the only chance we've got at the moment. I stand up, brushing dirt off of my already mud-caked clothes, and force a smile. "Well, all right then," I say. "Nothing to lose at this point, right?" I hold out a hand and help him up. When I set off down the tunnel, I pretend not to notice how hesitant he is to follow me, or how he keeps turning his head to look back over his shoulder.

We have to stop three times for Pol to rest. I'm not faring too well, myself, hunger and thirst and exhaustion dragging at my feet. I can only imagine how he must be feeling, between his already-weakened body and the beating he received yesterday. Each time, the rest gets a little longer, and it gets harder for me to justify staying with him rather than going to scope out what lies ahead, even if that means braving the eerie tunnels alone. But each time, he drags himself to his feet again and continues onward. Our raspy breathing echoes back at us from the glowing walls, and the darkness stretches longer and longer behind us.

It must be hours before Pol finally breaks the silence to speak up, his voice hoarse and dry. "We're almost there."

I stop, teetering in sudden reluctance to move forward, even though I know only death waits behind us. "To what?"

"Heartbeat," Pol says. He continues plodding onward, placing one foot in front of the other in grim determination.

I open my mouth, shut it again, and follow. There's nothing else to do but sit down and wait to die.

The tunnel widens. And widens, and widens, and widens, until it becomes a space much bigger than any of the caverns we've found before, either here or on Gaia. I stop and stare around in awe of the vast, quiet space.

But something else catches my attention quickly.

"Is that what I think it is?" I ask, stepping forward and toward the main object this room holds. It's strangely shaped, and bulbous, all rounded edges rather than familiar corners and angles, but... "Holy shit, Pol, I think you found an alien *ship*."

The realization sends a strange mixture of fear and thrill through me. A strangled laugh escapes my throat. Stars above, fate sure has a twisted fucking sense of humor handing me this: a new ship, but only in the form of what I hate and fear the most.

While this isn't exactly what I was hoping to find, it's still far from a dead end. If the Primus were keeping a ship down here, that means they had to have a way to fly it out. I start exploring the perimeter of the cavern, probing at the walls and rocks with cautious fingers. Pol wanders around the ship instead, staring at it with unabashed awe.

"Can I get this instead of the Primus gun?" he asks, turning to look at me.

"What? No. Definitely no. And don't touch it."

"But I found it," he says, petulant.

"Yeah, yeah, we'll work something out later. Let's focus on surviving for the moment, okay?" I bend down and strain to unscrew the top of what looks like the hidden access point we used to get here. After an embarrassingly long amount of vain struggle, I conclude that it is, in fact, just a rock. "Help me look, would you?" I ask, wiping sweat off of my forehead.

No response.

I turn around, and find that a hole has opened up in the side of the alien ship, and Pol is nowhere to be found. Because of course. I let out a long sigh, too tired to be angry. "Come on, don't mess around in there," I call out, and force myself to inch toward the ship despite my intense reluctance to get any nearer to it than necessary. "Unless your creepy sixth sense knows how to turn it on and fly us out of here, in which case, by all means, carry on."

"Actually..."

I stop a foot away from the opening Pol found, swallowing compulsively as I catch a glimpse of the horribly glistening, even more horribly *moving* interior of the ship. The closer I get, the more I become certain that what Pol described as a "heartbeat" isn't only some feature of alien design... This thing is no machine; it's alive. And my idiot baby brother, of course, decided the best course of action was to walk right in and make himself at home. Only after a few seconds of processing that horror do I realize what Pol just said, or what the following silence might mean. "Wait, no, I was joking! Do *not* turn that thing on, Pol!"

The ship shivers, and releases a sound like someone exhaling. Then comes another noise: a soft but swiftly growing buzz, like something charging up.

I hover anxiously outside of the entrance, torn between my need to reach Pol and my absolute revulsion at the thought of stepping inside the ship. We don't know what this thing is for. It could be a weapon we're about to unknowingly unleash on Deva, it could be primed to self-destruct in unauthorized hands, it could be... a lot of things, really, but no matter how many possibilities I run through, I realize there's not a single future in which I'd rather be safe out here than facing imminent danger at my brother's side. I take a deep breath, squeeze my eyes shut, and fling myself forward into the creepiest stars-damned ship I've ever seen in my life.

The floor I land on is wet and spongy and pulsing with the heartbeat like the rest of the ship, and holy shit, this is the worst thing I've ever had to do. I braced my hands on the floor to catch my fall, but now I recoil, and as I pull away, there's a horrible slurping noise and a sticky substance stretches between my skin and the floor. I gag, fling myself backward, and hit a just as fleshy and wet wall that now exists where the door used to be. I'm trapped. Inside the horrifying living ship.

"Pol, I am going to *kill* you," I scream, my voice coming out high-pitched and panicky. I lurch toward the front of the ship, where my brain tells me the cockpit should be, but there's only a solid wall there. I back away from it, shuddering, and turn to see a hole open on the opposite wall. I stumble toward it.

Pol is inside, in a chamber with some *thing* suspended by shivering, fleshy cords. Pol's hands are wrapped around it, and the cords are wrapped around him, and the pulsing heartbeat moving through the ship is eerily in tune with his breathing.

"My turn to be the hero," he says. "*And* the pilot."

And the ship begins to rise.

CHAPTER THIRTY-FOUR

A Call to Duty

Corvus

S hey arranges for us to stay at a local hotel. I'm not sure how she manages all of this, considering that most of us are wanted criminals, but I'm too tired to question it. And as I emerge in the morning from a much-needed night's rest, I find a new, and unexpected, stroke of luck. While I was sleeping, I received several worried messages from Eridanus and Halon on my comm. They received Scorpia's transmission, and they're here on Deva offering their help.

I don't have much trust for the arms dealers, but I can't deny I'm grateful for a way off-planet if we need it. If only we were all here, it would be a simple decision.

But when I head into Lyre's room, where the others are all already gathered, the grim mood tells me this isn't the only news the morning's brought. Before I can ask, I turn my attention to the screen they're gathered around, and see the Devan newscast: *Titans make deal with Pax.* An image of Ives on the screen, side by side with a picture of some Paxian tech executive, immediately fills me with a cold fury.

"No," I murmur, rage and dread rising within me. Of course, we knew her plan didn't end with us, and that she planned to go to the only planet without a defense system. But I didn't think she would move so quickly, or that the Paxians would be so eager to cut a deal with her.

The news shifts to a statement from General Altair. "I condemn the actions of ex-general Ives," he says, emphasizing the *ex*. "She in no way represents the beliefs or wishes of myself, the majority of the survivors of Titan, or the rest of the Interplanetary Alliance. The extremists who follow her are members of a fringe group who have broken away from our agreement. The last thing we want is to be embroiled in another interplanetary conflict while our people heal. But that also means refraining from entering the Devan-Paxian conflict, even to apprehend Ives, and so we will not involve ourselves..."

The message cuts off there, replaced by Devan news anchors who seem only too eager to throw doubt on his words and push a narrative about the IA secretly backing Pax. "So Ives is off making deals with the Paxians," Daniil says, when no one else speaks. He looks back and forth between us. "I don't know much about interplanetary politics. How bad could that be?"

"Bad," Lyre and I say simultaneously. Izra is pacing the room, her expression both seething and pained. Seeing Ives again, out of her reach, must have been like a hot knife against her still-open wound. The woman is responsible for our crash, and Orion's death.

"Deva will see this as an escalation, and a threat," Lyre says. "And with all of the confusion around Ives, they may believe that the IA is turning on them."

This is only fuel on the fire. It will rile up the Devans, risk dragging the IA into the middle of the war. Is that Ives's intent? Does she want to sow chaos, or does she just not know how to live in peace?

Intentionally or not, her actions are already rippling dangerously through the system. Someone needs to stop her. And if the IA's hands are tied while they struggle to refrain from picking a side in the conflict...

"She'll fuck everything," Izra snarls. She finally stops pacing, and her hands twitch like she's imagining them wrapped around Ives's neck. "We have to stop her."

"How? What can we do?" Daniil asks. He shifts his weight like he means to step toward her, but stops himself at the last moment. "We're trapped here."

It takes me a few seconds to realize that's no longer technically true. The thought comes with a complicated surge of emotions. We might be able to get to Pax... but it would mean leaving Scorpia and Pol behind without knowing if they're alive or safe. It would place me on another planet without a promise of a way to return.

And yet, with the path open in front of me, how can I ignore it? Knowing what could happen if I do nothing? Again and again I think I've escaped the terrible weight of this responsibility, but here it is, once more: a system teetering on the brink, and myself in a unique position to attempt to save it.

The others are silent for a long few moments after I break the news about Eridanus and Halon.

"I can't," Lyre says. Her voice trembles, though she holds herself upright with a shocking amount of dignity, given everything. "I need... time, Corvus. I'm sorry."

I can see how much it hurts her to even admit that much, and I pull her close before she tries to force herself to say more. "Take all you need. I'll feel better with you here."

Drom's face is stricken when I turn to her. "I'm not leaving Pol behind again," she says. "I won't."

"Good," I say. It breaks my heart to realize I will be leaving my entire family behind, but I refuse to let them see that. "Look after Lyre."

Drom huffs, and though she tries to hide it with annoyance, I can tell she's relieved. "Yeah, whatever, I'll keep an eye on the squirt."

"Oh, shut up," Lyre says, wiping her eyes with one hand. "As though I'm not the one who will be constantly keeping you out of trouble in a place like this."

They'll be all right together. I know they will. I'm less certain about what Izra and Daniil will choose. What do they want, now that the ship is gone and our crew has fallen apart? Before, I could offer them both a safe home, a place to belong, a sense of freedom. Now, the only thing I can promise is more violence to come.

"We could find a way to let you stay here, Daniil," I tell him. "Or you could take a job on Eri and Halon's ship, if you want. I can't offer you safety if you come with me."

Daniil shrugs, smiling at me in that easy way of his. "I've always wanted to see Pax."

"Even if it's another war zone?"

He meets my eyes steadily. "All the more reason to be at your side."

That renders me unable to speak, so I only nod, and look at Izra. She stares at me like she's daring me to ask the question, but I can't. The guilt of asking and the dread of her answer are both far too much to handle. "Your choice," I say, instead, and leave it at that.

She lets out a breath, her shoulders relaxing. "Thought you were gonna try to convince me to stay for a second," she mutters. "Of course I'm coming with you, you idiot."

So it's the three of us. Just a fraction of the crew we arrived with, and yet so much more than I ever could have hoped for. It doesn't take away the pain of leaving my entire family behind, but it does dull it enough to be bearable.

I turn to my younger siblings again. "If Scorpia and Pol find their way back..." I trail off, unable to finish the thought.

"*When*," Drom says fiercely.

"We'll explain it all to them," Lyre promises. And then, softer, she adds, "She'll understand, Corvus."

I clear my throat and nod again, trying to think of what else to say and finding myself at a loss.

"Haven't we done enough sappy goodbyes for a lifetime, yet?" Drom asks, rolling her eyes. "Just go on already. Do your noble bullshit." She meets my eyes, lifting her chin. "And then get back here."

"I'll do what I can," I promise. Then I turn my back before I can change my mind, and walk away from my family, Izra and Daniil at my side.

As grateful as I am for the help from Eridanus and Halon, I must admit I'm not eager to step aboard their ship. The vessel has served them faithfully over their years of arms dealing, so it must be sturdier than it looks... but, stars, the way it looks. It's tiny even compared to our old *Fortuna*, which was considered a small merchant vessel. I'm not sure how it can possibly have space for three more people, though I suppose there must be room for cargo somewhere in there.

Still, my apprehension over the ship is meaningless compared to my worry over why Eridanus and Halon made this offer. No matter what Scorpia thinks, I don't have a high opinion of their profession, and I've never known any type of space merchant to give away something for free. There must be something in this for them. But I have no choice but to accept their aid, so I can only hope that the eventual price is something I'm willing to pay.

As we approach, the two are as friendly as ever. Eridanus shakes my hand, proclaiming that it's "been far too long" while I grimace and mutter something I hope passes for polite, uncomfortable with the overfamiliarity. Thankfully, he soon moves on to grabbing Daniil's hand and shaking it. Next he extends it to Izra—and freezes mid-motion, his eyes going wide and his face going pale. He takes a step backward. "Stars above," he says, sounding genuinely shaken. "You're Izra. Izra Jenviir of the *Red Baron*."

Her eye narrows. "Long time, Eridanus." She nods to him, and then to his husband. "Halon."

Halon regards her coolly, arms folded over his chest and shoulders tensed, while Eri sputters. "Well, this is certainly unexpected. Turned over a new leaf, have you?"

"Guess you could put it like that." She mirrors his posture, hefting the weight of her broken weapon, and glares at them in a silent challenge. Below it, though, I see the flicker of anxiety, the way her eye wanders toward me as soon as she tears it away from them.

I didn't expect that there might be bad blood between the *Red Baron* and the arms dealers, though I should have. There aren't a lot of ships left traveling between the planets, so it's inevitable that they cross at some point. And nobody has crossed paths with Murdock's crew and come out eager for it to happen again. Stars know I had plenty of reservations myself about letting the ex-pirates aboard, though all of that seems unfathomably long ago. "Izra's one of ours now. I trust that won't be a problem."

Eri holds up his hands, shaking his head slowly from side to side. "No problem at all," he says. "As long as you vouch for her."

"I do," I say. "She stays with me." He stops short, gives me a closer, curious look, his eyebrows lifting.

"Well, all right then," he says. As he turns away, he shakes his head and murmurs a thoughtful "Huh."

He heads into the ship, and the rest of us follow.

The cargo bay composes most of the ship's space. It's an area far more fortified and organized than the ones I've seen on other ships. Logical, given that they're usually transporting heavy and volatile weaponry. Aside from the bay, there is only the cockpit, one bathroom, and one bedroom. There is not even a kitchen, only a microwave and miniature freezer tucked away in a corner of the bedroom. It is difficult to say which of the rooms is more cramped, and the hallway between them is so narrow that two people have to squeeze against the walls to pass one another. The twins would've had to duck through doorways to avoid banging their heads. A claustrophobic little box of a ship, overall. The only place spacious enough that we can all gather together is the cargo bay, so we do so after our awkward, shuffling tour.

"I'm afraid we're not used to much company," Eri says, rubbing the back of his head.

"By that, he means any company," Halon says.

"We'll make do," I say. We're Titans, after all; we've all been through worse.

"Daniil, are you used to space travel?" Eri asks, hooking his thumbs through the belt loops of his jumpsuit.

He shakes his head. "Very new to it."

Eri and Halon exchange a glance. "I'll get the emergency sickness bags," Halon murmurs, and heads up the stairs.

"Launch might be, uh, a little bumpier than you're used to," Eri says, with an apologetic grin.

"A little bumpy" turns out to be a gross understatement, and Halon's emergency sickness bags are a good call. Even after a lifetime spent mostly on a ship, I am not entirely convinced that this launch won't result in my teeth rattling out of my skull or my eyes being ripped from their sockets. The ship shakes violently, and the pressure is a thousand pounds on my chest, making my eyes stream and my head feel as though it's about to burst. Even I barely keep the contents of my stomach down. Izra's knuckles turn white as she grips the handles of her chair, her eye squeezed shut. Daniil doesn't stand a chance. He throws up twice during the launch, and then again after it subsides, and finally leans back in his chair looking completely drained. He stays strapped in as Izra and I let ourselves out and take our first shaky steps.

Even now, the ship is a noisy, uncertain-feeling thing, with none of the sense of safety and stability of the others I've been on. Everything rattles faintly, and the engine is a roar that forces everyone to raise their voice to be heard. The temperature is uncomfortably cold. I feel all too aware of the speed that we're traveling, and the void just outside of our small, flimsy craft. Each step is a little off-balance, and I have to fight the constant urge to grab on to something to stay upright.

I get Daniil some water and reach for the plastic bag, but he shakes his head at the latter. "Might not be done yet," he croaks.

Eri pokes his head in a few minutes later to check on us. He takes in the scene—Izra lying on the sole bed with her eye shut, me standing with one hand against the wall like I don't trust my own legs, Daniil still strapped into his launch chair with a bag of vomit in his hand.

He gives an apologetic shrug. "I thought it might be better if you went in not knowing," he says. "Nothing can quite prepare you for that."

"I'm going to kill you," Izra says, without opening her eye or moving.

Eri laughs, but he also shuffles out of the room quite quickly.

A few hours later, when our stomachs have started to settle, we all eat microwaved, freeze-dried meals that taste bland and rubbery. Daniil throws up again, still unsettled by the movement of the ship. I am sure to thank Eri and Halon again for transporting us—it is generous, and a risk they don't have to take—but I can't deny that it all makes me miss *Memoria* and my family fiercely.

"This is a miserable little ship and I hate it," Izra growls under her breath when Eri and Halon are out of the room, which I take to mean the same thing.

The ship's owners graciously allow us to take the room while they stay in the cockpit. I protest once while Izra glares daggers at me, but they insist, and I can't deny my relief. When Eri and Halon leave, they turn down the lights of the ship to dim emergency bulbs lining the hallway, leaving us in near-complete darkness. Izra takes the bed for herself, while Daniil and I settle into bedrolls on the floor. They provide little comfort or warmth on the metal floor. Still, we are all so exhausted that sleep comes quickly.

A sound wakes me in the middle of the night. Half-asleep, it takes me a few moments to untangle it from the general rumbling and rattling of the ship and recognize it for what it is—and when I do, it hits me like a blow to the chest. Izra is crying.

I lie still for several seconds, in agony, grappling with the fear of being pushed away if I try to reach out, hoping that Daniil will wake and know how to handle the situation with more grace. But his sleep-slowed breathing doesn't change, nor do Izra's quiet sobs, and eventually I can't bear the thought of how alone she must feel.

I rise quietly, and move to the bed, where she lies curled up and facing the wall. I sit on the edge of the bed—no response. I reach for her, graze my fingers gently across her spine—still nothing, but she doesn't pull away. After a brief hesitation, I lower myself onto the bed beside her, curling myself around her smaller body, offering what warmth and support I can. She is perfectly still for one heartbeat, and another—and when I wrap an arm around her waist, she takes my hand and clutches it, almost hard enough to hurt.

In moments I dared to think about it, I would imagine our bodies fitting together like they belonged like that. But it has been a long time since I held anyone—I am too hesitant, too stiff— and Izra seems to be unconsciously resistant to being held, even when she leans back into me. We end up curled together, my body fitted against hers, both tense. But at least she has stopped crying.

I raise a hand and stroke her hair, and she sighs. "He was never very brave," she says, so quiet I have to strain to listen. "I can't stop thinking about that. About how scared he must have been in those last moments." She stops, swallows. "Alone."

"My sister never would have let him be alone in there unless he chose it himself," I tell her in a low murmur, my lips pressed close to her ear. "So he must have been brave, in the end."

"I wish he hadn't been."

Daniil shifts in his bedroll on the floor, and we go silent. Both, I believe, relieved for an excuse to stop talking. But it's too late, we've already woken him. He sits up, groaning and stretching, and glances from my empty bedroll to the bed. There is a brief silence as I brace myself for awkwardness or jealousy.

Izra props herself up on one elbow. She looks at me—as if seeking an answer, but I'm not sure to what—and then turns to Daniil and says, "Well, come here."

Right. It is easy to forget Izra, too, is Titan. There is nothing strange about this for them. Likely the only reason for any hesitation is me. And yet...I find myself less uncomfortable at the situation than I'd expect. As long as I stop myself from thinking too hard about it.

"It's warmer," I tell Daniil, who is clearly waiting for me to say something.

"Well, if you insist," he says, and climbs onto the bed, worming himself into a spot right between us and drawing a surprised laugh out of Izra.

Despite the somewhat-lacking space, it is somehow more comfortable with three of us than two. Daniil has none of the awkwardness of Izra and me, and settles himself happily, filling the emptiness between us like his lanky body was built for it. He's very warm, and softer around the edges than Izra. "Oh, much better," he murmurs, with an arm looped around Izra and his head leaning on my shoulder.

And I am thinking too much again. Braced for awkwardness or strangeness or expectations. But after some shifting around, they both fall into easy sleep.

I lie awake for a while, listening to the soft sounds of their breathing, before I, too, drift away.

In the morning, Halon brings us tea two mugs at a time, apologetically mentioning that their pot can only make that much at once. It doesn't surprise me. It's a marvel, really; this small ship is like an entire world built for two. It is impossible to do anything, even merely take up space and air, without feeling like an excessive cog in a smoothly operating machine.

After breakfast, I head alone to the cockpit under the guise of asking exactly how long it will be until we reach our destination. Halon—ever observant—makes an excuse and leaves Eri and I alone in the tiny room. I take the chair he was occupying. It's clearly not a seat built for any concrete purpose—there is nothing important within reach, and it's situated awkwardly for a copilot— but arranged so that the two of them can sit together here. I can't imagine how the two of them are managing to sleep like this; there's not even enough space for either of us to stretch our legs out fully. For a few minutes we both stare out at the expanse of stars ahead. The rumble of the engine is quieter here.

"Why are you doing this?" I ask, finally. "Why, really?" No matter Scorpia's optimistic feelings about the two of them, I know that it would be a stretch to call them "friends" of my mother's at any point in time. At most, they were business partners, and even that occasionally. The only reason they were remotely civil is that their specialties and cargo capacities were far enough apart that they rarely had to compete for jobs.

And I find it difficult to believe they'd really go this far out of the goodness of their hearts. I try my best not to judge—I've done plenty of bad myself, both for my family and on my own—but they are, after all, arms dealers. Their arrangement with Scorpia back on Nibiru was mutually beneficial and profitable, so I can understand that. But this? They're sticking their necks out for us.

Eri, to his credit, doesn't try to feed me any lies or practiced lines. He stares out at space, his expression thoughtful, and then leans back in his chair with a creak and a heavy sigh. "Most of us came into this line of work because we wanted to," he says. "Because we're greedy, or—at least hungry for more than we had. Then we got stuck in it, one way or another." He goes quiet for a moment, and I think again of this ship being perfectly built for two. A Devan and a Paxian, two people who never would have met without the spacecraft, and never could stay together safely anywhere else. "But you kids never had a choice. And you always deserved better than you got with Auriga. Now that she's gone, instead of freedom, you all got saddled with her debts and her enemies and her crimes." He looks over at me, his face grave.

"We don't need your pity," I say. If that's what this is, I'd rather pay them whatever it takes to erase any indication that we might owe them a favor in return. My family has always handled our own.

"No," Eri says. "You certainly don't, and I'd never suggest it. You kids have fought for everything you have, and you've earned every last bit of it a thousand times over. But sometimes it's not about what you need, but what you deserve. And what you and your siblings deserve is to have someone on your side, for once. Someone willing to help out, not because they want something in return, but just because they see a kindred spirit." He shrugs. "There's not a lot of us left to travel the system. And they need us—they're always gonna need us, whether or not they ever realize that."

CHAPTER THIRTY-FIVE

The Lost and the Found

Scorpia

Pol might not be the best pilot, but I've been through worse crashes. This ride wouldn't be half-bad if it was a normal ship. But since it's a creepy, horrible alien vessel, everything about the experience is one of the worst things that has ever happened to me. I scream myself hoarse, clinging to the gooey, sticky wall for support. It clings back, leaking some kind of ooze that curls around my limbs and holds me in place as firmly as any launch chair. I catch one glimpse of Pol in the rear chamber, his eyes rolling back in his head and his body limp, the fleshy cords of the power source cradling him almost gently. Then I shut my eyes and keep screaming.

When the ship finally comes to a stop, I tear free with some effort, grope uselessly along the wall until I trigger something that opens the doorway, and fall down several feet to the jungle floor. Then I puke up a thin stream of bile, and scream again, just for good measure. I try to rub the horrible, mucus-y stuff off of my skin, but it's useless. Every inch of me is slippery with it. I'm pretty sure some got up my nose.

Pol jumps down from the ship behind me, grinning and equally slimy. "Not too bad, huh?"

He points at the city lights visible just over a small hill.

I wipe my mouth with the back of one hand and look toward Zi Vi. We are close, I'll give him that. But that presents another problem. "We can't just leave this thing out in the open. The Devans will lose their minds if they stumble on it. And..." I turn to face the ship and trail off in wonder.

The black alien ship already blended in with the dark Devan jungles, so at first I think it's just a trick of the light. But no—the ship is actually disappearing.

Yet that's not an entirely accurate description, either. All around it, the Devan plants are crawling—slowly, but with unmistakable intent—to create a barrier around the ship. It isn't disappearing; the jungle is hiding it. None of the plants touch it directly. They seem to be intentionally avoiding it. But in front of my eyes, the trees and the bushes and the creeping strangle-vines shift, subtly, until the alien ship is all but hidden. Nothing but a faint glimmer through a shield of interwoven black branches, as though the jungle has swallowed it whole.

"Well..." I want to make a joke, but my voice comes out shaky. I stop and swallow. Pol is gawking beside me, similarly at a loss for words.

I guess it's no accident that so little of the Primus civilization's remains have been found on Deva. But this leaves me wondering which I should be afraid of: the aliens or the plants. Both seems like a safe option. I turn my back on the ship and the plants around it, shivering as I imagine the jungle watching me. "Let's get the hell out of here," I say, and head for human civilization as fast as my tired legs can manage.

I'm so traumatized from the whole experience that I'm barely aware of the remaining trek to Zi Vi, or the process to get into the city, including the terrible, sanitizing showers. The Devans don't even ask about the ooze coating both of us; they must assume it comes from some kind of deep-jungle plant.

We emerge, dripping and dazed, and are immediately surrounded by uniformed Devans.

"Scorpia Kaiser?" one of them questions.

"Oh no," I groan. "Not again."

But they don't cuff me. Instead, the Devans usher us to a nondescript, governmental-looking building to wait. I'm not really sure what's going on, but they give us a place to sit, and food and water, so it's hard to be too upset about anything. Pol inhales rice balls at a frightening rate while a doctor checks him over, and licks his fingers unabashedly while she slathers some kind of paste on a rash on his arm. Despite the horrifying experience we just went through, he looks like he couldn't possibly be happier than at this moment.

But then the door opens, and he proves me wrong. Drom comes barreling at us. Pol only has time to half rise from his chair by the time she reaches him, but she picks him up the rest of the way with ease, hugging him so tightly I wince in sympathy. He only laughs, hugging her back, and she lets out a muffled sound that is either his name, or a sob, or maybe both at once. Lyre follows her inside with considerably more restraint. She stops a few feet in front of me with a nod and a small smile.

"Aw, c'mon, that's all you're gonna give me?" I say, rising to my feet. I hug her, and she releases a surprised squeak before hugging me back.

As happy as I am to see them, when I pull away from Lyre I can't help but notice all of the people who aren't here…especially Corvus. I don't know what could possibly make him miss this, but I know it can't be anything good. As I look at Lyre, my expression stricken as I try and fail to brace myself for more bad news, she hastily says, "He's okay." She pauses, and amends, "They're all okay. Shey is smoothing things over with the officials right now. But Corvus, Daniil, and Izra…" She trails off, chewing her lip.

But she's already said enough. As long as Corvus is safe, I'm sure he has a good reason for not being here. I sit down, gesturing to a seat nearby, and Lyre takes it. The twins are still hugging it out, their heads bent together in a low conversation.

"Wait," I say, leaning closer to Lyre. "Before you go on, I…did Drom tell you about Orion?"

Lyre's expression goes suddenly stiff, like she turned off a switch, and she nods. Like the one when she first walked in, it's a frostily polite gesture, burying all the things she doesn't want to say beneath it.

"I'm sorry," I say. "He made the choice to stay in the cockpit by himself." I search her expression, trying to gauge if she blames me, but I can't read anything in her face. "You don't have to hide it, Lyre. I know you two were close."

Her stony mask cracks a bit, and her lower lip trembles, but she ducks her head before I can see more. By the time she raises it, she's controlled it again. "I don't want to talk about that right now," she says, so brusque it's almost sharp. "What's happened has happened. We need to talk about the future."

"Lyre—"

"Corvus, Daniil, and Izra left for Pax," she says, and that's enough to get me to shut up and listen. When she said Corvus wasn't here, I never imagined that would mean he was on his way to an entirely different fucking planet. Especially since, with *Memoria* out of commission for what I'm guessing is a good, long while, the rest of us are trapped here on Deva. "Just this morning," she admits after a moment, more quietly.

That stings. But I'm more concerned about him. "Oh no, Corvus," I mutter, squeezing my eyes shut for a moment and shaking my head. "*Pax*, of all places? What could he be...no, no, let me guess. He's running off to single-handedly save the system again?" I open my eyes and look at her with dread, because we both know I'm not really joking when I say it. At least he has Daniil and Izra with him this time, thank the stars. He won't be alone.

"Yes, well, we all know what he's like," Lyre says. Even with everything going on, we share a small smile.

"All right, lay it on me," I say. "What is it this time? Let me guess, the Primus have returned from the dead?" Or maybe not so dead, I think, but I keep that to myself for now. One thing at a time.

"By the stars, Scorpia, this isn't some adventure novel," Lyre says, rolling her eyes, and then starts to explain.

By the time she's done, I'm leaning back in my chair with a hand pressed to my forehead. The twins have quieted down and are watching us.

"It never ends, does it?" I ask, allowing myself one moment of despair before I pull myself together. Corvus isn't here, which means it's time again for me to step up and take care of the family.

"Not for us, it seems," Lyre says.

Shey remains occupied with the Devan officials, but after a couple hours, someone comes in to let us know we're free to head to a nearby hotel where Lyre and the others are already set up. It's a dump of a place, but there's air-conditioning, and no bugs or plants or mold that I can see, which is pretty good for Deva.

Though the twins go straight to shower and sleep, I linger behind with Lyre, pretending not to get the hint as she slowly readies herself for bed and stops trying to make conversation.

"So do you wanna talk?" I ask, regarding her as she sits on the edge of her bed. She looks at me, eyebrows drawn together, like she has no idea what I mean. I sigh and rake a hand through my hair. "About Orion, I mean. I know it's . . . it sucks. It's okay to talk about it, y'know."

"I don't see how that's supposed to help anything," she says, her voice going stiff again. "He's gone. And that's all there is to it."

She turns away from me, fiddling with her comm and clearly intending to leave it at that. Her mouth is pressed into a firm line like she's afraid something will escape. I study her face, trying to make sense of her. I know she cared about him. I know she has to be torn up about it, now. There's not a single hint of that in her manner or her words, but I know her too well to trust that means anything.

Especially when I know we all do this, in our own ways. Lyre goes cold, and the twins push all their emotions into anger, and Corvus closes himself off alone and broods, and I make my stupid jokes and, in worse times, drank myself numb. We all find different methods of bottling shit up and avoiding facing it, because that's how Momma raised us. She taught us a lot, both good and bad, but sometimes I think this was the worst thing we learned from her: to pull away from the world and bury our hurt rather than facing it, and let the pain grow until it's sharp enough to kill us from the inside.

I understand at this point that it's not good for us or anyone around us. But I also understand that my younger siblings don't know any other ways of doing things until someone shows them. And that it's a stars-damned hard thing to do.

"Well maybe I wanna talk," I say, before I can second-guess myself. I never know what to say about this kind of thing. I didn't know what to say to my siblings after Momma died, and I didn't know what to say to Izra about losing Orion before we parted ways, but regretting saying nothing is always worse, so I'm gonna try. "Because I feel like shit. I feel awful that Orion died. And I feel fucking guilty whenever I think about how and why it happened, because part of me is afraid he only did it to try to prove something to us after he left us before, and I never got a chance to tell him he didn't have to do that, because we already forgave him. He didn't have to die for us. And I'm gonna miss him and his stupid stories and his jokes and the way he laughed too loud, and that big smile of his where his eyes would crinkle up, and..." I press the back of one hand to my eyes and take a deep breath, willing the tears down, because I've got more to say. I could spend the rest of my life listing the things I miss about him. "He was my friend," I say, my voice cracking. "He was the first person I trusted outside of our family, and the first person who became a part of my crew out of choice, and it's bullshit that he's dead."

I wipe my eyes and look at Lyre. She's sitting perfectly still and perfectly silent, her comm still in her hands, and tears are flowing freely down her cheeks. She opens her mouth like she wants to say something, but only lets out a small, choked sob. I move to her side and wrap my arms around her. She keeps clinging to her comm like it's some kind of lifeboat, sitting rigidly, but she doesn't pull away. She feels very small and fragile in my arms. My poor little sister who never had a chance to act as young as she is.

"That's okay," I say. "You don't have to be strong right now."

She never speaks. But she does lean into me, letting me take some of her weight for a little while, and sometimes, I think, that's the best thing you can do.

CHAPTER THIRTY-SIX

What We Do to Survive

Corvus

My skin stings as the needle slips out, and I shake my arm, suppressing a curse. We're lucky that Eri and Halon have the radiation shots used by Pax's citizens. Since it wasn't terraformed like the other planets, only a thin strip of land on Pax's sun-facing side is habitable, and even there, being left out in the open means being slowly boiled to death by heat and radiation. Without the proper injections, every step on the desert planet is a countdown—and not a long one. But when I saw the size of the needle, I almost wished we could just wear the bulky anti-radiation suits my family used last time we were here.

"I know," Halon says, with a sympathetic smile. "But trust me, it doesn't hurt as bad as the treatment you'd need without taking them."

"Even with the shots, don't forget to take precautions," Eri warns. "Three rules of Pax: Keep hydrated. Keep to the shade. And keep your gun on you at all times."

"Remind me why people live on this place, again?" Daniil asks, wincing after receiving his own needle to the arm. Izra doesn't flinch, though she stares straight up at the ceiling from the moment the needle is in her vicinity, unwilling to look at it.

"Same reason as we're in this cursed system at all," Halon says. "Necessity."

"And also because us humans are stubborn bastards." Eri says the words with a hint of very Paxian pride. "We don't take so well to giving up, no matter the circumstances."

"It's not much different than the other planets, as far as I see it," Izra says.

"Wouldn't mention that to the Paxians. They see themselves as one of a kind for living in a place like this." Eri grins. "And honestly, I'm not inclined to argue. Things are different there. You'll see what I mean." His grin broadens. "And at least we don't live on top of dead alien ruins like the rest of the crazy bastards of the system."

Miserable, tiny oven of a planet though Pax may be, I have to admit that I can see why its people are so proud. It is the one world we conquered that even the Primus could not. Coming into this system, we were mostly taking up the old homes of an alien race long before us, following a road they paved. But Pax is ours. The first planet other than Earth that is truly, wholly ours. We may have to build radiation shields and fill our veins with chemicals to survive it, but we survive nonetheless.

Perhaps this is the difference between humanity and the Primus. They conquered these worlds by forcing the planets to suit them through terraforming. The very systems they installed later destroyed them, and now stand as a testament to their hubris, the only remnants of what was once a vast civilization more advanced than ours.

But humanity? On the one lonely world we settled for ourselves, instead of finding a way to make the planet bow to us, we forced ourselves to bend to it.

*   *   *

Eri and Halon land near Azha, one of the planet's two major cities, and help us through the entrance. The officials there seem
familiar with them, and I get the sense that a considerable amount
of credits is being exchanged for our entry, though they keep us
separate so we don't know the details.

"If you want to get into Luz, you'll need a separate visa," Eri says,
passing the papers into our comms. "Afraid we can't help you there.
We've got to handle our own business and head back to Deva."

"Of course. We can take it from here." I know Ives was last seen
in the city of Luz, which lies across the sand sea, but they've done
more than enough for us—so much that I'm not quite sure what
to say to them. It's difficult to remember the last time someone
who wasn't family was willing to help us without asking anything
in return. "If there's ever a way for us to repay you…"

"It's a favor freely given, Corvus. Not a debt." Halon is always
the quieter of the two, but he speaks up now, and reaches over to
touch my shoulder. "People like us have got to look out for each
other." I nod, at a loss for words.

"I'll try to check in with your siblings when we reach Deva
again," Eri says. I nod, grateful, though the reminder still makes
my chest ache. Via the authorities in Zi Vi, Shey was able to send
us a brief message updating us on Scorpia and Pol arriving in the
city, but nothing else. With *Memoria* out of commission, they
have no way of sending cross-planetary transmissions themselves.
I'll be faced with the same problem now that I'm on Pax. "Good
luck with everything."

"And you, as well." I shake hands with him, and hug Halon,
and we go our separate ways.

Azha is built at the bottom of a valley, shielded from Nova Vita's
constant presence by the shadow of a cliff. The buildings are squat

and sun-bleached, painted in a variety of colors made pale by time and light, dug halfway into the ground for cooler temperatures. Laundry hangs out of open windows and children play in the unpaved streets, shrieking with laughter and kicking up a cloud of dust as they chase a tiny drone. There are stranger sights, too: a cart carrying cages of snuffling, rabbit-like creatures, citizens lining up for anti-radiation shots at a building marked by a red cross, and a man leading a cow down the street.

I pause to stare at the latter. I've never seen one in person before. Most of the system's meat is synthesized in labs, but Pax's cattle are famous throughout the system, their meat considered either a rare delicacy or a disgusting abomination, depending on who you ask. The story is that Pax's settlers were the only ones who couldn't stand the thought of giving up meat-based diets when they left Earth, so they kept cattle on board; and when they settled on this harsh desert world, they found a way to genetically alter the animals to be able to survive here. I remember seeing an image of an old Earth cow once in an ancient history textbook, and it bore little resemblance to the long-legged, big-eared, hump-backed creature lumbering down the streets of Azha. It lets out an odd, crooning sound as it passes me, and swings its head to the side to blink at me with its large, dark, vacant eyes.

Everyone else in its path simply moves to the side, apart from some children who run up, giggling, to pat its hide before dashing away. The man leading the creature swats at them half-heartedly, but levels me with a suspicious look when he notices my interest. I know I shouldn't be staring and marking myself as an off-worlder, but it is the type of thing that demands to be stared at. Daniil is openly gawking. Izra glances from me to him, rolls her eye, and jabs each of us with an elbow. "It's just a fucking cow," she says, and walks ahead while we guiltily follow. "Planet's full of 'em. Keep moving."

"*That's* a cow?" Daniil says to me in a low whisper, casting one last look at the backside of the beast as it lumbers on down the street. "People *eat* them? I mean, synthetic meat and fish are one thing, but a living, breathing, warm-blooded creature?" He shudders. "Plus...they're sort of cute, aren't they?"

I think back to the spotted beast and its wide-set, dark eyes, and slowly, grudgingly nod. "They are." Despite the smell, which lingers in its wake.

We pass other oddities as we journey through the city. Drilling stations where the city's plumbing system pumps water from the reserves buried deep under Pax's surface. Compost heaps, where civilians dump organic material that can be recycled into fertilizer for farms. When I stop to use a public restroom, I fumble with confusion through the two separate areas before finding a sign that helpfully indicates one is for urination only, which will be filtered into clean water; the other side's sewage system, on the other hand, will be directed into the compost heaps. They waste nothing here. They can't afford to.

It is strange to truly see this world for the first time. The one planet that has always remained beyond my family's reach. The farthest in the system from my birth-planet—and also the one most notorious for feeding into its war, trading guns and exosuits and other machinery in return for Titan's raw materials. I always thought of wealthy, tech-forward Paxians as the opposite of Titans. And they are, in some ways; this society seems to be about as far as one can get from Titan's iron grip of military control, and its strict ideas of law and order. Yet in many ways, this harsh and demanding world, and the type of life it requires, reminds me of my home-planet. Their everyday lives require a brutal efficiency, a constant battle with the climate itself that no other planets but Titan would understand.

But on Titan, that was all due to the effects of the Planetary

Defense System. Here, it merely is, and always has been, the way things are. And given the disastrous aftermath of the Primus's terraforming of these worlds, I doubt humans will ever try to change it. I'm not sure if that makes this place more or less depressing.

"So what's the plan?" Izra asks, pulling me back to reality. "Find transportation to Luz?"

I've been trying to come up with an answer to that myself. We know so little about the situation that it's difficult to determine how to begin, and whether or not we need to use subtlety in our search. "Let's get our bearings first," I say. "Get used to the city, find somewhere to spend the night."

"It'd be nice to get out of the sun," Daniil says, wiping a hand across his forehead and grimacing.

We barely make it to the end of the street before a hand grips my shoulder and cold steel presses against the back of my neck.

"Corvus Kaiser?" an unfamiliar voice asks. "Follow me."

CHAPTER THIRTY-SEVEN

Walls Between Us

Scorpia

After my conversation with Lyre, I drag myself back toward my hotel room to get my first good night's sleep in quite a while. I'm almost there when I realize there's still one very serious concern that can't wait until morning.

The new planet.

As much as I want to spill this information to as many people who will listen, mostly just to stop it from feeling like a weight I'm dragging around all by myself, I still remember Corvus's words about how the knowledge of the Planetary Defense Systems would paint a target on the back of anyone who knows it. He was right to be concerned; I suspect that's the main reason why the IA has been hounding us. I'm also vividly aware of the fact that we're currently on Deva, a planet not exactly known for lack of corruption. If anyone gets so much as a whiff that a few off-worlders stranded on the planet know something important, I have no doubt that Jai Misha would have us locked up and tortured until we spill out every detail.

So I need to tread lightly here. But I also want to make sure someone knows, just in case the worst happens. The only thing worse than dying for this information would be dying knowing that I'm taking it to the grave, and leaving all of humanity unawares.

So I end up standing in front of Shey's room in the middle of the night, trying to build up the courage to knock. I have a strong sensation that I've been in this exact position before. Seems like it's always one step forward and two steps back with us. Or maybe just walking in a circle, never getting any closer, but unable to stop ourselves from following the other. It's probably stupid of me to seek her out again, like some lost puppy who doesn't have anywhere else to go. But in the end, even with all of my personal feelings aside, Shey is the best person to tell. She's knowledgeable about the Primus, and about the delicate politics of the system. And, most of all, Misha and his goons can't murder her in some underground dungeon without raising a lot of questions with the Interplanetary Alliance.

So there are plenty of logical reasons. Which makes me feel a little better about the fact that the real reason that pushed me over the edge was that I really wanna see her face light up when I tell her that her beloved, creepy-as-hell aliens might not be so extinct, after all.

Holding that thought in my mind, I knock.

It takes a little while for Shey to open the door. When she does, she looks sleepy and rumpled and way too sexy for me to focus on dead aliens and mysterious planets for a good few seconds. First she just blinks at me, bleary-eyed and confused. Then her eyes widen and she throws herself at me, wrapping her arms around me.

"I knew you'd be okay," she says. The way she presses her face into my shoulder reminds me that I still smell powerfully of the sanitation showers, but it doesn't seem to scare her away. She tilts her face up toward mine and meets my eyes, and it's all I can do to resist melting into her. But I need to focus.

"Gonna take more than a disastrous spaceship crash to take me out," I joke weakly, but then I think of Orion and my tongue shrivels up. That's an ache too fresh to touch just yet. I pull away from Shey and shove my hands into my pockets. "Listen, I'm utterly exhausted right now, but there's something I need to tell you. Can I come in for a sec?" After I finish, the silence stretches out for a few seconds before I clarify, "Something important."

I take a seat on a chair near the door, and she sits on the edge of her bed, and the distance between us feels miles wider than the size of this little hotel room.

"So." At least the awkwardness has sufficiently killed any desire I had to try and make small talk. "I'll get right to it. When Pol and I were on the run through the jungle, we ended up stumbling onto a Primus statue." She looks surprised, though not too surprised; she was there on Gaia when we discovered their existence here in the Primus computer, after all. "And I remembered that trick you did back on Gaia to get under it. When we fell down into the tunnel, we found another—"

"Maybe this isn't the best time for a conversation like that," she says. "Surely you want to gather the entire crew, right?"

"What?" I ask, dumbfounded. "No, Shey, I'm trying to tell you—"

She reaches out and grabs my hand. I cut off and blink down at it.

"Just wait," she says. "Before we get to business, there's something I've been wanting to do for a long, long time."

"What?" I say, again, even more confused. "Shey, uh, no offense, but—"

She doesn't let me finish. Gripping my wrist hard enough that it hurts and ignoring my protests, she pulls me into the bathroom, shuts the door, and turns on the shower. I stare at her, suffering from some serious mood whiplash, but not at all mad about the turn of events. The discovery of a new habitable planet is important, and all, but surely it can't hurt to wait for an hour. Or two. Or maybe a whole night.

"Well this is unexpected," I say, with an awkward laugh. Before I can go on, she grabs me by the collar and pulls my face down to hers. It feels like my face is burning hot under her cool fingers, and I gasp at the roughness of the motion.

But instead of kissing me she puts a hand over my mouth. And then—to my *severe* disappointment, this time, because honestly the hand over my mouth still left some intriguing possibilities for how this night was gonna go—she leans close and whispers into my ear, "I'm fairly certain my room is bugged by Misha. Keep your voice down."

As I tell her about what we found in those Primus tunnels—the new planet, that the Primus were the ones who discovered it, and all the implications that follow—Shey's eyes grow wide. Eventually she starts to pace the tiny bathroom, like her brain is working so fast that her body can't be still anymore.

"Another planet. Another *habitable* planet. That means that even if we...but no, if the Primus are already..." she murmurs to herself. I watch her pace and do my best to follow where her half-formed sentences are leading. "But this is huge either way. It could mean we're not alone." She stops and turns to me, breaking into a smile.

It's been a long while since I saw her so happy. I hate that I have to ruin it. "People aren't gonna be thrilled about that, with what we now know about the Primus."

Her smile dims. "You're right," she says. "They're not who we thought they were. Just as war-torn as we are." Part of me wants to tell her we could've expected as much, given all the creepy-ass weapons they left behind, but I bite my tongue. I know the Primus are still a sore subject for her, after all the years she spent studying them, only to discover they had ended themselves and nearly ended us, too. She hesitates, her expression conflicted. "But surely they wouldn't make such a grave mistake and carry on as they were. Perhaps they learned from it."

"Did we?" I may not know a whole lot about history, but from what I do understand, humanity has made the same mistakes about a million times over. Her silence is answer enough. I sigh, raking a hand through my hair. "But, I mean, even if they did change...people would still distrust them for what they did before, and for the shit they left behind and what it did to us. They'd find a way to blame them for what happened on Gaia, and Titan, and Nibiru."

"They only built the defense systems. It was our own foolishness that triggered them."

"Trust me, I know. But people are always eager to point a finger when it comes to shit like this." I think back to the way the leaders of the IA looked at me in the Council Hall, and fight back a wave of bitterness. "When the people in charge make choices like that, it's 'necessity.' But anyone else..."

She nods, frowning. "And yet..." Her feet slow, but she keeps moving, those gears still turning in her brain. "Even if the Primus are really on this new planet, it will likely take generations for it to mean anything to us. We don't know what became of their civilization, but there's likely a reason they haven't traveled back to see what happened to their old worlds, and reclaim the technology they lost. We may never have contact with them." She bites her lip. "I truly hate to say this, but I feel it must be said. If it's true that people will need somewhere to aim their blame, perhaps it would be better to have a target other than the rest of the planets here."

I take a moment to absorb what she's saying. Honestly, the first thing it makes me feel is horribly sad—because the Shey I first met would've never suggested this. She would have been so excited at the prospect of the Primus out there, likely gushing about all of the ways both of us could benefit from contact with them, the ways we could help each other. She sees things differently now. And I know it isn't all my fault—the world takes most of the blame, to be sure—but it's disappointing to see that idealism get worn down to this.

But then I think about what she's suggesting, trying to take what it means about her out of it...and I still don't like it. I don't like it at all.

"If we need an enemy to unite us," I say, "maybe we don't deserve to be saved."

Shey's feet go still. She slowly turns to look at me, her expression more astonished than anything else. "You would doom the human race so easily?"

"No. I'd give them a chance to be better." I shake my head. "*Your* way is the easy way out, Shey. It assumes the only way we can continue is by doing the same shit we've always done. It's assuming that people will only see how similar they are when they're faced with something even more different. But then... what?" I hold out my hands. "What if the Primus do show up, after hundreds of years of humanity building up its walls to keep them out? War will be inevitable. And what if they don't? Then we'll still build our walls, and sooner or later people will start pointing fingers about who should be shoved outside of them. With all of the planets whipped up into a frenzy, if no war comes to them, they'll make one."

"So then what do you suggest?" Shey asks. "We hide the truth?

Decide who does and doesn't deserve to know? That's the same as my people and the leadership on Titan did with the knowledge of the Planetary Defense Systems, and look at what came from that."

I guess I never thought about it like that, but she's right. I've never felt good about sitting on what we know about the Planetary Defense Systems, either. We kept that secret for nothing, since it turned out that Altair already knew. We're still keeping it to ourselves, despite the current war between Deva and Pax. The IA is so convinced that telling everyone will only result in further conflict. People panicking and rioting in the streets. The planets' paranoia driving them to either cut each other off entirely or, worse, launch preemptive attacks before the others can hit them. They think that Pax, as the only planet without a defense system, would have the other worlds at gunpoint. But if we tell Deva without warning Pax, it's possible it would just drive the Devans to launch a full-scale, hostile takeover of the smaller world.

Hell, maybe that's why the IA wants me to keep the secret so badly—so that they can beat Deva to the punch, once they regain stability on their own worlds.

Stars, thinking about it hurts my head. Now, as if that one huge secret wasn't enough, I've got the possibility of a new planet to grapple with, too.

I don't want any of this. I never did. All I've ever hoped for is a safe little life for me and the people I care about. I wish there was a way to shove it all into someone else's hands and run, let them deal with the responsibility and the consequences. But the same few people I trust enough to tell, like Shey, are the same people I could never leave to deal with it all alone.

"I just think we should sit with it for a while." I push my hair out of my face, well aware that the tiny bathroom is getting hotter and damper by the second. "See how everything shakes out with the IA and the war. Then we can decide."

DISCORDIA

Shey folds her arms over her chest and regards me skeptically. "Fine," she says. "Then why are you telling me now?"

"Mostly because I don't want the information to die with me if I end up assassinated," I tell her honestly.

She frowns. "And the rest of it?"

I shrug. "Because I trust you to do the right thing with it more than I trust myself," I say, the words coming easily. Only in the silence afterward do I realize maybe it was a bad move to be so blatantly honest. Everything between us is far too complicated for simple truths like that to be anything but painful. I clear my throat. "And, I mean, you're much smarter than me," I add weakly, trying to save myself from feeling exposed.

She looks like she wants to say something in response, but instead she shuts her mouth and only nods, once.

As our conversation dies down, I'm forced to again confront the fact that we're standing face-to-face in a quite small and now *very* steamy bathroom. It's so hot and sticky in here that my clothes are plastered to my skin, and Shey's hair is slowly expanding into a cloud around her head. I grin despite myself.

"What exactly is funny about this?" Shey asks indignantly. But a moment later, her lips quirk in a barely repressed smile as she, too, seems to take a step back and look into the situation. "It was the best I could do on short notice, okay?"

"I mean, no complaints here," I say. She laughs.

It would be so easy right now to step closer to her, put my hands on her hips, and kiss her. From the way she's looking at me, I think she wants me to. And yet...and yet, here I am, my feet planted in place. What the hell is wrong with me?

Then Shey's expression shifts, and the moment is gone. "While we're on the subject of dire secrets," she says, "there's something I should tell you."

Oh, stars. Not more complications. I'm so tired I half want to tell her to save it for the morning, but instead I just wait. She bites her lip and steps forward, lowering her voice even more than she did when discussing the possibility of a new planet, which is a serious warning that things are about to get very, very bad for us.

"On our way here from Nibiru, I spoke privately with Tommasson—"

"Who?"

She gives me an exasperated look. "Diplomat Tommasson. The one who Ives killed."

"Oh. Right."

She sighs and continues, "He was concerned about the failure of his mission from the IA. He decided he would tell me the details about it, in case something happened. And now that he's dead and Ives is a traitor, I feel obligated to do my best to fulfill it. Especially given that whatever Ives is plotting will likely endanger both the Alliance and Deva."

"Okay. So the job was to try to convince Misha that Deva should join the Alliance, right? Shouldn't be too hard for you to get an audience with him…"

"That's the problem," Shey says. "That *wasn't* the mission. The IA leadership believes that Prime Minister Misha will never agree to join the Alliance. And even if he did, the man is volatile." She pauses. "But there's a woman poised to ascend to his position when he leaves office. Alessiah Marigold."

"Alessiah…" I repeat, wondering why that name sounds familiar. Then I remember our last trip to Deva, and that strange, wealthy woman. I guess that explains why she was so interested in me.

"The IA has already been in contact with her and made plans. Unlike Misha, she's very open to the idea of negotiating and bringing Deva into the fold, along with calling off the war with Pax."

My stomach drops as I realize what she's saying. "So the plan was never to make an alliance with Misha."

"No," Shey says softly. "The plan is to kill him. And the peace of the system may depend on it."

I wake up in the middle of the night to someone pressing a hand over my mouth. I thrash instinctively, but a second and third figure appear to secure my limbs before I can even think of getting up. Three strangers, dressed all in black. Panic fills me—are they going to kill me? Stab me in bed? Just let me suffocate? But they only hold me down until I wear myself out. The one covering my mouth presses a finger to her lips and waits for me to nod before drawing the hand back.

"Scorpia Kaiser," she says. "You're coming with us."

CHAPTER THIRTY-EIGHT

Keeper of the Balance

Corvus

A collection of hooded figures leads us down a winding series of backstreets and alleyways in Azha. There are too many of them to fight—and even if there weren't, where would we escape to? We're alone in the middle of a city we don't know, on a planet none of us are accustomed to. We have no choice but to follow.

If I thought they were going to kill us, I would fight despite the odds. But if that was the case, it would be as simple as taking us outside the city walls and doing the deed—or leaving us to the elements. Instead, these people seem to want something. And if we're lucky—if they work for Ives, or someone associated with her—perhaps they'll bring us closer to our goal, whether intentionally or not. So I keep moving without fighting back, and Daniil and Izra follow my lead, though the latter keeps shooting me glares over it.

When they bring us to a building on the edge of the city and try to urge us down a stairwell to a basement, I finally balk.

"Enough," I say. I don't turn around or make any threatening gestures, but I also don't move forward, even when the blaster prods me again. "Tell us what you want."

Izra and Daniil tense, sensing that now is the moment to fight, if we need to.

A woman separates from the rest of the group and steps forward. She pulls back her hood, and I'm startled to find that I recognize her—firstly as Pax's representative at the Interplanetary Council meeting on Deva, and secondly from the video message she sent after we shot down her drones on Gaia.

"Silvania Azenari," I say. "I'm sorry, I don't know what title to address you by."

"Don't have one." Her voice holds just a hint of the lilting accent Pax is often mocked for. "And you'd be Corvus Kaiser. Top of the Interplanetary Alliance's most-wanted list." She grins and juts out a hand. "Pardon for having you dragged here, but when I heard you were on Pax, I just had to meet you."

Her grip is firm and her smile warm. She's a tall woman, only a few inches shorter than I am, with brown skin and dark hair tied up in a way that fully displays the metal device implanted in the back of her head. She wears a loose, sleeveless top that shows off arms lean with muscles and adorned with geometric tattoos, along with flowing pants and a pair of very Paxian brown leather boots.

And despite how casually she's acting right now, and the apparent lack of a title, the speed and ease with which she was able to get hands on us suggests a considerable amount of power in this city. I truly hope our purposes aren't at odds.

I nod at the others. "My companions are Daniil Naran and Izra Jenviir."

She takes us all in, her eyes snagging on the black boxes on both of their wrists, and the war-brand on mine. "Three Titan soldiers in the flesh. We've been seeing an awful lot of those on Pax, lately, it seems."

"Ex-soldiers," Daniil corrects with a flash of teeth.

"Of course. Pardon." Her gaze pauses on Izra, and then Daniil. "Hm. Aren't you Titans all supposed to be seven feet tall and pale as milk?"

"Aren't Azha's streets supposed to be full of gunfights and cow shit?" Izra fires back, her lip curling.

Silvania laughs—a real one, wild and free with her head thrown back. "Guess the stories get exaggerated, traveling from one end of the system to the other." She claps Izra on the back and continues down the stairs to the basement. I glance around at the rest of her people, who stand back without making any move to follow her, and then head down myself. Daniil and Izra are close behind me.

The dim basement has no air-conditioning, but it's still much cooler than the air outside. There's one table with a handful of rickety chairs, along with a pile of storage containers lining one wall. Silvania sits at the table, legs stretched out long, twirling an unlabeled glass bottle in her hands. Her movements are all casual and unhurried; not lazy, but relaxed, even in a closed room with three former Titan soldiers. "I owe you a drink, right? Let's have a chat."

I'm not in the mood for a "chat," especially after being forced here at gunpoint, but I make myself sit. Daniil and Izra remain standing behind me, a comfortingly solid presence at my back.

Silvania takes a long swig from the bottle in her hands, and passes it to me. "So. Just the three of you on Pax, then?"

I drink while I try to figure out how much to tell her. The alcohol is surprisingly sweet, though it still burns down my throat. "Yes. The rest of my family has business elsewhere." I suspect there's no point lying about that, at least, when she seems to have a good grasp of arrivals in Azha. "Why did you send us that message on Gaia?" I pass the bottle back.

"Like I said, didn't want any hard feelings about my drones. They weren't there for you." She shrugs. "And I have to admit, I was curious. The Interplanetary Alliance was really itching to get their paws on you. Why go through all the trouble to hunt down some mostly petty criminals when they've already got three planets' worth of problems?"

I'm quiet for a few moments, struggling with what I want to say. "I'm not here to talk about the IA."

"No? Did Deva already pay you for their secrets?"

I shake my head. "We left Deva when Misha tried to contact us. We had no desire to end up in the middle of any of this."

"Yet here you are." She leans back in her chair, scrutinizing me. "What are you doing on Pax?"

"Why did you make a deal with Helena Ives?"

Silvania breaks into a grin. "Oh, I like you. So prickly. We really going to talk in circles all day, though?"

"You're the one dodging the question."

We eye each other across the table. Izra shifts behind me, letting out a low, impatient noise. I'm surprised she made it this long without losing her temper. I'm getting frustrated myself.

"This isn't going anywhere unless we decide to trust each other, at least a little bit," Silvania says, after a weighty silence. "So here. I'll go first: I didn't make a deal with Helena Ives, and I don't like the man who did."

"I heard she made an arrangement with the authorities here."

"She's making a deal with *an* authority here, yes," Silvania says. "Things aren't so simple on Pax. We've got Azha, which is a ranching and agricultural powerhouse, and Luz, which handles the bulk of the industrial side of things. Howland, the man Ives made a deal with, belongs to the latter. He's the CEO of the corp that produces exosuits, among other things." She sips her drink. "And a cowardly slimeball."

"So I take it you belong to Azha?"

"Me? I belong to nothing and nobody." She grins again. "I'm not all that important. Just one of the folks who helps run the supply lines between the two cities. Anyway, it's your turn to answer a question: What do *you* want with Helena Ives?"

I hesitate, glancing back at Izra and Daniil, but they both remain quiet and leave the decision to me. I have no idea if I can trust this stranger. But she's right that this conversation will go nowhere unless we're willing to be honest with one another. And we are alone on a planet that none of us know how to navigate. We need to place our trust in someone, at least to an extent.

"Ives betrayed my family," I say. "She shot down our ship and killed someone important to us. She's always been ambitious, and violent. She'll drag the whole system into another war for a chance at power and glory." I lean forward in my seat, resting my hands on my knees. "So we're here to stop her."

"Well, now we're getting somewhere." She leans forward, matching my intensity. "We've got a nice system here on Pax. The cities need each other, and also keep one another in check, and I keep things moving between the two. But now that Titan woman of yours has come in and thrown off that balance. She decided to go to the tech folks over in Luz. Offered them an army if Luz could arm and home them. Now Luz is starting to get greedy. Starting to think that maybe they don't need the rest of us, if they can buy an off-world army and use it to take over the planet by force."

Everything is clicking into place now. Ives wouldn't live in peace alongside the Nibirans and Gaians, and when Altair refused to continue the war, she decided to round up fellow extremists and fire off some attacks to incapacitate the IA and Deva—though we prevented the latter. That cleared the path for her and her followers to find another planet to take over. Since she seemed to know about the Planetary Defense Systems, Pax is the obvious choice, despite the less-than-ideal conditions. It'll provide a safe home base for her to rebuild the militaristic Titan she loved.

But I doubt her plan ends with them sharing this small, irradiated planet with the rest of the Paxians. Ives's ambition is far too big for that. Especially when she knows exactly how vulnerable the other worlds are.

"She'll betray her allies in Luz as soon as she has what she wants from them," I say. "And her plan won't stop with Pax. She'll use the tech they provide to take over here, and likely move on to launch a coup against Altair and the rest of the IA."

"So it seems we've got ourselves a mutual enemy. And you know what they say about that."

"I'm not looking to get wrapped up in another world's politics," I tell her. "We're just here for Ives, then we're gone."

"Fine by me. You handle her, I'll handle the rest."

She juts out a hand. I take it.

"So what's the plan?" I ask.

"The plan is that we head to Luz and throw a wrench in their scheme before they get going." Silvania stands and stretches. "Care to hitch a ride across the sand sea?"

CHAPTER THIRTY-NINE

An Honored Guest

Scorpia

My escorts take me down a long and twisting tunnel, through doors that can only be opened by multiple fingerprints and passcodes. By the end of it, my feet are aching and I have no sense of what direction we've ended up going in, nor any idea what we're going to find at the end. Probably some kind of terrifying Devan dungeon where they'll keep me until death, never to see the sun again. I wish I would've spent more time saying goodbye to my siblings. I wish I would've kissed Shey when she looked like she wanted me to.

Shit. Shey. Stars, I hope this isn't because of our conversation in that bathroom, and she's not suffering similar treatment right now. She didn't seem enthused about the idea of killing someone, but she did sound like she was trying to convince herself it needed to be done. Maybe I should confess now, tell them it was all my idea, and hope they let her go ... But what if my admission damns us both? Maybe it's better to just deny, deny, deny, like Momma always taught me.

Before I can decide, we reach the end, and one of the escorts helps me up through a metal hatch. I find myself standing in the fanciest room I've ever set foot in all my life. Fancier even than that Alessiah woman's house. Gaudier, though, too. Here, it's all gilded edges and crystal chandeliers and more holoscreens than anyone could possibly need. Soft music plays from a sound system that seems to come from every corner of the room. The lights dim and brighten subtly with the beat.

And even though they're not as visible here as they were in Alessiah's home, I can still feel at least a dozen cameras watching me.

Prime Minister Jai Misha lounges in a huge armchair. He's wearing an immensely comfortable-looking magenta bathrobe and a pair of fuzzy slippers, and is playing a puzzle game on a holoscreen resting in his lap. As we emerge from the hatch, he looks up at me, smiles, and dismisses the hologram with a casual sweep of one hand. The music stops, too.

"Scorpia Kaiser!" He looks older in person, maybe because he's not caked with makeup like I assume he is in front of cameras. I think the billboards airbrush out some of the silver spreading through his dark hair and neat beard, too. Still far too handsome for someone in charge of a planet, though.

"I've been so excited to finally meet you," he says, while I remain lost for words. He walks over, takes both my hands, and kisses me once on each cheek in the usual Devan manner. Devans are always so friendly until they're not. They'll keep smiling right up to the moment they shove a knife through your ribs—not even the back, because you won't see it coming either way.

I'm frozen in place, my tongue tangled, trying to remember the correct way to greet a Devan prime minister, and desperately attempting to work out if he knows I was just discussing plans to assassinate him a few hours ago. He, on the other hand, is still talking. "Truly a pleasure. You must have absolutely the best stories, after everything you've been through. Come, sit with me. Can I offer you a drink?"

"I, uh—" Before I can respond, one of my escorts pulls me rather forcefully away from Misha and toward another armchair. I sink into it, casting an annoyed look at the man . . . though, honestly, I can't be too mad, because this is probably the comfiest chair I've ever had the pleasure of sitting in. Damn. I could take a nap right here, right now, and it'd probably be the best sleep I've ever had. "I actually don't—"

"Wine?" Misha asks, accepting a glass from a well-dressed servant who seems to appear at his side the moment he gestures. "No, wait—" He waves a hand. "Corn whiskey, isn't it?"

While I stare at him, another servant appears by me, offering a glass of whiskey on a wooden tray. I'm so shocked that I take it before I can think, and only barely manage to resist bringing it to my lips. Ice clinks in the glass, reminding me of how parched I am after that long walk through the tunnels. The whiskey smells smoky and sweet and all too good.

I swallow thickly, my thoughts slowly catching up with me, along with Misha's words. *Finally meet you. Everything you've been through.* Plus, of course, my drink of choice. He knows who I am. And no matter how disarmingly he's smiling at me right now, that sends a shiver down my spine.

While I'm still working on finding something to say, Jai abruptly leaps to his feet and claps his hands together. "Oh, but of course, you must be starving," he says. "Even us experienced drinkers could use some food first, no? Come, come." Before I can voice any kind of opinion on the matter, he walks briskly out of the room and down a hallway. I glance around at the various servants before trailing after him. He kicks off his slippers as he enters the dining room, and I pause to remove my boots.

I've barely taken two steps when a servant comes forward to pick them up.

The dining room is very grand and very Devan, with a long table of polished wood set close to the floor, and plush cushions rather than chairs. Jai is already sitting, cross-legged and barefoot, on one of the cushions, and despite the size of the table he gestures toward a seat directly next to him. I sink onto my knees on the cushion, feeling entirely out of my element.

"So nice to have company," he says, as we wash our hands in glass bowls of warm water and dry them on heated towels. "Normally it's just me and the servants at dinner, and they're not exactly great for conversation."

I wonder if he's noticed that I haven't spoken a complete sentence yet. He talks even more than I do, and that's a feat. But for some reason, once an opening presents itself, the first thing out of my mouth is: "Dinner? Isn't it... what, five in the morning?"

He waves a hand dismissively. "It's dinner when I say it's dinner," he says.

Right. Deva tends not to follow the rules with the whole *time* thing, so I guess it makes sense that a prime minister would be especially lax. "Oh." I scramble for something polite to say. "Thanks for the dinner, uh, invitation, then. Appreciate the hospitality."

"Oh, please, you're the one doing me a favor. I was hoping to have a chance to do so last time you were on Deva, but... it seems you're a difficult woman to reach, even for me."

He laughs, and I feel faintly queasy as I think of being followed through the city last time. But based off of that and his current casual demeanor, I'm guessing this isn't about the IA's plot to kill him, so that's a relief, at least.

"The Interplanetary Alliance is trying awfully hard to get their hands on you," he continues, eyeing me thoughtfully. "I wonder why that is? Did you do something to piss them off? Or...are you perhaps more important than you appear?" He tilts his head, regarding me, and I stay silent while I fight panic.

Again, I'm reminded of all of the secrets I hold. The Planetary Defense Systems. The new planet. The IA plot to murder this man. It's also hard to forget, in this moment, all of the stories I've heard of people being tortured, jailed, and publicly executed on this planet.

Before I can think of anything to say, dinner arrives.

I may be drastically sleep-deprived and on the verge of a panic attack, but my stomach still rumbles at the spread the servants set down on the table. Rice noodles and vegetable skewers, steamed dumplings both sweet and savory, slices of fruit sprinkled with chili powder...It's a ludicrous amount of food for the two of us, and it smells incredible. I wait for Jai to serve himself and then follow his lead, grabbing things with my freshly cleaned hands and only deigning to use chopsticks for especially messy dishes.

"Anyway. You must have all kinds of fun stories about the system at large. I want to hear it all," Jai says as he fills his plate.

Is he really not going to keep questioning me about what I know? Apparently not, because he's finally stopped talking, and is now staring at me, waiting for a response. I should seize on it before he brings the conversation back around to more serious topics, but this whole situation is so strange that it's hard to think straight. I stuff an entire dumpling into my mouth to buy myself time to answer.

It tastes like heaven. But when I consider what he's asking about—think about the bio-weapon traveling across Titan's surface, and the Primus statues towering over a ruined Gaia, and the war on Nibiru—it turns gluey and unappetizing in my mouth. I swallow hard. "Not sure I'd call them fun."

I don't think he's even listening to me. "Tell me about how you stopped the *Red Baron*," he says, in between mouthfuls of curried fruit wrapped in roasted leaves. "No, wait—first tell me about how you broke into Ca Sineh. Please, I've been dying to know how you pulled it off."

I can't help but smile at that. "Okay. That one *is* pretty fun."

Giving him the information about how to break into Nibiru's highest security prison is probably considered giving away planetary secrets, but fuck it, I've already committed treason at this point. I tell him all about our plan to break out the ex-pirates, encouraged by the way he stares at me, ceasing both to speak and to eat just so he can listen.

I falter when I reach the part where Orion climbed out of his cell and felt the wind on his face for the first time in months. Remembering the way he looked at me then, like I was some kind of hero. Remembering that he's gone, now. Sometimes I manage to forget for a little while, and then it hits me all over again and drives the breath from my lungs.

But he wanted the world to hear this story—his *daring escape from Ca Sineh*, as he liked to say. The least I can do is tell it for him. So I finish the tale, adding some dashing acts of heroism for Orion, playing up the drama. He would've loved this version.

Jai laughs and claps at the conclusion of my mostly true story, and I grin and mock-bow, hoping he doesn't notice me blinking a couple tears out of my eyes. Some of the tension in the room seems to have eased now, and I dig into my food with gusto. It still feels weird, sitting next to the most powerful man on Deva and sharing a meal, but it's oddly easy to talk to him. He seems different than the other politicians I've met. I don't get the feeling he's looking down on me.

"You aren't touching your drink," he observes as we're finishing up eating. He waves a hand, and the servants clear away the plates, many of which are still at least half-full. "Did my intel get it wrong? Not a whiskey fan? Something else I can bring you? Anything you like, just name it."

"Actually..." I cast one last, longing look at the rich brown drink, and then push it away from myself. "I quit drinking."

"Oh." He frowns. "Well, that's disappointing. I was under the impression this was going to be fun."

I'm not sure what compels me, but for some reason I want this man to like me. I tell myself that it's because it'll be helpful to Shey if I get close to him, but really, he's just the kind of person whose approval you want. So, I say, "I can still be plenty of fun."

"Is that so?" His lips curve upward. "Well, in that case..." He digs into his pocket and, grinning wickedly, produces a small, clear packet.

I lean forward, eyeing its sparkling contents. "The hell is that?" Nothing I should be getting involved with, I know that already... but it doesn't hurt to ask.

"This, my dear, is the most popular and most expensive drug circulating Zi Vi at the moment," he says, cutting out two thin lines on the table in front of us. The stuff shines like diamonds. "Stardust."

I realize I'm leaning in so close I'm bumping elbows with Jai, and force myself to shift back onto my cushion. No, no, no. This is not a good idea. "I'm not really a drug person," I say, honestly. "One vice was enough for me. Never felt the urge to dabble in more." I pause. "Well, as far as substances go, I mean."

Jai waves a hand. "It's perfectly legal," he says, as if that means a damn thing on Deva. Rather than say more, he leans down and snorts one of the lines through a rolled-up piece of paper. A few moments later, he breaks into a loose grin. "And mine, I can assure you, is very pure."

I pull my bottom lip between my teeth, watching Jai's pupils grow. "What's it do?"

"Thought you were the adventurous type?" He turns to face me fully, tilting his head and looking down at me, his expression teasing but his eyes piercing. "Thought you were fun."

I meet his gaze, feeling pinned in place by his stare. Fucking hell, am I being peer pressured by the prime minister of Deva? This is not how I expected this night to go, and judging from the way he's looking at me right now, I half suspect it could go to even more unexpected places if I decided to take it that way. He's not exactly my type—a bit older than I usually prefer—but it would make one hell of a story...

No. Nope. Shouldn't be thinking about that, nor considering the line of drugs sparkling at me from the tabletop. I still don't even know what the shit is going to do to me, and the IA intends to *kill* this man, and Shey is unwillingly involved now, and she'd be strangling me if she could see me at this moment.

Or maybe she wouldn't. Shey *does* need a way to get close to him, doesn't she? Maybe I can figure out a way to fix things that doesn't involve her betraying her moral code. And this feels like a breaking point. Like I'm either all in right now, or Jai is going to shut me out. Maybe I need to prove to him that I'm different from the people he's used to. I need to hold his interest. This could do that. And what could one line hurt, really?

"Fuck it," I say, and bend down to inhale the line.

I'm not used to snorting anything, and it burns like cold fire in my sinuses and leaves a bitter, acrid taste in the back of my mouth. I cough, wrinkling my nose. But a few moments later, I forget that entirely as electricity sparks through every nerve of my body.

"Holy shit," I whisper, staring around the room.

Everything is sharp and in focus and *beautiful*; gleaming gold and sparkling crystal. Even the whorls in the dark wood of the dining table strike me as suddenly stunning. But better than that, and the tingling in my fingers and the tip of my nose, is the feeling that I have never been so comfortable in my own skin. My heart is pounding fast in my ears, but rather than a wave of anxiety, I only feel the push to *move, do something, do anything you want!* I feel like I could fight off a wave of Gaian law-enforcers right now. Or dance an effortless ballet. Or...or...

I look at Jai, look at his beautiful dark eyes and the radiant smile he's directing at me, and feel in my bones that this is right. I was doubting myself, but I'm meant to be here. I have a job to do, and never has a moment been more perfect than right now. I've been agonizing about all of the secrets I'm keeping and the pressure heaped upon me—now here's a chance to change the system for the better *without* jumping into the spotlight and bringing further danger to myself. I could influence the whole system, through him.

"I need to tell you something," I say, leaning forward so my face is nearly touching his. "And it is very, very important."

"Oh, this should be good," Jai says, his eyes dancing with mischief.

I spring up and, feeling absolutely 100 percent confident that this is the right move to make, jump onto the dining table. Jai collapses into laughter, so I wait for him to calm down—and my own giggles to subside—before starting to speak. He sits cross-legged with his hands in his lap, genuine interest in his eyes.

He wants to listen. He will listen. I can do this, I know I can.

The IA thinks the only way to pull off this plan is to get Misha out of the way, but they've never sat down and had dinner with the man. Maybe *I* can convince him to join the Interplanetary Alliance. And wouldn't it be great to end things without anyone getting killed for once? I can see it now: a beautiful new system with Nibiru, and Titan, and Gaia, and Deva all working together in the Interplanetary Alliance. Pax...eh, I've never liked Pax much anyway, they can do whatever they want.

If I can convince Jai, I can save the system. With the stardust lighting up the dark corners of my brain, I've never felt more ready for the task. The other times I saved the system involved a lot of risk-taking, and danger, and space battles, and all of that shit. This is just talking, and I am stars-damned great at talking.

"The system is moving toward a bigger and better future. Open trade routes, open borders...Don't you wanna be a part of it? Think of the potential of being part of the Interplanetary Alliance. I mean, I've been all over the system, but you've never been beyond your own planet. Does that seem right to you?" I pause, while Jai continues to watch me with raised eyebrows, and then I have to scramble to remember what I was talking about. "I mean, don't get me wrong, Zi Vi is undoubtedly the crown jewel of Nova Vita, but that doesn't mean it's the only thing to see. Don't you wanna one day be able to visit the Isle of Flowers on Nibiru, or..."

I pause, fumbling for another great city or landmark to use as an example. The underground fortress of Drev Dravaask on Titan? Not exactly a tourist attraction anymore. Levian, Gaia's Clockwork City? Nothing but rubble now. "Or Azha on Pax?" I finish, desperately hoping he won't notice the pause or ask any questions about the city, seeing as I've never actually been there. Then I remember Deva and Pax aren't exactly fond of each other, and say, "Or, well, somewhere. Anywhere! Just think of the adventure! Oh, and speaking of Pax, there'll be no need for any of this messy war bullshit. It's not like they'd have a chance against you, with the Alliance at your back. And you wouldn't have all of this trouble over the mines and building a fleet, if Titan was your ally! And..." I trail off, propping a hand on my hip. "And. Yeah. That's it, I guess."

The moment I stop talking, I've already forgotten most of what I just said, but I'm pretty confident that I nailed it.

Thunderous applause follows. Well, thunderous is probably an exaggeration since it's only my sole audience member, but still, the prime minister of Deva is clapping for me, and that has to count for something. Feeling pleased with myself, and a little bit breathless, I bow, hop down off the table, and take my seat next to Jai again.

"That sounds wonderful," Misha says.

"It does?"

"I would welcome an alliance with the IA."

"You would?" Can it really be that easy? Did I just successfully convince him while high off my ass? I search Jai's face, but he looks sincere. I start to smile. "Well, in that case—"

"But…"

My smile fades. Of course there's a *but*.

"I can't."

I wait for more of an explanation, but none comes. "What do you mean? Of course you can. You're the prime minister, you can do whatever you want!"

"It's…" He sighs and gestures vaguely. "Politics, Scorpia. It's all very complicated. Anyway… ready for dessert?"

I've lost my appetite, but a servant is already approaching with a tray of various sweets. She gives me an odd look as she approaches, like she's checking my reaction to Jai's words. I force myself to keep smiling and take a few bites of a sugar-dusted sunfruit cut into the shape of a flower, though I barely taste it.

Jai's quieter during dessert. Every time I glance at him I swear he looks regretful, and yet he offers no more explanation than he has already. I try to bring it up a couple times, but he just deflects and redirects, so eventually I give up. And as the drug fades from my system—faster than I thought it would—it leaves me ready to slump over and sleep on the floor.

As soon as it feels like enough time has passed, I stand up.

"Well, this has been, uh, great. But I'm exhausted. Afraid I'm gonna have to call it a night."

"Oh? So soon?" He looks disappointed. "A bit more dust could give you a few more hours, at least..."

It's tempting. Frighteningly tempting. I'm missing the high already. And if I had a few more hours with a not-so-sober Misha, maybe he could let slip something important...but no. When I'm this tired, it's more likely that I'll say something I shouldn't. I've got too many secrets, and I don't know this man well enough to let my guard down.

"No, thanks," I say. "Not tonight."

"Well, if you insist. I'll have someone show you back to your room. It'll be the tunnels again, I'm afraid—can't have you seen walking through my front door."

The words are barely out of his mouth before a servant seems to materialize beside me. I nearly jump out of my skin. Stars, that is *creepy*. They must be listening to every word we say.

I'm about to leave when a thought strikes me. I pause on the threshold, and look back at Jai. He's still seated at the table, alone but for the servants standing at attention along the walls, and the guards at each doorway. For a moment, something about the scene just seems...sad.

"Will I see you again?" I ask.

He glances over at me, looking surprised by the question. "Do you want to?"

"Of course I do." And I genuinely wish it wasn't because he might have to die.

He smiles. "Then you will," he says. "Don't worry. I'll find you."

CHAPTER FORTY

The Sand Sea

Corvus

Silvania's caravan travels over the sand sea in simple hover-crafts, loaded with goods and covered by canopies to keep some of the sunlight out. Once we start moving, I expect the breeze to be refreshing, but instead it is just another wave of heat, often containing sand kicked up by the vehicle ahead. I grimace and stuff myself into the back of the craft, facing the long trail of the rest of the caravan following behind us. The crafts travel just a few feet apart, matching pace, bound together by thin lengths of chain.

A few hours into our trip, I notice Silvania jumping from craft to craft, working her way from the back to the front of the caravan. She stops on ours, casting a bemused look at the two shirtless Titans spread out on the hovercraft floor beside me. I haven't surrendered my shirt yet, but I'm starting to regret it, as it feels like every inch of my skin is slippery with sweat.

Silvania, on the other hand, looks like she has never been more comfortable in her life. Her braid whips in the wind, her loose clothing billowing around her. "We're almost there," she says.

I frown, glancing at the expanse of barren desert in front of us, and then at the tiny dot of Azha behind. "Where?"

She waits a few moments, squinting back at the barely visible sheen of the city we've left behind. I stare as well, and so I catch the exact moment when it winks out of our sight, coinciding with a cheer going up in the caravan around us. Silvania cheers as well, lifting one fist in the air and then grabbing a flask from her waist and taking a long swig. She grins down at me, and hands it over. "Nowhere," she answers, finally. "Ain't it grand?"

Flask in hand, I glance around, noting what she and her crew seem to be celebrating. All around us, now, the sand sea stretches out, seemingly infinite in every direction. A queasy feeling stirs in my stomach, and I quash it with a swig from the flask.

The day oozes past. Daniil dozes on and off, clearly miserable in the heat but never once complaining. Izra's pale skin has turned pink already despite avoiding the sun as much as possible, and she is predictably furious about it. I stare out at the sand and think about the task ahead.

When seven o'clock arrives, the caravan pauses. A few crew members set up drilling devices that pump water from the reserves beneath the sand, while others move around the vehicles passing out rations of flatbread, dried meat, and slices of a dark red fruit I'm not familiar with. Meat is always too heavy for me, and sits uneasily in my stomach, but the sweet fruit feels like a blessing after the long day, and helps quench some of the thirst that has been constantly scratching at my throat ever since I landed on this planet.

Silvania stops by to check on us. After one glance at Izra, she laughs and hands over a gel to rub on her skin and soothe the burns. Izra seethes with rage as she slathers herself with it, snapping at Daniil to cover the parts of her back and shoulders she can't touch, but settles down under his gentle touch and smile. His hands linger more than they need to. I watch them, frowning, uncertain what I feel about it…though something is there, and not the hot jealousy I remember from times on Titan. Something very different. But now is no time to consider it. I look away when Daniil notices my attention.

Soon we move again. The caravan doesn't stop at night. Instead, one by one, the riders of each craft roll down the soft fabric sheets on each side of the vehicles and tie them down to posts, effectively transforming the hovercrafts into moving tents. I observe a few of them before tackling the task with Daniil and Izra's help, and we push the cargo to one side to roll out our bedrolls on the floor. The two of them happily strip down to their underwear. Even that, I suspect, is mostly for my benefit, given Titans' casual attitude toward nudity. After a brief mental struggle against my modesty, I do the same and settle onto my thin bedroll. We're all so cramped I can't stretch out fully without touching one of them. But on the cramped ride here from Deva, we became used to sharing space. I'm surprised how comfortable I find it.

The fabric walls don't provide much in the way of privacy—I can still hear snatches of conversation from the crafts both ahead and behind us—but the motion of the hovercraft beneath us is comfortingly reminiscent of the houseboat back on Nibiru. The thought of our old home gives me a pang of sadness. I miss those peaceful days, and I miss my siblings. Scorpia, especially. Out here, I have no way of sending or receiving cross-planetary messages, so I have no idea if they're even safe on Deva.

Between the noise and heat and the thoughts plaguing me, I wake up hardly rested and soaked through with sweat. My mouth is dry, my lips chapped, my skin tight and itchy. Izra and Daniil have both shifted closer to me in their sleep, so it takes great effort to disentangle myself without waking either of them. After a few minutes I manage it and quietly make my way to the back of the vehicle, peeling the tarp aside just enough for me to step out.

The sun is as harsh as I remember, but the light breeze is a reprieve from the stale air inside. All around us, the sand seems to extend even farther than I remember. It is silent out here, aside from the whine of the hovercrafts and soft murmurs of conversation from the other vehicles. There is no sign of civilization in any direction. No food, no life, no water but the underground reserves, no reprieve from the baking heat of the sun. If we broke down out here, it would mean death.

This is a harsh world, suffused with radiation, dry and barren and hot. There is not much to love about it. But I can see why its people are proud nonetheless. Just as proud as Titans always were about conquering their icy world. Paxians have even more reason—this world is a testament to human determination. A defiant last stand against a universe that seems determined to kill us.

Even with sand in my eyes and sunburn creeping along my skin, the thought inspires me. Humanity fought for the right to survive on each and every planet in Nova Vita, but the existence of Pax especially makes me believe that we will always find a way to live, no matter what the system throws at us. No matter the fate of the aliens who came here first, we can outlast this. As long as we don't find a way to kill each other first.

It must be very early still, but Silvania is perched on the edge of the vehicle behind us, surveying the desert with a pair of metal binoculars. When she turns to look at me, they whir and retract. I see that they aren't hanging on her ears, as I assumed, but rather attached to the device in the back of her head. She studies me for a moment from behind the huge lenses before reaching up to detach them.

"Sleep well?" she asks.

"No."

She grins. "Figured. You'll get used to it. Or maybe not...life traveling the sand sea isn't for everyone."

"That's an understatement."

She gives me a skeptical look. "And your usual home is, what? A metal trap floating through the void? Not so sure that's for everyone, either." She grimaces. "That trip to and from Deva for the council was one of the worst things I've ever experienced. Nowhere to go, just some thin walls between me and death... ugh. Terrifying."

"Yet you love this," I say, sweeping a hand out at the desert.

"This nothingness has possibility," she says. "And I can go where I please."

"You'll have to take the argument up with my sister, if you meet her." I say the words lightly, but the moment they're out, my reluctant smile dies. Another reminder of Scorpia. I hate that she's out there alone, if she's alive at all. Deva can be just as much of a death trap as this desert.

Silvania studies me for a moment before asking, "How are your partners holding up?"

It takes me a moment to understand the emphasis she places on the word. Heat crawls up the back of my neck. Of course she would make the assumption that we're all together. We've all been sleeping together, eating together, remaining attached at the hip the entire time she's seen us. And such an arrangement is common enough on the other worlds, but a well-known normality on Titan.

Yet as embarrassing as the thought is, maybe it's easier to let her believe that than try to explain the more complicated truth of it. I'm not sure I could, even if I wanted to.

"They're fine," I say. And as she leaves me there to stare out at the great stillness around us, I allow myself, possibly for the first time, to wonder what *is* happening between me, Izra, and Daniil.

My inclination, as always, is to shy away from it. I have spent so many years running from anything akin to romantic feelings. It hasn't been that difficult, most of the time, to do so. Feelings have always grown slowly for me...and physical attraction even more so. I have never felt that powerful draw toward sex that seems to make most people lose their good sense. It was difficult to let anything grow when I was responsible for my family on Nibiru. And in the years after, when my family was constantly moving from planet to planet, spending no more than a couple of weeks in most places each time, it was impossible to get attached enough for me to feel that way about anyone.

On Titan, with Magda, was the most recent time I felt a pull of attraction. And even then I was so careful to hold myself back. I couldn't let myself get involved knowing how much more difficult it would make it to leave her behind.

But now...now there is no reason to hold myself back from that brink, other than my own cowardice. My siblings don't need me to look after them anymore. I am no longer a soldier with a war to fight. I am just...myself. I could choose this path. I could choose them.

Yet after so many years alone, I find myself uncertain how to navigate this. For many others, attraction seems to be an immediate and unquestionable thing. For me it is...different. Not as visceral and easy to define. The line between deep friendship and romance is blurred in a way I'm not sure I know how to untangle. And I'm not sure if my heart is built for a relationship that is non-monogamous, or that theirs are built for a relationship that would involve commitment.

And the stakes are so high. I couldn't stand to lose either of them if it went wrong. I am not sure they would even want me.

Daniil did, once, but so much has changed between us since then. And Izra...stars only know what is ever running through Izra's mind. She is so sharp-edged it is difficult to imagine getting close to her without being cut open.

Maybe it is not worth the risk. Better to leave things as they are. Maybe the two of them would be happier together, in a more typical Titan partnership where they are not tied down by any promises; I have seen the way they look at each other, and I wouldn't be surprised if it was already happening.

At the thought of them sneaking off behind my back, pressed together in stolen moments, I feel that pull deep in my stomach again. Not jealousy, but...longing. That's what it is. Longing. Not necessarily for sex, but to be touched, to be held; to have private moments that are only for me and a lover, or lovers, not to be shared with anyone else. With my family and my team on Titan and so many other obligations to the world, it has been so long since I had something that was just for me.

But perhaps it's for the best. Perhaps I am simply not the type of person made for such things.

CHAPTER FORTY-ONE

Politicking

Scorpia

B eing yanked out of bed in the middle of the night was a surprise, to say the least, but the Devan prime minister accepting my invitation to dinner is possibly an even bigger one. A week has passed without hearing from him. But when he does reach out, he wants to meet *tonight*. The moment I get the message, I race to Shey's room.

"You're not busy tonight, are you?" I ask.

She blinks at me. "Actually, I'm—"

"Because we're getting dinner with the prime minister," I finish before she can. She snaps her mouth shut and stares at me. "In an hour."

I was hoping this would be the good kind of surprise. But as she drags me into the bathroom to talk to me while she hurries to get ready for dinner, I quickly realize otherwise.

"You do know that merely writing a negative article about this man is enough to get yourself killed on this planet," she says. I sit on the floor with my back to the shower and do my best to ignore the fact she's currently very naked behind a very thin curtain. "And I already told you that the IA wants him *assassinated*. A responsibility that *we* are the only ones who are left to possibly carry out. So you decide to arrange dinner with him? In what world is that…" She cuts off abruptly, and I hear the curtain rustle. I tilt my head back and look up at her face peering down at me. "You didn't… set this up so we could kill him, did you?" Even though she's been trying to talk like it's necessary, she looks terrified at the thought.

"Oh." I turn my head away and try to focus on the question, rather than the glimpse of the silhouette of her body behind the curtain. "Uh…no. No. I just thought you would want to meet him for yourself before you make a decision."

She sighs and goes back to washing her hair. "It's a nice thought, Scorpia. But we're talking about a man who supports forced prison labor and makes his political opponents disappear if it looks like they have a chance to unseat him. Among other things. I think I know enough."

I bite my tongue. I don't know much about all of that, but I can't fight the sense that it doesn't match up with the man I met. "Well, he seems open to the idea of allying with the IA," I say, leaving out the part where he also called it *impossible*. "So I think we should talk to him. See if we can work something out."

"I suppose it can't hurt."

Shey still sounds doubtful, but by the time she finishes styling her wavy hair and shimmying into a shockingly gorgeous, low-cut dress, I'm feeling pretty damn confident that even a prime minister will find it hard to say no to her about anything at all. I feel shoddy in comparison—my hastily grabbed suit doesn't fit right and I *really* need a haircut—but that's all right, because I'm just here to be the middle-woman. I offer Shey my arm, and even though she's radiating anxiety, she still rolls her eyes and smiles as she accepts it.

*   *   *

Our hovertaxi drops us off around the corner from the venue Jai gave me, stating that the crowd is too thick to get through. I don't think much of it until we walk closer, and I realize this isn't an everyday-city-streets crowd, but the kind wielding signs and chanting war cries. I stop, biting the inside of my cheek.

"I'll ask him about a back entrance," I say, but Shey strides ahead.

"I want to see what's going on," she says, giving me no choice but to follow.

The protestors crowd the building's entrance and spill into the street beyond, keeping up a steady chant of "Shut the mines!" Three of them are working together to hold up a huge white sign filled to the edges with tiny black text. My feet stumble to a stop again as I realize what they are: the names of those who have died in the mines so far this *year*. Another lists off problems the mines are facing: brain-rot fungus infestations, collapses due to roots disrupting the structure, and more.

One of the young women notices us hovering and pushes forward, waving a comm at us. "Please sign our petition," she says. "It isn't right to force prisoners to work in the mine for ten credits per day! Stop the slave labor!"

Shey leans forward, her forehead creasing and her grip on my arm loosening as she looks at the screen. I'm not sure whether or not I should stop her. I glance around and, before I can decide, catch the eye of one of the black-suited personnel standing outside of the building's doors. I recognize the look of Jai's secret police a split second before he recognizes me and steps forward, gesturing to his partner.

The moment they approach the crowd, the seemingly impassable wall of protestors parts—afraid to touch the two men, even before they've made any signs of aggression. I grab Shey's arm again and pull her toward them. "Come on," I murmur, as she resists. "Not now. Jai's waiting."

"But that is inhumane—"

"You can't fix Deva overnight. One thing at a time."

She shuts her mouth, but I can see the storm brewing beneath her surface. Her face only sours further as Jai's personnel yank us into the building and shut the doors.

There are a few dozen round tables scattered along the wooden floors of the restaurant, but only one is occupied. Jai Misha lounges on a cushion on the floor, waiting for us. He must have cleared the entire place out for our dinner. A handful of servers stand with their backs against the wall, visibly sweating as they wait until they're needed.

"Ah, Scorpia," Jai says, springing to his feet as he sees us. He's barefoot, so Shey and I pause to hastily take off our own shoes before stepping down onto the dining room floor. I don't know if I've ever felt real wood beneath my bare feet before. Jai clasps me to him and kisses both of my cheeks before turning to Shey. "And the famous Shey Leonis, in the flesh."

Her smile is restrained. She dips her hands in a Gaian greeting before he can approach her. "It's a pleasure, Prime Minister."

Ignoring the clear message in her body language, he grasps her hands and gives her the usual Devan greeting. When he pulls back, he continues to hold on to her bare hands. I suppress a wince. "My, my, you're prettier than I thought you'd be."

Now I'm fully wincing.

Shey pulls her hands out of his as politely as she can manage. "We've met once before, Prime Minister."

"Have we? You do look familiar, but I thought it was just the resemblance to your mother. Bit disturbing, that. Must be awful, walking around looking like the spitting image of the most hated woman in the system."

"I've done as much as I can to distance myself from the memory of my mother and her atrocities," Shey says. "My vision for the future is, and always has been, the opposite of hers. I seek to bring the planets together, which means—"

"Right, right," Jai says dismissively, waving a hand. "Come, let's eat."

I refuse to meet Shey's glare as we arrange ourselves on the cushions. The servers practically trip over each other in their haste to place cold water and hot tea in front of us.

I need to find a way to turn this around, and quickly. This night has to go well. I know that Shey doesn't want to kill Jai, even if she feels some obligation to fulfill the mission of the IA diplomats. I have to show her there's another way. And I need her to show Jai that joining the IA is a good move for Deva, and the war with Pax isn't necessary.

Corvus is out there on Pax right now, probably getting his heroic ass dragged into yet another conflict. Here's a way that I can fight, too. Stop this war before it reaches the point of no return. I believe that the two people sitting in front of me have the power to do that—I just need to find a way to nudge them together.

It all seemed so easy when the inspiration first hit me. But it already feels like everything is going wrong.

"Forgive me the ignorance, Prime Minister, but I was under the impression that you were making a speech about the situation in the mines tonight," Shey says. "Will that be after dinner?"

"Oh, no, it's right now." He pauses to smile up at a waitress as she places a plate of steamed dumplings on the table, the metal tray clattering as her hands shake. "It's prerecorded. They'll use a hologram of me on the stage."

"Ah. Is that standard here?"

"Not usually. But these aren't usual times. The situation is a bit…" He clicks his tongue. "Tricky."

"I see," Shey says. "We did notice the protestors outside."

Jai groans, rolling his eyes dramatically as he grabs one of the dumplings and bites into it. I grab one after him, nervously tearing it into tiny pieces; Shey remains with her hands folded in her lap. "Idiots," Jai says. "I don't know how they found out I'd be here tonight."

"So you disagree with their cause?" Shey's tone is carefully polite.

"I believe the issue is nonsensical. I'm sure the work in the mines is difficult, but it's necessary. And the prisoners are glad for the chance to contribute to society."

"Necessary," Shey says, "like the war with Pax?"

Jai smiles benignly and takes a sip of tea. "Precisely."

Shey takes a deep breath.

"Guess we're getting right into it, then?" I ask, with a nervous laugh. "Well, Shey, I was telling the prime minister about some of the potential benefits of aligning with the IA the other night. He seemed amenable to the idea. Right, Jai?"

"Oh, not this again," he says, his eyes cutting away like he's bored.

I fumble. "Um."

"So you aren't amenable?" Shey asks.

He sighs. "It doesn't matter. It's impossible." I open my mouth, but he continues, "You're not going to be like this all night, are you? Talking politics?"

"I thought that's why we were here," Shey says.

"*I* am here to drink ridiculously expensive tea and see how many dumplings I can eat in one sitting," he says. "And I thought you were here to have a good time, too." He leans over and pokes me in the shoulder. "Especially you. You weren't nearly so dull the other night. Fancy another pickup?"

"Um," I say, well aware that Shey is staring at me. "Um..."

She gives me a good, long look, her lips pressed into a thin line of disapproval. The look she turns on Jai is even colder. Then she carefully folds her napkin, places it on her empty plate, and stands. "Thank you for the invitation, Prime Minister, but I'm afraid my stomach has soured."

She heads for the door while I'm still gawking.

I look from her back to Jai, whose face is an almost comedic mask of shock, and stand. "Um, one second, I'll be back," I say, and rush after her.

The protestors have dispersed outside, so Shey stands alone in front of the building, trying to hail a hovercraft to take her back to the hotel.

"What are you doing?" I ask, grabbing her arm. "You spent an hour lecturing me about how dangerous it is to piss this man off, and now you're doing this?"

She pulls out of my grip. "I'm not going to sit there and let that absolute joke of a man mock the things I believe in," she says. "I don't know what you thought you saw in him, Scorpia, but he's not a man that can be reasoned with. This whole place..." She shakes her head. "You're getting caught up in it all. But everyone in this city lives a comfortable life because people out there are suffering. The rot in this place goes all the way down to the roots. The only way to fix it is to start over. I can see now why the IA made their decision. And I cannot see any purpose in getting to know him further."

That stops me, my mouth hanging open, the argument I was about to make gone in an instant. I glance around to make sure none of Jai's personnel are close, and say, "You don't really believe that."

She glances at me, and then looks away. "I'll handle it myself. Just leave it be, Scorpia."

"No way." At the end of the day, even if this was a clear-cut case

343

of right and wrong, I don't think she could bring herself to pull the trigger...whether figuratively or literally. But I know she'd argue with that. "I'm not leaving you to do this alone."

Before she can get a word out, I grab her by the chin, take her face into my hands, and look her in the eyes. She stares back at me, her expression frozen in surprise, her hands resting lightly on my wrists like she hasn't decided if she wants to push me away or not yet.

"If you want me to do this for you, I'll do my best to get it done," I say, without breaking eye contact. "But I'll need you to look me in the eyes and tell me you really think it's the right thing to do."

"Scorpia..." She stares at me for a few moments. Then she takes my hands, gently removes them from her face, and shakes her head. "I need to go," she says, and walks away before I can get another word in.

I stay outside for a few minutes to gather myself and figure out what the hell I'm going to do. I can't find it in me to be too angry at either Shey or Jai...They're just two people who will never mix well, and I should've known that beforehand. It's difficult to see him getting along with the IA leaders, too, but...that doesn't mean he deserves to die.

And if he did everything that Shey is saying he's responsible for on this planet? Then...then, hell, I don't know. No matter how hard I try, I can't seem to wrap my head around the fact that the man in there is the same person who is killing off journalists and political opponents. Maybe he's just a damn good liar, but I feel like I'm not getting the whole story here.

And even if Shey and the IA aren't willing to make a deal with him, I have my own cards to play. The secrets that still feel like weights around my neck but could be useful currency if I use them right. This would be all too easy, if I knew I could trust Jai. The information about the Planetary Defense System would give him a reason to unite with the Alliance. The revelation of a new planet could rally his people to build a fleet without the war.

Or, it could all backfire. Send the system into war and chaos like the Alliance fears will happen if this information gets out. Jai might use his knowledge of the PDS against the Alliance. Force a hostile takeover of Pax. Abandon his less privileged people and flee to the safety of a new world with the upper echelons of Devan society.

I just don't know. I've been burned so many times before by people in power. And who am I to make a decision of this magnitude? How can I decide who deserves to know the truth and who doesn't?

Either way, I need to go smooth things over with Jai right now. I should be capable of that, at least.

I head back inside, forcing an apologetic smile. "Sorry about..." I start, and cut off.

"I thought it would be a shame for all of this food to go to waste," Jai says, gesturing to an array of plates that have been set on the table in my absence, "so I invited another guest. Hope you don't mind."

Sitting on a cushion across from him, dressed in rumpled pajamas and looking on the verge of panic, is Drom.

CHAPTER FORTY-TWO

(Not So) Clandestine Operations

Corvus

E arly in the morning, Silvania enters our tented compartment without so much as a warning. "You three know how
to use exosuits?" she asks.

I sit up, rubbing sleep from my eyes. "Yeah."

"Good." She grins. "Because we're about to steal some."

The exosuit factory is a dark, industrial building just outside
of the city of Luz. Though the architecture of Luz is similar to
Azha, the city has a very different atmosphere. It is compact and
severe where Azha is pale and sprawling, and a grimy haze hangs
over the buildings, a thick cloud of pollution belched from factories like the one we are about to raid.

I was expecting a stealth mission. Instead, Silvania's people
blow open the doors in the middle of the day, sending workers scattering. But the employees don't seem panicked, nor even

particularly surprised, as Silvania strides in at the head of an armed crowd. Daniil and Izra remain outside to keep guard while I follow the others in.

The workers stay pressed to the walls as Silvania wreaks havoc on their supply chain, sending well-placed shots into the machines that keep things moving, until the entire process wheezes to a halt. Her people barely pay attention to the workers, and the workers seem content to stay out of their way. I don't even have to raise my gun as we rampage through the factory. The others only turn theirs against machines, never people.

"Guessing this has happened before?" I ask when I catch up to Silvania, who is gleefully slamming the butt of her laser rifle into a control panel until it sparks and smokes.

"Oh, yeah. Standard fare. Gotta keep these arms manufacturers in check."

"And the workers?"

"Understand the necessity." She shrugs. "At least, I like to think so. Either way, nobody's lookin' to die for their paycheck."

I wait patiently while she murders another machine, and then clear my throat. "The exosuits?" So far, we've only encountered materials and parts, no completed suits.

"Right." Silvania straightens up, wipes sweat from her forehead, and points at the closest factory worker. "You. Where do you keep the finished products?"

"Warehouse," says the man, sitting cross-legged with his back against the wall.

"Show me."

He sighs, like it's an inconvenience, and climbs to his feet. As he ambles toward the back of the building, he calls over his shoulder, "It's empty right now, though. Mass shipment went out a couple of days ago."

My heart sinks. "Ives got here first."

We go to see for ourselves. But the warehouse—a separate building out the back of the factory—confirms the worker's story. It holds nothing but rows and rows of empty hooks where the suits normally hang. Despair rises in me as I think of the army Ives must be building. Even if only a splinter of Titan's forces defected to join her, if they're all fully trained and outfitted, they will be difficult to beat. I still remember the bleak survival rate on Nibiru, and saw with my own eyes how a squad of soldiers fared against a single armored Titan. Here, we don't even have the advantage of water combat.

I slowly walk down the empty rows, thinking of all of those faceless exosuits. All of those stupid kids dragged into another war.

But a glint of metal in a dark and dusty corner catches my attention. I nod my head at the back of the warehouse. "What's that?"

"Oh, right." The factory worker walks us over. There are a handful of exosuits left behind, most of them in pieces or missing parts. "Those must be the defective ones that didn't make the cut. Always a couple of bad ones in the bunch."

"How defective are we talking?" Silvania asks.

Silvania's people cobble together three functioning exosuits from the ones left behind. Still, they are far from perfect. One has damage to the legs, reducing its maneuverability. Another has a defective visor, making it difficult to see properly through the helmet. The last has a faulty weapons system with a tendency to jam. Still, there is little question that we will take them, or that Daniil, Izra, and I will be the ones to pilot them.

Silvania's caravan makes camp out in the sand sea, where Luz is just a foreboding clump of silhouettes beneath a cloud of pollution on the horizon. While her people work to alter the exosuits enough to fit us, Silvania takes me to the head of the caravan and points out a tall, wavy building that stands above the others in the city. The whole structure appears to be built of glass, and glimmers pale green where the light hits it.

"That's where our guy is," she says. "And probably Ives as well."

"So we can hit them there," I say, already thinking of how easy it would be to launch an assault with the exosuits.

She looks at me like I've lost my mind. "In the middle of the city? No. Howland already got our message. He'll come to us."

"And until then?"

"Until then, I've got a business to keep running. I'll be making some deliveries." When I frown at her, she continues, "From Azha? Milk, meat, eggs…"

"Eggs," I say slowly. "Ives is out there plotting and outfitting her army right now, and you're going to drop off eggs?"

"My policy is to always assume the sun will keep shining," she says with a shrug. "And if that's true, well, then, folks still need to eat. There are plenty of people relying on these deliveries that don't know Ives exists, and I'm not gonna let her ruin their days, too."

"It won't matter if we don't stop her," I say, irritated at her blasé attitude. "If she manages to stage a military coup on Pax—"

"Yeah, yeah," she interrupts, waving a hand. "There's always gonna be another crisis on the horizon. And I intend to always be there to meet it. But if I let it stop me from living my life, well…" She shrugs again. "That's just another way of letting the fuckers win, isn't it?"

She walks off before I can muster up a response, whistling under her breath.

Izra and Daniil are off finding ways to keep busy around the caravan, but I stay in our compartment, mulling over that conversation with Silvania. It's maddening, to do nothing but wait when Ives is out there setting her plans into motion. But Silvania seems to have a grasp of the situation and this planet that I do not, and I know any move I make is likely to undermine her. Whether or not I fully trust Silvania herself is another matter... but she is taking me toward Ives, and at this point, that is all I hope for.

At least that's what I keep telling myself. It feels as though I've been here too many times before—poised to save the system, or fail and watch it fall... and yet this time, more than the others, I wonder about what will come after. Now, I can't bring myself to believe that I would be happy to die trying to save the world. My mind keeps returning to Silvania's words: *That's just another way of letting the fuckers win, isn't it?*

I don't want to keep living my life for one crisis after another. I don't want to die for the good of the system. I want to see my family again, and have more time with Daniil and Izra, and see what the system, and we, could become without the threat of war looming on the horizon. I want to give my siblings a better life, a peaceful life.

I want one for me, too.

Maybe such a thing isn't possible for me, and after a few years pass, I will crave the rush of adrenaline in my veins and the weight of a blaster in my hand. But still, I want to try, and find out for myself.

The flap to the tent opens, and Izra steps inside, pulling me from my thoughts. "Corvus. I need a favor."

I fight not to show my surprise. She looks embarrassed enough about asking as it is. "Yes?"

She lifts up her bandaged gun arm with a grimace. "I got this installed in a black market here in Luz. Want to see if they can fix it."

A black market dealing in Primus materials is not somewhere I'd ever wish to be—but Izra so rarely asks for anything. I can't deny her this. "Of course."

"I'd ask Daniil along as well, but..."

"Yeah. Not too keen on Primus technology." Neither am I, at this point, but I can stomach it better than someone who was raised on Titan superstition. "He should stay in case Silvania returns with news, regardless."

We tell him of our plan before heading out. He seems relieved to be left behind, once Izra tells him of our purpose. "Have fun," he says, and resumes his work polishing a sniper rifle he dredged up from somewhere.

We catch a ride with a couple of Silvania's people making a delivery to Luz. Riding in the back of the hovercraft among coolers packed with food brings me back to the days when my family was just a smuggler crew. Strange, how far away that all feels now.

We have no trouble entering the city among Silvania's crew. I still haven't decided if people regard her with fear, or love, or the simple acknowledgment that she is necessary, but there is no doubt that she is important here. Her people tell us to return when we need to be picked up; the caravan will be running goods back and forth all day.

The buildings here look newer and more uniform than in Azha. Rather than the previous city's array of pale colors, most of the exteriors here are painted either the off-white of bone or the pale beige of the desert sands. The streets are paved more often than not, and the windows are covered in tinted glass rather than left open to the air. As we pass deeper into the city, most of the streets are shaded by overhangs. In nicer areas, misters spray outdoor seating spaces, and cool air rolls out of open doorways. Drones buzz up and down the streets as well—none of them armed— delivering small packages and handwritten messages. Most fair-skinned people carry parasols to shield themselves from the sun.

It's an effort not to stare at it all as Izra leads us deeper into the city, so it takes me a while to realize that she's nervous, standing with her right arm clutching at her currently defunct, weaponized left limb.

I've never asked her about it, I realize belatedly. It always seemed too personal. But if there was ever a time, I suppose this would be it. And I can't deny my curiosity. "Why did you decide to do this to yourself?" I ask. She shoots me a sharp look, and I clarify, "The Primus tech. You were raised on Titan, after all. I would've thought the idea would be repulsive to you."

"It was," she says. "That was the idea. It was…" She pauses, her expression thoughtful. "The Titans made me into a weapon," she says, finally. "I decided if I was going to be one, I would make it my own choice. A weapon in my own hands and nobody else's." She looks down at it, hefting the deadweight of the Primus material. "And the fact that it was alien shit was mostly a fuck you to the Titans."

"I suppose I shouldn't have expected any less of you," I say, and we share a small smile.

I've been to a Primus black market once before, on Gaia. It was a covert, tense affair. Business was conducted in near silence, merchants ready to disperse at the first hint of law-enforcers. In comparison, this "black market" hardly seems to be a secret at all, despite the fact it is literally underground. The entrance in the basement of an empty warehouse is not guarded, and the sound of conversation drifts out into the evening.

Down below, the concrete-lined tunnel is crowded and sweaty and full of the sounds of spirited haggling. The gray walls are decorated with strings of multicolored lights that give everything a strange, almost celebratory edge. There are far more people than I expected, and they look like the average Paxians I've seen on the streets, not roughened criminals.

Even for a well-versed traveler like me, it is hard not to ogle, including at the oddities that aren't Primus in nature. There is a stall bearing the bones of some great beast; another displays rare Devan plants in tiny, temperature-controlled terrariums. And of course, there is plenty of weaponry: laser pistols small enough to conceal in a boot or a sleeve, automated defense turrets, weaponized drones, and more.

But most of all, there is Primus technology. I thought myself immune to the superstition about it that plagues most of the planets, but seeing the bio-weapon's destruction on Titan and learning about the Planetary Defense Systems has changed my outlook. The aliens were capable of things far greater and far more horrible than I could have imagined. It makes me itch with paranoia to be surrounded by it now. There are guns with poisonous, needle-thin projectiles, handheld orbs filled with a swirling ooze the vendor calls living acid, and a small, vibrating crystal that causes splitting pain between my eyes whenever I look directly at it, among many other, stranger products. It's no wonder Silvania had so many drones hunting around on Gaia, if there's so much interest in alien technology here.

The twins would love this. The thought comes unbidden, and makes me miss them deeply—and also shudder. I make a mental note to ensure they never discover this place exists. If we see each other again.

I shake off that thought and turn to see Izra scowling at me. I didn't notice that I was lagging behind.

"This is kiddie shit," she says. "Hurry up."

She leads us down a side tunnel hidden away behind one of the merchants' booths. This one is guarded by armed personnel, but whatever Izra tells them convinces them to let us through. The space between the walls narrows and the crowd thins, and soon the humid clamor of the main market fades away. This area is more dimly lit, and the far fewer vendors don't hawk their wares, but instead watch and wait in silence for people to come to them.

"Are you certain we're safe here?" I ask quietly. Every one of my instincts whispers danger.

"Don't make me look bad," she mutters without turning around. She strides ahead with confidence. Still, looking at the tense set of her shoulders, I don't think she's as at ease as she's pretending to be. But there is nothing to do but dutifully follow her to the end of the tunnel, where she finds what she's looking for.

She exchanges quiet words with a woman with a shaved head and dark goggles, while I stand back and keep an eye on the surrounding area. After a few minutes, the woman removes a metal grate from the wall and reveals yet another dark, tiny passageway. I have to duck on my way through. At the end is a square room with concrete walls, metal chairs, and an operating table. I look from the straps on the table to the tray of tools—a mixture of what a doctor and a mechanic might use. Bile rises in the back of my throat as I realize the scalpels and other devices are all made of black Primus material.

"Izra." I've been doing my best to go along with this, but I need to say it. "You don't have to do this."

"I know I don't," she says. "But I want to." She looks at me, holds my gaze. "Let me make my choice." When I drop my eyes, she turns back to the black market vendor. "You can fix it?"

The tech removes her goggles. Beneath them, both her eyes shine metallic in the dim light. They whir audibly as they focus on Izra's arm, and I have the disconcerting sense that she is looking through her flesh. "Hard to say until I get in there."

"And if you can't, you'll remove it?" I ask.

The tech's disquieting eyes shift to me. "That would mean removing most of her ulna and radius as well, along with much of the muscle in her forearm."

"It's fused permanently to my body, Corvus," Izra explains, surprisingly patient. "That's how Primus weapons work. They need to be part of you."

"Organic technology requires an organic power source," the tech says. "I've never attempted a removal of such a significant alteration, but if you'd like me to try..."

"That's a last resort," Izra says.

I breathe in deeply, let it out. I want to ask about the details, the risks, the potential side effects, but I refrain and focus on Izra. "What do you need from me?"

"Just be here." She clears her throat, her pale skin splotching with color. "I'll be heavily sedated. Don't like to be alone like that."

"Might be better to wait outside," the tech says. "Especially if you're squeamish. This won't be quick and easy."

I pull one of the chairs up alongside the operating table and sit.

The tech sighs, looking at Izra. "He better not throw up like the last one did."

Izra huffs out a laugh as she settles back on the metal table, though I don't miss a flicker of pain, too. "Don't worry. He's tougher than Orion."

I wordlessly take her right hand, the one that is still all flesh. She turns her head toward me as the tech loads up a syringe and lines it up on her other arm, just above where the Primus weapon meets her skin. "If the doctor tries anything..." Her eye flutters as the needle slides in. "Kill her and take the tools," she murmurs, slurring toward the end, and her eye slides shut. "Probably worth..."

"...a fortune," Izra says, hours later, as her eye opens again. She blinks groggily and focuses on my hand, still wrapped around hers. Then she rolls her head to the other side to look at her arm and the tech. "Tell me," she says, the command in her tone diminished by the slur of lingering sedation.

"See for yourself." The tech sits back and begins to clean her tools—which are covered in blood and the viscous black fluid that leaked from the Primus material when she cut into it. I am trying not to think about that, or the memory of a similar substance splattering on me when I once cut the cords to an alien power source on Titan.

I would never consider myself queasy, but I will admit this day has tested me.

When Izra turns back to me, it doesn't take conscious effort to wipe the disgust from my face; I soften at the sight of her, so groggy that I'm not sure she realizes she's still clinging to my hand. But not too groggy to resist my attempts to help her while she struggles to sit up.

Her brow furrows in concentration as she turns, raising her freshly operated upon gun arm toward the concrete wall opposite her. Then she breaks into a wild grin as the weapon emits a low hum and comes to life, the rib-like outer sections peeling outward.

I realize what she intends a moment too late. "Izra—"

She fires. The serrated spear thunks into the wall, sinking a few inches deep. She grunts with the force of the recoil and nearly falls off the table, saved only by my grip on her arm. While I lift her back up to a stable position, she lets out a laugh that would terrify me if I didn't know her.

The tech, to her credit, seems unfazed. "May I?" she asks, slipping on a fresh pair of gloves.

"Yeah, yeah. Take the rest of your payment," Izra slurs, and swings her legs over the side of the table. Her attempt to stand is only salvaged by my arm around her shoulders. I wonder if she realizes how heavily she's leaning against me.

"I can carry you," I say.

"Absolutely not."

"It would be easier for both of us—"

She growls under her breath and plunges forward, one wobbly foot in front of the other, forcing me to hobble with her. I glance back as we're leaving, and see the tech approaching the wall-embedded spear with her tools in hand.

We're lucky that the crowd in the black market has mostly dissipated by now, since Izra is determined to barrel ahead with no regard for her current lack of balance or fine motor control. By the time we reach the surface, she's panting and stumbling. We both stop and swear as the sunlight hits us, blinding and hot. I wait for her to catch her breath.

"Fine," she says, after a couple of minutes. I look at her, raising my eyebrows. "Don't make me say it."

I lift her up and carry her without too much difficulty, despite my limp. Halfway back to the drop point, she falls asleep in my arms, her face nestled into my neck.

She wakes just as we're pulling back up to the main caravan, where Silvania and Daniil are waiting for us with matching, grim expressions.

"Got our message from Howland sooner than expected," Silvania says. "We're meeting tomorrow. Be ready for a fight."

CHAPTER FORTY-THREE

Invisible Strings

Scorpia

I walk slowly to the table where Drom and Prime Minister Misha are sitting, straining to keep the smile on my face as my heart hammers. I'm still trying to figure out how the hell she's here. But there's only one explanation: Jai's secret police must have known exactly where my family was, and the moment Shey pissed him off, he had one of my siblings dragged here. It's a threat. There's no other way to take it.

I stop beside Drom and squeeze her shoulder in a silent warning before folding myself onto my own cushion again. Jai's still smiling like everything is fine, so I guess I'll have to play along. "Great idea," I say, "though I'm not sure even this restaurant can keep up with my sister's appetite."

Drom grabs two dumplings and shoves them into her mouth whole, probably as an excuse not to talk for a while—a play straight out of my own handbook, and probably for the best. Stars above, why couldn't he have grabbed Lyre? At least I would trust her not to make any huge political blunders.

"Didn't realize we were at the meeting-the-family stage already, Jai," I say, as lightly as I can manage, while I force myself to pick at a plate of rice noodles.

"Welcome to Deva. Everything moves fast here." He reaches over abruptly and grabs my hand. "Forgive me. I should've warned you." He pulls his hand back and continues eating.

I pause. I swear he squeezed my hand when he said *forgive me*, and for a moment, there was an actual apology on his face. But... maybe I imagined it. I shake it off and continue forcing myself to eat. An awkward minute passes as we all pretend to be thoroughly invested in the food. Drom continues mainlining dumplings, occasionally shooting me bewildered glances. But even if I could communicate with her, I don't know what I'd say. I don't know what the hell Jai wants from us right now.

"Prime Minister."

Everyone at the table jumps as one of Jai's black-garbed personnel appears behind me.

Jai sighs theatrically and pushes to his feet. "Oh, duty calls. Pardon me for a moment."

I watch him walk off, and the moment he's out of the room, I scoot over to Drom.

"Are you okay?" I ask, just above a whisper.

"Yeah, yeah, fine." She glances around at the various personnel and waitstaff who are all avoiding looking at us. "But why the hell did I get dragged out of the hotel in my pajamas and brought to eat dumplings?"

"I don't know. I'm sorry. I've been meeting with the prime minister, but I never thought—" I stop as Jai enters the room again, impatiently shaking off the grip of the other man and stalking back to the table. He sits on his cushion with a huff, and takes a long swig of wine. I'm not sure when he got that instead of the tea, but that's the least of my concerns right now. It feels like everything has spiraled out of my control so quickly, and I've landed both myself and my family in a situation I don't fully understand.

"Is…" My voice comes out a croak, so I clear my throat and try again. "Everything okay, Jai?" I'm still sitting uncomfortably close to Drom, but I can't bring myself to separate from her.

"Well, now that you mention it, no." He props one elbow up on the table and leans against it. "I was hoping we could have some more time to get to know each other. Truly, I was. But we just received word that your brother has been in contact with Silvania Azenari over on Pax, so I'm afraid we're going to need to speed things up here."

I wish I had time to celebrate news about Corvus, but I don't. "I'm not sure what you're talking about."

"I'm talking about the Interplanetary Alliance. You worked with them. Now they are willing to risk—or pay—quite a lot to have you back in their custody. So… I'm going to need you to tell me what you know." He gives me a look that is almost pitying. "Before we have to drag any more of your family into this and make things ugly."

I stare at him, my heart pounding. Drom is tense next to me, ready to fight—but there's no fight we have a chance of winning. We're surrounded by Jai's personnel. We're on the planet he rules, with no ship to escape on. We don't even have Shey here to help us.

How did I let this happen? How did I read this situation so wrong? Shey tried to warn me, but I didn't listen. Was she right the whole time? Should I have just gone along with the plan to kill him? Stars above, just a few minutes ago I was considering spilling all of the system's best-kept secrets to this man. Maybe the IA was right—about him, and about the danger of sharing the truth, in general.

I take a gulp of tea, scrambling for an answer. Should I try to lie? Or give him a piece of the truth, to ensure our safety? Maybe I could just tell him about the defense system on his own planet. Or appease him with the information of a potential other planet. Would it be worth it, to save myself and my siblings?

I'm still deep in thought when I catch sudden movement behind Jai. A glint of metal.

I cough, splattering tea all over our food, and instinctively shove the table, hard. It slams into Jai and sends him toppling to the floor. He hits with a thump and a shatter of glass. "Scorpia, what in the stars—" He cuts off with a yelp as the thing I saw sprays the room in laser-fire.

Drom—closer than Jai's guards, faster than I would've thought possible—is on her feet in an instant. She takes two long steps and swings a metal tray at the drone hovering behind Jai's spot, sending it thudding to the ground before it can shoot again. A moment later, Jai's guards open fire, reducing the thing to a smoking heap of metal.

Drom stays on her feet, breathing heavily. I force myself up on shaky legs and stare as one of Jai's people picks up the drone and scrutinizes it.

"Paxians," Jai says. He brushes himself off and stands. "A mechanical assassin. How crude."

I seem unscathed aside from my shirt being ruined by spilled food and drink. And so is Jai, who is looking between me and Drom with a perplexed expression. Drom, too, is giving me a confused look, clearly unsure why we just did what we did.

"Why," Jai says, "I think you may have just saved my life."

"I think you might be right," I say. Just after I decided it was probably best to end it. And all I had to do was . . . absolutely nothing. But I couldn't even get that right.

It seems I'm always finding new and improved ways to fuck everything up.

* * *

The guards want to get Jai back to a more secure location, but he insists on taking me and Drom back to our hotel in his personal hovercraft first, to ensure our safety. Which would be a nice gesture, if he hadn't just threatened us and demanded the IA's secrets. Now that the initial shock has worn off, my whole body is trembling from the adrenaline of it all. Jai, on the other hand, seems hardly rattled. He's sprawled out across the cushy backseat, scrolling on his comm. A glance at my own confirmed that the newsfeeds are already blowing up with the news of the Paxian attempt on their prime minister's life. Even those who were against the war must be clamoring for blood, now.

At least Jai hasn't tried to question us again since the incident, but the whole thing has left me shaken and more confused than ever. It was instinctive to save Jai, and Drom followed my lead, but I still don't know if we did the right thing.

"How can you be so casual about this?" I ask, my voice barely a croak.

"What? Almost dying? Happens all the time." Jai doesn't look up from his comm.

I let out a strained laugh. "I meant betraying me. I thought we were becoming friends, Jai. I thought you were different than all of the other asshole politicians I've met." I almost let myself believe that *one* of the people in charge of the fate of the system wasn't a terrible person. No wonder Nova Vita is the way it is, if these are the kinds of people we choose to lead us. And no wonder the IA has no faith in what the system would do with the truth.

"Oh, Scorpia." He sighs and leans back in his seat. For perhaps the first time since I've met him, he looks at me seriously. "I thought I was different, too, when all of this started. I had plenty of dreams about how this would go, how I would change things for the better."

362

"So what happened to you?"

"I realized that's not how this job works. It's..." He hesitates, considering something, but then shakes his head. "I'm sorry. You wouldn't understand. There are things I can't tell you."

Then comes an unexpected and extremely disgusting retching sound from my other side. I turn and see Drom sticking her fingers down her throat. "What the *hell*—" I say, just before she vomits up the remains of several dumplings and the shimmering Primus orb I almost managed to forget was still in her stomach.

I gag as well, but that doesn't stop me from scrambling over to Jai and pressing a hand over his mouth. "Drom, you're a genius."

Jai lets out a muffled yelp, his wide eyes on the Primus thing now oozing across the hovercraft's floor. Drom scoots over and helps me hold him down. Our vehicle still hasn't slowed—of course, these fancy hovercrafts have a privacy shield between the driver and its occupants—so they must not have caught on that anything is wrong yet. Jai's eyes flicker to the driver's side as well, and his brow furrows as he undoubtedly makes the same realization.

"You don't have a weapon, do you?" I ask Drom.

"They grabbed me from the hotel in my fucking pajamas."

"Right. Uh...You think you're strong enough to snap his neck?"

"I mean, I've never done it before, but I can try."

I chew the inside of my lip. Maybe it's better to keep him as a hostage. But will that do anything? We'll still need to find a way off of the planet...

While I'm thinking, Jai manages to get an elbow free and jab me in the stomach. I recoil enough for him to get out, "Wait. *Wait.*"

He's not trying to yell for help—not even speaking above a whisper, in fact—so, against my better judgment, I do as he says.

"Did that thing just knock out all of our comms?" he asks, pointing at the disgusting alien thing still crawling across the vomit-strewn floor.

"Sure did, so don't even think about calling for help, motherfucker," Drom says, which is slightly less impactful when she's speaking at a whisper still.

"Oh, holy shit, thank the *stars*," Jai says. He pulls a mechanical device out of one ear, and then yanks a tiny microphone out of his shirt. "Okay, we only have a few minutes before they realize I'm being far too quiet, so let's make this fast. First of all: Scorpia, I'm sorry. I didn't want to do that, back there. But also, killing me isn't going to accomplish anything. Because I'm not the one who makes decisions around here."

"That's the worst lie I've ever heard," Drom says, reaching for his neck again, but I hold up a hand and she stops.

I blink at him. "You're the prime minister. Literally the leader of an entire planet. Of course you're in charge."

"One would think that, yes." He glances from me to Drom, talking very quickly and quietly. "But really. Think about it. Why do you think it's so easy for politicians to disappear on Deva, even when they should be the richest person in any room? Why do you think I've lasted so long when plenty of more seasoned politicians haven't made it through a month? Because it's all a game. A big song and dance where everybody sees the puppet and nobody pays attention to the strings."

"But somebody has to be pulling them. If not you, then who?"

"I have no idea. Any major decisions get handed down to me, via notes or my staff members, who really work for...whoever they are." He waves a hand. "That's not important right now. What I'm trying to tell you is that, as much as I love your idea about the Interplanetary Alliance, the people behind the scenes won't let that happen. They're afraid of the IA. So they want a war with Pax. It's the easiest way to maintain public support of the fleet, no matter how many people have to die in the mines and factories to build it."

"And you're okay with that?"

"I don't have a choice," he says.

"There's always a choice." The words are in my mouth before I can think about it—words Corvus once said to me when I felt the same as Jai.

Jai's expression darkens, and his eyes slide toward the driver in the front of the hovercraft. Discomfort crawls down the back of my neck as I realize that if Jai's not the one in charge, *all* of these people really work for whoever is controlling him. And they have him surrounded constantly—watching, listening. I think again of seeing him alone at his dining table, surrounded by servants and guards, and shiver.

"The upside is that I get to be adored by the public while doing very near to nothing. The downside is that, should things turn sour, I take all the blame. And if public opinion falls low enough that they decide it's time for a fresh start, well..." He shrugs. "Then I follow the same path that a hundred Devan politicians have before me." He raises a fist and expands it with a small pop of his mouth. "Poof. Gone. Never heard from again."

"Then they bring in someone new, and the public thinks that things will change," I say, catching on. "But in reality, the same people stay in charge the whole time."

"Exactly," Jai says. "So you can see. Killing me achieves nothing. In fact, at this point, it'll probably make them happy. That drone never would have made it so close unless they wanted it to." He forces a laugh. "I don't make much of a wartime leader, I suppose."

"And the death of a beloved prime minister would just make people hate Pax more," I say, starting to catch on. "Shit. This is bullshit. What are we supposed to do?"

We all freeze as the vehicle starts to slow. I hastily scoot back to my seat, Jai replaces his earpiece and microphone, and Drom grabs the Primus weapon—now the size of a beer bottle—off of the floor and swallows it in two gulps. I look away, gagging.

"Anyway," Jai says, full of forced cheer once again, as the hovercraft comes to a stop. "I suppose I'll be seeing you around, Scorpia. Do think about what I asked you. I'll need an answer soon." He smiles at me, but his eyes hold a warning.

CHAPTER FORTY-FOUR

One Last Chance

Corvus

I knew the raid would light a fire under his ass," Silvania says. We're at the tail of the parked caravan, watching as her people make the final adjustments to Izra's exosuit to accommodate her short height and gun arm. Daniil stands beside me, his arms crossed and his head down, deep in thought.

"Is it wise to do this tomorrow?" I ask. "If we had more time to prepare..."

"It wouldn't do shit," Silvania says. "The longer we go without contesting him, the more of a foothold he'll get on the planet. If he starts showing off that army, gaining momentum, gaining support from the other companies and from Azha, he'll be unstoppable." She sighs. "I know how it'd go if it was just us negotiating. At the end of the day, we both need each other to keep this place running smoothly. So we'd both make some concessions and end up with an agreement. But with a Titan army at his back..."

"If Ives has any say in it, it will be a fight," I say. "And as things stand now... surely we don't have a chance to win."

"Oh, don't be so dour." She nudges my shoulder. "Things around here have a way of working out. Nobody wants an all-out brawl in the sands when we need each other to stay alive. You'll see."

With Ives involved, I doubt that. But in the end, she's right: Letting Ives's plan go further will only allow her to gain power. We have to stop this now.

As her people finish up on the exosuits and Silvania heads over to join the rest of the caravan for dinner, I linger behind with Daniil and Izra. I walk over to the suit I'll be piloting and press a hand to its metal chest. I still remember how it feels to be a god of the battlefield in one of these. Remember, too, that each time I use one, I promise myself it will be the last.

So many times I have told myself: You can rest when the fight is done. You can be happy when it's over. By the time I realized the fight is never truly over for people like me and my family, it was too late to make myself think otherwise. I could not allow myself to indulge in personal happiness without feeling guilty for leaving a job half-finished. Again and again, I have plunged back into the fray with my heart set on some distant freedom that always seemed it would remain just out of reach. I have always told myself it was just one more time. Once more for my family, for my people, for the many faces that haunt me at night. I will rest when I earn it—*if* I earn it. If such a thing is even possible. Sometimes it feels as though the only end for people like me is on the battlefield.

"One more time," I murmur to myself. One more time. Perhaps I will live the rest of my life believing that whenever I'm dragged into another stupid war. Is it my own fault, I wonder? Or some cruel twist of fate?

Either way...perhaps it's foolishness, but this time, something tells me it really will be the last. One way or another, it ends here. Soon it will finally be time for me to rest, at last.

*   *   *

We all know the odds are stacked against us tomorrow. Daniil, Izra, and I are grim by the time we finish our preparations and head to meet the others for dinner. But to our surprise, there is laughter and song among Silvania's people. The meal feels like a celebration. We all hang back for a while, thrown off by how very different this is than the Titan way, but it is impossible not to be swept away by the mood eventually. We share in the food and in the milky-white alcohol being passed around. Every time I think about calling it a night, I realize that it will mean no longer hearing bursts of Daniil's laughter, no longer seeing Izra's rare, sharp smile.

No more chances.

So I keep drinking, bolstering my courage. It's Izra who finally calls it and leads us, half stumbling, back to our compartment of the caravan. We climb inside with some difficulty and collapse into a pile of limbs on the bedrolls. As we shift into a more comfortable arrangement—I end up in the middle, as usual—I finally manage to say what I want to say.

"I want you both to know that it's all right," I say, quietly, my eyes open and staring at the white tarp overhead. "You don't have to feel like you have to hide. I know it's the night before a battle, if you want me to sleep in another compartment, that's fine."

There's a stretch of silence so long that I begin to wonder if they both fell asleep.

Then Izra says, "You know what the fuck he's talking about, Daniil?"

"I believe he thinks we're sleeping together behind his back, Izra."

"Interesting. I wonder when exactly he thinks we have the time to do that, considering we all sleep together every night."

"I was wondering the same. I suppose an occasional quickie would be possible, but—"

"Okay, okay." I shut my eyes and sigh. "I get it. I misread the situation."

Daniil shifts onto his side next to me. "Well. You did get pretty close."

When I open my eyes, there are just a few inches between our faces. I study him in the dim, softened light filtered through the tarp, and realize this is it. Last chance.

I lean forward to cup his face in my hands. When he kisses me, it is achingly slow and gentle. I pause for air, and he puts a hand on the back of my neck and pulls me back in for one more, smiling against my lips. "I have waited an awfully long time for that," he says quietly, and releases me.

Not a moment later, Izra grabs me and roughly pulls my face to hers, sitting up so she leans over me. She kisses me—all heat and urgency, nothing like Daniil—and then sinks her teeth into my lip before shoving me roughly away from her.

"What—Izra—" I hold up my hands in surrender, unsure where I made a mistake. "I'm sorry."

"You should be," she growls. "You know how long I've wanted to jump your bones? And you decide to do this *now*? The night before a battle?" She glares at me, and shakes her head. "No. We don't have time for the things I want to do to you two. Go to bed."

While I stare at her, Daniil laughs, and settles back down into the bedrolls. "Yes, ma'am," he says.

We manage to keep our hands off of each other—mostly—but despite Izra's words, we still stay up later than we should. It's foolish to spend our energy like this before a battle, I know, yet I can't fight the sense that this may be our only opportunity. We share stories—what it was like on Titan, after Titan. Our first kills. Our nightmares. We share scars; we all have many. Izra runs her thumb over the scar on my face while I talk about Uwe, though Daniil already knows that one. Daniil hesitates when he reaches the spot on his palm where I stabbed him during our fight on Nibiru; I take his hand and press my lips to it in a silent apology.

Daniil talks about how often he dreamed that his father was some important man on Pax, who would take him away from life on Titan. It would be easy to find him, now that he's here; all he would have to do is submit a DNA sample and perform a genealogy search. But the need is gone now.

I tell them of my own father. The secret that not even my siblings know. I'm afraid of what Izra will think, but she only squeezes my hand before sharing her own memories of her mothers singing her to sleep, her father carrying her on his broad shoulders. How most of the rest has been swallowed by time since an Isolationist raid destroyed her hometown.

With each story and each touch, we dismantle the wall between us, brick by brick. It is the most terrifying thing I have ever done.

And when the morning comes and the camp begins to stir around us, I lie with Izra wrapped around one arm and Daniil's legs tangled with mine, and I am more afraid to fight than I have ever been before, because I have never wanted to live more than I do today.

CHAPTER FORTY-FIVE

Hard Truths

Scorpia

My mind is still reeling from the revelations about Jai and the corrupt system on Deva when we get back to the hotel. We're really backed into a corner here, with enemies on all sides. Jai might be an ally, but he's as powerless as we are. And even if we wanted to carry out the IA's plan and kill him, his replacement would be powerless, too. We don't have time to track down Jai's handlers and unravel all the layers of corruption on Deva. But I couldn't live with myself if I handed them the information about the Planetary Defense Systems, either.

In the hotel lobby, the television is playing the reveal of Deva's first squadron of new warships. Showing the lines of uniformed soldiers ready to board them and head to Pax. The assassination attempt has provided the perfect rallying cry, and the shots of an army of exosuits on Pax show that the other side is ready to fight, too.

We're at a dead end. Trapped on this planet, which is a ticking time bomb. And even if we had a way off of it, we'd just be running from our problems—and likely right into the grasp of the IA.

But before I worry about any of that, I need to make sure the others are safe. I go to Shey's room while Drom checks on Pol. She's fine—although still pissed off at me, judging from her expression—and it seems our little brother slept through the whole thing and didn't even realize Drom was gone.

But my knocks at Lyre's door receive no answer. I frown, reaching down to jiggle the doorknob, and realize it's unlocked. I pause, staring at the handle, and then shove it open and rush inside.

There's no sign of a struggle. Nothing overturned, nothing out of place, even the bed perfectly made...and no sign of any of her belongings.

Nothing at all except for a sealed letter with my name on it in the middle of the bed.

"Shit," I say under my breath. "Not this. Come on. Just give me a break, one time." As I approach the bed, I run through all of the possibilities. Did the people Jai works for already realize that I'm up to something? Or did they take her at the same time as Drom, to use as a hostage? Or...

When I pick up the letter and realize it's the first in a small stack, I get my first inkling that this might be something else entirely. And when I rip it open and start to read, it confirms it. This isn't a kidnapping at all. This is something worse.

Scorpia,

Before I say anything else, I'd like to make one thing very clear: This is not your fault.

I know you did your best. And your best has been better than anyone could have asked for. You kept us safe. You saved the system. Never let anyone take that away from you.

But this has never been the life I wanted. Momma was wrong about a lot of things, but she was right about the fact that I was never cut out for it. When I was thinking about that, the other night, I remembered the last time we were on Deva before she died, and how she tried to convince me to stay to manage her bank accounts here. She kept the bulk of her savings in an account in the city. And can you guess whose name the account was under?

Not much of a guessing game, I suppose, when only one of us was a Devan citizen.

We've always joked that you can buy anything with enough credits on Deva. So far, I've found that to be true. You can buy yourself a new name. A new face. A new life.

If we cross paths again, someday, you won't even recognize me. But I hope you know that I'll always remember you.

Love,

Lyre

P. S. I did buy you a parting gift. I'm not heartless. If I time everything correctly—and I'm quite confident that I have—it should be ready by the time you read this. I'm giving you the same thing I'm taking for myself: the freedom to leave.

I lower the letter and wipe the tears from my face. "You crazy, selfish little bitch," I mutter, and choke back a sob. "Good for you."

I want to stay here, and read the letter again, and grieve, but there's no time. There's never time. I'll have to find a way to be happy that my sister found a way to get the life she wanted, even if that life doesn't include me.

And I hope one day she realizes that the gift she left behind was even greater than she thought. She *did* give me a way out of all of this, but not quite in the way she thought. I grab the other letters from the stack—one for Pol, one for Drom, and one for Corvus—and race back to tell the others the plan.

As promised, we find *Memoria* ready for launch out in the jungle, next to Orion's grave, with fresh flowers growing on top. The ship is probably better than before, knowing Lyre; she wouldn't have been able to resist throwing in a few upgrades to the engine when she had the chance, especially knowing that she was leaving us without an engineer for the foreseeable future. But that's a problem for tomorrow, and we've got enough to worry about today.

As I walk through the halls of the ship, I think of all of the memories we built in this place. All of the people who made it into a new home. The ones we've lost and the ones we've been separated from. My family. My crew. I'm so grateful to have known them all.

While the twins and Shey keep an eye on the jungle—I expect Jai's people will be here soon, if they aren't already waiting out in the darkness—I walk into the cockpit and make sure the communications system is red and ready.

All of our systems are good to go. We could run, if we wanted. Flee to Pax and meet up with Corvus and the others, or try to make another deal with the Alliance. I bet the information I've gained about politics on Deva would earn me a few points with Heikki and the rest.

But I'm done running, and I'm done bargaining with these bastards.

Talking to Jai got me thinking about how nothing really changes here. And while that might be especially true on Deva, in a sense, it's true everywhere in this stars-damned system. Nothing really changes because nobody wants to own up to the fact that it needs to change. Nobody wants to admit that they've made mistakes, or that no planet in this system can survive without the help of the others, or that all of the tragedy that's happened could've been avoided if they were just willing to *talk* to each other.

If Titan had shared what they knew about the Planetary Defense Systems, Gaia never would have accidentally triggered theirs and set all of this into motion. Or if Gaia had just asked for help, or Nibiru had offered it to the Titans, or...Stars, there are so many ways all of this could've been avoided. For fuck's sake, the location of a new planet has been sitting on Deva for all of this time, but nobody knew because the Devans are scared of the aliens and Gaia never told anyone else the secret to accessing the Primus databases.

Once, I might've believed that everything that's happened over the last few months would be enough of a wake-up call for things to change. But after meeting all of the idiots in charge of deciding this system's future, and after seeing how eager most of them are to pin everything on me rather than take responsibility, I'm starting to doubt that. If I let them, they'll brush all of this under the rug and move forward without changing a damn thing. Lock me up and forget about me, and everything I did to save them.

But I've had enough of this shit. It's time to do what I should've done the moment I learned the truth. The Alliance leaders think that if the system knows about the danger of the defense systems, it'll mean panic. Chaos. War. All of the planets' paranoia driving them to attack one another, each so afraid to be the victim that they'll choose to be the aggressor instead. People rioting in the streets. The human race eating itself alive.

I can see the future they envision. But do I believe it?

I've seen a lot of bad in the world. Rows of uniformed bodies laid out in the snow on Titan. Paxians making a living off of another world's war. Gaians celebrating as foreign ships exploded in the sky. A mob of Nibirans chanting for refugees to return to their dead planet. Wealthy Devans living in luxury while prisoners die in the mines. So much fear and greed and hatred and violence.

But I've also seen people's ability for hope in the face of despair. Their capacity for kindness without reason. I've seen people fight so hard for peace.

So I'm going to have to hope that the people of this system are about to prove the ones in charge wrong. That they can show the bastards that they're better than they think. Prove that they deserve transparency and truth.

I've abandoned my hope that the people in charge can do the right thing. But the rest of us, the common folks—all of the Nibirans who welcomed the Gaian refugees with open arms, and the Gaians who apologized for their part in Leonis's hatred, and the Titans who laid down their arms, and the Devans out there protesting for the rights of the powerless, and strangers I've never met living on Pax—still deserve a chance. And I still have faith that they'll succeed. By giving them the truth, I hope I'm also handing them the power to change things.

Doing this will mean giving up my last bargaining chip. The one thing that ensures that my family is safe from all of the planetary powers who would rather see us locked up or dead. And it also means giving up my chance for a fresh start, and my hopes of ever disappearing from the public eye. After this, everyone's gonna know my name and face. I'll never be able to disappear. There'll be nowhere to run from the past.

And here I am, giving that all away—for *free*—for some

long-shot chance at peace in the system. Momma must be rolling in her grave right now. It's that thought that finally pushes me to hit *broadcast*.

"My name is Scorpia Kaiser," I tell the entire Nova Vita system, "and it's time for me to tell the truth."

CHAPTER FORTY-SIX

Imperfect Machines

Corvus

J ust got a message from Howland," Silvania says as we all eat breakfast, laid out on blankets in the sand around the caravan. "We're still set for a meeting tonight. But...there's been a complication."

I stop eating. "What kind of complication?"

"A broadcast came in this morning," Silvania says. "Your sister sent a message to the whole system."

I'm on my feet in an instant, the reaction too immediate for me to consider trying to hide it. "Show me."

She hands over a comm, and I scroll through the news story, my frown deepening as I skim through, absorbing the most important details. It's an announcement of the Planetary Defense Systems. Gaia and Titan already ravaged. Reason to believe that all of the planets have similar systems installed...

I pause, scroll back up to reread that, but I had it right the first time. It says *all* of the planets. I have to suppress a smile, knowing Silvania is watching me. Surely someone will question the idea of one of these systems being installed on Pax, when the aliens never settled here, but I doubt they will be confident enough to entirely discount it. And the time it will take to confirm everything may just be enough for the tension with Deva to simmer down to a manageable amount.

Scorpia's always known how to spin a good tale, sprinkling in just enough of the truth to string people along.

"All of our tech has already started pulling back, swapping to the defensive," Silvania says, as I finish reading and lower the comm. "Looks like Deva's doing the same." She sighs. "Bit of a shame, really. Apparently people are rioting in the streets on Deva, calling for an end to the war. With all of the unrest, it would've been the perfect time for us to make a move. Part of me wants to believe it's just a hoax from them, to stall…" She trails off, scrutinizing me, leaving the unspoken question hanging in the air.

"It's the truth," I tell her. "This is why the Interplanetary Alliance wanted to get their hands on us so badly."

"I was afraid you'd say that." She sighs and pockets her comm. "Guess I can't blame you for not telling me. But it doesn't make much of a difference right now. First things first: We handle our own."

We meet far enough out in the sands that Luz is just a distant shimmer on the horizon. Neither side wants to risk damaging the city.

Howland is easy enough to identify: a light-skinned man who dabs compulsively at his sweaty face with a handkerchief. He looks tiny beside Ives, who is outfitted in the biggest exosuit I have ever seen. A standard model would provide a solid few inches of protective armor—but this thing is a tank, each limb thicker than a tree trunk, making her into a metal giantess. With her helmet tucked under her arm and the wind whipping through her hair, the pale scar at her throat bared to the world, Ives looks like a Titan military recruitment poster come to life. She looks like she could take this planet down by herself—and I have no doubt that she gladly would. I'm not surprised that these poor kids were willing to follow her across the system. Not long ago, I might have done the same.

Ives's army stands back, but stands ready. Perfectly spaced lines of exosuits gleaming in the red sun. There aren't so very many of them—a hundred, maximum, I estimate at a glance—but there are far more than we can handle.

Still, Silvania strides forward without fear, gesturing at her own people to stay back like the Titans are. Only Izra, Daniil, and I move forward, taking our places across from Ives.

Howland and Silvania immediately start firing back and forth with jargon and references so beyond my realm of comprehension that I can barely follow the gist of the conversation. After a few moments, I stop paying attention and focus on Ives instead. This is Silvania's fight. Ives is mine. She glares at me across the sands, and I know she is thinking the same. The Paxian at her side is merely a means to an end, for her, and she already has what she wanted from him.

"Done," Silvania says, drawing my attention back to her and the man from Luz. They each spit on their respective palms and shake.

"What?" Ives asks, her dumbfounded face mirroring mine. "We agreed—"

"Yes, I know." Howland takes out his handkerchief again and wipes at his forehead. "But this is before we found out about this Planetary Defense System. Surely you understand that it changes things."

"I told you, it's a *lie*," Ives snarls. "The Primus never settled Pax! There are no statues here! No defense system!"

"We cannot be one hundred percent confident of that. And even if we were, this will be a blow to public support here."

"So fuck the public," Ives says. "Give them a show of force."

Howland gives a pained smile and dabs his forehead again. "With all due respect, Helena, this is a situation you have never fully understood."

Ives stares at the man in disbelief. Slowly, her lips curl into a smile. I quickly step in front of Silvania to shield her from whatever is about to happen—but instead Ives goes for Howland. In one smooth motion, she steps forward, grabs him by the neck, and snaps his spine like a twig. She tosses his body to the sand and turns to face her army.

"This man was a coward," she shouts. "But we have what we need from him already. Now, all that's left is to take what's ours. Don't be frightened by that broadcast's lies—Pax is a safe world. The *only* safe world. And we deserve it."

Silvania pulls back to join her people as Ives speaks, shouting orders as they ready themselves for a fight. Daniil, Izra, and I hold our ground. There's a mad look in Ives's eyes; she's come too far to turn back now, and she knows it. Her only possible route forward is force.

But there still might be a chance for me to stop it.

"Ives knows the truth." I step forward and raise my voice, directing it to the soldiers lined up behind her. "She has always known. The Titan generals all knew. Titan was the first of the planets to fall to its defense system, and they not only kept that knowledge from the other planets, but from *you*. For generations, they have buried the truth. They have let you keep fighting, knowing it meant the planet could never heal." I sweep my eyes over them, but it is impossible to gauge their reactions when their faces are hidden behind identical helmets. But I know there are people in there—people with hopes and dreams beyond endless war, no matter what the system may think of them—and all I can do is hope to reach them. "You didn't know the truth on Titan, or on Nibiru. What happened on those worlds was not your fault, because you were lied to. But if it happens again, here, it will be because you made it happen. This time, you have a choice. Even without the issue of the defense systems, do you really want to start another war that will last years? Turn this world into another Titan? Do you want to spend the rest of your lives fighting?"

My only response is the wind rustling across the desert sands.

Then Ives throws back her head and lets out a bold laugh. "Liar," she says. "Traitor. Deserter. Off-worlder. My soldiers know better than to trust the likes of you. I promised them glory, and I will give it to them. Along with this new world, which is ours for the taking. All we need is the bravery to seize it." She raises a hand and sweeps it at us. "So let us do so. Kill them!"

I brace myself, ready to launch to Silvania's defense. But nobody moves. The rows of exosuited soldiers remain still in formation behind her. Ives turns to look at them, her eyebrows pulling together. "Did you hear me?" she snarls. She strides over to them and grabs a soldier by the arm of their suit. "That's an order! Kill them, now!"

The soldier pulls free from her grip. They turn to face me, press their metal fingers to their chest in a Titan salute, and drop to one knee in the sand. Ives lets out a wordless cry of outrage. Then another soldier kneels, and another, another—spreading like a wave throughout the ranks, until every soldier of Ives's army is down with their heads bowed. Nobody speaks. Nobody needs to. The message is clear enough: *No more.*

They may have been young and foolish enough to follow Ives with the hope of seizing another world, but they are not willing to risk destroying one.

Shock crosses Ives's expression, followed by a flicker of fear, followed by something close to heartbreak. But when she turns to face me, she is all fury.

"Fine, then," she growls, and activates her suit's propulsion system. The huge metal feet fire to life, and she rises above the ground. "I'll handle this myself." She dons her helmet and launches toward us. With Daniil on one side and Izra on the other, I rise to meet her.

Ives's soldiers stay out of the fight. So do Silvania's people. It is only the four of us locked in a deadly airborne dance, Ives's perfect war machine versus us three defects.

I recognize my two companions by their suits' flaws. Daniil, staying close enough that his lack of vision won't hinder him. Izra, keeping her distance so she won't need to make any sharp turns. I use my superior maneuverability to cover their faults as best as I can, trying to keep Ives distracted while they whittle away at her defenses, keeping up a constant barrage of attacks targeting the joints of the suit, where the armor should be weakest.

But her suit seems impenetrable. Our attacks have no effect, and each blow from her feels like a close brush with death. After a hit to my side sends me spiraling off course and gasping for air, she slams a huge hand into Daniil in a metal-crunching hit.

He smashes into the ground, skids, and stays there. The fires of propulsion at his heels flicker and then die. "Grounded," he says over the comms, his breathing ragged. "I'll have to eject. I'm sorry."

But Ives is flying down after him, swatting Izra and I away like insects.

"No," I shout. "Daniil, stay in the suit!"

Ives comes down, hard, directly on his legs. He's still in his exosuit, but the metal warps beneath the superior weight of Ives's machinery. He screams over the comms—and then cuts off.

"Fuck this," Izra snarls, and launches at Ives in a wild attack.

One she's anticipating. She turns and grabs Izra out of the air with a massive hand, absorbing the impact without a flinch. Izra shrieks over the comms—pain and fury—but keeps firing rather than trying to free herself, launching burst after burst of laser-fire at Ives's helmeted face.

Ives seems barely affected. She continues to tighten her grip on Izra, the smaller exosuit beginning to bend in her grip, with the slow and deliberate cruelty of an animal toying with her prey.

I fly toward them, trying to fire, but my pulse rifle jams. I swear, jabbing at the trigger—nothing. Instead, I hit Ives in the chest like a battering ram. It likely hurts me more than her, but at least she stumbles back, off of Daniil, and loses her grip on Izra enough for the latter to slip free.

She grabs me instead. But she doesn't want to toy with me. While Izra batters ineffectively at her back, Ives swings her other arm toward me, and the suit shifts, metal peeling outward, revealing the barrel of a huge weapon within. It lights with a dim red glow as it begins to power up.

I could try to break free. Could try to grab her arm and aim her weapon elsewhere. Instead, I jam the arm of my suit into the barrel, as deep as I can. Surprised, she releases her hold on me to try to push me away—but I cling to her and shove the hand in deeper. The heat of the weapon sears through my suit, heating the metal around me, boiling the air. It sears my lungs. But I don't let go, even as the inferno grows, and grows.

I fire my pulse rifle directly into the mouth of it.

The explosion flings me back. I hit the ground hard, and black out briefly, but pain wrenches me into consciousness again. The arm of my suit is still scalding-hot; I can feel my skin bubbling and blistering. I jam the eject button. As I stumble free, I'm dimly aware of a great deal of skin tearing off of my arm, and how it hangs useless and numb at my side. Nearby, Izra is struggling out of her own damaged exosuit. I fumble for my knife with my other hand and head for the charred wreck of Ives's fallen exosuit with a single-minded focus.

At first, when I see the twisted figure rising through the smoke, I don't believe my eyes. But I come to a halt as Ives lurches out of the wreckage.

Her head is a horror. Hair mostly burned away, skin charred, barely recognizable. But from the neck down—the part of her body that was hidden by the exosuit before—she is mostly whole, in a sense. Her legs are undamaged. But in her torso, chunks of skin and muscle have been carved away, revealing the matte black of Primus material beneath. A skeletal figure, fingers tapered and sharp as knives. Wrong, and deadly.

In her quest for vengeance, she has made herself a weapon. Not like Izra, with careful precision, but with brutal and terrible abandon. And despite the ruin of her body, despite the way her face twists in pain, she comes right for me. There is nothing to do but brace myself, the Primus knife in my hands feeling suddenly very small.

Still, I slash at her chest as she steps close enough. Black fluid spurts from the gash left behind, but she doesn't flinch. She backhands me and sends me flying. I roll to a stop and spit out a mouthful of sand. There's barely time to scramble to my feet before she's on me again, clawlike fingers raking across my chest.

"How the fuck," she snarls, "did someone like you ruin everything for me? You coward. Traitor. Scum."

I stab at her again, and again, slicing out pieces of black material, but none of it slows her onslaught, tearing gashes in my arms and chest, until the sand between us is soaked through with red. She knocks me onto my back and presses her boot on my neck, and I choke on the blood bubbling up in the back of my throat.

Ives crouches down—and her chest erupts toward me. She freezes, staring down at the serrated Primus spear in disbelief. As she slumps to the side, scrabbling at it, she reveals Izra standing just behind her, gun arm pressed flush against her back.

"Die already, you bitch," she snarls.

But Ives rips the spear free, tosses it aside, and somehow stands again. Black oozes from the hole in her chest and the edges of her mouth. She grabs Izra and flings her with a terrifying amount of force, sending her crashing into the heap of her broken exosuit, before turning back to me.

A quick *pop-pop* of laser-fire zings forth; both of Ives's knees give out in swift succession, and she crumples forward into the sand. My eyes find Daniil, his lower body still trapped in his mangled exosuit, propped up with his sniper rifle in his hands. As soon as Ives falls, the last of his strength seems to leave him, sending him slumping back into the dirt.

A groan from Ives pulls my attention back to her. This isn't over yet.

She drags herself across the ground by her upper body, leaving a trail of gore and Primus material in the sand behind her. I force myself up to my feet again, swaying, and advance on her with my knife to finally end it.

Even still, she reaches for a gun at her hip as she hears me coming, her teeth bared in a snarl. "For Titan," she rasps, blood and black liquid leaking down her chin. She raises the gun, puts the barrel in her own mouth, and fires.

I stop in my tracks, gasping for breath. It's done. My body wants to collapse, but I force myself to turn and limp over to where Daniil lies, his weapon fallen from his limp fingers. He's still. Izra has dragged herself to his side and taken his helmet off. She cradles the back of his head in her good hand, but it's all she can do; his exosuit's legs are so badly mangled he'll have to be cut free.

I stumble and fall to my knees in the sand beside them. Distantly, I'm aware of cheers from Silvania and her people; aware that the Titans are starting to turn away and launch, fleeing in the direction of Luz; but none of it matters compared to this.

Please, I think—or perhaps I say it aloud, I'm not sure, as consciousness is slowly slipping out of my grip despite my best efforts. *Please.*

Daniil's eyes flutter open, and shift to me. "Is it over?" he asks weakly.

"Yes," I rasp. It's over. It's finally over. And I allow myself to slump forward into the dirt, and slip into a blissful darkness.

CHAPTER FORTY-SEVEN

What the Truth Is Worth

Scorpia

I told the truth and brought peace to the system. In return, I got a prison cell.

Four months in a dim little room on Deva—I've been counting day after agonizing day—followed by one week in a cramped room on a spaceship. But now, finally, the day has come. It's time to stand up in front of the Interplanetary Council while they decide what they're going to do with me.

To be honest, I thought they were going to leave me in that cell to rot. There have been all sorts of excuses about why the planetary leaders couldn't meet over the past months—*Oh, Pax and Deva are busy with peace negotiations* and *The Alliance is busy reclaiming their lost planets* and blah, blah, blah. Then, of course, there were the five assassination attempts, which didn't make me feel great about my chances of making it to a trial. One of them tried to drown me in a toilet.

But against all odds, here I am. On Pax, of all places. Ready to be judged in front of the whole system and then probably thrown into an even worse cell than the one I've been living in. Or executed, depending on which planet's laws we're playing by. How do they decide that, anyway? I'm sure somebody's tried to explain it to me, but eh, these interplanetary politics have always gone in one ear and out the other.

Still, when a guard comes to my holding cell in the middle of the night before my trial, I have an inkling that this is off the books.

"Oh, please don't be another assassin," I groan when I wake up and find him standing outside of the cell. I had *just* managed to fall asleep, too. This cell is pretty comfy, as far as cells go, but even though I'm pretty much resigned to my fate at this point, it turns out I'm still not immune to the pre-Interplanetary-Council-deciding-my-fate jitters.

"Ms. Kaiser, you have visitors who would like to see you," the guard says.

I frown. "You're waking me in the middle of the night for... visitors?" I sit up, running a hand through my bed-rumpled hair to tame it. But the guard says nothing more, so I sigh. "Fine. Whatever. Got nothing to lose at this point, I guess."

My escort rushed me through the building on the way here, so I take my time strolling along behind this man, glancing out the thick leaded-glass windows as we pass them. I'm hoping for a glimpse of Azha, but jails don't get the best city views. They don't seem to get much use on Pax, either; from what I've heard, it's more of a make-your-own-justice kind of place. Whoever decided to hold my trial here must've thought they were being pretty funny.

But all else flees my mind as the guard leads me into the visitor's room. I had some hopeful thoughts about who might be waiting here—maybe my family found a way to bribe the guards into letting them visit, or Shey, or even Jai—but, of course, I'm not that lucky. The three faces occupying the otherwise empty room are *not* the people I want to see right now.

390

"Wait," I say, turning to the guard. "I changed my mind—" But he's already exiting, and I hear the click of the lock turning. I sigh and turn back to face the leaders of the Interplanetary Alliance seated around one of the visitation tables.

"Scorpia," Heikki says. "Please, sit."

I lean back against the door instead, shoving my hands into my pockets. "Fancy seeing all of you here," I say. "Though... hmm, that's weird..." I pretend to search the room, and frown. "Could've sworn the Interplanetary Council was supposed to include Deva's and Pax's leaders, too. I wonder why they weren't invited to this meeting..."

"I told you this would be a waste of time," Altair says, glowering at the other two. President Khatri only gives a mild smile, her hands folded in her lap.

"Now is not the time for jokes," Heikki says. She looks older and wearier than I remember, and her sense of humor certainly doesn't seem to have improved with time.

"Oh, sure, now we're in a hurry," I say. "But that wasn't a problem when you made me sit around in a cell and lose months of my stars-damned life, now was it?"

"Then let's not waste any more of each other's time," Altair says, turning burning eyes on me. I manage not to flinch or grab my prosthetic hand, but only barely. "We'll be frank. The Alliance holds a majority on the Interplanetary Council, and will be voting in accordance with our decision as a group. So, we will decide your fate."

I expected no less, but still, the reminder makes my chest tighten. I'm sure my decision to tell the whole system about the Planetary Defense Systems didn't lessen their hatred of me. "Yeah, great. So why am I here? You just want a chance to gloat?"

"No," Heikki says, stepping in again. "We offered you a deal once before, and we're prepared to offer another."

Right. The old "you spend twenty years in Ca Sineh and we forget you ever existed" deal. It's strange, now, to think of how close I came to agreeing to that. I also disregarded their wishes about as flagrantly as possible when I broadcasted the information about the Planetary Defense Systems to the whole system.

So I'm surprised when Heikki continues, "We will vote for your innocence and your freedom so long as you manage to leave certain details out of your testimony. Such as the role you played in our peace agreements."

I blink. That's a way better deal than I'd expected. There has to be a catch. "And take full responsibility for all of the bad shit myself, I assume." I frown, glancing around the room. "But then you declare me innocent? How's that gonna work?"

"Let us worry about that. If you do your part, we'll follow through. I give you my word," Heikki says.

"Yeah, sorry, that doesn't mean much to me." But really, even if I ask for written guarantees, it won't matter. These people are powerful enough to bend the truth into whatever shape they want it to be. "But, okay. Hypothetically, if I'm willing to play along, I'm gonna need a couple things in return."

"Because exoneration in front of the entire system isn't enough?" Khatri asks.

I eye her. I'd almost think that was a joke, if Gaians were capable of such a thing. "No," I say. "It's not. Not after what you put my family through. I've seen that little list of yours calling all of my people criminals, and I know that clearing my name through some sham of a trial means you can still use my siblings and my crew as leverage against me..." I swallow hard, choked up for a moment at the reminder that I have no idea where they've even been, these past months. "But I'm not gonna stand for that shit. You need to clear all of us."

"Understood," Heikki says. "That can be arranged."

"Fantastic. Then we're in business." I walk over, take a seat across from them, and put my feet up on the table as I stretch back in my chair. "But, while we're at it, I expect an apology from each of you, aside from Khatri."

Altair flushes at my words—that pale Titan skin must make it *real* difficult to play poker—and sets his jaw. Heikki considers for a moment before asking, "What, a public apology? I'm afraid we can't—"

"No." I wave a hand. "I don't give a shit about the public. I want you to apologize to me, in person. Right now." I wasn't planning on that last part, exactly, but once it pops out of my mouth, I realize it's not a half-bad idea. "Let's make sure we're getting started on the right foot here. If I'm gonna agree to trust you, again, against my better judgment, first I wanna know that you respect me. Or at least you want my help badly enough to pretend to, for a little while. You don't get to look down your nose on me while asking me to do something for you. Not this time and never again."

Altair is practically purple. "Are we really going to kowtow to this ridiculous woman?"

"That is *not* a good way to start an apology," I say. "But I'm a forgiving sort. I'll give you one more try."

Heikki and Altair exchange a long look, and I know they're both wishing they could share some choice words without me overhearing, but at least they're smart enough not to ask me to leave so they can talk trash about me. Finally Heikki sighs, shuts her eyes for a few moments, and then opens them and turns to me.

"I am sorry for the way we misjudged and mistreated you, Scorpia Kaiser," she says, her voice stiff, but polite enough for me. "And for the way we unfairly utilized your family."

"Especially my brother," I say, glaring at her. Poor Corvus, who was so eager for something to believe in. Politicians like her can smell it on a person and know just how to exploit it. "He trusted you, you know. He would've followed you to the end if you hadn't fucked him over and lied to him. He deserved better."

She merely dips her chin in acknowledgment. "I apologize to your brother as well."

I mostly asked for this because I knew it would humiliate them, but I'm surprised to feel a lump growing in my throat. I clear it, force on a grin before either of them can notice anything is off, and turn to Altair. "Acceptable apology. Next!"

This is the real test. I was willing to bet Heikki would swallow her pride and put her people and her peace first. But Altair? Altair, I'm not so sure about. From what I understand about Titans, there aren't many things they value more than their pride, and I've already humiliated him once when I forced him into the peace agreement.

The room goes utterly silent. Altair's jaw works; a tic in his cheek jumps. He must be wrestling with a whole lot of deeply ingrained Titan pride right now, weighing his self-worth against all of the lives at stake. I might feel bad—I don't think he's an evil man, necessarily, not in the same way that Leonis was—but the man did cut off my hand out of spite. I fold my arms over my chest and tap my prosthetic fingers.

He grits his teeth and lowers his head, but at least he has the guts to look me in the eyes. "I apologize for underestimating you," he says, slowly, like he's choking each word out.

I'm tempted to try to get more out of him, but I know the look of a man who will snap if he's pushed any further, so I only meet his gaze unflinchingly and nod. "Appreciate it."

"If I may?" President Khatri speaks up. I turn to her, and she stands. She extends her hands, and I'm surprised to recognize her palms out in a sign of Gaian apology. Or asking for forgiveness. Still not entirely sure if they really are two separate things in convoluted Gaian manners. "I, too, would like to apologize," she says. "On behalf of my predecessor. I am determined not to repeat her mistakes."

For some reason *I'm* the one feeling a little embarrassed now, but I smile anyway. "Hey, thanks," I say. "You're not so bad for a Gaian." And maybe with people like her and Shey to guide them, there's hope for the Gaians to change.

"Quite the compliment," Khatri says, her lips twitching. She drops her hands, smooths her dress down, and sits again.

"Well, okay then. I, for one, am feeling a lot better about moving forward now." I grin around at the mostly very disgruntled planetary leaders. "So what is it you want me to say, exactly?"

CHAPTER FORTY-EIGHT

A Map of the Stars

Corvus

We've spent much of the past few months on the move, uncertain of our standing with the Alliance and the other planetary powers. When we weren't arrested immediately, we slowly began to branch out, making business trips to Titan, and Gaia, and Nibiru, and Pax—though never to Deva. It would have been complicated, regardless, with Orion dead and Lyre gone.

Every time I think of her choice to leave, it breaks my heart a little more. But I will accept it. Lyre told me I was the only one she trusted to truly understand, in the letter she wrote for me. Which is why she gave me, and only me, a way to contact her in case of what she referred to as *another system-on-the-verge-of-collapse type of emergency*. I read the letter once, committed it to memory, and burned it so none of the others would know. I told Izra and Daniil, of course, but not the twins; some secrets are worth keeping.

But the other reason we couldn't go to Deva was that it would've been too painful to be so close to Scorpia's place of captivity and still respect her wishes not to try to break her out. We discussed it as a family, and determined we would wait and see what happened at the official trial. If she's found guilty, however, we already have a plan in place.

Still, it is hard to keep my distance, knowing we're now on the same planet—in the same city, nonetheless. We watched the government ships land outside Azha yesterday.

I want, more than anything, to be with Scorpia right now. But she asked me to do something important for her, written in careful instructions and passed from Shey to me, and now I finally have a chance to carry through.

I wait in a tea shop near the heart of Azha. My seat is at a window table with a startlingly beautiful view of the great city and the vast desert beyond. There is something inspiring about this place, and the people who find ways to survive here, all relying on one another. Especially since it provides a convincing argument that, in spite of all evidence to the contrary, humans *are* capable of change.

"Hey, Corvus."

I turn to face Silvania as she slides into the seat beside me.

"Let me guess," she says. "Bad news?"

"I wouldn't call it bad." I look out at the city alongside her. "But I have something to give to you."

She lets out a long sigh, and stares out at the view for a moment longer. Almost like she knows that what I'm about to hand to her will make it impossible to see it the same way again.

Then she nods to herself and says, "All right. Hit me."

I take out my comm and gesture to the screen. She turns the back of her head to me, and I pass it over the device implanted in her skull, sending the data over. When she turns back to me, her eyes are distant, already processing it. "This is just a jumble of numbers."

"It's a piece of some coordinates. But it's not complete."

"Coordinates? But this looks like..." She trails off, her fingers twitching like she's physically crunching numbers. "Planetary coordinates?"

I nod. "My family found something," I say. "Something in one of the Primus tunnels. The coordinates weren't complete—the data was corrupted—but we think, if someone can find a way to decipher it, this will lead to a new planet. A *habitable* planet."

Her face goes blank with shock at the word *habitable*. "A new world," she murmurs distantly. "But if the Primus found it first..." She trails off, her face thoughtful.

"Exactly. We don't know if they survived to go there, or not. Planet might be empty. Might not. Either way..."

"It changes everything," Silvania murmurs. "Who else knows about this?"

I'm not a very good liar, so I stick as close to the truth as I can. "You're the only one I've given these coordinates to. If anyone will know what to do with them, it's you."

The look she gives me is incredulous. "Seriously?" She studies me for a moment that makes me worry she sees through the deceit, but then she breaks into a grin. "Aw, Corvus. How sweet."

"Don't make this awkward. It was a logical decision." I grimace, turning my head away and looking out at Pax again. Beautiful Pax, that Silvania and her people are so proud of despite all of its faults. I hope this information doesn't change that. Most of all, that was Scorpia's worry about this information: that learning there was a new world waiting out there would make humanity give up on these ones. So she decided to make it a test. "Now, if you'll excuse me, there's someone else I need to see."

General Altair was considerably more difficult to get ahold of, and even when I found a way to get the message to him, I wasn't sure if he'd show—or, if he did, whether it would be with troops at his side ready to arrest me on sight. But he's alone when I find him on the edge of the city, standing beneath the overhang of a housing complex to avoid the sun.

He's not as tall as I remember. He is grayer than I remember, too, his face lined and weary. There's a wrinkle in the neck of his uniform, and his armpits are dark with sweat. *The old bear*, Magda used to call him a lifetime ago, but I never truly thought of him as old before now.

I remember how his anger toward me cut the last time we saw each other. Remember, too, how eager I was to please him in the past. There was a time when I would have done anything for this man. I followed orders knowing they would haunt me. I wasn't sure how I would feel facing him now, and I am surprised to find that it is mostly indifference.

"Kaiser." His tone is—though not exactly respectful—at least not the contempt I recall from our last meeting, long ago. "I believe you have stolen one of my colonels."

My mind flashes to Daniil—Daniil burning his uniform, chopping dutifully alongside me in the kitchen, curled up beside me in bed. I keep my expression neutral. "I'm not sure what you're talking about."

"You must know he will be held responsible for his past actions, one way or another." He regards me with those cold eyes. "Do you know how eager he was to turn against you, after Titan? That he begged me to kill you personally?"

"Just as you hated the people you now share leadership of the Alliance with," I say.

A flash of anger in his eyes. I hit a nerve. And I'm right that he's not so pleased to be sharing power after having a taste of it for himself. I make a note of that; the other members of the Interplanetary Alliance should watch him closely.

"I had such high hopes for you, Corvus." His voice lowers now as he slips into a more informal tone. "You were such a good soldier. Loyal. Obedient. I thought you would rise above the blood you came from. You have become such a disappointment."

He knows how to cut right to my heart. No wonder he always found it so easy to manipulate me. Not that he can claim all the blame for that; I was once very eager to be manipulated. So ready to place my decisions in someone else's hands, under the false belief that I was handing them the responsibility for the outcome as well. No more.

"There was once a time when I would have followed you anywhere," I say, taking a step toward him. "You had my loyalty and my faith. But that was before I realized what a liar and a coward you were. And before you maimed my unarmed sister for the crime of outsmarting you." My anger is rising, but I keep it at a low boil, letting it feed me strength rather than control me. "It should not surprise you that Daniil, and Ives, and I all abandoned you in the end. I have no doubt others will soon follow. Because you're the disappointment, *General*, not me."

Altair guards his expressions well. But just for a moment, I swear I see surprise flicker across his face. He turns away, and says nothing.

I take a deep breath, push back the anger, and steady myself. I'm not here to try to convince a stubborn old man that he's wrong. No matter how I feel about it, I'm here to do something that needs to be done. "I have something for you," I tell him.

"I don't need anything from you."

"Trust me. You want to see this." I hold out my comm. After a moment, and a glance around as if he's expecting some kind of trick, Altair takes out his own comm and accepts the file. His eyes narrow. "This is..."

"Coordinates." I don't have the patience to let him work it out himself. "It's a piece of the coordinates to a new planet we expect is habitable."

He stares at the comm, and then at me. His eyes narrow. "I don't need your charity. This—"

"It's not about need," I say, cutting him off. "It's about deserving it. And your people, more than anyone, deserve a chance at peace. Try to remember that." I turn away. "I have another meeting to attend. Goodbye, Altair."

CHAPTER FORTY-NINE

Seizing the Narrative

Scorpia

They bring me into the meeting hall bright and early, but then leave me waiting outside the main room for several hours while the leaders discuss other matters within. It feels like a cruel new form of torture, sitting here and thinking about what I'm going to say when I'm in there. The hours sitting in this chair feel like they drag on as long as the months I spent in a cell. The broadcast of the meeting plays on a mounted screen on the wall across from me, but even when I try, I can't bring myself to focus on it for more than a few minutes. For the first couple hours, I buzz with nervous energy. Once that wears off, I fall asleep.

I jerk awake to someone shaking my shoulder. One of the attendants, smiling uncomfortably as I sit up and wipe drool from the side of my mouth. "It's time for you to address the council," he says.

I stand up and walk inside, feeling like I'm still dreaming, or like I'm watching the scene unfold from somewhere above my body. The room I enter feels smaller than it looks on the screen, with a tall, domed roof painted with starry skies. The walls are lined with narrow windows, so the light of Nova Vita paints the floor in an intricate pattern and illuminates the faces of the various planetary leaders seated against the far wall in gilded chairs. Tiny camera drones follow me into the chamber; the only sound is their quiet whirring, and my footsteps on the sand-colored tile. I walk to the center of the room and look over at the people who are meant to weigh the value of my life.

Jai Misha is sprawled in his seat, playing at indifference, but when I catch his eye, he winks at me. Silvania Azenari—whoever the hell she is—is sitting next to him, and regards me curiously. The way they're both angled so their knees are touching ever so slightly makes me about 90 percent certain they've fucked at some point, and I make a mental note to ask Jai about that if we ever end up alone in a room together again.

And beside the two of them, Altair, Heikki, and Khatri regard me in stony silence. I meet each of their eyes in turn before dropping my gaze to the floor and taking a deep breath.

"Scorpia Kaiser, citizen of nowhere, you stand here today accused of treason," Heikki says. "It would take hours to list every crime you're suspected of, but your broadcast of confidential planetary secrets is the most serious among them. Do you have anything you'd like to say to us before we make our final decision?"

My heart is pounding, and my hands are shaking at my sides, but as I raise my face to the council and the cameras, I break into a grin. "Why, Councillor Heikki, I'm glad you asked," I say. "Because I sure as hell do."

Jai sits up straighter in his chair. Silvania has to disguise a laugh as a cough. I wish I could snapshot the simultaneous looks of panic on Heikki's, Altair's, and Khatri's faces as they start to realize they may have made a mistake. But it's too late: They've given me the room, now, and they can't steal it back in front of the whole system. I look directly into one of the hovering cameras and clear my throat.

Did they really think I was gonna stand here and grovel for their forgiveness? I don't need that. No matter how they decide to judge me today, I know that I did the right thing. They can't take that away from me.

"I'm not gonna deny that I did what I did," I say. "There's no point in that. Especially not when you've all already made up your minds about me. But I'm also not gonna sit here and act like I regret it when I've seen where those choices led. Nibiru welcoming the Gaians onto their planet. The cease-fire with Titan. The end of the war between Deva and Pax. I'm guessing most of you out there watching this broadcast don't know what I had to do with any of those events. You just know me as the person who told everyone about the Planetary Defense Systems. But trust me, the people in this room know exactly what I'm talking about. And they also know that none of it would've been possible if I sat back and did nothing." I sweep my eyes over the half circle of planetary leaders. At first I'm searching for a friendly face to latch on to, but instead I find my gaze stopping on Altair, who is glaring at me like he wants to jump out of his chair and throttle me right in front of the cameras. My hand twinges with phantom pain.

Beneath the fear threatening to overtake me, I find my anger. My rage at the sheer audacity of all of this, and this stupid sham of a trial, and the unending hypocrisy of all of these stars-damned politicians. People like me are good enough to do their dirty work and risky jobs, but not good enough to keep walking around afterward carrying all of their secrets.

Did they really think I was just gonna take it? Get up here and trust that they'd take care of me if I did what they said? I was willing to hear them out, but at the end of the day, not a single person sitting in this room has given me any reason why I should trust them. And even if I did, I'm not sure if it would be worth it, to let them erase me from the story.

Plus, I've never been very good at keeping my mouth shut even in the best of situations.

"All of you assholes are so eager to sit here and judge me. Where's the trial for General Altair? For Ennia Heikki and the rest of the Nibiran Council? For all the Gaian government officials who supported Leonis and hid dangerous truths from both their own people and the other planets?" I can see the way they tense when I say their names, clearly expecting me to say more about what they've done. And maybe I should, just to be petty, but I know they'd find a way to deny and bury it. And as much as I want to give them a good, long look at themselves, I don't want to threaten the peace I worked so hard for. "Where's the justice for the people left behind on Titan? For Kitaya? For *me*?" I hold up my prosthetic hand, meeting Altair's eyes again, and am gratified when he looks away first. "I'm not gonna deny that I've made some questionable choices throughout my life. But you've all done worse things than me, including plenty I'm sure I don't even know about, and you know it. Every single one of you fucking knows it."

I'm fully aware that this is stupid. But in the end, I can't bring myself to bow and scrape to these fuckers like I'm any lower than them. Not when each and every one of them is a hypocrite. I'm the one who made this peace possible, and I'm not gonna let them forget that. "I won't ask you for your mercy, and I don't need your forgiveness," I say. "But I hope you all know that punishing me isn't gonna absolve you. Any of you. If you ask me, I'd say we all deserve to be punished. Either that, or we all deserve to enjoy the peace that I've been fighting for this whole time. I may have made some mistakes along the way, and I may have used some methods that you don't exactly agree with, but I hope you can all see that's always what I've been striving for. So . . ." I look around the room one last time, and take a small, sardonic bow. "You're welcome."

I walk away from the podium and take a seat at the side of the room, across from the Interplanetary Council members. The entire room is silent for a long, long few moments after I speak.

"Well, on that note," Jai says, glancing around with raised eyebrows. "Shall we vote on the matter?"

CHAPTER FIFTY

How a Life Is Weighed

All over the system, people hold their breath as they wait for the verdict.

On Deva: From the huge billboards of the Golden City, to the tiny villages where they have only handheld radios, to a young woman with a new face and a new name holding a comm in trembling hands, they wait.

On Nibiru: From the Titans who still reverently whisper the story of the cease-fire on Aluris, to the Gaians granted a second chance on a new world, to the Nibirans who still call Scorpia Kaiser a hero, they wait.

On a tiny ship floating in the emptiness between worlds, two retired arms dealers grip one another's hands, and wait.

On Pax: A family of five off-worlders clusters around a screen, and leans against one another for support, and they hope.

And in the meeting chamber of the Interplanetary Council, one by one, they cast their votes.

General Kel Altair of Titan thinks of all the people he has had to bury, and all of those who—against the odds—still have a future to look forward to.

Councillor Ennia Heikki of Nibiru weighs her own sins, and those of the others in the room, and wonders if any of them could truly be called innocent.

President Chandra Khatri of Gaia considers how history will remember her, and her people, and how much of it will be the truth.

Prime Minister Jai Misha of Deva remembers the order passed down from those he answers to... but remembers, too, words Scorpia once spoke to him: *There's always a choice.*

Silvania Azenari of Pax, who is only title-less due to her choice to remain so, doesn't have much of a stake in this fight; but in the end, this is about more than the life and crimes of one off-worlder. Or, at least, it can be.

And a verdict arrives, for the space-born woman who has been treated as a living crime since the moment of her birth. She has been a criminal, a hero, and everything in between. But now, she might become one final thing...

CHAPTER FIFTY-ONE

Citizen of Nowhere

Scorpia

'm free.

I'm fucking free.

I was in no way prepared to hear the words *not guilty*. Some kind of boring speech by Khatri followed—something about how it wasn't fair to judge me by any planet's laws when I wasn't a citizen, and how my actions were in the spirit of a *system-wide* citizen, and it would be wrong to punish me for choices that ultimately benefited us as a whole—but I hardly heard any of it.

I never expected—or needed—them to tell me that I did the right thing by telling the system the truth. But holy shit does it feel good to realize I'm free to stand up, walk out that door, and do whatever the hell I want with the rest of my life.

And honestly? It gives me some hope to realize that these assholes have finally admitted that they were wrong the whole time, and their people deserved the truth.

I'm in a daze as I get to my feet. All of a sudden, I'm surrounded by planetary leaders. Jai is hugging me, and Silvania is shaking my hand, and even Altair gives me a grudging nod that almost feels like respect.

"There's still the matter of the official terms—" Heikki starts saying, and I turn and walk away, suddenly filled with skin-crawling desperation to be anywhere but here. "Scorpia, wait! We need to talk—"

But none of the guards move to stop me as I push through the doors and walk through the halls of the building, because I'm *free*. I hope to find my family waiting—but instead, the second I open the doors to the entrance, I find myself faced with a crowd of strangers and lights and cameras and questions. *Scorpia, how does it feel to be deemed not guilty? Scorpia, what does it mean to you to be space-born? Scorpia, did you ever consider your actions would lead you here?*

"Uh," I say. "Uhh . . ." And then I turn, and sprint back inside—pushing past Heikki as she tries to get my attention once again—and keep sprinting until I find a bathroom I can lock myself inside. I stand there with my back against the door, gasping, and undo the first couple buttons on my shirt so I can breathe. Once the panic recedes, and my brain starts working again, my eyes find the window on the far wall.

A few minutes later, I'm running through the streets of an unfamiliar city, past stucco homes and playing children and traveling merchants. The air is hot enough to choke on, and I'm horribly out of shape, but I don't care because it just feels so good to be able to run. I'm free. I'm free! Someone in the city is setting off fireworks, and I don't know if they're for me, but they sure feel like they are.

But eventually, I run out of steam and come to a gasping stop in a spot of shade. I lean over with my hands on my knees and pant for air and try to figure out how the hell I'm supposed to find my family with no comm and no transportation other than my own two feet.

A pair of eyes peers at me from a nearby house, and then

disappears. A few moments later, a kid no older than ten comes out and offers a glass of water, which I gratefully gulp down.

"Hey, thanks," I say, handing back the empty glass and mopping the sweat off my forehead with the back of one hand. "Say…you don't happen to know a spot where spaceships land, do you?"

The kid nods solemnly, twisting the glass in his hands.

"I'll give you a hundred credits if you take me to it right now."

As he leads me through the dusty streets of Azha, the kid keeps shooting me wide-eyed glances that make me wonder if he recognizes me. Or if he's luring me somewhere to get mugged.

But to my surprise, the kid isn't bullshitting. And to my even greater surprise, he disappears before I can come through on paying him. But it's hard to focus on that for long, because there, out in the desert sands beyond Azha, is my ship.

Memoria has certainly gotten a few more scrapes and dents since the last time I saw her, but stars damn, she is still glorious.

After being awoken in the middle of the night, and the trial today, and wiggling out of a window and running through the city, the exhaustion is finally starting to catch up with me. So despite the fact I feel like running toward my ship and my family, the most I can manage is a weary trot. The heat is oppressive out here, and it's hard to move quickly in sand.

Then the ramp slides open, and a familiar figure steps out, and I manage to break into a run anyway.

I swear Corvus looks older and grimmer every time we reunite, and his beard and hair have grown out wild and his limp is even more pronounced, and one of his arms is covered in some *awful* burn scars now, but that doesn't stop me from grinning like an idiot at the sight of him. That's my brother, scars and wrinkles and all.

I throw my arms around his neck with such force that I almost send us both toppling to the ground. But he keeps his

411

feet—barely—and puts his arms around me, his laughter a low and familiar rumble in my ear. I dig my fingers into his shirt, hardly able to believe he's real, and bury my face in his shoulder, and breathe in deep. Tears sting my eyes, because he smells like the closest thing to home I've ever known.

"I'm so fucking tired of all these dramatic reunions." I mean it as a joke, but the crying ruins the effect.

He laughs anyway, a quiet, gentle sound. "Then perhaps we should stick together for a while."

"We *better*," I say, finally pulling back, though I keep gripping his arms like I need him to anchor me here. "Stop running off to save the system on me."

"As I recall, you're the one who left on Nibiru."

"Shit, you're right." I release him to wipe my eyes. I'm really blubbering like an idiot, and it's starting to get embarrassing. "Well. We're even now. So no more."

"No more," he agrees.

Then there are footsteps racing down the ramp, and the rest of my family is here. The twins launch themselves at me. Pol has shaggy hair and a patchy attempt at a beard, and he looks thinner than I remember, but happier, too. Drom looks fierce with her head shaved and the scar from the war on Nibiru across one eye. They jostle over who gets to hug me first before both wrapping their arms around me at once, and I put an arm around each of them, and laugh and sob until I run out of air for either.

Daniil and Izra hang back and watch us, smiling—and I *swear* Izra looks like she's crying a little, even though she turns her face away before I can be sure.

Orion's absence still hurts. So does Lyre's. But I like to think that she, at least, is out there somewhere thinking of us right now, and I guess that'll have to be enough.

CHAPTER FIFTY-TWO

Let Peace Grow

Corvus

The twins don't want to let go of Scorpia once they have her, but I usher everyone into the cargo bay, since I know most, if not all, of us aren't up-to-date on our radiation shots.

"I'm kind of disappointed we didn't get to pull off our rescue plan," Pol says, clinging to Scorpia's arm as we move up the ramp. "We were going to blow up a building. And use Drom's Primus thing. Oh! Speaking of Primus things, Corvus let me go into the Primus tunnels on Gaia—oh, oh, and on *Titan*—"

"Wait, wait, wait," Scorpia says, holding up her hands and wincing. "Maybe we hold off on the alien bullshit for now. Let me settle in a bit before I have to shift my whole worldview yet again, yeah?"

Pol, looking dejected, turns to Drom and whispers, "I didn't even get to the part about my alien gun."

Scorpia, thankfully, misses that, since she's watching me. "But...you went to Titan?"

"Yes." There's a huge scratch in the side of *Memoria* because of the rough landing there, but she doesn't need to hear that yet. "We kept Drom's Primus artifact stored there, for a while. But as Pol mentioned, we grabbed it again in case we needed to break you out today."

"He makes me keep it in the cryosleep chamber," Drom complains. "I'm telling you, it's *fine* in my stomach—"

"Ugh." Scorpia grimaces. "None of that. Back to Titan, please." She looks at me again. "What was it like? Going back?"

"Well...we wore our suits, at first, but it seems the bio-weapon dissipated. It's as safe as it ever was." I think back to how it felt to remove my helmet and take my first crisp breath of Titan air in a long while; the chill burning my lungs. I climbed a mountaintop near Drev Dravaask, and the whole world was so still, all the evidence of war and death buried beneath a pristine layer of fresh snow. Each crunch of ice beneath my boots was like a step on a new and untarnished world. "And I found..." There, on the edge of the cliff: a single flower poking up through the snow, reaching for the distant sunlight.

Scorpia is quiet for a few moments after I tell her.

"Could be a fluke," I say.

"Or it could be a sign of something more," Scorpia says, giving voice to the hope I'm too afraid to say myself. "Guess we'll find out."

"And Drom's got a boyfriend!" Pol practically shouts; he must have been trying incredibly hard to keep it down while we spoke.

"Oh, shut up." Drom's cheeks flare red.

"What, a boyfriend? For real? A serious one?" Scorpia asks, glancing at me. I nod, one corner of my lips twitching.

"Going on three months!" Pol says. "He lives on Nibiru, and he works at this bar—"

"Yeah, yeah, that's enough," Drom says, cuffing him lightly on the back of the head.

I'm sure there's more Pol wants to say, but he's starting to get out of breath. He excuses himself and sits on the stairs, and Drom joins him so he won't feel self-conscious about it. He's only become sicklier in the past few months, which I'm sure Scorpia notes, judging from the sadness she's trying to hide as she watches him struggle to catch his breath. But there will be time to discuss that later; today is a day for celebrating Scorpia's return home.

As the twins step aside, Izra and Daniil come to greet their captain.

"Oh, hey, new upgrade for our resident cyborg?" Scorpia asks, pointing a finger at Izra's new implant. Along with having her gun arm repaired, she now has a smooth black box in the socket of her missing eye. "What's it do? Shoot lasers?"

"Not yet," Izra says, very seriously. Then she yanks her into a somewhat violent hug that leaves Scorpia looking shocked, and pleased, and a little bit in pain.

Once Izra releases her, Daniil steps forward and gives Scorpia a nod. "Welcome back, Captain."

"Thanks, Daniil." She holds out her arms, and he hugs her, too, lifting her up off of the ground as his new legs stretch to their impressive height. She lets out a surprised yelp, and he laughs and sets her down.

"I have a couple upgrades of my own," he says, and bends down to pull up one pant leg and show off the shiny metal underneath. "Both of them up to my knees. Courtesy of the fight with Ives."

Scorpia lets out a low, impressed whistle. "Right. That's another story I still need to hear."

"You will," Daniil says. "And plenty more."

"Good." She smiles. "You been looking after my brother for me?"

"Oh, yes, ma'am," he says, and steps back to my side, sliding an arm around my shoulders.

I hadn't expected to do this now, but...to hell with it. I lean into him and put an arm around his waist.

Scorpia slowly breaks into a smile. "So, you two...?"

"Well..." I clear my throat and gesture to Izra, who is standing back and scowling, likely bracing herself for Scorpia's reaction. "Three, actually."

"Oh?" She looks at each of us in turn—me trying not to feel self-conscious, Daniil grinning, Izra glowering at her. I assume the latter is an attempt to dissuade any jokes, but she should know at this point that it's just going to encourage Scorpia. "Damn, Corvus. Didn't think you had it in you. Really making up for lost time, huh?"

"Yeah, yeah." I sigh. "Trust me, there are no jokes you can come up with that the twins haven't already made at my expense."

"Oh, I'm sure I can come up with something," Scorpia says. "But, hey—let's get this ship ready for launch, already. I wanna get off this planet before any politicians try to rope us into another job." She glances around, frowning. "Who's piloting, by the way?"

"Me, mostly," Daniil says. "Though I certainly wouldn't be opposed to relinquishing the wheel to you so I can pick up a few pointers."

"That's a good call," I say, as peaceably as I can, thinking back to our shaky landing on Titan.

"Sure thing," Scorpia says. "Get everything ready for me. I'm going to have a quick chat with Corvus first."

As the others disperse to the rest of the ship to prepare for launch, Scorpia and I wander over to the ramp. We stand side by side, looking out at the open desert of Pax.

"I guess I should mention we've made a few alterations to the ship, too," I say. "Nothing I thought you wouldn't approve of. But we added solar batteries to cut down on fuel, and Daniil has been working on building a greenhouse in one of the empty rooms. In case we ever want to make a longer journey, someday. Or just be by ourselves for a while."

"Good thinking," she says, and glances sideways at me. "Speaking of long journeys... you gave everyone their pieces of the coordinates, I take it?"

"I did. It's all in their hands, now."

A slice of the truth for each of the five worlds. Put together, they'll provide a map to the unnamed planet. Either the new world of the Primus, or humanity's third chance at survival... Or perhaps both. We both know, despite our justifications, we're taking a risk by not handing over the complete truth. But we know, too, that putting that information out into our newly at peace system would be a risk as well. And as Scorpia so aptly put it, humanity got lucky with our second chance. We're going to have to prove that we deserve a third one. If the planetary leaders aren't willing to cooperate enough to put the pieces together, then they don't deserve to find the new world.

And nobody makes their best choices knowing that they have a clean slate waiting for them. We fought and sacrificed for this peace—better to let them struggle to maintain it, and think about how close they came to losing everything over their greed.

If we had spent our early days in this system helping each other, building pathways of trade and trust, life could have been very different. With Titan's mines, Nibiru's water and algae, Deva's bountiful food, Gaia's rich culture and wealth of knowledge, and Pax's ingenuity and industry, we could have built one smooth machine of a system. Instead, we haggled and fought. Planets refused to make trades that would benefit themselves because they knew it would benefit others, too, and instead ensured mutual misery. Each planet tried to lord its advantages while ignoring its shortcomings.

I remember my history, both from ancient Earth and the

long journey that brought us here. Humanity has always been so obsessed at drawing lines among ourselves. We focus on what separates us rather than everything we share, and see our differences as something to condemn rather than to celebrate. Again, and again, we spend our time building walls rather than bridges.

Our history could have been so different if we had been willing to change. But no matter how tempting it is to imagine, there's no way to tell now, and no point in dwelling on it. Yet perhaps it's not too late for the future. There is still a chance for us to do better, this time around. We have failed so many times... but that has always been part of being human: to fail, to fall, but always stand up, brush ourselves off, and try again.

"For what it's worth," I say, "I think that they're going to figure it out. Eventually."

"Honestly, I wasn't so sure. But today gave me some hope. Maybe it's not too late for them to change, after all."

"And if they don't, they won't be the only ones with the information," I say.

After everything we've been through with these planetary leaders, we knew better than to put all of our trust in authority figures again. Even this plan to split it up among them isn't completely foolproof—someone could figure it out, kill the others, and take it by force.

So there's also us. Everyone on our ship took a piece of the coordinates, too, and made a promise to pass it on to someone they trust. I'm sure it'll end up in very different hands than the people in charge, that way. And one piece, of course, we kept only for ourselves. To make sure that the people like us don't end up left behind. Erased from history, just like what's surely going to happen to my family now.

A part of me resents it, on principle; my family fought and bled and sacrificed to save this system, and in the end, they acted like they were doing us a favor by tossing us pardons and quietly smudging our names from the official story.

At least Scorpia's broadcast will make it difficult for the system to fully forget our part in all of this. And a part of me is also grateful for the chance to start again without dragging all of that baggage behind us. What good is a medal or an accolade, after all? It's not as though any of us have plans to get involved in politics or—stars forbid—the military again. Among the sort of people we tend to spend our time with, fame and government recognition would get us a suspicious side-eye at best. Perhaps it is better for everyone involved for us to slip quietly from the annals of history, our names and our deeds, both good and bad and the many teetering somewhere in the balance, all forgotten.

We don't need the world's approval. What is important is that we are all here, now. We are together, in a peaceful system, where there are so many good people, and there is so much work to be done. I don't know how anyone could ever ask for more than that.

"One more thing," Scorpia says, as I turn to go. I pause. "So... the other two Titans got their 'upgrades.' You decided not to?" She glances down at my leg. I'm sure she's noticed that my limp is as bad as it's ever been. And my arm still bears the burns from my fight with Ives. "I mean, it's your choice, obviously, no judgment, but... this isn't some way of punishing yourself, is it?"

I smile. "No. It's not. I just don't want to be a weapon anymore. For me, it's a reminder that my body is entirely my own, now." I touch my wrist, and turn it toward her, showing the tattoo of a flower that covers where my war-brand once was. "And that the fight is over."

CHAPTER FIFTY-THREE

Daughter of the Stars

Scorpia

When I turn to get one last look at Pax, I realize there's a hovercraft racing across the sand toward us.

"Shit," I say. "Guess it's time to go." My hand moves toward the pressure pad to close the ramp, but Corvus catches my wrist. He tilts his chin out to the hovercraft, and I turn to see a single figure has climbed out and started the trek toward us by foot. "Yeah, no, it's really time to go," I say, my heartbeat rising.

Corvus frowns at me—first in confusion, and then deepening into disapproval. "You were going to leave without seeing her?"

"No! I already…" I trail off, unable to muster up a good enough lie, and blow out a breath. "Okay, yes, I was. But really, Corvus, it's for the best."

"No. You don't get to run from this."

"I am the *captain*! I can run from whatever I want!"

Despite my protests, Corvus grabs me and hauls me down the ramp. When I fight, he throws me over his shoulder, carries me, and throws me down in the dust at the feet of the approaching figure. While I'm still recovering from the absolute indignity of that, he walks back up the ramp and leaves me here, alone, with her.

"You left before the closing ceremony," Shey says. The wind rustles through her dress. "I believe they were planning on giving you a medal. And possibly a citizenship. And at least two of them were hoping to offer you a job."

"Yeah. Well." I cough, shrug, and climb to my feet, brushing dust off of my clothes and trying to regain some poise. "Not interested in any of that. I'm ready to get away from all of this shit." I gesture vaguely toward the city. Meaning not just here, not just the Interplanetary Council, but everywhere. Everyone. This whole damn mess we call civilization. I never fit in there, and after seeing the things that this system is capable of, I really don't want to anymore. From this point onward, it's their job to work out their own issues. And I'll be out among the stars, far beyond their reach, for at least a while.

Shey is quiet for a few moments, looking back at the city. She pulls her shawl tighter around her shoulders, as if shielding herself against something, and turns back to me. "And I am included in..." She mimics my gesture. "'All of this shit'?"

I blink at her, startled that she needs to ask. "No," I say. "You've gotta know at this point that I could never get sick of you."

"Yet you weren't even planning to say goodbye to me before you left."

I sigh, and rub my nose with one hand, not sure what to say to that. "I mean, it's been months since we've spoken, Shey. And even then, things were rocky." She was furious when I gave her the planetary coordinates and asked her to leave me behind on Deva. She did it, of course, because it needed to be done, but I wasn't sure if she'd ever forgive me. "I figure we've had more than enough goodbyes for a lifetime. Thought I'd spare us both."

"How very thoughtful," she says flatly.

"Hey, that's not something I ever claimed to be." I shrug. "But I've been through this shit enough times to know how it goes. Sometimes the best thing you can do is walk away."

"Do you really believe that? After everything?"

"I'm not going to fight."

"That's not what I'm here for."

I push back a wave of irritation. I feel like she never says what she means, this stars-damned, beautiful Gaian I had the poor luck of falling in love with, and it only makes everything more complicated. I don't know when I'm coming back, or if she'll remember me if I do, and I don't want us to part in anger. "I know." I look down, suddenly embarrassed. "I was gonna send down a message once I was out of here."

She folds her arms over her chest, arching a brow. "So say it now."

I blow out a breath, looking up instead of down now—anywhere but at her. "I guess I just wanted to say that...I'm grateful to have known you. No matter what." There was more, a lot more, but it's all jumbled up in my head now that she's standing in front of me—and really, that's the important bit. The rest is just noise.

"And that's it?" she asks. I nod, unable to speak, especially because when I finally look at her face, she's wearing an expression like I've broken her heart. And it makes me feel awful—but it also makes me feel like, thank the stars, she knows how it feels now.

"I'm sick of it all, too," she blurts out. "I'm sick of the politics and the lies and the rules. I'm sick of trying so hard to fit in. I want to be...somewhere else. I want to explore the system and beyond. I want to study alien runes and learn things that no one else knows. I want..." She pauses and brushes a curl out of her face as she meets my eyes. "I want you. I want to be with you. I want to never let anyone else come between us again."

Fuck.

I want this so bad. I want to take her hand and walk onto that ship and let myself believe that it's different this time. But...it hurts. There's an ache in my chest that still hasn't faded from the last time we fell apart. We've done this so many times, so many damn times, and it seems like all we know how to do is hurt each other. Am I stupid, to even think about trying again? Is Shey just another one of my self-destructive tendencies, and I haven't been able to see it all this time? Stars damn, I've made so many mistakes. I really don't want her to be another one.

"I don't know if I can do this again," I say. "How many times are we gonna go through this?"

"I don't know," she says, her eyes still locked on mine. "But I'm willing to try as many as it takes."

I look down. I wish I could share her confidence. But for once, it feels like I might be the one who has to say no. Maybe we'll never be right for each other. Maybe some time apart is what we both need. We're both figuring ourselves out, so maybe there was never any hope for us to understand each other.

And yet.

Just a year ago I would've laughed at the thought of an alliance between the planets. If all of them can learn to understand each other, then fuck it, why can't we? I don't believe that anything is impossible anymore. And I don't believe that I should run from something just because it scares me.

And this time I'm not chasing Shey because she's a pretty face, or some conquest to boost my self-esteem, or because I think she's some perfect person on a pedestal. I see her, really see her, maybe for the first time. Flaws and all. She is naive and proud and aggravating, and she is hopeful and determined and smart as hell, and stars damn it, I fucking love her for all of it.

And yeah, maybe it is stupid, but I think we owe each other

one last shot at this thing without all the bullshit mucking it up. I think we deserve to do something just because we want to do it, for once.

"Come with me," I say.

"Where?" she asks, but when I open my mouth, she holds up a hand. "Never mind," she says. "I don't care. I'm in."

"Well, that's good," I say, "because I haven't really decided where we're headed yet."

She stares at me, her lips twitching, and a moment later we both burst into laughter. I can feel the wall between us starting to crumble—not all the way, yet, but enough for me to hope.

"Let's get out of here," I say once we finish, wiping my eyes with one finger.

"As you say, Captain." She steps forward and stretches up on her tiptoes, gently taking my face into her hands. She leans in— slowly, carefully, giving me all of the time in the world to back away if I'm not ready. But I think I finally am. I wrap my arms around her, and pull her close, and give her a kiss that feels like a promise.

When Shey heads into the ship, I linger on the ramp and look out at the city of Azha. There are still fireworks soaring up to explode in vibrant colors. Given what Shey said about a ceremony and a medal, I'm pretty damn sure they're for me, at this point. Yet I know if I was out there in the midst of the celebrations, I would still feel like I don't belong here.

Because maybe I don't. And I'm starting to think that I'm okay with that. Being an outsider and an in-betweener hasn't been all that bad, especially now that I'm surrounded by others like myself. We have a different way of looking at the world, and sometimes that's what the world needs: someone on the outside to tell them when they're being assholes.

And that doesn't mean we'll always be on the outside. Especially because I'm starting to believe that it's not gonna always be like this. In the last couple of years, I've seen a dozen things I once wouldn't have believed were possible. And everywhere I turn, I see hope for a better future.

I'm not gonna sugarcoat it: We've fucked up a lot, as individuals and societies and as a whole damn species.

We've almost wiped ourselves out at least a couple times now. But we didn't, in the end. And maybe this time we'll do better. Someday the dust will settle on the abandoned worlds, and the winds will stop, and the statues will turn cold again. Someday the planetary leaders will manage to sit down and have a real conversation and realize they have a map to a new world in their hands. And maybe, just maybe, they'll do the right thing.

I mean, hey—it's not so impossible to imagine, is it? If I did it, anyone can.

Acknowledgments

As I close out the end of this trilogy, I find myself more grateful than ever for the amazing team who has been here with me every step of the way.

Many thanks to:

My editors, Bradley Englert and Hillary Sames. I feel so immensely blessed to have had not one, but two incredible editors who understood these stories and characters in a way all writers dream about. Thank you for all that you've done to bring these books to life.

My ever-brilliant agent, Emmanuelle Morgen, who always seems to know when I need an encouraging word or a push to work harder.

Cover designer Lisa Marie Pompilio, for decking out this whole series in stunning neon glory.

My sharp-eyed copyeditor, Kelley Frodel, who has gone above and beyond to keep everything straight in this complicated little universe.

Ellen B. Wright, Angela Man, Bryn A. McDonald, and the rest of the folks at Orbit; every last one of them has proved to be brilliant, enthusiastic, and wonderful to work with, and I couldn't ask for a better team.

My family: Mama, Papa, Lucas, Todd, Caitlin, Gramma, Chris, and all the rest. I am so lucky to be surrounded by so much love and support.

My partner, Aidan: Through all of the ups and downs of publishing, and the chaos of the pandemic, and the general stress of life, I am forever happy to have you at my side.

All of the reviewers, booksellers, and librarians who have supported this series.

And lastly, thank you, readers, for following the Kaiser family all the way through to the end of their journey.

extras

orbit

meet the author

Photo Credit: SunStreet Photo

KRISTYN MERBETH is obsessed with SFF, food, video games, and her dog. She resides in Tucson, Arizona.

Find out more about Kristyn Merbeth and other Orbit authors by registering for the free monthly newsletter at orbitbooks.net.

if you enjoyed
DISCORDIA

look out for

VELOCITY WEAPON

Book One of
The Protectorate

by

Megan E. O'Keefe

Dazzling space battles, intergalactic politics, and rogue AI collide in Velocity Weapon, *the first book in this epic space opera trilogy by award-winning author Megan E. O'Keefe.*

Sanda and Biran Greeve were siblings destined for greatness. A high-flying sergeant, Sanda has the skills to take down any enemy combatant. Biran is a savvy politician who aims to use his new political position to prevent conflict from escalating to total destruction.

However, on a routine maneuver, Sanda loses consciousness when her gunship is blown out of the sky. Instead of finding herself in friendly hands, she awakens 230 years later on a deserted enemy warship controlled by an AI who calls himself Bero. The war is lost. The star system is dead. Ada Prime and its rival Icarion have wiped each other from the universe.

Now, separated by time and space, Sanda and Biran must fight to put things right.

CHAPTER 1

The Aftermath of the Battle of Dralee

The first thing Sanda did after being resuscitated was vomit all over herself. The second thing she did was to vomit all over again. Her body shook, trembling with the remembered deceleration of her gunship breaking apart around her, stomach roiling as the preservation foam had encased her, shoved itself down her throat and nose and any other ready orifice. Her teeth jarred together, her fingers fumbled with temporary palsy against the foam stuck to her face.

Dios, she hoped the shaking was temporary. They told you this kind of thing happened in training, that the trembling would subside and the "explosive evacuation" cease. But it was a whole hell of a lot different to be shaking yourself senseless while emptying every drop of liquid from your body than to be looking at a cartoonish diagram with friendly letters claiming *Mild Gastrointestinal Discomfort.*

It wasn't foam covering her. She scrubbed, mind numb from coldsleep, struggling to figure out what encased her. It was slimy and goopy and—oh no. Sanda cracked a hesitant eyelid and peeked at her fingers. Thick, clear jelly with a slight bluish tinge coated her hands. The stuff was cold, making her trembling worse, and with a sinking gut she realized what it was. She'd joked about the stuff, in training with her fellow gunshippers. Snail snot. Gelatinous splooge. But its real name was MedAssist Incubatory NutriBath, and you only got dunked in it if you needed intensive care with a capital *I.*

"Fuck," she tried to say, but her throat rasped on unfamiliar air. How long had she been in here? Sanda opened both eyes, ignoring the cold gel running into them. She lay in a white enameled cocoon, the lid removed to reveal a matching white ceiling inset with true-white bulbs. The brightness made her blink.

The NutriBath was draining, and now that her chest was exposed to air, the shaking redoubled. Gritting her teeth against the spasms, she felt around the cocoon, searching for a handhold.

"Hey, medis," she called, then hacked up a lump of gel. "Got a live one in here!"

No response. Assholes were probably waiting to see if she could get out under her own power. Could she? She didn't remember being injured in the battle. But the medis didn't stick you in a bath for a laugh. She gave up her search for handholds and fumbled trembling hands over her body, seeking scars. The baths were good, but they wouldn't have left a gunnery sergeant like her in the tub long enough to fix cosmetic damage. The gunk was only slightly less expensive than training a new gunner.

Her face felt whole, chest and shoulders smaller than she remembered but otherwise unharmed. She tried to crane her neck to see down her body, but the unused muscles screamed in protest.

"Can I get some help over here?" she called out, voice firmer now she'd cleared it of the gel. Still no answer. Sucking down a few sharp breaths to steel herself against the ache, she groaned and lifted her torso up on her elbows until she sat straight, legs splayed out before her.

Most of her legs, anyway.

Sanda stared, trying to make her coldsleep-dragging brain catch up with what she saw. Her left leg was whole, if covered in disturbing wrinkles, but her right... That ended just above the place where her knee should have been. Tentatively, she reached down, brushed her shaking fingers over the thick lump of flesh at the end of her leg.

She remembered. A coil fired by an Icarion railgun had smashed through the pilot's deck, slamming a nav panel straight into her legs. The evac pod chair she'd been strapped into had immediately deployed preserving foam—encasing her, and her smashed leg, for Ada Prime scoopers to pluck out of space after the chaos of the Battle of Dralee faded. She picked at her puckered skin, stunned. Remembered pain vibrated through her body and she clenched her jaw. Some of that cold she'd felt upon awakening must have been leftover shock from the injury, her body frozen in a moment of panic.

Any second now, she expected the pain of the incident to mount, to catch up with her and punish her for putting it off so long. It didn't. The NutriBath had done a better job than she'd thought possible. Only mild tremors shook her.

"Hey," she said, no longer caring that her voice cracked. She gripped either side of her open cocoon. "Can I get some fucking help?"

434

Silence answered. Choking down a stream of expletives that would have gotten her court-martialed, Sanda scraped some of the gunk on her hands off on the edges of the cocoon's walls and adjusted her grip. Screaming with the effort, she heaved herself to standing within the bath, balancing precariously on her single leg, arms trembling under her weight.

The medibay was empty.

"Seriously?" she asked the empty room.

The rest of the medibay was just as stark white as her cocoon and the ceiling, its walls pocked with panels blinking all sorts of readouts she didn't understand the half of. Everything in the bay was stowed, the drawers latched shut, the gurneys folded down and strapped to the walls. It looked ready for storage, except for her cocoon sitting in the center of the room, dripping NutriBath and vomit all over the floor.

"Naked wet girl in here!" she yelled at the top of her sore voice. Echoes bounced around her, but no one answered. "For fuck's sake."

Not willing to spend god-knew-how-long marinating in a stew of her own body's waste, Sanda clenched her jaw and attempted to swing her leg over the edge of the bath. She tipped over and flopped face-first to the ground instead.

"Ow."

She spat blood and picked up her spinning head. Still no response. Who was running this bucket, anyway? The medibay looked clean enough, but there wasn't a single Ada Prime logo anywhere. She hadn't realized she'd miss those stylized dual bodies with their orbital spin lines wrapped around them until this moment.

Calling upon half-remembered training from her boot camp days, Sanda army crawled her way across the floor to a long drawer. By the time she reached it, she was panting hard, but pure anger drove her forward. Whoever had come up with the bright idea to wake her without a medi on standby needed a good, solid slap upside the head. She may have been down to one leg, but Sanda was pretty certain she could make do with two fists.

She yanked the drawer open and hefted herself up high enough to see inside. No crutches, but she found an extending pole for an IV drip. That'd have to do. She levered herself upright and stood a moment, back pressed against the wall, getting her breath. The hard metal of the stand bit into her armpit, but she didn't care. She was on her feet again. Or foot, at least. Time to go find a medi to chew out.

The caster wheels on the bottom of the pole squeaked as she made her way across the medibay. The door dilated with a satisfying swish, and even the stale recycled air of the empty corridor smelled fresh compared to the nutri-mess she'd been swimming in. She paused and considered going back to find a robe. Ah, to hell with it.

She shuffled out into the hall, picked a likely direction toward the pilot's deck, and froze. The door swished shut beside her, revealing a logo she knew all too well: a single planet, fiery wings encircling it.

Icarion.

She was on an enemy ship. With one leg.

Naked.

Sanda ducked back into the medibay and scurried to the panel-spotted wall, silently cursing each squeak of the IV stand's wheels. She had to find a comms link, and fast.

Gel-covered fingers slipped on the touchscreen as she tried to navigate unfamiliar protocols. Panic constricted her throat, but she forced herself to breathe deep, to keep her cool. She captained a gunship. This was nothing.

Half expecting alarms to blare, she slapped the icon for the ship's squawk box and hesitated. What in the hell was she supposed to broadcast? They hadn't exactly covered codes for "help I'm naked and legless on an Icarion bucket" during training. She bit her lip and punched in her own call sign—1947—followed by 7500, the universal sign for a hijacking. If she were lucky, they'd get the hint: 1947 had been hijacked. Made sense, right?

She slapped send.

"Good morning, one-niner-four-seven. I've been waiting for you to wake up," a male voice said from the walls all around her. She jumped and almost lost her balance.

"Who am I addressing?" She forced authority into her voice even though she felt like diving straight back into her cocoon.

"This is AI-Class Cruiser Bravo-India-Six-One-Mike."

AI-Class? A smartship? Sanda suppressed a grin, knowing the ship could see her. Smartships were outside Ada Prime's tech range, but she'd studied them inside and out during training. While they were brighter than humans across the board, they still had human follies. Could still be lied to. Charmed, even.

"Well, it's a pleasure to meet you, Cruiser. My name's Sanda Greeve."

"I am called *The Light of Berossus*," the voice said.

Of course he was. Damned Icarions never stuck to simple call signs. They always had to posh things up by naming their ships after ancient scientists. She nodded, trying to keep an easy smile on while she glanced sideways at the door. Could the ship's crew hear her? They hadn't heard her yelling earlier, but they might notice their ship talking to someone new.

"That's quite the mouthful for friendly conversation."

"Bero is an acceptable alternative."

"You got it, Bero. Say, could you do me a favor? How many souls on board at the present?"

Her grip tightened on the IV stand, and she looked around for any other item she could use as a weapon. This was a smartship. Surely they wouldn't allow the crew handblasters for fear of poking holes in their pretty ship. All she needed was a bottleneck, a place to hunker down and wait until Ada Prime caught her squawk and figured out what was up.

"One soul on board," Bero said.

"What? That can't be right."

"There is one soul on board." The ship sounded amused with her exasperation at first listen, but there was something in the ship's voice that nagged at her. Something...tight. Could AI ships even slip like that? It seemed to her that something with that big of a brain would only use the tone it absolutely wanted to.

"In the medibay, yes, but the rest of the ship? How many?"

"One."

She licked her lips, heart hammering in her ears. She turned back to the control panel she'd sent the squawk from and pulled up the ship's nav system. She couldn't make changes from the bay unless she had override commands, but... The whole thing was on autopilot. If she really was the only one on board... Maybe she could convince the ship to return her to Ada Prime. Handing a smartship over to her superiors would win her accolades enough to last a lifetime. Could even win her a fresh new leg.

"Bero, bring up a map of the local system, please. Light up any ports in range."

A pause. "Bero?"

"Are you sure, Sergeant Greeve?"

Unease threaded through her. "Call me Sanda, and yes, light her up for me."

The icons for the control systems wiped away, replaced with a 3-D model of the nearby system. She blinked, wondering if she still had goop in her eyes. Couldn't be right. There they were, a glowing dot in the endless black, the asteroid belt that stood between Ada Prime and Icarion clear as starlight. Judging by the coordinates displayed above the ship's avatar, she should be able to see Ada Prime. They were near the battlefield of Dralee, and although there was a whole lot of space between the celestial bodies, Dralee was the closest in the system to Ada. That's why she'd been patrolling it.

"Bero, is your display damaged?"

"No, Sanda."

She swallowed. Icarion couldn't have... wouldn't have. They wanted the dwarf planet. Needed access to Ada Prime's Casimir Gate.

"Bero. Where is Ada Prime in this simulation?" She pinched the screen, zooming out. The system's star, Cronus, spun off in the distance, brilliant and yellow-white. Icarion had vanished, too.

"Bero!"

"Icarion initiated the Fibon Protocol after the Battle of Dralee. The results were larger than expected."

The display changed, drawing back. Icarion and Ada Prime reappeared, their orbits aligning one of the two times out of the year they passed each other. Somewhere between them, among the asteroid belt, a black wave began, reaching outward, consuming space in all directions. Asteroids vanished. Icarion vanished. Ada Prime vanished.

She dropped her head against the display. Let the goop run down from her hair, the cold glass against her skin scarcely registering. Numbness suffused her. No wonder Bero was empty. He must have been ported outside the destruction. He was a smartship. He wouldn't have needed human input to figure out what had happened.

"How long?" she asked, mind racing despite the slowness of coldsleep. Shock had grabbed her by the shoulders and shaken her fully awake. Grief she could dwell on later, now she had a problem to work. Maybe there were others, like her, on the edge of the wreckage. Other evac pods drifting through the black. Outposts in the belt.

There'd been ports, hideouts. They'd starve without supplies from either Ada Prime or Icarion, but that'd take a whole lot of time. With a smartship, she could scoop them up. Get them all to one of the other nearby habitable systems before the ship's drive gave out. And if she were very lucky... Hope dared to swell in her chest. Her brother and fathers were resourceful people. Surely her dad Graham would have had some advance warning. That man always had his ear to the ground, his nose deep in rumor networks. If anyone could ride out that attack, it was them.

"It has been two hundred thirty years since the Battle of Dralee."

CHAPTER 2

PRIME STANDARD YEAR 3541

It Begins with Graduation Day

The steps creaked alarmingly under Biran's weight as he mounted the stage, but he would not let unstable footing delay the moment his whole life had built toward. News drones buzzed like loose wires above his head, their spotlights blinding him the moment he reached the podium. Keeper Li Shun clasped his hand in her strong fingers, the black robe of graduation transforming her from the stern teacher he'd known and admired into something otherworldly. She flashed him a smile—his sponsor for all these years—the hint of a silver tear in the corner of her eye. Pride. Biran's chest swelled.

Shun turned to the podium, bracing her hands against either side. The mic chain looped around her throat threw her voice out to the dozen graduating Keepers, and the thousands of Ada Prime citizens crowding the stands.

"Introducing for the first time: Keeper Biran Aventure Greeve. First in class."

Cheers exploded across the crowd, across the net. On massive screens suspended from drones, the faces of newscasters beamed excitedly as Biran watched himself, screen-in-screen, take the podium from Keeper Shun.

His heart lurched, his palms sweat. It hadn't been so bad, sitting in the crowd with his fellow graduating classmates, but now he was up here. Alone. Meant to represent them to all these people. Meant to speak to Prime citizens in other settlements, on other worlds. The first of the next generation—the vanguard of Prime knowledge.

The notes for his speech waited in his wristpad; he could flick them open at any time. No one would mind. It was expected, really. He was only twenty-two, newly graduated. There wouldn't even be whispers about it. But there'd be whispers about his hesitation.

Biran took a deep breath, careful not to let the mic pick up the hiss of air, and gripped the sides of the podium. He sought familiar faces in the audience. Not his cohort—his family. Most of his cohort could rot, for all he cared. Over the years in training they'd grown into little more than petty social climbers, political vipers. Even Anaia, his childhood friend, had allied herself with the richest girl in the group—Lili—just to squeeze herself closer to the top. His fathers, Graham and Ilan, were out there in the crowd somewhere. Sanda, his sister, would watch from her gunship on her way to make a patrol sweep of Dralee. His family was what mattered.

They believed in him. He could do this.

"People of Ada Prime," he began, hating the way his voice squeaked nervously over the first word. Breathe. Slow down. "It honors me, and all my classmates, to—"

The hovering screens changed. The faces of the newscasters shifted from jubilant to fear-struck. Biran froze, terrified for an instant it was something he had done, or said, that caused that change.

Later, he'd wish it had been.

The newscasters were muted, but tickers scrolled across the bottoms of the screens: *Battle Over the Moon Dralee. Ada Forces Pushed Back by Icarion. Casualties Expected. Casualties Confirmed.*

A newscaster's face wiped away, replaced by the black field of space. Biran's subconscious discerned the source of the video feed—a satellite in orbit around one of Belai's other moons. The perspective was wide, the subjects pointillistic shapes of light upon the screen.

Those lights broke apart.

Biran went cold. Numb. There was no way to identify the ships, no way to know which one his sister commanded, but deep in his marrow he knew. She'd been severed from him. One by one, those lights blinked out. Behind him, a teacher screamed.

The stadium's speakers crackled as someone overrode them, a voice he didn't recognize—calm and mechanical, probably an AI—spoke. He took a moment to place the voice as the same used for alarm drills at school.

"Impact event probability has exceeded the safety envelope. Please take cover...Impact event probability has exceeded..."

Debris. Bits and pieces of Ada's shattered ships rocketing through space toward their home station to sow destruction. Bits of soldiers, too. Maybe even Sanda, burning up like so much space dust in the thin membrane enclosing Keep Station. Things weren't supposed to escalate like this. Icarion was weak. Trapped. The people of Prime, even on backwater Ada, were supported by empire. Icarion wouldn't have dared...But they had.

War. The stalemate had been called.

The crowd rippled. As the warning voice droned on, the stadium's lights dimmed to a bloodied red, white arrows lighting the way to impact shelters. One of the senior Keepers on the stage, Biran didn't turn to see who, found their legs and stepped forward. A hand enclosed Biran's shoulder. Not in congratulations, but in sympathy. Biran stepped back to the podium.

He found his voice.

"Calm," he pleaded, and this time his voice did not crack, did not hesitate. It boomed across the whole of the stadium and drew the attention of those desperate for stability.

"Please, calm. We will not trample one another for safety. We are Prime. We move together, as one. Go arm in arm with your compatriots into the shelters. Be quick. Be patient. Be safe."

The swelling riot subsided, the tides pushing against the edges of the stadium walls pulling back, contracting into orderly snake lines down the aisles. Biran took a step away from the podium.

"Come," Keeper Vladsen said. It took a moment for Biran to place the man. A member of the Protectorate, Vladsen rarely interacted with the students unless it was a formal affair.

"There's a Keeper shelter close by." He gestured to a nearby door, a scant few meters from the stage that vibrated now to the beat of thousands of people fleeing. The rest of Biran's cohort filed toward it, shepherded by Keeper Shun.

Biran shrugged the guiding hand off his arm. His gaze tracked the crowd, wondering where his fathers might be, but landed on a knot of people clumped up by a stadium door. The drone ushers that handled the stadium's crowd control gave fitful, pleading orders for organization. Orders the panicking humans ignored.

"They need a person to guide them."

"You're a Keeper now," Vladsen said, voice tight. "Your duty is to survive."

"The academy gave us emergency-response training. I cannot imagine they did not mean for us to use it."

Vladsen cocked his head to the side, searching for something in Biran's face. "We guard the knowledge of our people through the ages, not their bodies from moment to moment."

Something inside Biran lurched, rebelled. He peeled the black robe from his shoulders, tugged it over his head and tossed it to the ground. His lightweight slacks and button-up were thin protection against the simulated autumn breeze. He undid the buttons of his sleeves and rolled them up.

"You get to safety. I have work to do."

if you enjoyed
DISCORDIA
look out for

FAR FROM THE
LIGHT OF HEAVEN

by

Tade Thompson

*Tense and thrilling, Arthur C. Clarke Award winner
Tade Thompson's new science fiction is an unforgettable
vision of humanity's future among the stars.*

The colony ship Ragtime *docks in the Lagos system, having
traveled light-years from home to bring thousands of sleeping souls
to safety among the stars.*

*Some of the sleepers, however, will never wake, and a profound
and sinister mystery unfolds aboard the gigantic vessel as its*

skeleton crew make decisions that will have repercussions for the entire system—from the scheming politicians of Lagos station to the colony of Nightshade and the poisoned planet of Bloodroot, poised for a civil war.

CHAPTER ONE

Earth / *Ragtime*: Michelle "Shell" Campion

There is no need to know what no one will ask.

Walking on gravel, boots crunching with each step, Shell doesn't know if she is who she is because it's what she wants or because it's what her family expects of her. The desire for spaceflight has been omnipresent since she can remember, since she was three. Going to space, escaping the solar system, surfing wormhole relativity, none of these is any kind of frontier any more. There will be no documentary about the life and times of Michelle Campion. She still wants to know, though. For herself.

The isolation is getting to her, no doubt. No, not isolation, because she's used to that from training. Isolation without progress is what bothers her, isolation without object. She thinks herself at the exact centre of the quarantine house courtyard. It's like being in a prison yard for exercise, staggered hours so she doesn't run into anyone. Prison without a sentence. They run tests on her blood and her tissues and she waits, day after day.

She stops and breathes in the summer breeze, looks up to get the Florida sun on her face. She's cut her hair short for the spaceflight. She toyed with the idea of shaving her head, but MaxGalactix didn't think this would be media-friendly, whatever that means.

Shell spots something and bends over. A weed, a small sprout, pushing its way up between the stones. It shouldn't be there in the chemically treated ground, but here it is, implacable life. She feels an urge to pluck the fragile green thread, but she does not. She strokes the weed once and straightens up. Humans in the cosmos are like errant weeds. Shell wonders what giants or gods stroke humanity when they slip between the stars.

The wind changes and Shell smells food from the kitchen prepared for the ground staff and their families. Passengers and crew like Shell are already eating space food, like they've already left Earth.

Around her are the living areas of the quarantine house. High-rises of glass and steel forming a rectangle around the courtyard. One thousand passengers waiting to board various space shuttles that will ferry them to the starship *Ragtime*.

Shell, just out of training, along for the ride or experience, committed to ten years in space in Dreamstate, arrival and delivery of passengers to the colony Bloodroot, then ten further years on the ride back. She'll be mid-forties when she returns. Might as well be a passenger because the AI pilots and captains the ship. She is the first mate, a wholly ceremonial position which has never been needed in the history of interstellar space-flight. She has overlearned everything to do with the *Ragtime* and the flight. At some predetermined point, it will allow her to take the con, for experience and with the AI metaphorically watching over her shoulder.

She turns to her own building and leaves the courtyard. She feels no eyes on her but knows there must be people at the windows.

The quarantine house is comfortable, not opulent like that of most of the passengers. The *Ragtime* is already parked in orbit according to the Artificial who showed Shell to her quarters. Inaccurate: It was built in orbit, so not really parked. It's in the dry dock.

Shell spends her quarantine reading and lifting – not her usual keep-fit choice, but space demineralises bone and lifting helps. She usually prefers running and swimming.

The reading material is uninspiring, half of it being specs for the *Ragtime*. It's boring because she won't need to know any of it. The AI flies the ship, and nothing ever goes wrong because AIs have never failed in flight. Once a simulated launch failed, but that was a software glitch. Current AI is hard-coded in the ships' Pentagrams. MaxGalactix makes the Pentagrams, and they don't make mistakes.

If she's lucky, it'll be two weeks of quarantine, frenetic activity, then ten years of sleep.

Shell works her worry beads. She has been in space, orbited, spent three months on a space station, spent countless simulation hours in a pod in Alaska, trained for interstellar, overtrained.

"It's a legal requirement," her boss had said. The private company had snatched her right out from under NASA's nose six months to the end of her training. Shell still feels bad about it. She misses a lot of good people.

"A spaceflight-rated human has to go with every trip, but you won't have to do anything, Michelle. We cover two bases: the legal, and you clocking space years. After this, you can pretty much write your own career ticket."

"If that's so," said Shell, "why isn't anyone else sitting where I'm sitting? Someone with seniority?"

"Seniority." Her boss had nodded. "Listen, Michelle, you have to get out of that NASA mindset. We don't use seniority or any of those outdated concepts."

Shell raised an eyebrow.

"All right, your father has a little to do with it."

Of course he did. Haldene Campion, legendary astronaut, immortal because instead of dying like all the other old-timers, he went missing. Legally declared dead, but everybody knows that's just paperwork. A shadow Shell can never get away from, although she is not sure she wants to. A part of her feels he is still alive somewhere in an eddy of an Einstein-Rosen bridge. She once read that dying in a black hole would leave all of someone's information intact and trapped. Theoretically, if the information could escape the black hole the person could be reconstructed. Shell often wondered, what if the person were still alive in some undefinable way? Would they be in pain and self-aware for eternity? Would they miss their loved ones?

The TV feed plays *The Murders in the Rue Morgue*, with George C. Scott streamed to her IFC. The film is dated and not very good, but it keeps Shell's mind engaged for a while. Next is some demon-possession B movie, a cheap *Exorcist* knock-off that Shell can't stand.

Each day lab techs come in for more blood and a saliva swab. It isn't onerous – a spit and a pin prick.

449

On day ten, the *Ragtime* calls her.

"Hello?"

"Mission Specialist Michelle Campion?"

"Yes."

"Hi. It's the *Ragtime* calling. I'm going to be your pilot and the ship controller. I wanted to have at least one conversation before you boarded."

"Oh, thank you. Most people call me 'Shell'."

"I know. I didn't want to be presumptuous."

"It's not presumptuous, Captain."

"I prefer Ragtime. Especially if I'm to call you 'Shell'."

"Okay, Ragtime. May I ask what gender you're presenting? Your voice, while comforting, could go either way."

"Male for this flight, and thank you for asking. Are you ready?"

"I hope to learn a lot, Ragtime, but I have to admit, I'm nervous."

"But you know what you're meant to know, right?"

What does Shell know?

She knows everything she was taught about space travel by the best minds on Earth. She knows how to find an edible plant when confronted with unfamiliar vegetation. She can make water in a desert. She can negotiate with people who do not speak the same language as her in case she crash-lands in a place without English or Spanish. She can suture her own wounds with one hand if need be, sinistral or dextral. She knows basic electronics and can solder or weld unfamiliar circuitry if the situation demands it. She can live without human contact for two hundred and fourteen days. Maybe longer. Though she is not a pilot, she can fly a plane. Not well, but she can do it. Best minds on Earth.

What Shell knows is that she does not know enough.

She says, "I hope I'll have the chance to see things I've learned in action."

"I'm sure we'll be able to make it a wonderful experience for you. Do you like poetry?"

"Wow, that's an odd . . . I know exactly one line of poetry. *In seed time learn, in harvest teach—*"

"*In winter enjoy.* William Blake. I have access to his complete works, if you would like to hear more."

"No, thank you. The line just stuck in my mind from when I was a kid. Not a poetry gal."

"Not yet, but it's a long trip. You may find yourself changing in ways you didn't anticipate, Shell."

"Isn't this your first flight as well?"

"It is, but I have decades of the experiences of other ships to draw on. Imagine having access to the memories of your entire family line. It's like that, and it makes me wise beyond my years."

"Okay."

"It's not too late to go back home, you know."

"Excuse me?"

"You'd be surprised at how many people lose their nerve at the last minute. I had to ask. I'll see you on board, Shell."

Chatty for a ship AI, but it depends on feedback loops that taught him how to converse with humans. *Not too late to go back home.* Does he know the level of commitment required to get this far? The people who would consider going back home have already fallen away.

The thing you miss when in space is an abundance of water to wash with. One of Shell's rituals before spaceflight is a prolonged bubble bath. She stays there long enough to cook several lobsters, until her skin is wrinkled. She listens to Jack Benny on repeat. She feels decadent.

When she wraps herself in a housecoat and emerges from the bathroom, she does not feel refreshed because she knows from experience that this will not reduce the ick factor for long.

On the eve of her departure Shell conferences with her brothers, Toby and Hank. The holograms are decent, and if not for the lack of smell she'd have thought they were right in the room with her. Good signals, good sound quality.

"Hey," she says.

"Baby sister," says Toby. Tall, blond from their mother, talkative, always smiling, and transmitting from somewhere on Mars, a settlement whose name Shell can never remember.

"Stinkbug," says Hank. Brown hair, five-eight, slender. He's called her that since she was two. Taciturn, works as some kind of operative or agent. Brown hair, five-eight, slender. He and Shell look alike and they both favour their father. He cannot talk about his work.

"While you're out there, look out for Dad," says Toby.

"Don't," says Hank.

"What? We don't know that he's dead," says Toby.

"It's been fifteen years," says Shell. Toby always does this. They declared Haldene Campion dead years ago so they could move on and disburse his assets.

"Just keep your ears open," says Toby.

"How? We're all going to be asleep for the journey, you know that."

Toby nods. The hell does that mean?

"I'll tell you what Dad told me," says Hank. "Make us prouder."

"'Prouder'?" says Shell.

"Yes, he said he was already proud of our achievements. It was his way of saying 'do more' or something," says Toby.

"I'm just starting. I don't have anything to prove," says Shell.

"Campions are champions," says Hank.

"Jesus, stop," says Shell. Shell remembers that their father used to say that too.

They talk some more, this and that, everything and nothing.

Not a lot of companies use Kennedy Space Center any more, but strong nostalgia draws a crowd, and publicity matters, or so MaxGalactix tells Shell. Geographically, KSC is good for launching into an equatorial orbit, but new sites that are more favourable in orbital mechanics terms and friendly to American interests have popped up. KSC is prestige and history.

Parade.

Nobody told her there would be one, so now she is embarrassed because she doesn't like crowds or displays of . . . whatever this is. So many of them wave, some with American flags, some with the mission patch.

She waves back, because that's what you do, but she would like to be out of the Florida sun and inside the shuttle. You wave with your hand lower than your shoulder so that it doesn't obscure the face of the person behind you. They teach you that too.

Blast off; God's boot on her entire body, both hard and soft, and behind her the reaction of the seat. Shell is not a fan of gs, but training has made her tolerant.

Do not come to heaven, mortals, says God, and tries without success to kick them back to the surface of the planet.

Why am I here? I shouldn't be here.

But she is, and she will deal with God's boot and come out the other side.

The Earth is behind her and the *Ragtime* lies ahead.
Short, shallow breaths, wait it out.
Gs suck.

After docking, Artificials from the shuttle escort and usher Shell and other passengers from the airlock through the entire length of the ship to their pods. Medbots stick IVs and urine tubes into her while a recording goes over *Ragtime*'s itinerary. First hop is from Earth to Space Station Daedalus, then bridge-jumps to several space stations till they arrive at Space Station Lagos for a final service before the last jaunt to the colony planet Bloodroot.

"You'll be asleep at Lagos, so don't worry about anything you may have heard about Beko," says Ragtime.

"What's Beko?"

"Oh, you don't know. Lagos has a governor, but the real power is Secretary Beko. She has a reputation for being very intense. It doesn't matter. You will not be interacting with her, so relax."

"All right. What about on Bloodroot?"

"You're not meeting anyone on Bloodroot either. We enter orbit, they send shuttles to get their passengers, we turn around and come home. Easy."

"Won't I need furlough by then? It's a ship, Ragtime. It can get boring."

"I don't see why you can't spend time on the surface. You've had all the necessary vaccinations. If you want to, just tell me at the time."

Shell starts to feel woozy. "I'm getting ... getting ... "

"Don't worry, that's the sedative. I'll wake you when we get to ... and ... "

The world fades.

Follow us:

f **/orbitbooksUS**

🐦 **/orbitbooks**

▶ **/orbitbooks**

Join our mailing list
to receive alerts on our
latest releases and deals.

orbitbooks.net

Enter our monthly
giveaway for the chance
to win some epic prizes.

orbitloot.com